Nefarious

MARY ANN MARLOWE

Published by Mary Ann Marlowe
www.maryannmarlowe.com

To Jen Hawkins
When the night was cloudy
You were the light that shined on me

Week 1

Monday

Dane sat in his office, hiding from the gaggle of pimply new interns invading the trading floor. On the task bar of his open laptop, the IM program flashed continually. There was no point clicking on it; the instant he acknowledged the message, someone else would vie for his attention.

I oughta just shut that down and make them knock on my door.

As if he'd conjured it, a light tap brought his gaze up. The door opened a crack, and he caught the backside of Val as she turned and walked away.

He slid open the bottom drawer of his desk and rummaged for the crumpled pack of cigarettes. He'd let it be known he was trying to quit so nobody would question why he rarely smoked. Out of sympathy, they never questioned him when he did. Not that he ever did. The cigarettes were nothing more than a prop, a means to an end. He'd bought the current pack a year ago. The half-empty pint of Maker's

Mark lying under the cigarettes, however, had only been there a day.

As he left his office, he deliberately lifted the pack and slid it into his suit coat pocket for all the world to see him slinking down for a secret smoke. He glanced furtively but conspicuously from side to side until he'd left the trading floor. Once in the first-floor lobby, he resumed his natural confident gait, lending him an air of aristocracy.

Out in the smoking area, Val waited, arms crossed, cigarette hand resting on her elbow. Juxtaposed to the warping picnic table and patchy, trash-strewn grass, Val glittered like fool's gold. Her perfectly coiffed blond hair shone in the sun but didn't budge despite a mild June wind. Everything about Val was anchored, moored, unyielding. Only Dane knew how to make that rock bend. And only sometimes.

Val faced the four-story structure but kept her eyes trained on Dane and nodded once in greeting. The temptation to look up at the office windows for observers might overwhelm anyone else, despite the inability to penetrate the glass. Whoever might be watching them would see nothing but a casual encounter.

Dane passed her and sat on top of the picnic table, faced at an angle away from the building, feet on the bench. He hunched over and focused on the unlit cigarette in his hand. "You know we can't meet here again for at least two weeks."

She turned a quarter of the way toward him, enough to appear to be conversing as one would expect of two people sharing the same space. Not enough to show interest in the topic. "I did message you, but you were ignoring me."

"Don't take it so personally. I ignore everyone."

She took a long drag and exhaled. "We only have a minute before they start to show up."

"Right. Interns." If any of the new kids saw them out there alone together, they'd scrounge up a cigarette just to

4

come and cozy up. *It's what I would have done in their place.* Admirable, but irritating. "So get to the point."

"Selena Valencia. Have you met her?"

He rubbed his chin and tried to place the name. "Valencia? Any relation to Geraldo?"

"It's Geraldo's daughter. She took an internship here under me. Isn't that delicious?"

"Geraldo sent his daughter *here*?"

"No, that's the delightful part. He doesn't know she came here. Apparently, he's occupied with some business in Germany and told his daughter to find an internship, probably expecting her to stay in the city at one of the obvious financial firms. But she's apparently eager. She wants to learn from the best."

Dane yawned. "And so she came here. Fascinating. You dragged me out here to gossip."

"Of course not." She snapped at him but then slicked her gold hair back and smiled at him, adjusting her tone to match. "Of course not. I have a favor to ask of you."

Across the yard, a young man had opened the door and paced in a narrow circle, gathering his courage to approach the infamous pair.

"You'd better spit it out. We've got company."

Val's smile twisted wickedly. She sat on the picnic bench, beside Dane's feet, and ran a finger under the hem of his slacks, lightly brushing along the edge of his sock. "Do you ever think about when we started together? The exhilarating risks we took?" She inched up the inside of his calf. "Do you ever think about that one night? Do you even remember it?"

Dane shifted, but left his foot firmly planted. He knew what she was up to, but he wanted to know why. "Of course I remember." He remembered waking up to find her gone. "Is that why we're here? Do you want to take me home, Val?"

She withdrew her hand. "When it comes time to decide which intern you'll mentor, I want you to pick Selena."

"To what end?"

"To train her to bend rules and skirt the law. I want her to leave here an expert in ethical violations, without even knowing how amoral she's become. I want to send her back to her daddy with an appetite for corruption."

"Why would I want to do that?" Dane watched the awkward boy make up his mind. He'd taken a few hesitant steps toward the picnic table, still out of earshot.

"You have as much cause for vengeance as I do. If it weren't for Geraldo, we'd still have our company." She snarled. "R&M was *our* company."

He knew he ought to feel touched she'd taken his ouster to heart, but he'd spent the past three years moving on. Val was never as forgiving.

Dane rested his elbows on his knees. "You could have stayed on without me. I hope you don't think I'm to blame for your current situation. I shudder to think of how you'd punish me."

"Very funny. You know I'm only loyal to you, Dane."

He doubted she was loyal to anyone, but she had left their company to follow him to the Midwest, and he couldn't forget that. "And I'm forever grateful. Truly, I'm humbled."

Val narrowed an eye as though she could parse his bullshit enough to detect the sincerity behind his sarcastic tone. "Then you'll help me set the girl on a ruinous path?"

Dane slid the unlit cigarette back in the pack. "I'm afraid I'm going to be distracted with another endeavor for some time."

"Let me guess. Seducing the head of accounting? She seems like your type."

He gave Val one long look. "No. I plan to seduce our new CEO."

"Noelle?" Val scoffed. "How is that any kind of challenge? You could do that this morning and spend the rest of your summer with Selena."

"You seem to forget history."

"Oh, are you still nursing that wound? Or is this about Dane's ego? She spurned you before you could bed her, and you'll never rest until you check that box. Is that it?"

Dane clenched a fist. "I was so close. Until she shot me down with no explanation."

Val frowned. "And publicly, too. Yes. How humiliating. If I'd known you carried a torch, I might not have insisted the board offer her the job."

"Why did you? You never cared for her."

"Perhaps not, but she might prove useful to me. There's a story to her sudden resignation from R&M, and I intend to find out what it is. Maybe she holds a grudge against Geraldo as well. I could exploit that." She dropped her cigarette and ground it out. "If you don't spook her. What do you have planned?"

"What I failed to do last time." He leaned forward to whisper in Val's ear. "I'm going to seduce her before she realizes what happened. I want her to think she's resisting me only to find she can't."

Val rolled her eyes. "Pedestrian. Let me guess. Was Noelle the last person to break your heart?"

"No." Dane stepped off the table and tilted his head toward Val. "You were."

The corner of Val's mouth curled up slightly. "I believe I've rectified that."

"Right. And then substituted rejection with betrayal." He enjoyed seeing the color drain from her face.

She recovered enough to whisper harshly, "Let it go, Dane."

He pushed the knife in another inch. "I already have."

The awkward boy had circled around them and made his approach. Val regained the beneficent facade she reserved for the rest of the world. A strand of hair had escaped her tight control, and she tucked it behind her ear, head held high. She shot one more calculated glance at Dane. "Hurry along. This one looks ripe for the picking."

Dane popped the pack of cigarettes back into his pocket and left Val to her games.

Email recovered from the corporate hard drive.

Sophie,

Guess where I am? Did you notice my new Fleetwood Capital email address? I'm here! I don't know if I'm supposed to be writing personal emails from here, but I couldn't resist breaking in my brand-new account!

I'm sitting in my cube! I have my own cube!! Okay, so it's more like a shallow desk, but there is a small partition between computers. I don't have anything to do here just yet but swivel in my office chair. We'll be in training for a week before (I hope) they place us with mentors. Two more before we get to even touch the system. But then six weeks working in a real trading environment!

I hadn't seen Val Montgomery since she and my father had their falling out years ago. I was nervous to speak to her considering, but she was so sweet. She complimented me on my glasses. I just stood there half stuttering and half rambling on about what an honor it was to be here.

I've yet to meet Dane Russ. But I did see him going into his office earlier. I cannot believe I'm going to be working under them. They were so young when they founded their company, and I know if I pay attention, I can learn so much. Maybe I'll even be able to pick their brains and find out how they managed to get so successful so fast.

We have our first meeting with Val in a few minutes. The other interns look about as nervous and eager as me. I hope I'm not the worst one here. They're probably all top of their classes, too.

Write me back and tell me about summer school. I don't envy you stuck in class while I'm getting first-hand knowledge in the real world.

Much love,
Selena

Val surveyed the room. Fifteen interns squeezed around the long table. Every chair was occupied. Not a single one of these kids exuded the boredom she felt. They watched her as if they were in the bear exhibit at the zoo. *Will she come out of the cave? Will she attack?* They thought they were as safe as if they were on the other side of the barricades. And they normally would be. The innocent ones no longer interested her. Except one.

Selena wore a smart new suit. Crisp. Probably purchased a month ago in anticipation of this day. She had a fresh-scrubbed glow about her. With her pen poised above a perfectly blank notepad, she clearly expected to leave this room with her mind expanded. As if it were so easy. It would take all summer to mold her brain the way Val planned.

She scanned the other interns, chess pieces on her board, sizing up their value to her. So far, the only one with the chutzpah to approach her sat at the far corner of the table. *Anthony*. He stood out in the way he sat. Leaning back in his chair, one foot crossed on his knee. Val raised an eyebrow at him, and he straightened up and put his forearms on the table. Now they were all a neat row of matching pawns.

The screen behind her came to life with the first of many PowerPoint slides. She could give this speech in her sleep, but she'd learned that the interns would try to write down her every word. The slides would at least help them get it right. The pens flew across the notebooks already, and she saw the words *Welcome to Fleetwood Capital* in fifteen different sets of handwriting.

She sighed. "Good morning and welcome to Fleetwood. We're so glad to have all of you here today. I trust you've settled into your new desks. If you have any remaining issues, please contact Rosamund Shirley. She'll make sure you have everything you need. Now, for the next hour, I'll be taking you through some basics about our company, who we are, what we stand for, how we stand in the market today, and of course what we are aiming to achieve."

The door swung open, and Dane waltzed in. Fifteen intern heads swiveled away from Val and gawked at him. Anthony vacated his chair with alacrity, as though he feared someone else might beat him to it. He gestured for Dane to sit, but Dane's lip curled up on one side in disdain, and he simply leaned against the back wall, languidly pushing a stir stick around his Styrofoam coffee cup. Dane never sat at meetings. *These kids will learn.*

Anthony sheepishly pulled his chair back and returned to his place at the table.

As Val waited for order to return, she let her gaze linger on Dane, draped against the wall in all his languorous beauty. She knew he'd spent a fortune to look like he did, but knowing it didn't make her appreciate it less. Of course, she'd seen him before he'd learned to groom himself so handsomely. She'd taught him after all. But he'd been born with those dark sultry eyes and that decadent luscious mouth. Fully aware she was drinking in her fill, he puckered his lips like he might blow her a kiss.

She inhaled, searching for a hint of his scent. If it wouldn't be considered unseemly, she might be tempted to cross the room and take him up on his implied offer.

Instead she turned her attention to the interns, now waiting for her lead.

"This company," she continued, "was founded by Martin Fleetwood in 1957 with a specialization in mortgage trading." Val clicked through the slides, expanding on the historical events that nobody wanted or needed to know. Martin Fleetwood had died years ago. Besides Rosamund Shirley, nobody currently here had ever worked under that scrupulous man. He'd roll over in his grave if he knew the stewardship had passed on to the likes of Dane Russ. And Val, though her reputation was spotless. The only stain on her record was her connection with Dane. But as the worshipful faces in the room could attest, she couldn't be blamed for following him into exile.

The subject of the slides moved on to the current state of the company. "Have any of you researched the company's stock position?"

Anthony raised his hand. "Yes, ma'am. Stocks are trading at thirty-eight as of this morning."

Val glanced at Dane. "Are we up or down?"

Anthony opened his mouth, but Dane's voice command-ed the room's attention. "The market's hot, and our stock is rising."

Val controlled her expression, but the corner of her mouth rose slightly. "What do you make of our throughput?"

Dane lifted his shoulders from the wall, engaged now. "I like our position with regard to market penetration."

The interns had stopped taking notes, and their heads followed the volley as though they were spectators at a tennis match.

Val set up the shot. "And the projected yield?"

"Coming together." Dane crumpled the Styrofoam and tossed it into the trash bin.

Val exhaled. "Our stockholders will be very satisfied."

Dane reached in his pocket and produced a single cigarette. He toyed with it for a heartbeat before walking out the door.

Val bit the end of her pen. *My most valuable chess piece moves in every direction.*

Except into her bed.

No, she wouldn't cede that game until she knew how they could both win.

With all the eyes back on Val, she proceeded to lecture them on expectations of ethics and compliance, chuckling to herself as they diligently took notes.

Dane tucked the cigarette back into the pack in his pocket and entered the stairwell. For the past week, he'd been keeping tabs on Noelle's daily routine and was reasonably sure she'd take a coffee break within the next thirty minutes. There was no good reason for him to be using the kitchen on her floor of the building, but he'd spent three years cultivating an eccentric behavior pattern, and nobody was likely to question his decision to get his coffee from the third floor. Of course, he realized that this would likely permanently alter Noelle's own morning routine if she thought she might run into him on her coffee break.

The kitchen was empty except for the elderly Rosamund Shirley. Rosamund was a short woman, as wide as she was tall. He'd overheard co-workers refer to her as Violet Bowling Ball. What they couldn't know was that she was once a striking beauty who nearly brought the company to an end when she caught Martin Fleetwood's eye. Their affair was brief but notorious at the time. Dane marveled that even someone as upstanding as Martin Fleetwood could be brought down by love. Or lust more accurately. He did right by Rosamund by allowing her to remain on as the head of human resources, but he repaired his marriage. And Rosamund repaired to the Old Country Buffet.

That was already ancient history when Dane was a kid and his dad sat on the board. He'd overheard his parents dissecting the gossip, cringing at their judgmental tone. When Dane got dragged to the office, Rosamund had been the only person who ever took a moment to talk to him like he was more than his father's son.

Dane approached her quietly and laid his arm across her shoulders. "Hello, doll. What's shakin'?"

She took a step back and assessed him over the top of her half-moon glasses. "Dane!" Her orange lipstick had escaped the confines of her mouth, giving her the smile of a clown. "Your hair gets darker every time I see you."

Dane bit back the fact that she said that to him every time she saw him. His hair had always been so dark it bordered on black. If anything, he'd begun to notice the appearance of a few grays at his temple. He winked. "When will I convince you to run away with me?"

"You incorrigible flirt." She giggled like a young girl—a young girl suffering from the early signs of emphysema. "My running days are behind me now, but we could always sneak off for a quick roll in the hay."

"Don't tease me. You know you'd just break my heart." His smile melted, and he touched her arm. "But now, how are you doing, Rose?"

She pulled her coffee from the machine and ripped open a packet of fake sweetener with arthritic fingers. "You know how it goes. One foot in the grave. One foot dancing a congo line."

"You scared me this year with your heart." He eyed her mug. "Shouldn't you watch your caffeine intake?"

"And you need to cut back on the cigarettes. I worry about you, Dane. You don't take good care of yourself."

"Don't worry, Rose. It's not so bad. I can quit anytime." He flashed her a grin to let her know he was aware that's what an addict would say.

She shook her head. "I don't see you enough. You always keep my wit sharp. Come visit me when you have a chance." She started to move toward the kitchen door but stopped and placed her hand on his cheek. "You know, your father was always so proud of you."

Dane swallowed. His dad had been proud of him, of all his accomplishments, up until his disgraceful expulsion from his own company. "*Your problem is we spoiled you. You think you're impervious to consequence.*" He hadn't spoken to his dad again after that. And now he never would. At least the old bastard had never gotten around to disinheriting him before he dropped dead of a heart attack. *Who's impervious to consequence now, Dad?*

Rosamund's bony fingers dragged across his skin, a tender caress from a crone. Dane laid his hand on hers. "Thanks, Rose. That means a lot."

Once Rosamund had left, Dane stood in front of the coffee machine with a packet half in the slot and waited. Within five minutes, he heard the clack of heels on the floor in the hallway and snapped the coffee maker shut. The machine kicked into gear with the fizz of pressurized water forced through the narrow package, exploding into the cup below. Dane leaned casually against the counter and lifted his eyes as Noelle entered the kitchen, a model of professional poise.

She stopped short. "Oh. Dane. Hello."

Dane let his gaze travel down her body, openly assessing her. The new job suited her. She was a picture-perfect CEO in her smartly tailored navy business jacket and skirt with an unfortunately modest white blouse. Her blond hair had been severely tamed in a twist at her neck.

She seemed even more confident, more stylish, and somehow more beautiful than ever. Colder, too.

When she'd encountered Dane on her first day, she'd glared so disdainfully, he'd nearly dropped his nonchalant facade to ask her what he'd done to earn her scorn. But he'd spent too much time in Val's company, and rather than react emotionally, his brain immediately calculated the long game: vindication.

Studying her now, Dane wished they had no history together, that they could start fresh. He imagined freeing her hair, loosening her buttons, coaxing a human response from her. His pants tightened at the fantasy.

If he could crack through Noelle's marble exterior, he might just stand a chance. He almost did once.

He grinned. "Noelle. I'm glad to run into you. I was hoping to set up a time to come to your office and talk about my needs."

A spot of crimson appeared on her neck and rose. She dropped her gaze. "Your *needs*?"

"Servers. We're nearly over capacity as it is. The production servers are under considerable load. If we don't take care of servicing them soon, they could overheat."

The red reached her cheeks. She laid her hand on the counter. "Well, of course, you need to order new hardware."

"Right. But before I can put in a request for acquisition, I'm going to need your consent." He leveled his eyes at her, enjoying all the signs of her discomfort. She controlled her facial features, but her chest rose and fell quickly. When she lifted her hand off the counter, she left behind a damp print. Dane took a step toward her and laughed when she jumped back a foot. "Do I make you nervous?"

Noelle backed away from Dane until she reached the door frame. "Of course not. Email me the necessary paperwork." And coffee forgotten, she turned and walked away.

Dane followed her to the edge of the kitchen and made eye contact with Leonard in support. Leonard nodded once, and Dane headed back to his office secure in the knowledge he'd learn Noelle's new coffee routine soon enough.

Back in his office, he poured the coffee into the dirt surrounding the fake cactus and filled his mug with bourbon.

Val scrolled through the Facebook gallery. In every picture, Geraldo had the same twenty-something platinum blond on his arm. He had a consistent type, it seemed.

She slid his worn business card from her wallet and tapped it on the desk. She'd been twenty-six when Geraldo joined the board at R&M eager to put his stamp on the company. She might have been a bit older than his usual crop of arm candy, but she had something those other girls didn't; she kept his mind engaged. They'd been well-matched in that regard. His clever banter and diabolical sense of humor amused her enough to intrigue her. By the time she discovered his possessive jealousy, they were more than friends.

For her part, Geraldo's philandering had never made her feel jealous so much as wronged; he'd expected more fidelity from her than he'd ever given in return. He had a particularly irrational concern about her relationship with Dane—to Val's never-ending amusement. Of all the men in her life, Dane had always been the one Geraldo never need fear.

She'd cultivated this jealousy like a meth addiction. As long as his focus was trained on Dane, he missed any signs she was seeing other men. She never had difficulty keeping her affairs secret, but pretending she pined for Dane proved deliciously fun and effective, especially since it had a kernel of truth. But Geraldo could never prove his suspicions because things between Val and Dane had been settled for years. Ever since they'd met in college, they'd worked together, flirted openly, but kept the romance safely at bay.

Until that New Year's Eve.

Val's eyes closed, and she let herself relive that earth-shattering night, wondering again what would have happened if she'd followed her heart instead of her head.

She stood alone in the middle of the crowd, one minute before midnight. As the partygoers counted down the last seconds of the year, she scanned the room, tapping her foot and searching for Geraldo. That man didn't have a sentimental bone in his body, so it wouldn't have surprised her if he'd left early, but she felt like a fool, and there would be hell to pay.

An airhorn blared, and all heads swiveled toward the giant monitors displaying cheesy animatronics counting down to midnight.

She had no intention of staying a second longer, but then her eyes landed on Dane, cutting across the floor, and *his* eyes landed on *her*. He changed direction, heading straight for her.

He pushed through the swaying crowd, getting closer. He'd come a long way from the day she'd met him in college, back when he'd worn T-shirts sporting video game references. In that ridiculously expensive suit, he could have graced the glossy pages of a *World's Most Eligible Millionaires* article—and he had. *I created a monster.* A beautiful monster. He walked toward her with an elegance that denoted confidence and style.

He must have noticed she'd been abandoned and wanted to slip over to make sure she wasn't alone at the start of the new year. She was surprised, but delighted he wasn't orbiting Noelle. Her hope flickered.

She watched him avoid the grasping hands of other partiers, anticipating the moment he'd say something saucy like, "How 'bout a kiss, doll."

He stopped several feet from her and let his gaze drag down her entire body. She wore a silky black dress for the occasion, and her blond hair fell in careful tendrils thanks to an afternoon at the salon. Geraldo's eye tended to wander, so she'd make an extra effort whenever they'd be in a sea of other women. In all probability, he'd wandered right off with one of the wait staff despite her attention to appearances.

The way Dane raked his eyes over her, she didn't think she'd been the one at fault for Geraldo's disappearance.

As Dane continued toward her, she noticed for the first time that he staggered. He had a drink in one hand, and she was willing to bet it wasn't his first. Or his third. A lazy smile crept across his face, and she'd been about to ask him if he was drunk when he took one last stuttering step toward her and lifted his hand toward her face. But he stumbled forward, and his hand landed on her shoulder, throwing her backward. "Hey, Dane. What's going on?"

He recovered his balance and stared into her eyes. He said words she hadn't heard from him in years. "You look fucking beautiful tonight, Val."

It took her off guard, and she gasped. "Whoa, Dane. Steady."

He leaned forward, his forehead pressing into hers, eyes closed, just breathing her in. He smelled of bourbon. His fingers twisted in her hair, and his lips stopped inches from hers. Just the memory of it made her ache. He fell so quiet, she wondered if he'd drifted off to sleep.

Then the room exploded around them as everyone screamed, hugged, kissed. Dane and Val stood dead still, pressed against one another, swaying like a couple in the final hours of a dance marathon.

Dane's eyes opened, and he peered into her soul. She couldn't resist the temptation to reach up and touch his hand against her cheek. "What are you doing, Dane? Where's Noelle?"

"Fuck her." His breath tickled her ear.

Val pushed at his shoulders until she could see his expression. "Why? What happened?"

He shrugged like it didn't matter. "She doesn't want to have anything to do with me."

Val glanced around, but everyone was preoccupied with their own revelries. She grinned as she considered the possibilities. "So it's New Year's Eve, and we're both alone." Her voice came out low and husky.

"Do you want to be?"

She wrapped her hand around Dane's tie and dragged him closer. "No."

When his lips met hers, she would have sworn the world dropped to complete silence. He kissed her soft at first, but then her lips parted, and his tongue brushed against hers, deliciously alcohol tinged. His hands found her neck, and he crashed into her with so much passion, she lost her balance and wobbled on her spike heels.

Without calculating the risks, she grabbed Dane's hand and urged him to follow her to the lobby where he paid for a room.

If he looked unbelievable in his tuxedo, he looked even better out of it. They spent the night whispering in each other's ears, confessing frustrated desire. She told him she'd always loved him. He told her he always would. They were both lying. And they had it backwards, besides.

The next morning, she found Geraldo's business card pushed under the hotel room door and made the only rational decision open to her at the moment, sacrificing a relationship with Dane in the short term to save face with Geraldo for the longer game.

That decision had cost her more than either man would ever know.

In ordinary circumstances, she would have coerced Geraldo to step aside and let her have Dane. But she'd already given Geraldo too much power in the boardroom. She knew he'd crush them both if she didn't cede to him in the bedroom. She'd been cocky enough to think she could appease Geraldo, salvage the company, and earn back Dane's trust.

If only . . .

If only Geraldo hadn't been so intent on a takeover, he might have granted her her freedom. She and Dane might have been a power couple—the unlikely union of two best friends who'd built an empire and fallen in love.

It was a fantasy that could never be.

Instead, they chased away boredom playing a game of cat and mouse—and neither one knew which was which.

In hindsight, she'd learned a valuable lesson—she should have cut her losses and picked one winning hand. By trying to play all sides, she'd lost Geraldo's trust, her company, and Dane's affections. And she no longer cared about the first.

But even though Geraldo had won that round, she was still playing a longer game, moving her chess pieces deliberately, slowly—not to mention rigging the board. She intended to even the score. If she could ignite Dane's dormant sense of indignation, they could move to regain control of their company. And once she toppled Geraldo, she'd get Dane back.

If she ever had him.

She sighed. Dane had been drunk that night. Drunker than usual. Had it meant anything? He probably didn't even remember half of what he'd said.

She did.

She put the business card back into her wallet, wondering if he'd kept any physical souvenirs of the night she'd lost everything.

Sophie,

It's begun. I sat in on the first training session with Val herself. And Dane made an appearance. The two of them got into a discussion of the company that broke the speed of sound. It's so weird seeing them together. She's so sweet and above board. But Dane. Let's just say his reputation does not appear unfounded. He comes and goes as he pleases, broods most of the time, and when he speaks, somehow he makes everything sound sexy—and I don't mean his voice turns me on (though it is lovely). It's like he's talking about sex when he talks about finance. I can't explain it. You'd have to hear it. And no, I'm not projecting. I heard the other interns mention it, too. I don't know how Val stood there so calm while he made me blush.

To be honest, though, he makes me a little nervous. I didn't expect him to be so . . . I don't know. Dan-

gerous? Even though that is his name, lol. One of the interns swears he smelled like booze. But he's undeniably attractive.

Anyway, I'm not obsessing over Dane. You wanted a report, and I'm giving you one. Day one has ended. I can't wait until tomorrow.

Sorry that your summer is so boring. I wish you were here. I haven't managed to make any friends yet. Even my roommates keep to themselves. I know I'm not here to make friends, but still, it would be nice to have someone to talk to. Yeah, I know. I'm lucky to have been chosen and it's only for the summer. Still. I miss you.

Love you,
Selena

Tuesday

V al had set up interviews in fifteen-minute intervals throughout the morning and sent the meeting invites out at the beginning of the day. She'd spoken to all these kids back when they'd applied for the program, but it had been a few months since she'd given any thought to them, and she still needed to put names to faces. And besides, she wanted a chance to play with her food.

The knock came right on time. She closed her laptop and said, "Come in."

Selena stood in the entrance, squeezing her hands together. "Ms. Montgomery? Are you ready to see me?"

Val forced the muscles in her face into a smile. "Selena, won't you please come in?"

Selena hesitated, and Val turned up the wattage, flashing her teeth and willing her eyes to feign sincerity. She rolled her hand toward an open chair. "Please, have a seat. I'd like to chat for a moment."

Selena closed the door, and Val thought, "*Welcome to my parlor.*"

As Selena stepped slowly across the room, Val sized her up. She was almost the same age as the girl currently dangling off Geraldo's arm somewhere near Heidelberg, but the similarities stopped there. Selena had thick brown hair falling out of a braid, large brown eyes hiding behind tortoise-shell glasses, an angelic face, and five feet of rail-thin physique. She'd dressed the part of the intern—conservative and not too flashy. In ordinary circumstances, Val might not have noticed her.

Val realized she'd steepled her hands as she assessed her prey and deliberately dropped them. She picked up a pen and began to jot a note on the legal pad before her. *Selena Valencia. June 11.*

"Tell me why you're here. There must have been ample opportunity back in New York. At R&M?"

Selena had the good grace to drop her eyes to her lap. "I knew you'd bring up my dad."

"Look. We host interns every summer in the hopes that they'll learn something, we'll like them, they'll like us, and we'll find a love connection. But realistically, a large number of our interns move on to other firms. I'm not under the illusion that you'll return to us once you've earned your degree, but I'm curious to know what your intentions are. Will you be heading to work for your father in a year?"

Selena shifted in her chair, and Val wondered for a heartbeat if she'd miscalculated. She didn't intend to send the girl running back to her dad that minute, nor did she want a vow of eternal loyalty. But in order to establish trust, she had to first display the level of mistrust Selena would have been expecting. Val took a deep breath, preparing to soften her approach, but Selena lifted her eyes and spoke.

"I know what happened at R&M, or at least I know the tabloid version of events. My father has never given me the entire story, and I'm hopeful that I won't be punished for my connection to him. Yes, he expects me to return to work for him, but I plan to make my own decisions when the time comes."

Val sat back in her chair. "Just remember that the interns compete to earn a guaranteed job offer for next year. If you do take that honor, we hope you'll at least consider us. Of course, if that's not something you'd be interested in, we'd be happy to give you a recommendation."

"Thank you. I came here because I want to learn everything there is to know about digital trading, and who else would I want to work with other than the two tech wizards who took the world by storm before—"

Selena closed her mouth on the faux pas. Val's eye twitched, but she recovered from the unintentional slight enough to pretend she'd only heard the compliment.

"That's very flattering. You will learn here if you work hard and keep your eyes and ears open. I'll expect you to follow my direction, or another trader's should one take an interest in your training. For now, I'll be pairing you with another intern." She glanced at her notebook as if to confirm the assignment. "Anthony Knight."

Corrupting Selena wouldn't bring down Geraldo's operations. For that she needed information she hoped Noelle could provide. Still, she wouldn't resist the opportunity to subvert the girl. After all, a little vengeance was more satisfying than none.

With or without Dane, she planned to lay the groundwork by getting Selena to start breaking little rules, and what better motivation was there than a summer crush? Of all the interns, that hapless fool Anthony seemed the most tractable. He might be talented in finance, but he had about as much social intelligence as Dane had at that age.

Selena's eyes grew wide for a beat. She'd clearly noticed the attractive, albeit inept, young man. *Perfect.* "Of course. Thank you. I'll work hard and learn everything I can."

"And Selena. Please come to me directly if you have any questions at all."

Selena stood and headed toward the door, hesitating only a moment before turning back. "But will we eventually be working with mentors this year?" She twisted her hands. "When I researched the internship, I noticed that last year—"

Val held up a hand. "Oh, yes. We will make sure you're each partnered with an experienced trader. I have big plans for you." At Selena's grin, Val added, "For all of you."

Sophie,

Of course I realize that using my work email could infringe on corporate policy, but I read through the handbook last night, and I don't think I'm breaking any rules. They discourage abusing the company email for personal business but allow that it is occasionally necessary, as long as it remains appropriate. And since I'm not supposed to play on my phone or browse the Internet while I'm here, you might be getting a few more emails than usual. At least if I have free time.

Guess what I found out today? If I win some intern competition, I'll have a guaranteed job waiting for me right here. After this internship, I'm going to be able to get a job anywhere, and Dad won't be able to make me come work with him. I know you think I'm trying to get back at him, but you're wrong, Ms. Psych major. Not everything is a Daddy issue, you know. I barely know him anymore, anyway. I just want to choose my own path. To be the best you need to train with the best, right? Doesn't that fit in with your feminist theory? You should be more supportive, my friend.

I'll talk to you later.
Selena

The invitation slipped in between a series of change request notifications. Dane nearly missed it as he held his delete key down and watched the unread emails scroll up and disappear into the ether.

Dane,

Please come to my office at 4. We can discuss your inventory needs then.

Best,
Noelle Constance | CEO Fleetwood Capital LLC

He read the message several times for any hidden meaning. An invitation in the late afternoon could lead to a proposition to an early evening. But Dane doubted Noelle was making any overtures. She'd been far too skittish the day before, and she had a long history of saying no to him. It had taken him months of slow, purposeful courting to wear her down before. God, he'd brought her right to the brink of saying yes. He'd manage it again.

Perhaps the late hour would give her an excuse to cut the meeting short if she needed an escape. She'd only recently settled into the position. He hadn't been able to discern a pattern to any of the one-on-one meetings she'd held. Mostly just getting to know her staff. Maybe she wanted to reconnect with him. She couldn't avoid him indefinitely.

He closed his laptop at three fifty-seven and headed to Noelle's office. When he entered the hallway, he overheard a burst of laughter coming from the open door. Before he could stop and knock, he realized every chair in the room was occupied by the heads of other groups. His shoulders dropped. Of course. It was one of *those* meetings. He'd avoided them for the past three years but had walked right into this one. And it was too late to turn and leave. Hal from QA stood and waved him over. "Take my chair, Dane."

With no other choice, Dane slipped in but stepped around Hal's proffered chair. He leaned against the wall as he always did in group meetings—the easier to slip back out without drawing too much attention. Hal sat back down and chatted with Julie from Sales. "It's about time she held this meeting. I need automation servers."

Servers. Dane was supposed to be asking about hardware. She'd called his bluff. He hadn't overseen the machines since he'd laid the network at his own company. Back then, he'd watched server load like a hawk. If their new systems had gone down before they'd reached maximum traffic, they might as well have gone home. What customers would trust their trades to an unreliable system? But even at his own company, a dev ops division had been created to monitor the day-to-day needs of the operation. That freed him to focus on software design, his real genius. He missed that work. He wasn't so bored when he was solving the myriad crises that arose in those days.

Stifling a yawn, he scanned the room. Noelle was punching the numbers on her conference phone with the help of Margo from Customer Support. There were two product managers here—Andre and Ernst. But Val was noticeably absent. Maybe

Noelle hadn't heard how instrumental Val had been in forcing out the last CEO. Or maybe she had. It was possible, though unlikely, that Val had been invited and chose not to show.

Dane rubbed his chin, trying to find the angle that profited him best.

If he could use one attack to capture two castles, so much the better. It made for a tricky end game, but Dane enjoyed the sport of playing as much as winning.

If Noelle had snubbed Val so quickly and openly, she risked creating a dangerous enemy. And a pissed-off Val would make an excellent accomplice—for him. Intent on destroying Noelle, Val would throw her full support behind Dane's attempts at seduction. He could never underestimate Val's acumen in matters of simple sexual attraction. She rarely kept her toys for long, but she certainly knew how to lure them in. He'd watched her in action, and even so he'd fallen victim to her charms, once. A willing victim to be sure, but he'd actually believed her when she'd coaxed his heart out of his chest.

But what if Val's absence revealed some jealousy toward her rival? Surely, Val was beyond such weak emotions. Then again, a jealous Val might lower her formidable drawbridge. She was too cunning to let him past her defenses, suspecting a Trojan horse intent on breaking her from within. And she thought *he* was paranoid. In reality, he'd forgiven but never forgotten her decision to abandon him years ago. She'd proven her loyalty lay with Dane, not the company they'd built, when she took a dive and quit. He could never forget that decision either.

Whatever was going on with Val, it was clear Noelle hadn't invited Dane to this meeting for any reasons that interested him. In fact, she'd probably only asked him there to put him in his place after his audacity the day before. It was a smart move, and ordinarily he might have counted it a setback, but he'd seen her flinch in the breakroom. This wouldn't be like before when she'd shut him out and he'd gone down without a fight. He'd had years to up his game, and he meant to make her experience desire and hope, followed immediately by loss and despair.

Truth be told, Val deserved the same, but he was willing to bide his time.

He watched for another minute as Noelle spoke crisply into the conference microphone. "Who's calling in? Is there anyone on the call?" She turned to Margo, "Are you sure it's connected?"

He slid around the outer wall and reached the hall. Once in his office, he pulled up the latest patch file one of the developers had sent him for code review. This was the closest he came to coding these days. Product overviews, design meetings, scrums, code reviews, long drawn-out discussions debating the merits of agile over waterfall development—these tedious chores fell into his daily purview. But the glory days of building a system from the ground up were light years behind him. Hell, he didn't even get to write the code for the solutions he designed.

The patch file looked clean, but Dane identified a small issue; the developer hadn't indented properly. Not a huge deal, but they had coding standards for a reason. He wrote the note into the defect and sent it back to the developer. It hadn't made him feel any better. The developer wasn't his problem. It was the goddamn invisible handcuffs he wore.

As an added kick to the groin, his current lack of freedom came courtesy of Geraldo, thanks to the way he'd overthrown Dane, making everyone doubt his integrity.

He dropped his head back. Maybe he *should* take Val up on her suggestion to ruin his daughter after all.

Maybe I should just take Val.

He packed up his computer and grabbed his gym bag. He took a quick tour of the floor to check in on his developers, then continued through the cubes to where the interns were stationed and stopped to learn their names.

Had he ever looked that optimistically hopeful?

That kid he'd seen outside yesterday morning stood and held out his hand. "Anthony Knight. Fourth year at Purdue. Pleased to finally make your acquaintance, Mr. Russ."

Dane took the kid's hand. "It's Dane. No need to get so formal."

"Oh, right. Sorry." He shuffled his feet. Suddenly, as if he'd remembered something urgent, he swung around and said, "I brought a copy of the *InterTech* magazine with you on the cover. I wondered if you'd sign it."

The other kids found something else to do. A pretty brunette girl to his right had the presence of mind to look embarrassed for him. Dane picked up a pen. "Sure. What do you want it to say? *To my biggest fan?*"

One of the other boys snickered, and Dane felt bad. He'd once been socially inept, and he certainly understood what it was like to be ostracized from one's peers. He signed the magazine and handed it back. "So what have you learned today?"

The question had been intended to give the guy some cool points back. A chance to have a conversation with his apparent hero and save face. Dane scratched his head and stifled the urge to narrow an eye. He knew one good glare from him could be blistering. And this poor soul hadn't quite earned his scorn. Just his boredom.

"Mr. Russ. I mean, Dane." He giggled. Dane squeezed his fists together and kept his face placid. It would be just great to come off as an asshole bully on the second day of their internship. "We've learned so much about the company. They've set us up on the system. It's intimidating, but I think we've all just about gotten the hang of our first assignment."

"Show me." Dane pulled up a chair and watched the kid painstakingly enter a single mortgage-backed security, one Loan ID at a time. "Did they teach you about servicers?"

"I learned all about that at school. I'm getting a degree in Finance."

Of course you are.

Dane stood and clapped Anthony's back. "That's great. I'm glad to see you all settling in. I trust Val's taking good care of you?"

All the interns nodded. They might have come looking to work under his shadow, but Val would have them eating out of her hand in a week. If she hadn't already. Putty.

His exit path took him along the corridor to Val's office—his true destination. He could see her working through the rectangular glass pane. As if she sensed his presence, she glanced up from her desk. He swung his gym bag around as he passed. She gave no sign of understanding, but she'd know where he wanted to meet.

A movement outside the door caught Val's eye. She glanced up from the mid-year reviews in time to catch Dane flashing his gym bag at her. She nodded one time, but as soon as he'd passed, the nod turned into a head shake with a roll of the eyes. She shouldn't mock his paranoia since she'd been the one to plant his initial insecurities. But there was obviously no reason for anyone to be tailing him here in the sticks. She wasn't about to give him hell about it; it served her purposes for him to mistrust everyone. Maybe she should hire someone to follow him for real to keep him on his toes. It made things more interesting.

Unlike Dane, she never left work before five, often working until late into the night. She knew all the unwritten corporate rules and followed them to the letter, at least as far as the eye could see.

She spent another ten minutes setting up appointments to meet with her subordinates the following day to discuss their performance. She'd assembled a top-notch team of traders, so the reviews were mere formality—paperwork to appease someone higher up the chain in some other city. Most of the goals were irrelevant in any case. She used the opportunity to make sure her team members were happy and unlikely to leave for a better position at a competing firm. In a way, this had become *her* performance review. She wanted to find out what she could do better. Bringing in new talent always led to months of retraining.

Dane never understood why she bothered to actually do the job she'd been hired for. But he was a man, and he'd been born into money and privilege. She'd fought and scraped her entire life, and she'd learned the value of a good cover story. In her backwoods hometown, nobody had praised her for the power of her mind. She'd cultivated a reputation for proper behavior in order to survive as a pawn in someone else's game. And she'd learned how to run the board without even looking like a player.

Dane could mock her for keeping up appearances. If he honestly believed she'd allowed him to see beyond her mask, he'd never figured out she simply had different masks for different suitors.

Or for different pawns.

Her mind returned to the interns. She'd left them alone for most of the afternoon to practice, but it was time to check on them and send them home. Maybe she should organize a socializing activity. She fished out her wallet and thumbed through the bills. *Twenty, forty, sixty* . . . She had less than one hundred, not enough to pay for a round of drinks for a dozen young interns, but the bar on Frederick had her card on file.

After a quick phone call, she grabbed her belongings and left her office. The interns all stopped working, fingers frozen on keyboards. Nobody appeared to be sleeping or playing on their phones, yet. They always started out so eager.

"Listen up. You've all worked hard today, and I'm proud of your enthusiasm. I'd like to reward you with dinner and drinks at Romano's a few blocks away. Just mention my name to the server, and the tab will be taken care of."

The kids' pudding faces almost warmed her heart. She glanced over at Selena, whose eyes flitted toward Anthony. *Good.*

"So finish up what you're working on, then you're free to go. Don't overdo it. You still have to be here bright and early tomorrow. And we'll be doing bond math." Several kids groaned. "Yeah, it wasn't my favorite when I was your age, but it won't be so bad. Maybe I'll order pizza and we'll have a working lunch."

With that, she swung out of the trading floor, climbed in her Honda Civic, and drove to the nail salon. She laid two twenties on the counter and said, "The private room, please."

Sophie,

Oh my gosh, I have so much to tell you.

Val came out a minute ago and told us to go have dinner on her. She's as nice and approachable as everyone says. I had a meeting with her earlier. She seemed genuinely interested in making sure I'm settled here. And then she put me on a team with the cutest boy in the group.

Don't worry. I'm not here to get a boyfriend. We've been working hard all day, learning our way around the software. But it can't hurt to have something nice to look at. I kind of got the feeling he was checking me out too. Maybe tonight when we go out, I'll get a chance to talk to him.

Oh, and Dane stopped by our desks on his way out tonight and sat down right next to the cute guy, Anthony, for like TEN minutes. I leaned in to eavesdrop and see if I could glean any information, and he smells unbelievably good. He emits a kind of power even when he's just standing there. For a second, he looked right at me, and his gaze is so intense that for a heartbeat, I was pinned in place. His eyes are hard and soft at the same time if that's possible. Such a vivid blue. I'll see if I can find any pics on the Internet that do him justice.

I'm sorry the dorm is so lonely. I miss you too, I have to tell you I'm loving the awesome apartment I have here, even though I have to room with a couple of the other girls. Good thing it's close by because with what they're paying us, I can't afford gas. I'd be okay if Dad hadn't decided I needed some "real world experience" and stopped sending me an allowance. Tonight's dinner will be a luxury. Then it's back to microwave food.

Cheers,
Selena

Dane pulled his Aston Martin into a parking space as far away from other cars as possible. Yes, the car cost more than a fair-sized house around here, but he didn't own a house. And other than his top-of-the-line wardrobe, five-star restaurant habit, and extravagant vacations at private resorts in exotic locales, he lived the life of a penniless miser. He had no wife running through his bank account, no kid to send to college. The car paid for itself in other ways. He'd never had to lay out a dime to get a woman to go home with him.

That wasn't why he'd bought the car. He'd bought it because he could. The value of that car represented a fraction of his net worth. His stock holdings at R&M alone had been substantial, and the severance package had made the news.

Plus he'd invested well of course. He wasn't one of the brightest minds in finance for nothing.

All that alone would have made him grotesquely wealthy. He didn't need to continue to work at all, but he grew bored without a toy, so he kept the position he held now at an ungodly salary.

Still he thought about retiring to Key West nearly every single day—but then he'd remember Val. He owed her so much. He wouldn't leave her behind until he'd paid her back. For everything. After all she'd made all this possible. His fortune. His freedom. His black heart.

Although he'd never been formally charged with malfeasance, the board at R&M had threatened him with a lawsuit if he refused to walk away from his own company. If he hadn't bent to their coercion, Geraldo would have kept on digging, and eventually he might have found the evidence of unscrupulous behavior they were lacking.

But that wasn't why he'd left without a fight. After Noelle, Val, and Geraldo had each made a fool of him within a mercilessly short period of time, he couldn't stand to be in the same room with the authors of his humiliation.

Dane never knew for sure whether Geraldo's crusade resulted from a vengeance of passion, payback for the night Dane had stolen with Val, or if he'd merely taken an opportunity to seize the reins of power. Intellectually, Dane respected the move, even if he'd been the victim. Val wanted to stoke his sense of righteous indignation to convert him to her plans to screw with Geraldo, but he didn't see the point in it. Dane had all the money he could ever need, and he had Val. He had no use for his old company, and Geraldo was no longer in any position to fuck with him.

The only actor in this drama he hadn't forgiven was Noelle. She'd stood there at that New Year's Eve party, in front of dozens of witnesses—his employees, co-workers, friends—and told him, "I could never love someone like you." He told himself it didn't matter, that he hadn't cared for her anyway. His crush had been nothing more than fascination. Like Val had said, he'd been charmed by the challenge. That's not what he'd told her that night, but in the blink of an eye his infatuation had turned to hatred. He wouldn't make the same mistake twice. He wouldn't fall for his own fiction.

True, Val had loved him and then devastated him. He ought to hold a grudge against her as well, and he did. He intended to even that score if she'd ever drop her defenses. But at least she'd tried to fix her error. Whether out of guilt or loyalty to Dane, she'd worked her magic to sweeten his exit. It was thanks to her the board had agreed to buy his shares and provide the golden parachute. It was her influence along with his father's name that had opened the doors for his job at Fleetwood.

At the time, Dane assumed Val wanted to expedite his ejection so Geraldo could replace him, so he and Val could become a power couple, running his company, laughing at Dane. He was ready to destroy them both, but then Val had surprised everyone when she resigned and followed Dane to the middle of nowhere. She'd chosen him over Geraldo, and now Dane was the one laughing.

With Val by his side, Dane had elected to lay low in the Midwest, but he knew nobody trusted him anymore. He was watched at all times, and his access to the system was restricted. He felt like a fucking figurehead, hired to attract people to breathe in his air, but he wasn't anything special. Not anymore. Other than Val, only Rosamund treated him like a human.

And so he owed her his gratitude, his loyalty, his friendship. But not his love. And some day he'd make her pay in kind for the night she'd left him feeling like a fool.

He occasionally considered starting another company, but owning a company had led to its own kind of drudgery. Even though he often missed the sense of purpose it gave him to extinguish the fires of a serious production issue, he now enjoyed the leisure to quietly fuck with anyone he liked.

Which was the only reason he was seriously considering telling Val to sign him up for her summer project.

He slid out of the Brioni suit jacket and laid it carefully over the passenger seat, obscuring his laptop bag. He slipped off the Salvatore Ferragamo dress shoes and laced up his Bottega Veneta leather gym shoes. He grabbed his bag and crossed the parking lot.

Once in the locker room, he took equal care hanging his slacks and dress shirt in the locker before changing into his T-shirt and shorts. He tucked a one-hundred-dollar bill into his pocket and headed to the weight room.

He pushed himself on the upper body machines for a round, then slung the towel over his neck and scanned the equipment. On the leg press, a toned college-aged blonde easily pumped out her reps. When she caught his eye, she smiled, strategically looking away. Her blush almost looked genuine. The girl-next-door routine intrigued him, but he hadn't come here to pick anyone up. Not tonight.

Just as he began to let down his guard, Morty Becker strode in. Casually. Dane sucked on his teeth. Had the internal auditor tailed him to the gym? Val could call him paranoid, but for the past several weeks, he knew someone had been watching his every move. Dane had taken precautions not to give anyone anything to go on. And Val could thank him for extending his care to her own reputation.

As soon as Morty lay on his back at the bench press, face directed at the ceiling, Dane took advantage of his blind spot. He crossed the room, leaned over the water fountain near the hallway, then turned and exited through the door into the alleyway.

The warm soapy water soothed Val's tired feet, and some of the tension she didn't know she'd been harboring seeped from her shoulders. She closed her eyes, focused on the peaceful music, and breathed in the smells of eucalyptus and mint. The sound of a door closing pulled her from the edge of sleep. Muted, high-pitched voices followed, and then Dane entered the small room.

He carefully removed his ridiculous sneakers and gingerly placed them on a shelf against the wall. Honestly, who paid several hundred dollars for European sneakers? There were better ways to spend money—less flashy, more effective. He sat in the leather chair and gently immersed his feet into the basin, sighing a groan of pleasure.

"Nice, isn't it?" She nodded to the technician to leave them in privacy. One of the many things money could buy.

"I've got ten, maybe fifteen minutes." He grinned. "I was right. I've got a tail."

"I never said they weren't out to get you. I just said you're paranoid. Those two statements are not mutually exclusive. So who is it?"

"Morty Becker."

"From internal audit? Why would he care what you do or who you see? You're far too circumspect to have raised any suspicions about your activities." Val frowned. "Not that you've done anything worth suspicion in a while. Speaking of which, how are things going with your girlfriend?"

When she'd floated Noelle's name for consideration for the CEO position, she'd known she'd prick Dane's vanity, and he'd have to react. She'd hoped the reality of this woman would put a final stake through Dane's perfected memory of her, or that he wouldn't find her as attractive as he once did. But there was always the possibility he'd want to assuage the anger that years had only ripened with time, that he'd have to rectify that slight to his ego.

Men are so weak.

And yet, she'd pushed for the board to hire Noelle because she could use her. Noelle had left R&M without so much as a promise of another job. According to insider gossip, Geraldo had done something that the precious Noelle Constance couldn't tolerate. Val intended to find out what. Had Geraldo's hands begun wandering once Val was no longer there to buffer his predatory tendencies? Or had Noelle discovered she was working for a criminal? Why hadn't Noelle reported anything?

She'd suffer through the theater of Dane's thwarted libido if it meant getting closer to Noelle. She could profit from his vanity. And there would be some entertainment watching him continually relive the night Noelle rebuffed him so brutally.

Val's ego could handle it. After all, she'd often suspected Noelle had been a subconscious substitute for Val since they did share some physical resemblance. But the joke was on

Dane for trying to thaw the ice queen. Surely, he'd figure out faster this time that Noelle was an impostor, a mere facsimile of the woman he wanted. And Val was sitting right here.

Dane scratched his chin. His facial hair grew faster than any man she knew. She often told him he had a five a.m. shadow. "It's going. Or it will be."

She exhaled a short laugh. "So, nothing. Are you going to give up on this embarrassing waste of time and focus on something of real substance?"

He narrowed his eyes and paused for a moment. "It will be easier when I can get her alone. I thought I'd make inroads this afternoon when she invited me to her office, but then that turned out to be an all-hands thing. Everyone was there."

Val ground her teeth. "What do you mean, 'all-hands?'"

"All-hands. Well, maybe 'all-heads' would be more accurate. Margo, Andre, Ernst . . ."

"She invited all the department heads to a meeting?" Val took her feet out of the basin and stood to reach for her purse. She pulled out her phone and scrolled through the corporate emails. There was nothing she'd missed. She sat back down. "Why wasn't I invited? Is that skinny bitch trying to squeeze me out? And what are you laughing at?"

Dane raised his hands in protest. "Whoa. I'm not laughing. Maybe she just forgot."

"Forgot?" Noelle would forget about Val to her peril. Val settled back into the leather chair and placed one foot at a time in the hot water. "So what did you say you needed to move along on your little seduction?"

Val could kill two birds with one stone by helping Dane quench his lust, the faster to cauterize his heart and leave Noelle's bleeding. Val could slide into the role of trusted confidante to whom Noelle would spill all her secrets.

Dane had laid his head back, eyes closed—the very image of relaxation. The curl of his lip on one side of his mouth gave away his amusement. "I need to draw her out. I need time with her to get under her skin. She's started building a wall. I need to get beyond it."

Val tapped the armrest for a moment, considering his problem. "I think I can arrange that." Yes, she had an idea what to do. She nodded and leaned toward Dane. "Now about *my* project . . ."

Dane sat up and looked at his watch. "Sorry, I need to get back. Morty will be looking for me." He stood and shook off his wet feet. "Maybe next time, I'll have time to get my nails painted."

"Maybe next time, we can meet in a less clandestine location."

He waggled his eyebrows. "My place? In an hour?"

She was tempted. Dane was a beautiful man who maintained his body like he maintained everything else. And his stamina matched that of his over-compensating sports car. It had been years since she'd run her hands across his chest and breathed in the intoxicating smell of him. But he was on a mission with another woman on his mind. "If you'll consider forgetting this whole ridiculous charade with Noelle."

"For you?" He sucked on his lower lip. "Maybe. But now that I've tasted the challenge, I'm afraid I won't know how to quit. The woman will come to want me against all her better instincts. I'm already visualizing the moment."

"So that's your angle? You're taking revenge on her for rejecting you? Is this going to become a new thing for you, Dane? Should I be worried?"

"How is that any different than your interminable war against Geraldo?" A smile played on his lips. "Think how satisfying it will be to see her fall all over me and humiliate herself as badly as I did back then."

"So true love then?"

He snorted. "What would you know about that?"

Val laid her hand over her heart. "You wound me."

"Is that a no?" He took a step back, and God help her, she wanted to follow him, she wanted to say yes.

She considered the lay of the land, the position of all her pieces. "I'll tell you what. You capture your little rabbit, and then we'll talk."

He slid the crisp Benjamin from his pocket and dropped it on the tip plate. "Is that a wager?"

She shrugged. "Sure, if you like. You finish up your little game with Noelle. If you can bring her to her knees and walk away, destroyed as you intend, I'll be all yours."

She flashed a smile that radiated self-confidence and total control. She could appear aloof and uncaring. Whatever he did, it couldn't bother her. Her smile communicated her power.

Dane moved toward her and bent so close she could feel his warm breath on her cheek. Her smile faltered, and without meaning to she leaned forward a half an inch into his space. His lips vibrated against her skin when he said, "You've got yourself a deal."

When he turned and left, Val swallowed hard and sucked in a deep, shuddering breath.

Wednesday

*S*ophie,

Life is good. The interns all went out to this near-by restaurant and got a long table. We started out trying to converse as a group, each sharing a bit about where we were from and why we'd decided to intern at Fleetwood. But then everyone ordered a couple of drinks, and after a bit, we were talking in small intimate pairs or trios, and it was brilliant. Val was so smart to send us out like this to bond. I'm sure she knows the value of close personal relationships in the workplace.

And then . . . that cute boy Anthony took a chair next to me and asked me who I was hoping to intern with. I told him Dane of course, and he said he'd also wanted to work with Dane, so maybe we'll be competing for the mentorship even before we're fighting over who will be the best here. Speaking of that contest, one of the guys drank a bit too much and started boasting about how he had a stronger background than any of us and would easily win the job. I probably could have dropped my dad's name, but I wonder if they'd assume I wasn't capable of winning on my own merits. What do you think? I'm here because I'm smart enough, right? I don't want to trade on my dad's reputation alone.

Anyway, we ended up being asked to leave after a loud argument broke out. I hope Val isn't mad at us.

How are your summer classes going? Make sure you have some fun. I highly recommend it.

Best,
Selena

The quarterly board meeting always came at an awkward time. Although Val's presence wasn't strictly required, she arranged for one of her new hires, Kyle, to take the interns through their first exposure to the bond trading software that would be their life for the next several days. They always grumbled about it, and she felt sorry for Kyle. He wasn't getting paid to babysit and hold hands. But there was nothing she could do. If she skipped the board meeting, they'd forget she existed. She'd spent too much time gaining their trust to let it slip away.

None of the board members would actually fly out to this meeting. Val could have stayed at her desk and dialed in, but she made it a point to move down to the larger conference room where a webcam had been set up for the remote. She wanted to make sure she'd be seen. She rarely talked at these meetings except when there was something she wanted. She had a small sphere of influence, and she tried to use her power judiciously.

Since this was Noelle's first official presentation, Val had extra incentive to attend to support their new local leader. It would consolidate Noelle's trust in her as well.

Val entered the meeting room. Most of the chairs around the long table were already occupied. She secured one of the remaining seats near the end of the table since it would put her closer to Noelle, who sat at the head.

The screen lit up with a Powerpoint and a list of all the attendees who had dialed in. Maxwell Baker, Aloysius Holstein, Amy Waterson, Louis Beauchamp, and the rest of the old guard who owned the umbrella company that had purchased Fleetwood several years back. Since Fleetwood was so small and so different than their other holdings—and so profitable—they had left the company alone rather than try to force it into the larger group. The board still had the power to make big decisions, but they usually needed reasons. And they rarely turned their eyes on the company beyond these quarterly reviews—unless things were going bad. Like when the company suffered the publicly devastating loss of their CEO last quarter.

Things were going quite better now that the problem had been addressed, but the board was still skittish.

Fortunately, Noelle had recently quit her position at R&M, and the board had hired her based on Val's strong recommendations, not realizing that Val was appraising her for qualities that didn't appear on her resume.

Noelle smiled into the webcam as she called the meeting to order with a "Good morning, everyone, and thank you all for calling in."

A small picture-in-picture flashed on the corner of the screen, and the board room displayed everyone present.

Noelle pressed the clicker, and the presentation began. Graphs showed the earnings for the prior quarter broken down by activity. Most of the revenue had come through brokering transactions for the day traders who used the software to make their own trades but relied on the added expertise of one of Fleetwood's real-live consultants. But Fleetwood in turn made its own investments by buying and selling mortgages, trading in stock, and maximizing any other financial tool they could master. For a small Midwestern company, they could compete with many of the bigger New York City banks. And this was thanks in large part to the experience of the staff.

Noelle clicked through to a slide that listed the players at the company. "As you know, we couldn't make this company run without the people. I'd like to give credit to some of our key personnel who have been instrumental in advancing our position in the market."

It was always the same people. Nobody from the technical department ever got a mention. It was as if the company truly believed that they thought up a product and it materialized out of nowhere for the sales staff to market. Val never brought this up, however. She liked it better when the board forgot Dane even worked here.

Noelle paused on the recent history she couldn't ignore: the firing of Ted Rasmussen. "As you are all aware, I am replacing the former CEO under considerable media attention. I appreciate your confidence. Be assured that we are taking the matter very seriously. We'll be training all of our employees to recognize and report sexual harassment."

Val stifled a yawn. Ted had been a legitimate pervert who came from a culture where men in power could openly terrorize the women in their employ, and the corporate blue dogs would turn a blind eye. Ted wasn't a cautionary tale so much as relic of another time. He hadn't learned to adjust to a modern workplace, and Val found it very easy to exploit his sexual appetite until he ceased to be useful. Until Val needed to make a place for Noelle.

It was only a matter of time before someone complained about his wandering hands. And Val had led the charge, knowing which women would come forth to make sure the allegations stuck. It was easier since it was all true. *Good riddance*.

Noelle's lip curled as she added, "Hopefully Ted's fate will serve as a warning that this behavior will not be tolerated."

Val appraised her for any other signs she might have had recent first-hand knowledge of unwanted sexual advances. Geraldo could be insistent, Val knew, but might he have come right out and threatened Noelle? Was she protecting his secret to avoid the controversy?

At last the slide show ended. Noelle took questions from the attendees and answered them with fluency. Val had to give her credit. She'd taken to the position.

Maxwell spoke up and mentioned that Noelle had failed to project the revenue for the fiscal year. "We need to be able to plan. Could you please get these numbers to us by next week?"

Noelle blushed with the realization that she'd completely dropped the ball on one of the main interests to the board. "Of course. I'll have it ready by Monday. If nobody else has anything—" She paused to make sure nobody piped up. "That will conclude our meeting."

Chairs pushed away from tables, and people left alone or in pairs, talking under their breaths about various things— none of which had anything to do with the meeting. Noelle sat in her chair, looking slightly defeated but fighting to regain her confidence.

Val moved over one seat to be closer. "That was a good presentation. I thought you did a wonderful job showing how we've remained competitive in the market despite the recent scandal."

Noelle didn't acknowledge Val and kept scrolling through her notes.

Val tried another tack. "You know, it's not a big deal to get them the fiscal projections a week late."

That did the trick. Noelle lifted her eyes. "Look, I know you helped me to get this job, but I can't honestly figure out why."

"You've got a great track record. And we've known each other a long time."

"Not exactly. We knew each other a long time ago. And we weren't exactly friends then."

"True. But we weren't exactly enemies." Val pursed her lips in thought. "Can you tell me why the cold shoulder? Have I done something to offend you?"

Noelle closed her laptop and looked Val directly in the eyes. "It's nothing personal against you. I'm simply baffled by your decision to follow Dane out here. After everything, why would you continue to associate with him?"

Val raised one eyebrow. "Why did you?"

Noelle's shoulders relaxed. "Valid question. Honestly, this was too tempting a promotion. How could I pass up on the chance to advance my career like this?"

Knowing she wouldn't likely get Noelle to confide in her so soon, Val couldn't resist asking the only question she wanted the answer to. "Why did you quit?"

It was too soon. Noelle gathered her papers together without another word.

Val started to stand but threw out like an afterthought. "Oh, I'm planning to bring a donut truck around the front of the building this afternoon as a social activity for the new interns. Do you think we could make it something for the whole company? My treat. It would be a good way to trick the other staff to come out and introduce themselves to our interns. In just a week, we're going to start the one-on-one mentorship. Wouldn't it be good for our experts and interns to mingle before that?"

Noelle squinted an eye but apparently couldn't find an angle she could disagree with because she finally nodded. "That sounds like a wonderful idea actually. I'll send out an invitation as soon as I get back to my desk." She slid her laptop into her bag. "And thank you."

"It's no big deal. Donuts aren't that expensive."

"No, I mean thank you for reaching out to me. Maybe I've been a little hasty in my judgment of you. Dane on the other hand—I think someone needs to keep an eye on him."

Val shook her head. "You don't need to trouble yourself with Dane. The company shackled him pretty tight." Nobody needed to know that those shackles were mostly imaginary. With a bit of incentive, Val had coerced the former CEO into giving Dane just enough freedom so he wouldn't want to leave, while keeping him dissatisfied enough that she'd become his sole source of amusement in this wasteland. "He can't cause you any trouble. Well, nothing you can't handle, right?"

Noelle smiled. "I handled it once before. I suppose I'll handle it again."

Despite the dim lighting in the meeting room, Val could make out a flush creeping across Noelle's cheek. She chuckled. "He is after all just a man."

"I used to think he seemed like a nice guy." Noelle shook her head. "But it doesn't matter. Besides, I'm way too busy to entertain any unwanted advances. I've been trying to avoid him altogether."

"Sounds like a good plan." They walked out into the hall together, and Val said, "So I'll see you at the social, right? It wouldn't be the same without our fearless leader."

"Sure. I'd be glad to come and mingle with the troops."

"Great. See you there."

Val left Noelle behind to go sit in the smoking area and think. She wished Dane would see her and come down to talk, but she also knew he was too paranoid to meet there again so soon.

One of these days, when it no longer served her, she'd have to cure him of his unfounded fears of being watched. Nobody here cared what they did. That was the beauty of their situation. But Dane had been burned before, and he wasn't about to drop his vigilance, even though, in the three years he'd worked here, nobody had ever sounded the alarm on any of his nefarious activities.

And they never would.

Dear colleagues,

Please join us this afternoon for a social event generously hosted by Val Montgomery. We'll enjoy the beautiful weather and partake of donuts and coffee brought direct to us from the D'oh! Nuts! traveling truck. This is a great opportunity to meet the new interns and connect with each other outside of the work place.

Come down to the parking lot at four. I hope to see you there.

Best,
Noelle Constance | CEO Fleetwood Capital LLC

The donut social was a clever ruse. Dane made a mental note to thank Val later, though if it gave him an advantage in his efforts, he'd be thanking Val soon. All night long. He knew Val got something out of this, too. Suggesting this event to Noelle and then offering to spring for it would raise her profile and secure her a stronger position. Next time Noelle invited the heads of departments, she wouldn't forget about Val.

His phone buzzed, and he opened the text message. Leonard. It didn't even matter what he'd said, but out of curiosity, Dane opened it. *Softball practice is on time.*

Dane walked over to the window. From his vantage point, he couldn't tell who milled about on the sidewalk or over by the picnic tables on the other side. He could see the edge of a red truck. And he had Leonard's message. Noelle was outside.

After taking an extra minute to repair his image—chewing an Altoid, reapplying the slightest hint of a musky lemon-tinged fragrance, straightening his dress shirt and suit coat, controlling his hair—he descended to join the others as though it was an afterthought.

The chatter grew louder as he approached the glass doors and more than doubled in intensity when he stepped into the June sunshine. The suit might have been overkill, but then again it gave him an air of elegance he couldn't achieve with a sweat-stained shirt.

Ignoring the donut truck entirely, he moved over to the picnic area. Noelle had stationed herself at one table and found herself flanked by sycophants. Her blond hair had started to unwind from a clasp at the back of her head, and wisps flew in front of her eyes. She ran a manicured finger across her forehead and tucked the gold strand behind one ear. The intimate gesture caused Dane to experience a twinge of unanticipated arousal. He shifted in his seat and enjoyed watching her field one employee after another, suitors presenting themselves at court.

He wondered if she would be as easily influenced by the suck ups as the last CEO. But when her eyes began to dart around, apparently searching for an escape, he guessed no. He leaned against a table and waited for his own ass kissers.

It only took a few minutes.

"Mr. Russ. I mean, Dane. Could I get you a coffee? There's a rather diverse selection. And the donuts are made to order."

"No, thanks."

"Tea? Water? Did you want to try a donut?"

"I'm good. Thanks . . . Andrew?" He knew the kid's name. He knew all their names now.

"It's Anthony. But that was close. You nearly had it." Anthony stepped closer, apparently thinking he'd scored a point with Dane.

Dane looked past Anthony and took in the social patterns of those who congregated. Val moved easily from group to group. She trailed a small posse of younger interns and introduced them around, staying put for the duration of a short exchange, then rotating out. She'd always had the gift of the social sociopath. Compared to the awkward clumping of everyone else, her moves looked as choreographed as a ballet. She was the black swan.

It was only a matter of time before she encircled him with her movable party.

"Dane. You know Elly, Kristin, Jennifer, Ron, Summer, and Selena. Just a few of our interns. The rest are scattered about here."

Dane nodded. "Yes. We met yesterday. How are you liking it here?"

They stood silent for a moment, maybe unsure who should go first. Dane inhaled. "I understand you worked on bond math today?"

Ron broke the awkward barriers. "That was balls." He accompanied his review with a wide grin, so Dane took that as a positive reaction to one of the less popular aspects of finance.

Dane made eye contact with Val, and she pulled the group behind her. The sun, trailing her solar system. A solar system composed of baby ducks.

Noelle's situation hadn't changed, but the players had. They came, wave upon wave, and pinned her. She'd never come out of her office again if she had encounters like this awaiting her every time. Dane took this as his moment to intervene.

He stepped behind her and tapped her shoulder. "Could I steal you away for a moment?" He leveled his eyes at Paul Lehman, who'd choked off a word mid-sentence. "You don't mind if I borrow her, do you?"

Noelle seemed torn, hesitant to leave with him. Paul's stammering protestation reeked of desperation, and on either side of Paul more eager staffers waited to bend the ear of the top dog. They had so many suggestions, so many accomplishments to share, so many empty praises to lay at her feet. Her decision made, she followed Dane toward an unoccupied table in the far corner.

"What can I help you with, Dane?"

"Honestly, nothing. I thought you might like a break from the henpecking. They don't mean any harm."

She cut her eyes back toward the table where Paul looked a little lost. "It's my job to listen." But she didn't make a move to return.

Paul waited, shifting from foot to foot, but his eyes wandered toward the donut truck.

Dane leaned in and whispered, narrating. "He's wondering if the donuts will run out before he's had a chance to try one. In a few minutes, he'll walk away and blend in with a more familiar group."

Paul threw a glance back at Noelle and then slowly turned and plodded to the truck. Noelle laughed. "There are others waiting. I really should—"

"It's almost five. They're about to realize they don't need to stay until the bitter end of the donut social. When they figure out they can sneak out of work a little early tonight, they'll be off to collect their things. Watch." Noelle kept her face turned toward Dane but watched from the corner of her eye as the eager beavers dropped off one by one.

And that left Dane sitting across from Noelle as the courtyard cleared out.

"Still playing *Age of Empires*, Dane?"

He was surprised she remembered his affinity for that old strategy video game. "I've just been to more of these things than I care to count."

"And yet you aren't eating the donuts, drinking the coffee, or last I checked, socializing."

He gave his most abashed half smile. "I'm talking to you."

That spot on her neck appeared.

Hit.

"I thought you were merely rescuing a damsel in distress."

He lifted his gaze and looked directly into her eyes. "I'm not in the business of rescuing damsels."

"Right. You have rather the history of putting damsels in distress."

"Is that so? Do I put you in distress, Miss Constance?" He touched her hand.

The red spot reached her cheek.

Another hit.

She pulled away. "Not in the least."

Her resistance might have hurt him years ago. He'd slowly courted her, taken his time to get to know her, letting

her get to know him. Not since college had he failed so spec-
tacularly to conquer, and it earned him Val's uniform mockery
then. He could see it in her disgust now. But there'd been more
to it than the challenge. Something about Noelle had intrigued
him back then. He'd stupidly thought if he could win someone
like her, it would mean he was worthy of more. Or it might
just mean she was worthy of less.

But then Noelle suddenly and without explanation cut
him off in the most humiliating fashion. He still found himself
prodding the wound to his ego, wondering what in the hell
had repelled her so profoundly she'd tell him off in a roomful
of co-workers.

The question danced on the tip of his tongue, but he
wouldn't open his veins in front of an emotional vampire. Instead, he focused on the current problem. "Then why have
you been avoiding me?"

"You have a number of off-putting habits, Mr. Russ."
She made to stand.

He grabbed her wrist. "No, wait. You can't drop that
and leave. Give me an example. How can I change for the better if nobody ever corrects me?" He flashed his most boyishly
charming smile.

The rest of her cheek flamed.

Battleship sunk.

She raised one eyebrow and considered. "For one thing,
you've taken up smoking."

"You're offended by my smoking?" He reached into his
pocket and retrieved the pack, thanking the gods he happened
to still have it on him. "Fine. I'll quit." He crumpled the package into a ball and shot it toward the large trash can at the
edge of the building. His shot fell short, and they both laughed.

"That was easy enough, Dane. But you can't just claim
to quit. You'll buy another pack tonight. You've never been
able to deny yourself whatever you want."

Her eyes narrowed, and he wondered what she meant by that. Was that a dig at the night he spent with Val that New Year's Eve? It wasn't like he'd cheated on her with Val. He'd taken his solace there, as misguided as that turned out.

"I won't buy another pack. But if you don't believe me, you can keep a watch on all the smoking areas tomorrow, and for the rest of the week. If I'm so incorrigible, I won't be able to make it through the entire work day without a smoke."

She tilted her head at him. "It's none of my concern whether you choose to smoke or not. Why would I spend any time monitoring your activities?"

Something in the way her eye twitched when she objected triggered a suspicion in him. Was she having him watched? Impulsively, he took both her hands in his. "Be my saving grace, Noelle." He chuckled. She surprised him by laughing, too. "And if I fail, then nothing will have changed. But I'll lay you a wager: if I can make it until Friday without a cigarette, I get to take you out to dinner."

She drew her hands back. Her movements were slow, however. She didn't appear repulsed, but her control troubled him. She stood and laughed awkwardly. "Mr. Russ, quitting smoking is its own reward. And I don't know why I'd lay a wager that I can in no way win."

"Fine, I'll up the stakes. If I fail, I won't ask you to dinner. Ever again."

"You know I could report you for harassment and get that same result."

He held a hand over his heart. "Shots fired." He let his most innocent smile spread across his face. "How about this: If you win, I won't bother you at all about anything that isn't work related ever again."

She tilted her head back and appraised him through narrowed eyes. "And you'll keep your word? If I catch you smoking at work, you have to respect my space."

"And if I make it through Friday, you will join me for dinner."

She hesitated. "That might look—"

"Like old friends catching up."

"Friends . . ."

He cut his eyes over to the trash can. "And besides, you're so sure you'll win."

She bit the inside of her lip for a beat. "Okay. That's a fair wager." She reached out her hand, and they shook. "I'll see you around the smoking court."

"I'll see you Friday at seven." He winked. "Dress nice."

When she disappeared around the corner, Dane tapped his phone and dialed L'Etoile. "Andre, I'd like a reservation for two on Friday at seven-thirty."

Thursday

*C*ontinued from Page 6

. . . met Val Montgomery and signed up for the Finance lecture she was attending, hoping to find common ground to talk with her. Although he had no trouble getting up to speed in the class, he soon discovered that Val's understanding of the material far surpassed his own. In order to keep up, he began reading everything he could find on the subject, and eventually he could maintain a conversation with her on diverse financial subjects.

But with his newly acquired interest in the world of finance, he began to consider ways to leverage his skills with the computer to make formerly inaccessible market analysis understandable to the average person. What began as a simple program to project bond yields grew into a more complex system for aggregating stock trends.

When he revealed to Val what he'd been working on, she immediately saw the value and suggested building a system where users could manage their own investments, trade stock, and maintain a portfolio of their own. Their first platform launched on . . .

Sophie,

One of the interns had an article about Dane and Val on his desk. I'm attaching a scanned page because there's a beautiful picture of Dane that looks more like him than any others I've seen before. He really does have teeth that white. His suits always look like he came straight from the tailor. Let's just say he's easy on the eyes. But there's something about him I can't place. We had a company social yesterday, and he just sat by himself. Val took us over to say hello (she's so gregarious and full of positive energy), but he looked like his mind was on something else. I bet he thinks in computer code all the time. And still, if he's half the financial genius Val is, there must be so much he can teach us. I'm still hoping he'll take some of us (me!) under his wing.

The attached article should prove that I'm not the only person who finds him worth discussing. I am not "mooning" after him as you put it. He's way too old for me anyway. He's like thirty-five. Just because you think I talked about him a "little too much" back at school doesn't mean I'm going to develop a crush on the man. You know he actually was a subject of conversation in my finance classes. And other than one short visit, he's barely acknowledged our existence.

Besides Anthony has been very flirty. I wouldn't be surprised if he asks me out for this weekend. (I swear I'm focusing on the work more than anything else.)

I'm taking care. I don't know what you're worried about.

How did you manage to get a cat past the RA? I don't want to sound bitchy, but you might have asked me before agreeing to take it in. Honestly, you're a stickler for rules until one cat needs a temporary home. I would have said no, but you've always been so sweet.

Hugs,
Selena

Val leaned against the door frame, observing the interns hard at work on a cooperative task. Anthony and Selena sat head to head, laughing. Confident she'd created some kind of connection between the two of them, she considered her next step. It would take a little more work, but if she could get Selena to trust Anthony, she might be able to coerce him to do the job Dane had refused to do. At least the first part of her new plan had clicked. Together, Anthony and Selena performed better than any of the other pairs. But they were both socially challenged, and at the rate of their tentative flirtation, it would take them months to forge the sort of bond Val could exploit. And she didn't have months.

Val drummed her fingers against the wall.

She let her mind drift back to when Dane and she had been like a well-oiled machine, always anticipating the other. Her lip twitched, recalling the day after graduation when Dane's father had insisted he get a proper job and stop fooling around with that amateurish start up. She told Dane not to pay it any mind, but Dane owed his father for the education he'd received, and his dad was sure to let him know. It was possible that the venture with Dane might have burned out in the months after they left school. They might have grown bored. Ironically, Dane's father's intervention was the best thing that could have happened to their company. More determined than ever, they kept in touch, worked long distance, through long nights, over chat windows and cell phones. There was an urgency and excitement to their forbidden activity.

That might do the trick.

Back at her desk, she drew up the list of intern teams. She printed it out and drew new lines between pairs. With a completed list, she returned to the training room and got the interns' attention.

"I apologize for neglecting to re-arrange you all earlier today. I'd like to make sure you have a chance to get to know each other better and so for the rest of the day, I'm going to pair you with a new partner." She caught the furtive glance Selena threw at Anthony. If he felt any disappointment, she couldn't read it. He'd mastered the art of sucking up and kept his eyes on Val until she gave them permission to move around the room. But just before he stood, he scribbled something on a piece of paper and slid it to Selena. Whatever it was caused Selena to blush.

Val leaned against the table only slightly pleased. Planting the seeds of a romantic entanglement would barely move her closer to her goal. She really needed Dane to bury the land mines that would detonate in time. Anthony would be a weak substitute, but Val used the weapons at her disposal.

When the kids had managed to pick up where they'd left off at her interruption, she prepared to leave. As she approached the door, she had the uncanny feeling of being watched and turned to find Anthony's head lifted, but his eyes darted back to the computer monitor so fast, Val couldn't be sure he'd ever looked elsewhere. Val cast a glance back at where Selena presented the picture of innocence. She narrowed her eyes. Without Dane, she'd need a year to destroy that girl.

Pssst - Selena. Sucks we got separated. I can totally still see you though. :) When we get a break, you wanna go get a coffee?

Anthony

The raucous clatter of the training room air conditioner completely obscured the *click clack* of fingers across keyboards. Dane peered through the door and observed the interns. It was a part of his high profile "Dane's in the building" campaign. He didn't want Noelle to forget he faced the quotidian struggles of the newly tobacco-free, so he paced the halls, fetched coffee, chatted with co-workers, and observed interns. By all appearances, he was shaking off the jitters of addiction.

The training room happened to be on the same floor as Noelle's office, so he figured it was in his interest to make an appearance. Maybe he'd give them some friendly advice. Although he didn't want to appear too friendly. After all, giving up cigarettes should make him more irritable. He ought to be taking advantage of that.

But he found himself amused by the theater of budding romance before him. While most of the interns kept their heads down, focused on the task of creating a loan bucket that matched some target dollar amount, that gawky kid Anthony kept lifting his eyes and casting dark, haunted glances at Selena on the far side of the room.

Dane chuckled. Val managed to create this drama in less than a week. Amazing. He pulled a chair up next to Anthony and checked his work. "You've gone over."

Anthony blushed and shook his hair into his face. "Oh, God."

"It's okay. Look." Dane dragged some numbers back across the screen. "Start again. It's not always about getting the fewest loans. You just have to meet collateral with whatever you have at hand. But you never want to go over." He let out a short burst of air. "One time, we were short on collateral and had to throw cash into the bucket."

Anthony's eyes were saucers. "I didn't think you could do that?"

"You can't do it in the software. We had to get creative."

Focused now on his screen, Anthony worked quickly and found a solution that was close enough. The numbers would never be exact. He clicked through to the next screen and sighed. "There's so much more to learn than I expected."

Dane placed a hand on the Anthony's shoulder. "Yeah, but you'll get it." He leaned in closer. "At least when you're not distracted by a pretty girl."

If Dane hadn't been sure the kid was harboring a crush, the speed with which Anthony's head swiveled up and his eyes flew over to the girl and back to Dane would have confirmed it. His shoulders dropped. "Is it that obvious?"

"Only if you've ever been there."

"Val?" Anthony sat up straight. "Oh, God. I'm so sorry. I didn't mean to pry. God. I'm an idiot."

Before the kid hurt himself, Dane shook his head. "No, you're right. I had a crush on Val for a long time in college. She was always so poised and confident, and there I was—this big nerd."

"You were never a—"

"Oh, yes. A big nerd."

"So what did you do?"

"I got her phone number and sent a text to her during a class. It was funny watching her glance around trying to guess where it came from. When she figured it out, she marched right up to me after class."

This was canon. The mythological genesis of Dane's friendship with Val was based in this socially inept attempt to ask her out. It was half right. She loved to tell tales of how woefully pathetic he'd been when he'd sought her out, how she'd had to remake his entire image once they'd founded the company. And he did start dressing sharper to appeal to investors, which in turn made him far more popular with the ladies. But he'd never lacked the confidence or ability to talk to girls before he met Val. He simply hadn't been interested in any specific women enough to drag his attention away from the video games he was trying to create. Okay, so the giant nerd part was one hundred percent accurate.

So was the part where he pursued Val to no avail which is why he'd never bothered to correct her version of events. The end result was the same: He'd fallen under her spell. But for months, no years, that frustrating girl had never given him any reason to hope for anything more than a partnership, barely even a true friendship.

Well, not never. Once. Close enough.

Anthony's jaw hung open. "Well? What did you say? What did she say?"

"Why? You want to crib my best material? I'm afraid you need to get your own."

"Would you believe I already tried? I sent her an email, but she shot me down dead. She said it was against policy to flirt over corporate resources." He sucked in his breath, terror writ large in his eyes. "Oh, God. Not that I—"

Dane raised a hand. "Hey, I'm not the corporate policies police. Besides, who doesn't abuse email?"

Anthony exhaled, but the sheepish wrinkle in his brow never quite relaxed. He twisted his mouth. "I thought we had a connection, when we were paired up. I guess it was just me."

"I'm sure you'll think of something. Maybe she'd be willing to talk over chat."

"The training machines don't have an app installed."

"What's to stop you from downloading one?"

Anthony furrowed his brow. "But wouldn't that violate Sarbanes-Oxley?"

How had Val stumbled on the two most ethical kids?

"Use your phone." Dane stood up and pushed his chair back in. "Nobody expects interns to follow all the policies to the letter."

He strode out of the room, smiling. Val owed him. Big.

Val,

I'm attaching this interview I came across from years ago. I have to confess I've always been curious about those early days when you first met. You always claimed you had no interest in Dane. Wonder when that changed.

Best,
Noelle Constance | CEO Fleetwood Capital LLC

Finance Weekly: *It's been said you met Dane in a Finance class. Do you mind sharing the true story behind your amazing partnership?*

Val Montgomery: *Not at all. It was our junior year in college when I first laid eyes on Dane Russ, although it's true that he'd seen me first. What people don't know is that I was taking a class Dane was helping teach for Independent Studies, and it had stumped me*—Introduction to Programming. *Every day, growing more and more frustrated at the failure of my code to compile, I was about to punch the monitor. One day, in the middle of Finance, a message popped up.* I'll help you with programming if you'll go out for coffee with me.

FW: *From Dane?*

VM: *I wasn't exactly sure at first. I looked around the class, eliminating potential sources of this aw-*

ful come on. The obvious answer hit me as soon as I noticed the tragic nerd casting furtive glances my way.

FW: This is Dane Russ you're talking about? A tragic nerd?

VM: Nerd would be an understatement. He wore a T-shirt that must have been some kind of obscure inside gamer humor. Or possibly some obscure indie band. He'd clearly ignored any advice on how to style his hair. I swear, if he wore glasses, they would've been taped on the corners and sliding down his nose. But he didn't wear glasses, and his eyes were a beautiful shade of blue. I'll admit, even then he had potential. With his dark hair, he had a vague Clark Kent thing going on.

FW: How did you respond?

VM: I walked directly up to him and asked him something like, "Is this how you get dates? Bribery?" And then he introduced himself and offered to help me with my homework.

FW: In exchange for a date?

VM: In exchange for a date.

Val didn't need an article to remind her of one of the most significant days in her life—the day she caught Dane. Their relationship could have very easily ended before it started.

When he offered to tutor her, she snorted. "But only if I go out with you? No offense, but no thanks."

"Just one date." He whispered it, and she nearly took pity on his pitiful self, but she had zero interest in him sexually, romantically, or otherwise. Still, she figured she could always use a nerd.

"I'm Val." She held out her hand. He wiped his on his knee before shaking hers. She closed her eyes in embarrassment for him. "Look. I'll accept your trade. You help me with this homework, and I'll go get coffee with you." At the hope blooming on his face, she added, "But it's not a date. Just coffee." His mouth rounded, like he was about to try to bargain, but she held up a hand. He didn't have a very strong position, and she did. "It will buy you some credibility to be seen out with a girl. You can't ask for much more than that."

Dane walked a half a step behind her as they headed to the coffee shop. Maybe he feared she might run away if he lost sight of her.

She stopped dead and faced him. "If you want a girl's respect, you need to believe you deserve it."

He swallowed. "Okay."

"And what's with your shirt? *Wanna play with me?* I don't get it."

His eyebrow dipped. "It's a joystick. Haven't you ever played a video game?" That was the first time he'd struck a tone of confidence since they'd left the classroom. It bordered on arrogance, and she liked it. So she teased him.

"You mean like *Solitaire*?"

He groaned. "No. Like *Diablo* or *Half-Life*."

It was too easy. Like shooting nerds in a barrel. "And those require a joystick?"

"No." He sighed heavily. "They're PC games."

She continued to needle him the rest of the way to the coffee shop, and he told her about the different games he liked

to play. She didn't pay much attention but faked enough interest to keep him talking. When they reached the door, she stood
by, waiting for him to open it for her. He registered where they
were and blinked. "I could show you sometime. Do you want
to come back to my place?"

She opened the door for herself and walked up to the
counter to order. As soon as they sat down, she explained how
things were going to be.

"Here's the deal. I need help with the programming class.
You need help with," she waved in his general direction, "everything. If you'll tutor me, I'll try to fix you up enough that
you can get a date without resorting to bargaining or seducing
people with video games."

"I can get dates."

"And sex?"

He slumped in his chair and pursed his lips. "What do
you propose?"

"First, sit up straight and master your expression. You
look like a sullen teenager."

He glared for a heartbeat but then obeyed her command.
"Okay. What else?"

She sucked on her lip, regarding him. "I don't know
if it's possible, but I'm willing to wager if we get you a new
wardrobe and work on your appearance . . . and find you a
non-nerd topic you can talk about as passionately as you do
your nerd things, you might be able to get a girl to your room
without all the tricks."

He leaned as far forward as the table would allow and
whispered, "What if I just want to get laid?"

She laughed. "Oh, you want me to work miracles."

He cocked his head now with one eyebrow raised. "And
you want what grade in your computer class?"

Oh, yes, she might like him after all. "Touché." She
looked at him for a minute. "We'll need to throw in some gym

time, too. But—" He had a decent build, and with work, he might even become attractive. "—if you do everything I ask and help me get an A in programming, I'll do my damndest to get you laid. Deal?"

"What if you get an A, but I don't get laid?"

She ran a tongue across her lip, thinking. "If you haven't gotten laid by New Year's Eve, I'll sleep with you myself."

His eyebrows shot up. "It's a deal."

Val's eyes refocused on the article before her. Ten years had elapsed between the New Year's Eve in question and the night they finally consummated that bet.

She'd never forgotten the morning she technically won that wager with Dane. The first time she lost him.

Finals had rolled around, and Val aced her Programming exam, but Dane still hadn't gotten laid. In just a couple of weeks, she'd have to fulfill her end of the bargain. His time for finding another willing partner was ticking away, and with the end of finals, the campus emptied. She'd begun to suspect he wasn't even trying anymore. She'd worked this miracle and had begun to hope he was stalling because he wanted her to be his first.

The holidays on campus were a depressing affair. Most of the students had gone home, so there weren't many parties. For New Year's Eve, Dane and Val were planning on a night out clubbing in town. She pictured them together at the stroke of midnight. He'd say to her, "You lost." But she'd be thinking that she'd really won. And they'd kiss and go back to his room since her roommate had stayed in town as well. She didn't know what would happen beyond that. They'd never talked about it.

She woke up at ten a.m. on New Year's Eve, just as her roommate, Kate, came crashing back in after an all-nighter. Kate was laughing when she dropped onto Val's bed.

Val yawned. "What's so funny?"

"I did it! I took pity on the poor boy!" Kate was cackling. "It's done."

Val sat bolt upright. "You did what?"

"I found Dane last night at a bar, and he was well lit. And hot. Honestly, he's one of the best-looking guys on campus right now. If you can get him to stop talking about computers for an entire night, he'll be damn near perfect."

"What happened, Kate? What did you do?"

"What you've been trying to make happen for the past three months." She grinned, pleased with herself. "I did you a favor and slept with him. You won your bet!"

Val pulled the pillow over her head, pretending to go back to sleep, hiding the tears.

She shook her head at the irony that here they sat years later with the exact reverse wager. But this time, she didn't intend to lose him.

She started to close the document when it occurred to her to wonder what Noelle had been doing with a nearly five-year-old article about Dane and her. What was she playing at with her passive aggressive email? Noelle was in no position to be angry or jealous about Val's relationship with Dane. Noelle couldn't cry foul now since she'd kicked Dane to the curb even before Geraldo made the entire board aware that Val had finally slept with Dane.

Then again, since Val had filled Noelle's head with Dane's many misdeeds of to lead her to his public humiliation, she could understand Noelle's confusion. Val bit her lip and giggled. That was bad of her, but she found it amusing how willing Noelle had been to believe the worst. If only Geraldo had been as pliable.

A light tap at the door disrupted Val's concentration. She lifted her head, but her eyes cut over a moment later, glued to the computer screen as long as possible. Selena waited in the threshold, passing her hand over her skirt to straighten out invisible wrinkles. Val nodded, inviting her in.

"Selena?"

"I'm so sorry to bother you, but I find myself in a bit of an ethical dilemma. I hate to tattle, but I'm concerned that I might get into trouble if I don't speak up now."

"Oh? What kind of trouble?" Val gestured to a chair across from her desk and leaned forward.

Selena sat and dropped her face into her hands. "I've always been taught that I need to follow not just the letter of the law but the spirit as well."

Val bit the inside of her lip to keep from laughing.

Selena lifted her head, eyes so sincere and guileless. "I wanted to do better than this."

Val closed her laptop and moved around her desk to a chair beside Selena. She took the girl's hands in hers. "Could you please just start at the beginning? What kind of trouble could you have gotten into running trade simulations?"

"It's not the work. It's personal. I've developed a bit of a relationship already with one of the interns."

"And? That's not off limits. It certainly can complicate things, but—"

"And after you separated us, he began sending me emails. I asked him not to, you know, because it's an abuse of company resources. I knew it was wrong."

"Okay. So then, what's the problem?"

Selena took a deep breath and looked at her hands. She glanced up at Val then dropped her gaze just as fast. "I—"

Val rolled her eyes. *Get to the point, girl.* "You what?"

"I installed a chat application on my phone." She swallowed hard. "It seemed like a way around the policy, but of course, we're still wasting company time, so it only skirts the issue."

Val snorted. "Do you honestly think that nobody has ever done this before?"

"Have you?" The girl's hands relaxed in Val's. Her eyes widened with an almost worshipful need for absolution.

"Ah, well, of course. Your father and I—"

"My father used chat software? But, didn't he fire you for breaking compliance?"

Val pulled her hands back. "I was never fired. Where did you hear that?" Her voice was too sharp, and the girl jerked. Val inhaled and corrected her tone. "I left the company of my own free will. I sold my shares. I no longer wanted any part of that company after everything."

"Wow. I'm sorry. I just thought."

"Anyway. Focus on your work and just be judicious with the time you spend on personal matters. But thank you for bringing it to my attention."

Selena grew serious. "I think I should uninstall the chat application. Right?"

"I suppose." Val couldn't openly press the girl to subvert the rules.

"It's just that Dane told Anthony—" Her hand covered her mouth, like she'd blurted out a secret.

"Dane?" What was he up to? She should have guessed he wouldn't be able to resist the lure of innocent blood in the water. When Selena winced and refused to reveal anything more, Val pressed her lips into a smile. "So, Anthony, huh?"

The girl's smile was genuine. "I think so." She hugged her shoulders. "He's been very helpful."

Val congratulated herself on the quick progress her little pawns were making. It was only the beginning. If only she could recruit Dane for real.

As Selena left the office, Val felt a stab of dissatisfaction at the assumption she'd been fired. It was true she'd followed Dane after he'd been forced out. Most people either correctly guessed she wanted to continue to work close to Dane or wrongly believed she'd been pressured to leave. She'd left on her own, but her reasons were more than blind loyalty to Dane.

Had she stayed on at R&M, she would have been an apparent owner, but in truth, she would have been working as an employee of Geraldo. Geraldo's control of the board made sure of that. If she had to work for someone else, she'd rather it be someone she could manipulate.

Here, at Fleetwood Capital, although she was an employee, she wielded as much power and influence as she'd ever had at R&M. With Dane at her side, she'd learned the infrastructure and the business from the ground up. She knew all the employees. If anyone figured out what she was up to, she saw to it they no longer worked at the company. She knew who she could trust for information, and she knew how to make things happen without ever alerting the board to her actual power. She'd found working from the shadows far more effective.

After the last CEO didn't work out, the board had almost voted to put Val in charge, but she'd suggested someone else. And within a week, Noelle Constance had been brought in. Val had expected her to be the same milquetoast girl she knew at R&M. Noelle surprised her. And that might become a problem.

It would be best to make sure the new CEO had an Achilles heel. Yes, she would leave Dane to his own devices for now.

Sophie,

God. Really. Please stop with your nagging. You have the wrong idea about Dane. Everything you're spouting is just hearsay. You don't think I've heard it all before? Your information about how he and Val were fired from their own company is completely unfounded. I heard it from Val herself. Dane and Val are two of the smartest peo-

ple in the industry, and if they wanted to leave their company and work elsewhere, they must have had a good reason.

Also, stop worrying about Anthony. You have no idea what it's like out in the real world. I mean, if you were so concerned with me breaking some ethical standards, you should have told me to stop writing you from my company email address a week ago. But whatever. You're living in the shelter of an academic world where harboring a cat is subordination. You couldn't possibly understand the nuances of the workplace. And you're not my dad. I expected you to be more supportive.

It's too bad your car broke down. I was looking forward to showing you around here. It would have put your mind at ease. Seriously.

Selena

Morty Becker made a terrible spy. He had no business being in the third-floor breakroom. Neither did Dane, but Leonard had seen Noelle in there for the past two days at around three, and he'd hoped to engage her in some conversation. She'd successfully avoided him since they'd made their wager, and he wanted to casually remind her without having to stoop to emailing her. But instead of Noelle, he found Morty. Or more accurately, Morty found him.

Dane stepped away from the coffee machine, blowing on the hot liquid. "Afternoon, Morty. Down here checking up on the customer support team?"

Morty's suit looked like he'd dunked it in water, rolled it into a ball, thrown it under his pillow, and slept on it all night. Dane had always thought of auditors as meticulous people, but Morty was a shabby mess. He had the appearance of a dime store gumshoe detective. Or maybe Dane thought so because Morty was so obviously keeping tabs on his every move.

"The breakroom on four didn't have the coffee I usually drink." He selected a packet of Sumatra and dropped it into the machine. Dane made a mental note to check the fourth-floor inventory on his way back to his office.

But he had a second idea.

He reached into his pocket and moved his hand about. The pocket was empty, but if he'd had a pack of cigarettes, that's where they'd be. He waited a beat for Morty's coffee to finish brewing, then stepped down the hall to the elevator bank. He hit the down button. When the doors slid open, he hesitated until he caught a glimpse of Morty coming around the corner. He entered and hit the button for the ground floor.

Once in the lobby, he dropped the coffee into the nearest trash can. He nodded to Eleanor, the receptionist, as he cut across to the entrance to the mailroom.

Charlie looked up from a stack of letters. "What can I do you for, Dane?"

Dane hadn't thought this through and stopped for a second to compose his plan. He turned in the doorway so he half faced Charlie but could still see the entire lobby. "I wanted to find out if the afternoon mail's already gone out."

"A-yup. Went out at two, same as always."

The stairwell door opened onto the lobby, and Morty stepped out. Dane dropped back farther into the mailroom and watched Morty stride across the floor toward the doors leading out to the courtyard. The poor bastard was completely out of breath. Apparently the gym workouts hadn't gotten him in any better shape. Dane should probably start going more often. For Morty's health.

"Thanks, Charlie. I'll leave a little early and stop by the post office."

"No problem."

Charlie went back to sorting the mail, and Dane crossed back to flirt with Eleanor, but then thought better of it. It would be satisfying to see Morty's face when he came back in with no evidence that Dane had been smoking. And even more amusing to watch him realize Dane knew he was trailing him. But as long as Morty didn't know he knew, it might be advantageous to him.

Instead, he took the elevator back up to his office, left the door open, and waited until Morty peeked through the crack as he passed by.

Sorry, buddy.

Friday

The interns had worked hard all week. Val considered letting them head out an hour early. It wasn't like they were doing any real work yet. But she didn't want to get them into thinking that Fridays ended at four by default. So she threw an extra challenge at them and promised they could leave once they finished it. It would take them an hour.

She was on her way back down to check on their progress when she passed Noelle's office and spied Dane through the window in her door. She slowed her pace but couldn't see more than Dane's back.

Of course Dane would kick off his plans to woo Noelle. And since the culmination of his efforts would win Val a night in his arms, she ought to be pleased that he'd made his first move. But she'd rather not know how the sausage got laid.

When she entered the training room, the interns' heads swiveled toward her.

She announced, "When you've finished, you're free to go."

They all turned back to their monitors with renewed fervor.

Val dropped into a chair and rested her hands on the table before her, wondering what Dane had been saying to Noelle. Surely he couldn't have wormed his way into her good graces already. She should convince him to change the wager somehow, make his goal more palatable, something that would serve her own purposes.

Maybe Val could drop the games altogether and let him take her home.

It was a constant temptation, but she worried if she gave him the opportunity, there was a better than average chance he'd use it to get even with her for leaving him that morning. She didn't want to wake up the day after, humiliated and alone, even though that's exactly what she'd done to him.

She'd been a fool.

That night, on the elevator, he pressed her against the wall, his hands on either side of her head.

"I've waited so long to do this." His body was flush against hers, his hard-on sending sky rockets in flight.

She ducked her head to ask him the question that had been on her mind for ten years to the day. "Dane, why did you do it? Why didn't you wait one more night?"

He stepped back just as the elevator came to a stop, and the doors opened. A wry smile crossed his face, but he held his hand out and said, "After you."

In the hallway, he wrapped an arm around her waist and held up the key card close to his face to verify the room number on the envelope. Once they crossed that threshold, she knew she wouldn't want to talk anymore, so she stopped walking. "Dane. We've never talked about it."

He leaned against a wall and ran his tongue across his lips. He smiled, all arrogance. "Are you admitting you wanted me to wait?"

"If that will get you to tell me. It was one more night, Dane."

The smug grin dropped from his face. "Truth?"

She tried to match his tone with open sincerity. "Please."

He let out a heavy sigh. "I was nervous, Val. I thought—" He raked a hand through his hair and stood up straight. He paced toward the elevator before spinning back to her. "I thought you would go through with it only to keep up your end of the bargain, but then that would ruin our friendship. And honestly, I was afraid you'd laugh at me."

She swallowed. "I wouldn't have laughed, Dane."

He took her hand. "I shouldn't have slept with that other girl. But I'd already fallen in love with you by then, and I'd gone out drinking to try to figure out what I was going to do. I couldn't think of any other way to slow things down. I should have known I'd ruin things either way."

Her mind snagged on one statement. "You'd fallen in love with me?" The words choked in her throat. Had he been in love with her all that time? He'd always been there, beside her, devoted in every way. But they were best friends. And sure, she'd never stopped wondering what might have been, but he'd gone on to sleep his way through half the college and then their company, while she'd patted herself on the back for a job well done.

He traced her cheek with his finger. "I'm still in love with you, Val. I always will be."

She wrapped her hand around his index finger. "It's New Year's. Is it too late to collect on a bet?"

His smile returned, but this time, there was no trace of teasing. He strode down the hall and threw open the door to a lavish honeymoon suite.

Val's mind returned to the training room, the kids clacking on keyboards, and the reality of her lost cause. She blinked to clear her eyes of the forming tears. All that time, he'd been right there.

And she'd let him go again.

If she gave him a third chance, she suspected he'd take her, then leave her as repayment for her betrayal. Wasn't that exactly what he intended to do with Noelle? Maybe Noelle would absorb his frustration with past regrets, leaving Val to receive a Dane ready to give their relationship another chance.

She could almost taste the ultimate satisfaction of rewarding Dane for using and losing Noelle while they laughed at the poor girl's naïveté.

Several interns stood and began packing up. As they filed out, Val said, "Good work this week, and I'll see you bright and early next Monday."

Once they'd all left, she slipped back into the now empty hallway. She overheard Noelle's voice through the opening in her door and wondered if it was possible Dane hadn't left.

A slight alcove a few feet from Noelle's door housed a copier and printer. Val laid her hands on the front panel of the copier and focused on the selection menu, but she keened her ears toward the conversation on the other side of the slightly ajar door.

"Geraldo, stop. It's not just the money."

Val's stomach lurched. Why was she talking to Geraldo? Was he trying to lure her back?

"You think I don't know that? I was there when you—"

Val urged her to finish that sentence.

The elevator doors opened down the hall, and Rosamund turned the corner toward Val. Val grabbed some abandoned print outs from the printer's collection bin. She tapped them into a neat pile and pantomimed the act of putting the papers into the copier. She nodded as Rosamund passed by without a word.

What had Geraldo done? Val slid as close to the door as she could, praying nobody would appear in the hallway.

"If you recall, you're the reason I'm even here." Pause. "I *am* being careful. You've always underestimated me."

Val peered through the crack. Noelle sat on the edge of her desk, one hand holding the phone to her ear, the other raking hair that had long fallen from its clasp.

"What do you propose? Am I supposed to go through Dane's emails or tap her phone?"

Val stifled a gasp. Was she doing Geraldo's bidding? Spying on them?

That little bitch.

Noelle stood, and Val fell out of sight. "Fine. I'll talk to a few board members."

Val's heart beat a mile a minute. What game were they playing? She needed to get Noelle to confide in her somehow.

She waited until Noelle said her goodbyes, then counted to thirty before tapping on the office door.

"Hi, Noelle. Got a minute?" Her voice dripped with sweetness.

Noelle turned, face flushed. "Val, what brings you here?" She leaned against the edge of the desk.

"It occurred to me that you're relatively new to the area, and I wanted to see if you'd like to go out tonight. I could show you around a little. We could grab a bite to eat."

Noelle's toothsome smile lit up her face, but Val no longer trusted the sincerity. "That is so nice of you. I haven't had a moment to get around and explore."

Val ignored the aversion. "So you'll come out?"

"Well, I would love to. Ordinarily. However, I've somehow managed to agree to dinner with Dane tonight."

Val widened her eyes, feigning surprise. "You've got a date with Dane? How—"

"It's not a date! It's just dinner."

"Oh, right. Of course. It wouldn't be a date." Val smiled as Noelle's body became fully erect. Dane had his work cut out for him. "Well, have a nice evening anyway."

Noelle held one hand up. "You know, if you're free tomorrow, maybe you could show me around?"

"Of course. I'd be more than happy to. I'll give you a call?" Val's smile showed all her teeth.

With his head against the steering wheel, Dane groped under his seat, feeling around the floorboard until his fingers brushed against a small plastic bottle. He reached across to the passenger side and checked for any other empty bourbon samples. It was lucky he'd decided to check because he found a still wrapped condom on the mat. He pocketed all the evidence and then double checked his teeth and hair. He'd gone home, showered, and dressed in a deceptively casual suit. He'd paid a fortune for the elegance of a custom-made sport coat and slacks. The cologne he wore smelled of citrus and cost two hundred dollars an ounce. Satisfied nothing about him would prove offensive, he climbed out of the car.

He tossed the empty into the street and transferred the condom to his wallet. He put his hand in his pocket and sauntered up to Noelle's front door. According to his watch, he'd arrived two minutes early. He hadn't come early to pick up a date in recent memory. Then again, he hadn't been out with anyone worth showing up on time for. But tonight, he played the part of the eager suitor. It wasn't hard to pretend. This was the first time he'd ever gotten her to agree to go out with him, even if he'd had to twist the circumstances to get there.

He rang the bell.

He'd expected Noelle to keep him waiting. He'd expected her to eventually appear wearing a professional button-down shirt and slacks combination. He was wrong on both counts.

Noelle answered the door immediately. She'd swept her blond hair up in some kind of tight twist at the nape of her neck, and she wore an elegant black dress and heels. It made Dane wish he'd gone for a more lavish restaurant. One with nearby rooms to rent. Not that L'Etoile was a dump. But he imagined himself decked in a tuxedo with Noelle on his arm as they crossed into a hotel room just before he unzipped her dress slowly.

The way he'd longed to undress her the night she'd pushed him away.

He caught himself mid-leer and forced a sheepish grin on his face. "You look stunning."

Noelle dipped her head, and Dane felt a stirring. It had been ages since he'd dated a girl who blushed.

He waited a beat for her to close the door and then held his elbow out to her. "My lady."

She hesitated but must have decided the gesture was innocuous enough and slipped her hand around his arm. "A true gentleman."

He led her back to his car and opened the door, but she looked doubtful. "Do you mind if I move the seat back?"

Dane took the opportunity to step away and admire her long legs. "The seat won't go back much farther, but there's plenty of leg room." He pointed at his own legs. "Promise."

As she made up her mind to climb into the sports car, he resisted an urge to lay a hand across her back. It might be natural enough to support her as she slid in, but she clearly mistrusted him. He waited until she was settled, closed the door, and jogged to his side, straightening his slacks before taking his own place in the driver's seat.

He pressed the ignition, and the engine purred. Noelle touched her flawless hair as though fixing an errant strand and said, "I confess, I've been admiring this car. I was looking forward to riding in it."

"That's good to know." He flashed a cheeky grin. "The car's just a metaphor for the driver."

"Is that so?" She snorted. "While I know you're expensive beyond reason, you don't appear to come with cup holders."

Her response relieved him. If she'd acted offended at his arrogance, he'd have to tone it way down. And he didn't want this seduction to take an ice age. He revved the engine with a roguish eyebrow waggle. "Are you ready to experience metaphorical horsepower?"

Now she smiled. "Let her rip."

His intended display of prowess was inhibited by the speed bumps through her neighborhood, but as soon as he hit open road, he floored it, letting the engine roar like a race car. He glanced at Noelle, pleased to see her face lit up with pleasure. The car was better than any aphrodisiac.

The restaurant was in the city on the top floor of one of the taller buildings. Dane slipped the maître d' a fifty for no other reason than to be remembered the next time he called at the last minute for a reservation. He had no doubt they'd held a table with a view for him. He hadn't needed to wait to be seated since he'd made his first million.

He pulled Noelle's chair back before taking his own seat. She admired the lights of the city below, and that led him to his opening gambit. "Do you miss New York City?"

She turned her sparkling eyes back to him and plucked her napkin off the table. "I do. But there's a quiet charm to the Midwest. Do you ever consider going back?"

"The quiet charm suits me," he lied. He'd never had a chance to miss the city. He returned whenever he got the urge.

"Well, don't take offense, but that surprises me. You went from the bleeding edge of technology to a glorified manager. You must miss the thrill of it."

A small part of him perked up at the opportunity to unload the bitterness of the past three years. It would feel wonderful to lay his burden at someone's feet, but as Noelle was the architect of his dissatisfaction, he gave her the magazine interview answer. "That was a once-in-a-lifetime experience. But it was exhausting and unrewarding. I never had a moment to enjoy any second of it." He smiled, all sincerity. "I hope you don't let the pressures of your new job make you forget to live a little."

With impeccable timing, the waiter arrived to recite the specials. It wasn't a coincidence. Tipping well had earned Dane a tailor-made dining atmosphere where a clandestine gesture would bring the servers to the table immediately. After asking Noelle if she drank red wine, Dane ordered a 1996 Château Lafite Rothschild. The restaurant kept this vintage on hand just for him. He paid a premium for that service—on top of the eight hundred dollars the bottle sold for at auction.

He didn't always spring for his personal reserve, but tonight's company was worth every expense.

When the server decanted the wine, Dane tilted his head toward Noelle. They both watched as an inch of the nearly black liquid filled her glass. She sipped it and nodded in approval. "You've started spending your money wisely, I see."

"I did mention I like to enjoy life."

Once the waiter had taken their orders and left, Dane struck a serious pose. "For too long, my money and my life were literally tied up in the stock market. When I was freed from the responsibilities of owning a company, I loosened up. And loosened my purse strings. What's the point of money if you don't spend it?"

"Freed from the responsibilities? That's an interesting way to say 'forced out.' Are you really over it?"

He shrugged. "Would I rather have my own company back? Honestly, I don't know."

"Geraldo believes you and Val are working to sabotage him. Is he wrong?"

Dane tapped his finger on the wine glass, filing away that slip of information for Val and pondering a proper response. "Do we seem to be plotting to overthrow him? You see how hard Val has worked on her internship program. And my life has never been easier."

Noelle's shoulders had relaxed. "That was my impression. But I'm learning that things aren't always as they appear."

He couldn't help but push the question. Val wouldn't forgive him if he didn't. "Did Geraldo do something?"

She laughed. "It's more what he didn't do." She shook her head and reached for her goblet, swirling the wine around in the glass. She breathed it in. "Tell me. Is wine another metaphor for the man?"

That brought a genuine laugh from Dane, and he gladly dropped the interrogation. He much preferred to talk about himself. "Elegant, dark, and brooding. Full of complexity, with a great nose and just a hint of floral notes."

She smiled. "That's an interesting description."

"And how would you characterize the wine?"

She thought a moment. "Ostentatious." At the first sign of Dane's protest, she raised a hand. "Though hardly subtle, it is surprisingly multi-layered." She held it up to the light. "And easy on the eyes."

Was she flirting with him? The slight stirring Dane had felt when he'd flattered Noelle earlier grew stronger with her own transparent attraction.

But then she added. "However, it's not a wine I'd choose to drink every day. I'm afraid I'm far too practical to develop a habit I can't maintain."

Dane lifted his glass. "To tonight, then."

She raised her own. "To tonight."

The food arrived, and the verbal sparring gave way to questions of "how's the steak?" and "have you ever tried charolais?"

They only hit one moment of awkwardness when Dane said, "This reminds me so much of that company party at Del Frisco's."

It had slipped out. He hadn't intended to reminisce. The look of pity that crossed Noelle's face at his accidental show of sentimentality made him curse himself.

Noelle's blush crept down her neck, and at last she broke the silence. "I believe that was the night you first asked me out."

Relieved, Dane let out a shuddering breath. "You remember."

She smiled gently, and he worried for a minute she'd rebuff him again, but she laid her fork across her plate and sat back. "How could I ever forget that?"

Dane started to ask her what happened. Why had things changed so abruptly? But the waiter arrived to clear their empty plates, and he regained control over his impulses.

When the dessert and coffee came, Dane realized his time was growing short. He'd need to decide soon whether to position himself as a seductive suitor or a vulnerable romantic. The first might land him in bed tonight—or it might put a permanent end to his attempts. The safe bet would be to hang back and let her desire for him develop. He had no doubt it would if he could overcome whatever mistrust she clearly had for him. If only he knew why she'd rejected him. He could afford to be patient. He'd coax an answer out of her before he finished this. Besides, she was as entertaining as ever, and it might be amusing to drag things out a bit.

And so he said, "Thank you for following through on your wager."

She ran her tongue across her lips, tasting the last of the chocolate before she blotted the rest with a napkin. "I don't know how you managed to do it, but I'm impressed you had the fortitude to give up cigarettes cold turkey like that."

"I should thank you for that as well. I've been trying for a while. I guess I lacked sufficient motivation."

"You weren't just pretending to smoke to trick me to go out with you?"

"That would have been a long con, don't you think?"

"You always were clever and determined."

Noelle's right hand rested on the table beside her coffee cup. Dane reached across and lifted it in his, and for a moment, she looked into his eyes. Unsure what she sought there, Dane instinctively went for the smolder. He'd successfully ended many dates with his intense gaze. Noelle's expression hardened, and he thought he saw desire there. He ran his thumb across her skin, but she withdrew her hand and laid it in her lap.

"I should be getting home. I need to research the projections for the fiscal year."

He didn't argue with her. He'd shown her he was interested, and now he had to let that seed grow. Instead, he stood and pulled her chair out for her.

They were quiet on the way back to her house, and Dane got out to walk her to her door, mentally coaching himself to leave her there without so much as a handshake. She fished her keys from her purse as soon as she exited the car and kept up a brisk pace. When she slid the key into the lock, she turned and said, "Thank you for dinner, Dane."

This is where he meant to tell her she was welcome and that he'd see her at work on Monday, but the skin on her face glowed soft under the porch light, and he couldn't resist the urge to reach up and drag his thumb across her cheek. Her eyes opened in surprise, but she didn't back away immediately.

Dane took advantage of her momentary shock and leaned in to press his lips against hers. It was like kissing a marble statue. But then she softened, and her lips responded to his. Her body relaxed. The low stirring of desire had been intensifying, and he gave it free rein. He slid his fingers around the back of her neck and tightened his grip, parting her lips with his tongue.

She jerked her head back. "Dane." She swallowed. "I'm sorry. I should have made it more clear. This wasn't a date."

He loosened his fingers and let her step out of his embrace, cursing himself for his weakness. "Have a good weekend, Noelle."

After she let herself in, he adjusted the crotch of his pants and pulled out his phone.

The phone dinged with Dane's ringtone. He so rarely communicated via technology, Val thought it might be urgent and climbed out of bed to read his text.

What are you doing?

She groaned. *Busy.*

The phone dinged again. Since she was up, she read his next message. *I want to see you.*

Are you drunk?

She drummed her fingers, now waiting for his answer.

No. I'm coming over.

She texted quickly, *Don't come over*, then waited. When he didn't respond, she sighed. "Ugh. I shouldn't have answered him."

She lay back down, distracted by the promise of Dane's imminent arrival. When the doorbell rang fifteen minutes later, she cursed. "I told him not to come over." She sat up and threw her legs out of bed. "I'll just send him away." She pulled on a silky dressing gown, cinched at the waist with a flimsy belt.

When she opened the door, Dane stood, leaning against the door frame, looking impossibly incorrigible—the way she loved him best. He pushed into her house uninvited. She moved ahead of him and led him back into a sitting room and closed the double French doors behind her. When she turned around, he was already pouring himself a tumbler of brandy.

"So you're not drunk yet, but well on your way?"

"It's my first drink, tonight." He took a sip. "My first real drink."

"Why are you here?"

He crossed to her and ran a finger along the front of her robe. "Is this how you always greet midnight visitors?"

She knocked his hand back. "Did you come bearing gifts?"

He moved closer into her space. "I was hoping I might come baring you."

"Hilarious." Val took a step back. "So you've already conquered Noelle?"

"You can't be serious."

"Oh, I see. Your dinner with Noelle came to an end, and you're bringing me your leftover hard-on. How cute." She crossed her arms. "But I'm not a backup, Dane."

He put his hand back on the silk neckline and ran his finger under the cloth. Val relaxed her arms, letting him slip past her defenses and caress her breast. Encouraged by her body's response, he loosened the tie around her waist, and the robe spilled open. He pushed her back against the glass doors and caught her in a kiss. His urgency heightened her desire. His erection pressed against her hip, and she fought her own urge to reach for him even as she failed to resist him.

His lips found her neck, and he dragged his teeth across her skin. When she shivered, he lifted his head and smiled that cocky grin. "Did you know Geraldo thinks we're plotting against him?"

Only Dane would know those words would turn her on. "Well, we are." Were they spying on each other? "Did Noelle tell you this?"

His only response was to press his mouth against her cheek with a groan. She ran her hands up the back of his neck, then pushed him back.

He stepped away and unclasped his belt. The idea of him taking her right there, right then made her pulse quicken. An agonizing throb accompanied every heartbeat. But she knew what Dane wanted. Fucking her and leaving her in emotional turmoil would be a revenge he'd savor.

She'd only let this happen on her own terms. She closed her robe. "Dane. This wasn't the deal. What are you doing?"

"What I should have done years ago when I first brought you here."

Her nostrils flared. "Are you starting to believe your own press? You didn't bring me to this God-forsaken backwater. If anything, you just prepared the way for me."

He caught her wrist and pulled her to him. "But you're here now. With me. I only ever wanted you." He was lying. And it was a lie she was only too eager to hear. "You know you want me, Val. Tell me you don't, and I'll leave."

She wouldn't answer that. He was right; she wanted him more than ever, but she didn't like his tone with her.

Instead, she reached behind her for the handle and threw open the double doors. She walked back to the front of the house, talking over her shoulder. "We have a deal, Dane. You can have me when you finish dallying with Miss Constance. Until then—" She motioned toward his way out.

He ran his hands through his hair in frustration. She adored him when he was falling apart, but not enough to give in to him. She wanted him, but she didn't need him.

Finally, he left her alone in the foyer. But not alone in the house.

When the door clicked closed, she swallowed down a lump in her throat. She allowed herself a moment of regret before taking control of her emotions. Then she climbed the stairs, opened the bedroom door and dropped her robe at her feet. When she slid under the sheets, her lover greeted her right where they'd left off, erect and ready for her, thank God.

He ran a hand across the same breast Dane had so recently excited. "What did he want?"

"Shut up," she said. She shoved his shoulder back onto the bed and threw her leg over him, straddling him to take what she wanted. And she indulged in a forbidden fantasy. Unfortunately, while her body could be fooled, her mind knew the difference between Dane and another.

But she gave her imagination free rein, picturing Dane tracing her cheek with his finger, like he'd done that night, saying, "I'm still in love with you, Val. I always will be."

She wrapped her hand around her lover's index finger, pretending it was Dane's. She used her lover's body, but in her mind she stood in that hotel, saying, "It's New Year's. Is it too late to collect on a bet?"

Val's lover flipped her onto her back, and she hooked her legs around his waist, remembering Dane rolling her onto her side, unzipping her dress.

Val rocked her hips up hard, and her lover grunted, meeting her frenzied rhythm.

Dane's words echoed in her ears. "I spent so many nights imagining what this might have been like." When he spoke, his breath whispered against her skin. Her spine tingled. He peeled the left side of her dress down her arm, and she let him slip the other side off. His eyes languorously followed the dress he slowly slid down her body. She lifted her hip and let him free the fabric completely.

Her chest rose and fell as her lungs sought oxygen to feed her pounding heart. Sweat dripped from her lover's brow, but she saw Dane, propped on one elbow, wearing far too many clothes. As she started to loosen his tie, he lay perfectly still, letting her work through one obstacle at a time. He only lifted a hand to help when her fingers got frustrated on the buttons of his shirt. His dress shirt fell to the floor, and the undershirt came up over his head. She stopped and sucked in a breath. He was tanned and fit. Her hands needed to run along his taut torso.

She unhooked his belt and unfastened the button on his pants. The zipper showed a pronounced strain, and he moaned softly as she ran her hand along the front where the fabric stretched tighter. She didn't want to waste time toying with him. She needed to see him, so she dug her nails over both waistbands and yanked his boxers off with his pants. God, he was glorious. She took in every inch of him, every hard inch.

As she reached for him, he grabbed her hand and said, "What about Geraldo?"

She froze. Her lover slowed, "Val? You okay?"

In response, she grabbed his ass and urged him on. He picked up his pace and lost himself again in his own pleasure. Val pushed through the motions, but her mind was troubled.

Val hadn't forgotten about Geraldo, but she'd processed him and conveniently decided he no longer mattered. Yes, they were an item, but it had been more for their own intellectual amusement than anything physical. He much preferred younger arm candy, and she had no doubt he was under one of them right then.

But that wasn't really what Dane had been asking. Despite their more model showroom than genuine relationship,

Geraldo didn't like to lose. Val—or anything else. His ruthlessness in business was what drew her to him in the first place after all. The question Dane wanted to know was whether Geraldo would have the power or intention to ruin them if he felt betrayed. It was too late to ask that question. Once she and Dane had entered that hotel room, everything would be assumed. There was no reason not to follow through.

Truth be told, she'd relished the promise of Geraldo's inevitable tirade. She'd wanted Noelle to feel justified in letting Dane go. She'd wanted Dane to forsake everyone and everything, including his company, for her. She'd wanted Dane.

And she was feeling reckless. "Screw him."

Dane chuckled. "I was hoping you'd screw me."

He knocked her onto her back and worshiped her. His hands ran over her exposed skin, down her length. He moved closer and just as his fingers slid between her legs, he kissed her.

"Mmmm. So wet," he said, slipping two fingers in her.

Her back arched. She was so ready for him. She glided her hand around his erection. She'd been desperate to touch him, and she'd reveled in the silky soft skin over his rock-hard cock. Pre-cum ran down from the tip, interfering with the smooth easy strokes. The look of desire in his eyes took her breath away.

Dane ran a hand through her hair and said, "I've wanted you since the first moment I saw you." He moved with practiced ease, and she lay on her back, his cock pressing against her.

She dragged her fingernails down her lover's back, holding on as he reached toward his own climax. She couldn't keep her hands off his body, although it wasn't Dane's.

But it was Dane she heard whispering her name, and the memory of it threw her over the edge. Her lover's whole body tightened, and she saw Dane groaning with his orgasm.

"Val?" Her lover rubbed her arm. "You called me Dane."

She opened her eyes and pushed him off her.

"I'd like you to leave now." She laid her head on her pillow and listened to the sounds of fabric over skin, pants zipping, feet on the carpet, a door closing.

She shook quietly, hating herself for reaching into the past to stoke a physical fire, for sullying a sublime memory in a moment of profane weakness. But once she'd peered into that abyss, she couldn't stop from conjuring up the most precious part of the night.

Dane fell beside her and gently traced her skin. She told him, "I love you." And he said the same. He promised he always would.

Maybe he'd been lying, too. Maybe she hadn't lost as much as she believed.

The next morning, she'd woken before Dane and climbed out of bed to take a shower and order room service. Near the door, a small scrap of paper had caught her eye. She'd reached down and discovered a business card. When she'd flipped it over, her heart sank. It read, "Geraldo Valencia."

He'd given her no time to plan a counterstrike, to arise victorious from one spontaneous decision. She'd had moments to make her decision based on what she knew of all the players.

She'd looked back at Dane's sleeping form and considered the many options. She'd tucked Geraldo's card into her purse and put her clothes on. Dane would have to understand.

She wiped away a tear and prayed he'd eventually forgive her.

Saturday

Val parked in the garage below the mall. "Have you been downtown since you got here?"

Noelle picked her purse up from the floor. "Actually, just last night. Dane took me out to dinner at L'Etoile."

Val turned the rearview mirror to face her and touched the edge of her lip to remove stray lipstick. "Oh, he must have really wanted to make an impression. That's a nice restaurant."

"Yeah, it was."

Val didn't continue to inquire. She didn't want to appear too eager to discuss it. "Do you want to start at Nordstrom's?"

Val's idea of showing Noelle around the city consisted of buying cute shoes and then stopping for a coffee at the in-store restaurant. The shopping wasn't just for show. Val prided herself in her neat appearance, and she'd spend a little more money to look professional and well-groomed. She wouldn't go to such a ridiculous extent as Dane. *He's so vain, he probably imports his barber.* She snickered to herself, imagining an opera singer prancing around Dane as he trimmed his hair. That sounded about right.

Dane hadn't always preened, not when she first met him. He'd come to appreciate the image she'd helped him cultivate. And then he'd become all image.

Once they'd tired of shoe shopping, Val and Noelle carried their bags to the bistro and took a table against the wall. Val insisted on paying for the coffee, and they sat across from each other making small talk. She waited until Noelle brought up the elephant in the room.

"Forgive me for prying. I'm sure everyone would love to ask you this, but why did you follow Dane out here? You could have stayed on at R&M, surely?"

Val blew on her coffee and bit back the venom the phrasing of that question always brought up her throat. She had no intention of confiding in Noelle. "Working there wasn't the same anymore. The soul of the company left with Dane. I realized I had no reason to stay, and Dane had such nice things to say about the ethical culture at Fleetwood. It seemed like a great place to restart."

"Dane praised the ethical culture of Fleetwood?" Noelle's eyebrow rose almost imperceptibly.

"Well, yes. You don't believe all those nasty things Geraldo said about him?"

The memory of Dane's thumb and forefinger pinching her nipple in her sitting room the night before flashed before her eyes.

Noelle scoffed. "Val, you don't think I've forgotten everything you yourself said about him? And Geraldo couldn't force Dane out of his position for unfounded charges." Her intonation gave away a hint of doubt.

"No?" Val picked at the edge of a napkin, shredding it into a tiny dusting of powder. "Then what reason did you have for going along with the decision to target Dane?"

"Are you telling me we were all duped by unfounded accusations? Were you as well?"

"Have you never had reason to mistrust Geraldo?"

Noelle narrowed an eye. "I've had reason to mistrust many people."

"Think about it. Dane had a sterling reputation. His contributions to the technology were enough to balance against a personal attack. What proof did Geraldo produce?"

"To be honest, I don't recall any. Dane agreed to the terms of his departure before we began to investigate. I confess I was relieved."

"And with Dane gone, Geraldo quietly became a majority shareholder. Do you think that was by accident? The takeover might not have been hostile, but as you may recall, it wasn't gentle."

"You make a compelling case. I knew Geraldo had a personal ax to grind, but I thought Dane would fight back if he were innocent of the charges. I suppose there may have been other reasons he wanted to leave."

Val bit her lip. Was Noelle looking for excuses to defend Dane now that he was casting a spell on her? She tucked that possibility away to share with him later. That could speed things along nicely. And the sooner Noelle was out of the way, the sooner she could give into the base desire Dane had ignited the night before.

But that wasn't why she'd corralled Noelle here today. "Come now. We're talking about Geraldo. He'll lie, cheat, manipulate, or coerce to get what he wants."

"Should I assume you're working to undermine him and get your company back?"

Wouldn't she like to know. "Why would I waste my time on that now?" Val paused and gave the appearance of entertaining a new thought. "Unless you have some compelling evidence against him."

Noelle held up her hands in surrender. "Not I. I was merely curious."

Disappointing. Dane might be able to help extricate whatever secret Noelle wasn't sharing.

"So, you and Dane?"

"No. That is definitely not happening."

"And yet, you had a date?"

"It wasn't a date. I made sure to let him know that."

Val winced but pretended to cover it.

"What?" Noelle leaned in.

Val needed to choose her words carefully now that she had the other woman on the hook. "Oh, nothing. You know men. Such touchy egos."

"Yeah, and?"

Val shrugged as though she relayed nothing more than a universal truth. "And well, Dane won't keep pursuing a woman who shoots him down cold." *Ludicrous lies, but what the hell.* "But that's probably for the best since you're not interested in him. You let him down easy after all. I'm sure he'll be fine."

Maybe she could convince Noelle that Dane was a delicate bird with a broken wing. Hilarious. But Noelle had never been difficult to manipulate.

"Are you afraid I'm going to hurt *him*?" Noelle's eyes rolled. "You'll have to forgive me if I'm a wee bit skeptical of his soft side."

"Yes. I know he has a bit of a reputation as a ladies' man."

"A bit? My God, Val." She shook her head. "And yet you let him in your bed not a day after you yourself warned me about his faithlessness."

Val took a moment to absorb Noelle's words and consider the next attack. "True. I think we can all agree that night was a mistake."

"And it would be a mistake for me to go out with Dane. Wouldn't you agree?"

"Not at all." Val found the angle she needed to sell. "The truth is, he hasn't been the same since you. He's very hesitant to ask a woman out." She held her breath to keep from laughing at this pile of bullshit. It wasn't altogether false that he'd changed since Noelle rebuffed him. But if anything, he was on the warpath, burning a hole in his mattress like he had something to prove.

"Dane? Hesitant? He didn't seem so when he asked me to dinner."

"Oh! He asked you out?"

"Well, no. He didn't ask me out so much as coerce me."

"What do you mean?"

"He made a bet. I lost. Would you call that a date?"

Val raised a corner of her mouth. "Interesting. I guess you're right then. Well, that's good."

"How so?"

"You seem like a nice, caring person. I'd hate to see him get hurt again. He's been so closed off for so long. For a minute, I thought maybe—"

"Maybe what?"

"Well, he doesn't confide in me like he used to, but I can tell you he's afraid to make himself vulnerable. I thought maybe if you were ready to give him a chance now, you might reach him. But as you said, it wasn't a date. That's probably best for both of you."

Noelle's brow wrinkled the slightest amount. Did she worry she might have hurt poor Dane? "I'm sorry. It's just that I can't reconcile what you're telling me with everything else I know."

"You don't know him like I do. He likes to keep up the image of the bad boy because it puts up a wall of protection."

"I find it hard to believe you right now. I took your word that he's a womanizer through and through. I turned him down based on the portrait *you* painted."

Val shook her head. "I was wrong."

Noelle wadded up her napkin. "No, you weren't. You were the next in line. Doesn't that bother you? Or was that what you'd intended?"

A brief image of Dane sprawled across her bed flashed in Val's mind. No, that did not bother her one bit. She reached across and took Noelle's hand. "He was hurt and embarrassed. I had no idea he would come to me, but he did."

"I've sometimes wondered why he went to you. Everyone knew you were friends, but you'd adamantly denied any romantic interest. It has occurred to me that perhaps he was trying to goad Geraldo."

Val kept her smile in place as she processed a move she'd never once considered. "It wouldn't make any sense for Dane to provoke Geraldo. What could he have possibly hoped to achieve?"

"Maybe exactly this? He doesn't seem terribly concerned about losing his own company. But like you say, I don't know him at all."

"Did it ever occur to you that perhaps I was the one wanting to goad Geraldo?"

Noelle's eyebrows rose. "Are you saying you used Dane to free yourself from Geraldo? I find that—"

"Weak?"

"No, I was going to say . . . calculated."

"That it was not." She didn't worry Noelle would relay this confession to Dane. He'd never believe Val spoke the truth here to this woman. "If I'd been more calculating, Geraldo would be here, and I'd be there."

"With Dane?"

If only. But that wasn't the narrative she wanted to sell. "Dane and I are friends, Noelle. Neither of us planned for that night to happen. Dane's heart was broken, and I was there for him." Until she wasn't. She'd let Noelle assume she was the heart breaker in question, when in reality, Val had done the deed herself. "I just don't want to see that happen again."

"His heart was broken? I'll bet." Noelle rolled her eyes. "He'll be fine."

The napkin in front of Noelle had been shredded. Dane either had a worthy adversary who would never yield to him or a reluctant lover who would fight in vain against her own growing desire. Time would tell. Perhaps time was the answer. But Val was running out of patience.

Val schooled her face in a tight insincere smile. "Yes. Don't worry. He got over rejection once before. He'll move on soon enough."

The pop of surprise in Noelle's eyes told Val all she needed to know. The clock was ticking, and Noelle now knew she had to make her decision before she lost her second chance.

Satisfied she'd at least planted a seed, Val suggested they take a look at the summer dresses. *Dane has no idea how much he owes me.*

Dane pushed his muscles as he ran up and down the trail hills, rivulets of sweat cooling his back slightly. When he reached the edge of the man-made lake, he dropped into a casual walk, hands on his sides as he sucked in lungfuls of air. He passed a family feeding the ducks, but he barely saw them. His sight was turned inward, calculating his next move. Did he have a next move? Chess was never Dane's game. Dane was more a *Diablo* guy; shoot everyone and collect the treasures. It was Val who could see the lay of the land, anticipate her opponent, and deliver at end game.

But what had she really ever won?

If she'd forfeited the game long ago, he might be with her today. She chose the game—and Geraldo—over the player.

Over the simplicity of a love affair. Of course, who's to say they wouldn't have ended in a murder-suicide.

Val wasn't his problem. She still wanted him, and she always would. Their friendship would survive his bungled attempt to bed her.

The real question was whether he could repair the damage he'd done last night with Noelle with his inept wooing. He botched that in the worst way—neither seductive nor vulnerable. Desperate and pathetic. Noelle would have every reason to disdain him and keep him far from her. She must think he was the worst creeper. He groaned recalling how she'd shut him down the last time.

It was New Year's Eve. Why was it always New Year's Eve?

He'd pursued Noelle nearly two months. He'd taken things slow because she intrigued him more than most of the women he'd hooked up with. Val mocked him when he confessed how much he liked Noelle, calling her—and he remembered this verbatim—colorless, flavorless, and odorless. But she was none of those things. Val was clearly jealous. Noelle was the first woman he'd ever truly courted. He barely recognized himself—or maybe he saw the person he'd been once years before, when he'd first met Val. Before he'd made a deal with the devil to hone him into a seduction machine.

He'd even sworn off other women while chasing after Noelle. And the weird thing was, he didn't miss any of it. He would have been happy taking as long as she needed.

But he wanted her in his bed. And she'd made him think he was getting somewhere. Even if she wouldn't agree to go out, she'd talked to him in the office, shared pieces of herself, listened to the things he'd confided. He'd gotten to know her every bit as well as any woman he'd ever dated. He'd planned to get her alone that New Year's Eve, just before midnight. And then, after a night of drinking and dancing, she'd be intoxicated by the desire to spend the night in his arms. He was going to kiss her.

Dane rubbed the sweat off his forehead, anger resurging at the memory of his worst humiliation.

When he found her at the party, she'd frowned at him then walked away. She looked like she'd lost someone she loved. He foolishly thought he might be able to help her with some personal trouble, but it turned out he was the trouble. She told him to leave her alone. She'd said, "Stop stalking me, Dane." And he'd asked her why. He'd been embarrassed by the way his voice had cracked, but he'd had to ask. "What did I do? I thought you liked me. I thought you could love me." Even now, he cringed as he pictured the audience gathering to watch as Noelle put a stake through him, when she'd told him she could never love him. Never love *someone like him*.

And so he'd done as she asked and left him alone.

Until now. Now he needed to gain her trust enough to bring her to the brink of desire again.

At least he'd partially succeeded. The date had gone better than he would have dreamed. Noelle was more beautiful than he remembered. He'd been charming and funny. She'd teased him and encouraged him. And they'd interacted like a romantic couple—up until that fumbled attempt at a good-night kiss. He chided himself for that slip. He'd meant it when he told Val he wanted to watch Noelle's resistance slip, but he didn't want to force himself on her. His ego would only be assuaged when she not only consented to spend time with him but pursued him. When she didn't recoil at his advances.

His only recourse to get back in the game would be to keep his distance and let things reset. Maybe in a week or two, she'd forget or think he wasn't that serious after all. Not that either of those were good, but better than a restraining order.

He retied his running shoes, stretched his calves, and began the return trip through the woods, completely oblivious to the perfect blue June sky.

Week 2

Monday

S*ophie,*

Finally, it's Monday again. I never thought I'd say that, but the weekend seriously dragged on. I'd kind of hoped the interns might all go out together, but everyone seems to have gone back home, and I was stuck here. Alone. I went shopping, trying to find something nice (on sale) to wear in case Anthony ever does ask me out—which he won't, but there's really no harm in daydreaming. About him—or Dane. (Sue me. He's hot.)

Oh, but today is the day! The heads of various special areas are coming in to pick an intern to shadow them for a week. I've boned up on securities and derivatives—even read up on futures and commodities. I'm gunning hard for Dane to pick me and spent most of the weekend reading everything

I could to impress him. I'm so nervous he won't pick me. Or at least Val. Fingers crossed for me. Think what you want, but even though he's most well -known for his computer skills, he knows the business. It doesn't hurt that he's easy to look at, obviously.

I might be wearing a new skirt and a flirty top to catch his attention, and I know I look cute because Anthony brought me some coffee this morning— free coffee from the breakroom, but still. It's sweet, but I'm annoyed that he didn't contact me at all over the weekend when I was so bored. Maybe he went home like everyone else? Anyway, I'm giving him the cold shoulder to see if he'll try a little harder.

I'm so ready for something interesting to happen.

Selena

Val waited for the interns to stop gossiping long enough to come to order. "Good morning, everyone. I trust you had a nice weekend. This week is going to stretch you, so if you're tired or hungover this morning, you're going to regret your life decisions very shortly."

The kids laughed at her joke. These were the top students at various schools around the country. They'd come to learn and wouldn't waste the opportunity partying. Although she noticed Anthony had moved his chair close to Selena and seemed to be trying to whisper something to her.

Val cleared her throat, eyes on Anthony. He looked up and had the good grace to appear abashed.

With everyone now paying her the same respect they had on day one, she began. "As you are all aware, we provide a mentorship opportunity that can't be found elsewhere. Fleetwood has among its staff some of the most illustrious financial minds in the world. Your peers might think they were smart to take a position at one of those Wall Street firms, but you all know better. Which is why you're here. And we expect a great deal from you in turn. By the end of this week, you should be competent enough to take a place on our trading floor in the capacity in which we train you."

The kids all shifted in their seats, excited at the prospect of real-world trading. Val oversold it a bit, but she was proud of the program she'd set up. Each year, she'd helped mold a cadre of young hopefuls into promising traders. And most of them applied to work for Fleetwood when they graduated. She knew it wasn't for the cultural attractions. They came to continue to work for her. And with her firsthand knowledge of them, she made quick work of weeding through them.

"Your progress this week will be scored and evaluated as a part of the competition for that coveted job offer to follow the internship, so you're going to want to show your mentor the same level of respect you've shown me and prove you deserve to work here."

It was all bullshit. There was no objective standard to base the final decision on. Whoever seemed like they'd take the job and fit in at the company would be considered. But she preferred carrots to sticks when dealing with employees, and the contest gave the interns motivation to behave which in turn kept her co-workers willing to participate in this extra work.

The first trader to show up was Steve Lewis who began asking the interns what they knew about hedge funds. Selena covered a yawn with her fist. If she'd been wearing a sorting hat, she would have muttered, "*Not hedge funds.*

NOT hedge funds." Fortunately, Kristin showed interest and aptitude for the topic, and Steve invited her to join him in his office later.

The same repeated with Lana Cornwall in commodities and Peter Green in bonds.

When Dane entered the room, all the kids sat up a little straighter. Val scanned the group of interns, trying to guess who he might pick. Thank God, Selena had chosen today to wear a short skirt and a blouse that opened enough to suggest a cleavage. Dane couldn't care less which of the interns could keep up with him. He'd go with whichever might entertain him.

He didn't bother to glance at Val, and she shook her head at his ridiculous compunction. As if she'd hold it against him for holding himself against her Friday night. Those five minutes had given her something worth thinking about all weekend. But if he wanted to play apologetic scamp, she'd amuse him.

He pulled up a chair and began questioning the interns in rapid fire on topics ranging from futures to securitizations. He even asked them about their experience with java and sql. Whenever the others faltered, Selena managed to answer more or less correctly.

"And who can explain what a shelf company is?"

Selena spoke up before anyone else could. "It's a company with no employees or fixed assets."

He nodded. "And what are they used for?" He kept his eyes on her, letting everyone know the question was hers to answer.

She paused, maybe believing her chances hinged on getting this right. "One use might be as a transition from a bank or other structure that is prohibited from selling to the street. The bank could sell assets to the shelf company, which would then be permitted to sell to the street."

"Good." He put his elbows on his knees and leaned forward. "Give me an example of a type of financial instrument that might be sold this way."

She didn't hesitate. "Asset-backed securities."

"One last question, Miss Valencia."

Val rolled her eyes at the drama. He'd decided to pick Selena from the minute he'd seen her legs. It was fortunate she'd been well-prepared for this harangue. Val figured he'd only let the question-answer session go on so long to amuse himself since the girl could obviously keep up.

Selena's expression held a nervous hope that the question wouldn't trip her up. "Yes?"

"Would you like to spend the next week securitizing assets with me?"

Val resisted the urge to tell them to get on with it. They had other interns, and the traders were starting to form a line at the door. Dane had to make a show of everything.

With no climactic surprise, Selena clapped her hands together and then pulled herself back into a professional restraint. "Yes! I'd love to."

"Great." He stood. "I'll see you this afternoon."

Val ushered Jai Patel in and tuned him out immediately, watching Selena intently. The girl glowed with a victorious glee. It was obvious Dane had been her first pick all along. Good. Maybe his dormant sense of retribution would finally wake up.

Transcript of second quarter board meeting addendum Page 4

Parties present: Noelle Constance, Maxwell Baker, Aloysius Holstein, Amy Waterson, Louis Beauchamp

Noelle Constance: *These added features will attract new customers as well as retain our existing client base, leading to increased revenue. And as I've demonstrated, the cost savings in our strategic initiatives, specifically as relates to our more efficient storage centers, will increase our overall margins. It is my conservative estimate that we should hit the projected growth of five percent, but of course, we hope to exceed expectations.*

Maxwell Baker: *Excellent. You've clearly done your homework.*

Amy Waterson: *Yes. It's quite a relief to have someone competent in your position. We can put that last chapter behind us.*

Louis Beauchamp: *We are all pleased to have someone of your impeccable reputation on the team.*

Noelle Constance: *If you don't mind me asking, what was it about my candidacy that caused you to select me. I understand Val Montgomery—*

Aloysius Holstein: *Val did direct our attention to your resume, but you have the background and credentials. We were obviously swayed by the ev-*

idence you won't be the sort to bring anymore of these sex scandals to the company.

Maxwell Baker: *Our investors won't stand for any hint of scandal. We believe we've won back their trust. Please prove our faith well founded.*

Noelle Constance: *I have every intention to.*

Dane's mood had increased with the possibility of working with Selena. She was both pretty and eager—his favorite combination. It would be the perfect distraction from his other affair. Plus, he'd been looking for a way to get back on the system. Since he oversaw technology, he had no real reason to work on live trading software in production. By the end of the week, they'd have to let him create a login for Selena. She'd be operating on the trading floor soon, and as her mentor, he'd get to play.

He spent the rest of the morning going through his email. He didn't even need to read the subject headers before hitting delete, delete, delete. So much garbage. He marked all the meeting requests with *Tentative*, but then stopped with one that stood out from the mass of *Release 4.2 deployment final code walk through for gold build* types of invitations.

The single-subject title almost registered as spam.

Coffee?

The request had been sent while he was grilling Selena. And it was from Noelle. He quickly checked the other invitees to verify it was sent to him alone. But to what end? She couldn't fire him. He held his cursor over the *Decline* button.

But his curiosity was piqued. What could she want? She'd made it clear she had no interest in him—not yet. His behavior had even grossed him out.

He stared at the email a moment longer, savoring what might be a small victory. She'd come to him.

Tempted to decline, he decided instead to delete the invitation without a response. Just in case things went bad, he wanted no record to exist anywhere in the system that indicated he'd encouraged her in anyway. But an outright refusal might turn her away right when she was coming around, no matter how unlikely that scenario.

Anyway, she'd set the time for later this morning, and he had so many meetings to attend. At least, on paper.

Sophie!!!

EEEEEEEEEEEEEEEEEEE! I got it! I get to work with Dane!

You should have seen the looks in the eyes of the other interns. I thought they might gang up to kill me. But I rocked the interview. He had no choice but to take me. OMG OMG OMG!

Selena

The sushi menu lay on the carpet just inside her door, slid there while she worked with the interns. She picked it up and opened it to find the time written in black felt pen. *11:45*

Never mind her own plans. *Drop everything, Val. Stay at my beck and call.* She nearly threw the menu into the trash can, but her vexation didn't last longer than it took to cross to her desk. Of course she'd meet him. He was the closest thing to fun around here.

The sushi restaurant was only a few blocks away and had the advantage of quaint private rooms with stereotypical sliding bamboo doors that used rice paper in place of windows. Val entered and slipped her shoes off. She knelt at the table across from Dane, who'd already ordered a pot of sake and checked off his sushi order.

Val did the same and handed their slips to the waitress. Then she settled in for whatever Dane needed to say.

"Do I owe you an apology?" He lifted the corner of his mouth in what he knew damn well was his apologetic grin. He could get away with murder with that look.

Val considered toying with his apparent sense of remorse, but she didn't believe he actually felt any. "You want to apologize for giving me a glimpse into what I have to look forward to when you finish your dalliance?"

His grin twisted into smug satisfaction. "I like the sound of that." He looked around. "This room is private. Would you like another sample of projected earnings?"

She shook her head. "You don't have to couch your seduction in ridiculous innuendo around me. Speak plainly."

"I thought I did on Friday. You didn't seem to like that so much then."

"Oh, I liked it plenty. I'll like it better when I'm not sharing your attention with your conquest."

"Say the word and I'll set that aside. It could be you and me. Noelle is just entertainment."

Val's breath caught. The offer tempted her, but words without action meant nothing. "Is she? I have to confess I have my doubts."

"About what exactly?"

"Honestly, Dane. I'm losing faith in your abilities. Are you really such a loser you can't seduce one girl?" Appealing to his vanity usually provoked him to show his hand.

"Well, that's flattering." He wasn't amused, she could see. Perhaps insulting him had been a misstep.

The door slid open, and a waitress placed plates before them. Dane poured soy sauce in a side dish, jammed a chopstick into the wasabi paste, and stirred a green glob into the brown liquid. Val poured him a cup of sake and waited for him to pour hers before biting into her sashimi.

She exhaled sharply before giving him a rare piece of honesty. "Look. You were supposed to take care of this quickly, but you're dragging it out. Why? I'm beginning to suspect she's the one seducing you."

He cocked an eyebrow. "And you think me moving in faster would prove she's not?"

"Why are you so obsessed, then? Is she really just the one you couldn't have?" Val smiled despite the twist in her gut. She'd been the one he couldn't have—until he'd had her. Had she blown her one chance? She raised an eyebrow. "Or is this a midlife event? Trying to prove you're still vital?"

"You're proof enough of that, my love." Was his hang-dog frown for real, or was he mugging for Val's amusement?

He always did know how to appease her. "You know what I mean. As long as you're fascinated with Noelle, I'm not about to be your side piece."

Dane dragged a California roll through his toxic sludge, musing as if it were an afterthought, "I could forget all about her right now. Trust me."

She didn't. She knew him too well. But she'd prepared for his reaction. "You might not forget her so quickly when I tell you about her phone call with Geraldo, Friday."

"What phone call?"

"I overheard her. I think he's asking her for dirt on you or me. Probably both of us."

Dane's cheeks flamed crimson. "Why is he still bothering? He got everything already. What more does he want?"

"I imagine he wants to finish ruining you—or me."

"Why would she help him?"

"That's what I'm trying to find out."

The napkin in his hand had crumpled to a wad. "And you expect me to do what exactly?"

She grinned. She knew he'd bite. "Hand me your phone."

Reluctantly, he slipped it from his breast pocket and unlocked it. She faced the screen toward him so he could see her scroll through his installed apps until she found the recording device. "Use this."

Dane visibly recoiled, paranoid by how technology was slowly invading even his most private moments.

"You go too far, Val."

Val tsked. "Oh, I don't want to hear you climax Dane. Unless it's with me. I just want you to get her talking about Geraldo. Surely you can do that much?"

"And if she doesn't want to tell either of us?"

"Maybe we can find some leverage to encourage her."

"Blackmail? That's so nasty."

"But effective."

"Look. I just want to get her in bed."

Valerie stifled a wince. "You can do both. I can make it worth your while."

"How?"

"Let's revise the wager. Get me something against Geraldo. Or against Noelle. I'm not picky."

"And you'll be mine?"

Val nodded. She'd be Dane's, but more importantly, Dane would be hers after he chose to betray Noelle. And Noelle would be forever out of his reach once he did that.

Dane picked up his sake cup and swirled the liquid around. "Noelle asked me for coffee today."

Val took pleasure in sharing one piece of good news. "Is that so? I took her out on Saturday and fed her an earful about poor lovesick Dane."

He chuckled. "After Friday night, I doubt she's interested in lovesick Dane."

She figured he'd earned the information. "Well, I played on her obvious interest in you. You know, I think she's convinced you've got a soft center under that bullshit demeanor you keep up."

"Seriously?" He leaned forward and ran a finger across Val's hand. "You may have saved me weeks of recovery."

She hated the way the concerned lines on his face smoothed, hated the dreamy grin that left her worrying her plan might backfire. It wouldn't do for him to become infatuated again. Maybe he needed a new distraction.

Val retracted her hand. "Yes, I know. And now you owe me."

Dane sucked on his teeth. "You want me to work on Selena?"

"You have the perfect opportunity to get even with Geraldo. He's probably working to sabotage your efforts with Noelle." The same way he'd forced her to sabotage her chance with Dane. "Think about how he drove you away from your company." *And from me.*

"I'm listening."

Val played her trump card. "Think about that pretty girl falling under your spell. You know they all look up to you."

Dane grabbed his shoes and began to put them back on. "Nice try, Val. But I'm not interested in seducing some insipid fan girl."

Val grimaced. "That isn't what I was suggesting."

He stood and threw two twenties on the table. "But since I have her under my tutelage anyway, I'll teach her some questionable little loopholes. I can at least lay that groundwork."

"Good."

Dane slid open the bamboo door, but before leaving, he said, "If Geraldo wants to keep up his vendetta, he'll find himself well matched."

As he took the elevator up, Dane fiddled with the recording app on his phone, messing around until he knew how to hit the On icon with his hand in his pocket. He turned the app off. It went against his instincts to capture himself even in writing. But Val's familiarity with the location of the app on his phone had left him unsettled. How many conversations had she recorded? Surely she'd only incriminate herself if she attempted to publicize anything said between them. And she had further to fall than him in the public eye. Still, he wondered if he ought to factory reset her device the next time she left it on her desk.

He exited the elevator to find Selena waiting outside his office door. He glanced at his watch to make sure he hadn't stayed away longer than he meant. But no. It wasn't even one yet. She bounced on her toes as he held the door open for her.

"Come right on in, Miss Valencia. I see you're eager to get started." He followed her in and unfastened the button on his suit coat. "I can't recall anyone so excited to securitize assets. Well, not since Val."

Selena beamed at the comparison. "If I can confess something . . . I came here to get a chance to work with you, so this is really a dream come true."

Jesus.

Dane smiled at her as if she wasn't being an insufferable suck up. "That's nice to hear. You might feel differently after today." He'd fully intended to start her off easy. The basics of structuring a security weren't complex. The realities were like walking a tight rope ever since the financial crisis with many opportunities to run afoul of ethics and possibly the law—all of which Dane hoped to exploit in the next week. With Selena ready to eat everything he fed her as though he were a god of finance, maybe he could ramp up his lessons.

He pulled a chair around the desk beside him and loaded the loan tracking software. "Can you log in? We should do this through your account."

Her jaw dropped. "Am I going to start trading?"

"Nope. This is a sandbox. You can do anything you want in here, and it won't affect the real world. Play around. Make mistakes. Break the law." He laughed, and she did, too, only a little harder than warranted.

"That's funny." She typed in her user name and password, and the page rendered with a menu for various activities.

Dane walked her through starting a new transaction, showing her how to choose the source of the assets, a shelf company for transfers if necessary, and a target buyer. "The system makes it pretty easy to create a sale. You'll obviously need to learn about all the players here, but the hard part is selecting the assets to include in the sale. We're just going to make a simple security to start."

She nodded. "We already did some of this last week, but the whole time I was looking forward to real world opportunities."

"We'll get there." He spent the next hour walking her through the different loan properties and showed her how loan buckets were created. Finally, he walked her up to how to build a tranche for the security. "And if we take loans from each of these buckets—"

She reviewed the loans he'd selected and turned to face him. "But some of these loans have really high interest rates."

He nodded. "I know. Whenever I see that I shake my head. Interest rates are so low these days. Why would anyone carry a thirty percent interest rate?"

"Wouldn't these be considered subprime?"

He affected an older brother look of approval. "Good catch. Ordinarily, yes."

She hesitated, apparently choosing her words carefully. "Then why would you include them in the security?"

"Because they are high-yield investments if they continue to pay. Higher risk, higher reward. And also because there are ample triple-A rated loans in the security to balance the risk."

She chewed on her lip, clearly uncomfortable. "But what about Dodd-Frank?"

He knew she'd initially bring up the financial regulations that were intended to prevent malfeasance. But Dane had not only read all eight hundred and forty-eight pages of the bill, he'd kept up on the court challenges. He'd never be allowed to play on the trading floor unsupervised, for good reason, but he'd learned more about financial instruments than the stressed-out traders down there today. They might know how to follow the laws, but Dane knew how to bend them.

He swiveled his chair toward Selena. "You've read Dodd-Frank?"

She sat up straight, defiant. "No. But I've read about it. We studied it last year."

"If you've already learned everything about securities, there are other interns who would happily switch places with you. I don't think anyone took Suzanne up on interest rate swaps."

She looked stricken. "No. I want to learn. I didn't mean to imply I already knew everything. I'm here to learn. I need to work with you because—" She gave him a devious grin. "—I want to beat all the other interns in the contest."

Bingo.

"Let me show you why Dodd-Frank doesn't apply here." He could talk circles around the regulations. And Selena nodded right along, sucking up every detail like the good student she'd probably always been. And she trusted him to tell her the truth.

Val spent her afternoon working with a pair of interns, building stock portfolios, diversifying for short-term and long-term goals. She'd opted to use the training room for her mentorship since she didn't want anyone messing with her own computer. Once she got them started, she exited into the hall. Noelle's office was a few feet away, door open. Val took a few steps and knocked.

Noelle glanced up from her laptop. "Oh, Val. Come in."

"I was in the neighborhood." Val threw a glance back over her shoulder at the training room.

"Have you started mentoring?"

"Yup. I've left them with a small exercise. I had a minute free, so I thought I'd come let you know I had a lovely time on Saturday. I need to spend more time with other women."

Noelle closed her laptop. "Can I ask you something?"

"Of course." Val stepped all the way into the office and closed the door. She sat in the chair facing Noelle's desk. "What's up?"

"Maybe nothing." She pursed her lips. "I sent Dane an invitation to coffee, but he never responded to it."

"You sent it how?"

"Through Outlook. I set it up like a meeting." She smiled ruefully. "I thought it would be easier to make it look as professional as I could. I don't want to give him the wrong idea."

"The wrong idea about coffee?"

"I know. It's mixed signals. But I'd kind of hoped to clear the air. After all, we have to work together."

"Well, I wouldn't read too much into it. He marks all his invitations tentative."

"He didn't though. I never got any response."

"Oh. That *is* odd." *Good boy, Dane.*

"You don't suppose it means he's angry?"

"Well, you know. I haven't discussed it with him. I'm not exactly his first choice of confidante in matters like this. Not since we were in college."

Val scanned the desk where Noelle tapped her fingernails. Other than a neat stack of paper and assorted pens, there weren't many potential sources of information. No hastily scrawled notes that might hide answers. Nowhere Val might leave a recording device.

Val waited for Noelle to speak again, hesitant to interrupt the momentum of her decision-making process. At last, she looked into Val's eyes. "I'm making more out of this than necessary. I really don't know why it even bothers me."

Val smiled, gentle. "Is it possible maybe you like him?" She held her breath, hoping she didn't rock the boat too far. But sometimes it only took recognizing feelings for them to begin to grow. Even when the feelings weren't actually there.

It was annoying to be doing Dane's work for him, but the last time he took months to attempt to seal the deal, and in that time, he'd discovered his emotions. Val needed him in Noelle's confidence today, and his hackneyed attempts at romance were getting him nowhere. If he could get her to trust him enough to share some intimate information, she'd have time enough after to throw a crowbar between them before things went too far. She'd done it before.

Noelle laughed. "Of course not." But her fidgety hands told another story. Val was reasonably certain Dane could hook her yet, but it would take an effort to haul her out of the water.

"Of course not." Val smoothed her skirt. "If you want to talk to Dane, you could just send him an email. Or stop by his office if he's avoiding you." She let out an exaggerated sigh. "He's probably nursing his wounds. Or embarrassed. He'll get over it."

"I hope so." Noelle stood, indicating the meeting was over. "And thanks, Val."

Sophie,

Look. I know I've only been out here a week, but I feel like I'm already way more experienced in the real world than you. You want to warn me about sexual harassment in the workplace because I chose to dress for success? Don't you realize that I can't harass anyone? And it's not like Dane is going to come on to me or something. A harmless crush can't hurt anyone.

Even my dad once dated Val, so clearly it's done.

Plus I am the most competent intern here. He didn't choose me just because of a skirt.

I basked in his brilliance for an hour this afternoon, and I promise you it was all professional. He's not this boogeyman everyone paints him as.

So calm down.

Selena.

Connor,

Please come see me in my office at your earliest convenience.

Dane G. Russ

Connor, one of the system admins, knocked on the door just before five. Dane waved him in. "Thanks for coming so quickly, Connor. Would you mind closing the door?"

Connor looked confused but did as he was asked. "What's this about?"

"I was hoping you could clear something up for me." He looked at his computer screen which currently displayed a couple of Putty sessions, black consoles that could be connected to a database or application servers. He had tailed a server log so the screen was littered with lines of garbage information. But he assumed Connor would never look too closely.

"Sure. What about?" Connor swallowed, and Dane hoped that meant he had a reason to feel nervous.

"I was going through some of the traffic logs from the past few months. You know we're obligated to monitor potential security holes, and I like to dig through the calls coming into and out of our network. You find interesting things there."

Connor stood still, giving away nothing to indicate if Dane's bluff would pan out. "Yeah. I suppose so."

"I found some calls to what seem to be porn sites. It appears to be downloaded files. I checked the computer name on the calls and, well, they led to you."

"I don't know why that would be. I mean, I don't look at porn." Connor shuffled his feet ever so slightly.

"I'm sure you don't. But I'd hate to have to ask Morty Becker to take a closer look into this. They tend to be a little less lenient about matters like this. I just want to make sure they don't happen again." He hoped he looked understanding. Connor could deny his accusation—hell, it wasn't really even an accusation. He'd be smart to walk away.

But he wasn't smart. "I swear it was only the one time. I was at home. Drunk. And I didn't realize I was tunneling in to the corporate network. It won't happen again. I swear it."

Dane hid his relief behind a wolf's grin. He'd wounded his prey, but now he needed to go in for the kill. "Good. I'm willing to let that go. But Connor, there's something you could do for me."

"Oh?" If he realized he'd been trapped, he didn't show it. Yet.

"I need you to route some information from the mail servers my way."

Connor's face lost color. "I can't do that. I'd get fired."

"You'd get fired for downloading porn, Connor. We could have someone go in and look to see what else we might find. And you know, when you get fired for downloading porn, that information doesn't remain private. Do you have a girlfriend, Connor?"

His shoulder's dropped. "What do you need?"

Dane produced a thumb drive and dropped the real bomb. "I need every piece of email to or from Noelle Constance."

Sophie,

I'm not sure why you have to be such a negative Nancy. I did read the articles you sent me, but I don't trust the sources. Why would Fleetwood hire Dane if he'd committed illegal activities? Wouldn't he be sitting in jail? Wouldn't there be some record of that? Sounds like people are really out to get him for whatever vindictive reasons. I bet he's made a lot of people jealous over the years. He was so young when he started his company. I can tell how brilliant he is just looking at him. And no, smarty pants, it's not the Kool-Aid talking. There's weirdly no cult around him here. It's like they've all forgotten who he is. He doesn't act like he's any big deal. He's been nice enough to come talk to the interns a couple of times.

But I haven't forgotten who he is. I'm angling to get closer—no, not like that, jeez (although, hmmm . . .).

I wish you'd just be happy for me instead of automatically assuming the worst. Give it a rest already.

Selena

Tuesday

*A*nthony,

I know I said we shouldn't use the company email to communicate, but I'm learning that maybe I need to relax a little. Seems like a lot of the rules are just guidelines. Anyway, I didn't get much of a chance to talk to you yesterday. I hope you enjoyed your first mentoring session as much as I did. I stayed up late last night reading about Dodd-Frank. I'd love to get together later and talk about the loopholes that are still present in the current legislation.

Are you free tonight?

Selena

The thumb drive arrived via interoffice mail just as Dane was settling in to delete all his emails. There was no note accompanying it, but still Dane didn't like that Connor had taken the risk of letting the memory stick out of sight. Then again, he didn't want people to see Connor entering his office regularly. And Dane had no reason to stop in to talk to the system administrators. He'd have to think of a better routine.

He slid the device into the port and opened the file. It contained only one email of interest.

Dear Noelle,

I'm surprised that you're writing to ask these questions after all this time. Honestly, I'm not sure what you're hoping to learn. At this point does it matter if Dane did everything Geraldo accused him of?

You probably know better than anyone that Dane's always had a rougher edge. He doesn't follow the rules, or more accurately, he doesn't bother to learn what they are. But he does know the law, and I never believed he was making unauthorized trades or any of the other charges. Where was the proof?

But since Dane stepped down willingly, what else could we think? We sure miss having him here. He's smart, loyal, and hard working.

Is that really what you wanted to ask about, sweetheart?

Kitty Monroe

Dane loved that Kitty didn't go overboard on the praise. Nobody would believe that he was an altar boy.

He'd never understood why they'd turned on him in the first place. Kitty wasn't lying that the accusations laid at his feet had been flimsy. Sure, he'd tweaked the code over the years to give himself a back door into the systems so he could dodge the business logic in the software meant to block shady transactions. But none of the board members were savvy enough to realize that. None of his deals had come under scrutiny. Everything Geraldo had trumped up had been completely baseless and offensive. Dane would have every right to nurse a grudge, if he didn't actually have arguably criminal activity to hide. But his execution had been masterful.

Dane reread the email, looking for clues to understand what Noelle was after. If she was a mole for Geraldo, why would she be talking to the board at R&M about what had happened years ago? Was she having a change of heart?

She wouldn't be the first. Over the years, different board members had contacted him to express remorse and wonder whether they'd moved too quickly. Encouraged by the ones who reached out to him, he'd made an effort to charm or seduce the ones who hadn't.

Kitty, in particular. Before he left the company, she had pursued him for months to no avail despite being married. Not that he cared about the oaths she was prepared to break. He balked at having a complicated affair. However, given the choice between an angry husband and a recalcitrant former board member, he opted to soothe the grudge. And he discovered that married women need the same amount of discretion as him. Ever since, he'd made a point to look Kitty up whenever she knew he'd be in town. A good thing, too. It bought him a recommendation.

It was too late to change the past, but at least their revised opinions might help his cause with Noelle.

He owed Val for planting the seeds of doubt in the first place. She'd pleaded his case and laid the groundwork for his rehabilitated image before she turned in her resignation and came out to join him at Fleetwood. He might be more grateful that Val had followed him into the "heartland" if she hadn't stabbed him in the back first.

Fucking New Year's Eve.

Though really, it was his own fault for giving into a decade-old fantasy. But how could he have turned her down when she stood alone at midnight, wanting him after so many years, giving him a chance he'd stopped even considering an option? When *she* kissed *him*, he went for it because that chance might never come again. He didn't really think through all the ramifications. And she'd reacted more passionately than he'd dared dream. That night, he opened himself up to her, gave himself totally, and believed it could be the first night in many.

He'd thrown his cards on the table and lost.

He sighed. *Women. Can't live with them, can't blackmail them into loving you forever.*

"""

Dane,

Hi. I sent you an invitation to meet me for coffee yesterday, but I don't think you ever saw it. I know you're busy during the day, but I'd really like to meet at some point and talk. Are you free later this afternoon? I'm not going to take silence as a refusal. Please respond.

Noelle Constance | CEO Fleetwood Capital LLC

Val's door opened, and Dane strode in without knocking first. He hadn't walked into her office in so long, he looked completely out of place. Val closed her laptop and leaned back in her chair, curious to find out what occasion had brought him out into the open.

"You sure you don't want to meet someplace more clandestine?" She'd never cared who saw them together, although with the events of the past week, it might be better for Noelle to remain unaware of their alliance.

He glanced back through the window in her door. "No, I just need you to answer a quick question. Have you been in touch with our old board members?"

Val scanned her memory. "Not lately. Why?"

"Apparently Noelle has been contacting them."

"Oh, has she? Interesting." Val filed that away. "That won't look good if she requires a restraining order after you dump her."

A line creased his forehead. "I hadn't thought of that." He settled into a chair. "Why is she investigating me in the first place?"

"Do you think it's a coincidence she started asking about you after you let her know you wanted to take her out?" Val held her hands on her lap so Dane wouldn't see them shake. It irritated her to have to turn him and push him in the right direction, especially when that direction was toward another woman.

"So you think she's vetting me?" He shifted his eyes. "This could work out in my favor."

When he looked that cocky, Val had an urge to grab his tie, wrap it around her wrist, and push his chair back into the corner, out of view of anyone peering through the small window. She'd lock the door and unzip his pants.

"Val?"

Val blinked. "Yes, yes. She'll find out what a great guy you are and fall into your arms. Wedding bells will ring. Now could you please get out of my office? Some of us actually do work around here."

Dane smiled as he left Val's office. He'd only stepped in to destabilize her. He knew how jealous she grew of other women, and he wanted to make sure she'd be eager to consummate the promised affair. She'd rebuffed him long enough.

When he returned to his office, Selena was swiveling in his chair. "Hello. Are you ready to show me more about securities?"

She'd dressed in quintessentially schoolgirl attire. Short skirt, high stockings, penny loafers, and a short plaid tie around her unbuttoned shirt collar. He swallowed. "Aren't you supposed to be with the other interns until noon?"

"Ugh. They're going through the Fair Credit Reporting Act." She rolled her eyes. "I'm already aware of the regulations."

He sat on the edge of his desk, conscious of the schoolmaster position this put him in. "What responsibilities does a bank have when it uses a consumer report?"

"It must disclose the cause of a denial of credit to the consumer."

"Does it?"

She hesitated with a pout. "No, wait. It just has to disclose that—"

"Off you go."

She wrinkled her nose. "I can read about all that later. I'd rather stay here and get the kind of training I won't get from the books."

A responsible mentor wouldn't have entertained her obvious manipulation. He had theoretical obligations after all. There was a weekly meeting with his developers that he really ought to attend. He rarely showed up for them though. He'd put project leads in place to handle the day to day. They'd alert him if they hit any major roadblocks or needed input. "Go grab your laptop."

She raced out of the room, beaming. Dane adjusted his pants.

What mischief could he get done today? And could he resist the damage she might do him? If she intended to continue the sex kitten routine, he might need to have her switched with another intern before anyone charged him with sexual harassment.

He settled into his desk and prepared to resist Selena's obvious attempt to come on to an older man, idly wondering if he could pull that off in total secrecy.

Selena,

Hey - that sounds like a fun night, however I'm going out with the group tonight. If you want to join us, we'll be going over right after work to the same bar we went to last week. And if you really want to, we can talk about Dodd-Frank.

Anthony

Geraldo,

This detective work feels shady. All I'm doing is irritating people who haven't spoken to Dane or

Val in years. Nothing I've learned comports at all with the things you've warned me about. Granted, I have personal reasons to mistrust Dane, but from a professional standpoint, I have no reason to think I've fallen into—what was it you called it? A nest of vipers?

Noelle Constance | CEO Fleetwood Capital LLC

Noelle,

They've clearly traced over their tracks to make sure they left no enemies behind. If you're willing to dig a little more, I am positive you'd discover those two are up to no good. They can't help it.

I'd be willing to give you firsthand knowledge, but I suspect you'd write it off as grievances from a spurned lover, so I'd prefer you figure it out on your own. Or not. It's no difference to me. I'm just looking out for your best interest as always.

Do you have an internal auditor? Hire him to follow them if you have to. Have their emails and mail intercepted. Tap their phones. They'll eventually show their true colors. Do not trust them.

Geraldo

Geraldo,

I do appreciate your warnings. But you're suggesting I spy on emails and tap phones? That seems extreme, and that would make me worse than anything I can even imagine I might find out about either of them.

But we do have an internal auditor who seems willing to do a little investigating on the side.

I confess I find it hard to take your apprehensions seriously when you sent your daughter here to work under them. I understand Dane's currently mentoring Selena. Can you explain to me why you're comfortable with that arrangement? Do you think I'm less capable than a twenty-year-old?

Noelle Constance | CEO Fleetwood Capital LLC

Dane found another orange envelope on his desk and shook out the memory stick within. There were several files on this thumb drive from earlier this morning. He considered everything he'd read. The first thing he needed to do was put an end to his investigation. He had enough information, and if Noelle started snooping through his interoffice mail, he'd be done.

Was she reading his email? Was she going to have him followed? If she hadn't already, who had? Nobody? Was he being paranoid? Should he be paranoid?

He slipped a note into the orange envelope.

Thank you for your hard work. I have everything I need.

He considered adding a fifty but thought better of it. The note by itself had nothing incriminating. He could have been asking for the sys admins to mount a shared directory or install a Linux library for him.

Selena returned with her laptop and started to come around the desk to his side, but he pointed to the chair facing him. She crossed her legs, showing smooth, brown knees and a thigh that disappeared under the skirt. He mentally dragged a finger along the skin, then closed his eyes and counted to five.

"So a group of us are going out tonight. I know you probably never hang out with the younger people, but it would be cool if you came out. A lot of them idolize you."

He rubbed his temples. She'd just made sure he'd never say yes to that. "I don't think that would be appropriate, Selena."

"And why not? Get to know the interns. There's nothing wrong with that."

The idea of someone following him to a bar only to find him regaling the interns with war stories amused him. "Maybe. But let's get back to work. We're going to talk about—"

"Can we talk about Dodd-Frank? I was up late last night reading about loopholes in the regulation." She uncrossed her legs, then recrossed them the other way. "I couldn't believe how defanged the law has become through lobbying efforts. I don't know why it never occurred to me that investors would find ways to profit from the laws meant to regulate profits."

Dane had to consciously wipe the look of shock from his face. He easily replaced it with one of pride. She was a hell of a student. He wondered what she looked like with her hair down, with her glasses off.

Stop it, Dane.

"Yeah, sure. There's a lot of ground to cover there. We can set up some securities today that would be technically legal, but borderline. If that's what you want to do. I'm not saying you should do this, of course."

The innocence of her smile clashed with her words. "Is that what you got in trouble for?"

"No. I didn't get in trouble for anything."

She bit her lip, thinking. "Can I ask you something?"

"Sure."

"Why'd you leave?"

"Oh, is that all? Can we leave it at loss of confidence?"

"It's just that, I've read all the articles, and there's always this hint of actual fraudulent activities. But they just went away. And now you're here. So did they just make everything up?" Her eyes were vast pools of curiosity. She looked like she'd swallow anything he fed her.

He crossed his arms. He'd been asked the same question, mostly from people who worshiped him, like this girl seemed to. Those who didn't worship him usually believed what they wanted and never asked him anything. "Would you believe me if I said, yes? They made everything up."

"I might. My dad's not the most honest man alive."

Dane's ears perked up. "How do you mean?"

She averted her eyes and tugged at the hem of her skirt. "Never mind. I don't want to talk about my dad."

"That makes two of us."

Her head lifted, and she bit her lip, like she was weighing the wisdom of her next words.

"Spit it out, Selena."

"Just. Why didn't you stay and fight?"

"That's two questions, Miss Valencia. Can we get to work now please?"

"And you'll come out with us tonight?"

"If it means you'll stop asking me questions."

She beamed. "Excellent."

Noelle,

Thank you for your invitation to coffee. I'm not sure it would be appropriate at this time.

Dane

Selena tapped on the door and looked through the small window until Val waved her in. Selena continued to dress provocatively, but her bloodshot eyes marred the effect she was likely aiming for. Perhaps she and Anthony had fought.

Val indicated the chair. "Is everything okay? You don't look well."

"Actually, I have something I need to discuss with you."

Was she already going to raise a warning flag about Dane? It wouldn't be surprising after her qualms about a simple chat program. Perhaps it had been a bad idea to push that so quickly. "Don't be shy. Whatever it is, I'm sure we can work it out."

Selena looked at her hands in her lap, scratching at fingernail polish that had begun to chip. "I need to find another mentor."

Val's hands went cold. Had Dane come on to her? That's not what she'd asked him to do. "You're not satisfied with the training?"

Selena looked up with tears in her eyes, and Val's mind raced with ways to contain this disaster. She wasn't at all prepared for what Selena said. "Dane's great. I've learned so much from him in just two days."

Val relaxed. Maybe this could be salvaged with some simple flattery. "That's good to hear. He's said wonderful things about you. He tells me you show great promise."

A blush crept up Selena's cheek.

Interesting.

Val had been so concerned that Dane had made an unwanted advance toward the child, she'd failed to notice the obvious. Selena might have consented to his overtures.

She filed that away as a potential solution to a bigger problem.

Selena twisted her hands. "That means so much to me, and trust me, I'd love to continue on with him, but my dad—"

"What about your dad?"

"He found out I'm here, and he's not at all happy about it. He says I can stay, but I have to promise him I'll find another mentor. So I can't work with Dane. It's not fair."

Val had to bite back a smile. This wasn't an ideal turn of events, but it might make Selena more eager to prove herself. "Oh, I didn't know your father was unaware you were here. How did he find out? Do you know?"

Selena shook her head, swallowing back her emotions. "I don't know. I don't know anybody here. I've only told my college roommate, but I don't think she'd tell on me. She doesn't like that I'm here, either, but I don't think she'd call my dad. She knows how I feel about him."

Val played that admission over in her head. Had she overlooked a potentially willing weapon sitting right in her hands?

"Well, I guess it doesn't matter. It's what we have to deal with now, right?" Val stood up and sat down next to Selena with her arm around the girl's shoulders. "How would you like to work with me? I have two interns now, but I can catch you up quickly."

Selena's whole body dissolved into Val's. "Oh, that would be wonderful."

"I know I'm not Dane, but I know a thing or two."

Selena sat up straight and shook her head. "No. I'd love to work with you. I never meant you to think otherwise. Thank you so much!"

Val patted her back. "Okay, then. Off you go. I'll see you back here tomorrow afternoon."

Selena wiped her eyes. Val would have liked to give her a tissue, but she didn't have any in her office. She should rectify that—Selena wasn't the first person to cry in her presence. Instead, she tightened her arm for a quick side hug and then stood with a hand held out to help Selena up. It was a kindly gesture, but Val just wanted Selena gone so she could concentrate on her own thoughts.

Selena closed the door, and Val immediately began pacing, trying to envision her battlefield. Someone had leaked to Geraldo, and that someone felt an awful lot like Noelle. Which side was she playing for?

More importantly, what issues did Selena have with her dad? Would she be willing to betray her own father? Could she?

Val stared out the window at the parking lot, tapping her fingernails on the glass. Her eyes fell on Dane's external phallus of an automobile parked at the far corner. It was a shame she couldn't use Dane to coerce her.

But maybe when he found out Geraldo had stripped him of his afternoon plaything, he'd be willing to return fire.

Val needed to talk to him right now.

The picnic tables wouldn't work, especially since Dane had purportedly quit smoking. She checked the time and stepped out of her office. She could catch him before he left.

Rosamund Shirley lurked outside her door like a ghoul.

"May I help you?"

The decrepit woman gave Val the creeps. Why hadn't she retired already? Shouldn't one of her relatives have shipped her to a nursing home by now?

Rosamund looked around. "I seem to have gotten off on the wrong floor."

Val gritted her teeth before pressing a smile across her face. "Let me walk you upstairs." It never hurt to keep up appearances.

She led Rosamund to the elevator and stayed with her until they'd reached her cube. Rosamund patted her hand. "Thank you, dear. You'd think I just started working here yesterday."

No. Val would never make that mistake. She shot a glance over at Morty on the other side of the room and caught his eye. She looked away immediately before he'd do something stupid, like wave at her.

Once she'd performed her act of charity, she made a beeline to Dane's office but found his door locked. And he was gone.

The kids all scooted around to make room for Dane. He flagged down the waitress and ordered a scotch, neat. Then he told her to put the whole tab on his credit card. At least if he was paying, he could pretend it was a company outing and stop feeling so creepy. Even the boys were practically leering at him.

A couple of them had been in the middle of a conversation when he arrived, and they kept arguing until others swatted at them and pointed toward Dane, as if royalty had arrived. Then in silence, they all stared, waiting for him to perform a circus act.

"So are you all enjoying the internship?" A dozen heads nodded and called out an assortment of agreements. They kept watching him. "And you're learning from your mentors?"

"Some more than others," said one of them.

"Ron, right?" He gave the kid a chance to correct him, but he knew he'd gotten it right. "Are you not satisfied with your assignment?" Ugh. He didn't like to be that prick. But arrogant interns pushed his buttons.

Anthony spoke up. "I think Ron's trying to say that Selena landed the best situation."

How humiliating to have misconstrued the intent. But he hated the ass kissing more than the arrogance. "Selena's a sharp student."

Ron laughed, too loud. "Selena seems to think there are loopholes in Dodd-Frank. Is that your definition of sharp?"

Dane was actually relieved Ron turned out to be an asshole because it would be a lot more fun this way. "She's right about that."

"Oh, please. Dodd-Frank is the greatest piece of regulatory law to be enacted since . . ."

"Since Glass-Steagall?" Dane offered helpfully.

"Well, yeah."

There were several empty mugs in front of Ron, and Dane realized the kid was running on liquid courage. But still. He couldn't resist.

"But that law was repealed." His scotch arrived, and he took a long sip. "Have any of you actually read Dodd-Frank?" Ron looked away. Dane glanced over at Selena. "Tell them."

She sat up straighter. "Glass-Steagall was only thirty-seven pages long, but Dodd-Frank is so complicated, the only people who really know what's in it are lawyers. And it keeps growing."

Before she could get going, Ron said, "You're not a lawyer. You're just a programmer, right? Wasn't your SEC license revoked?"

Dane pretended to adjust his collar. "Tough crowd." But the kids had probably never seen a live comedian. "First of all, where did you hear I lost my license? That's simply untrue.

Second, programmers have to know the rules of the game as well as any traders. After all, who puts the gatekeeping into the software you use to buy and sell? That software is complicated and always changing with regulations."

Ron sat down and shut up. Dane looked around to figure out if this was some kind of pitchfork-wielding mob or a case of drunken bravado.

Anthony looked abashed. "Hey, I'm sorry for that. Not that I have any connection to him whatsoever. We were all kind of thrown together, right?" He laughed awkwardly.

"No, problem. Listen, go ahead and order whatever. The bar will take care of it. I'd recommend not getting as drunk as your friend. Tomorrow is still a work day. I'm gonna head out."

Selena jumped up to follow him and caught his elbow. "I'm sorry. I had no idea they were going to be like that. Whenever they talk about you, it's like they're in the presence of a god. I don't know what got into Ron."

"He wanted to blood me. I get it. He's probably top of his class at some pretentious school. Whatever. He'll feel like an ass tomorrow—and next year if he puts in an application to work here." Dane grinned at Selena so she would see he was joking. He didn't need to tell her he'd much preferred Ron's attacks to her pawing at him. At least he could defend himself against Ron.

"So I was wondering if you could give me a ride home. I don't have a car here."

Dane scratched the back of his neck. If Noelle was having him followed, he didn't want to be seen driving a young intern home. "Let me call you a cab."

He waited out front with her until the cab arrived and handed the driver enough cash to get her home. Then he found his car and sped out of the parking lot. He went straight home.

When he pulled into his driveway, the cab stopped behind him on the street, and Selena climbed out.

Oh, God, now what?

She spoke to the driver, who drove off, leaving a twenty-something-year-old girl on his doorstep. He looked up and down the street for any signs of witnesses. He waved toward his car. He had to get her back home.

"Why are you here, Selena?"

She laughed. "I had the cab driver follow you." She staggered a little as she approached. How had Dane missed that she'd gotten good and drunk at the bar. He'd been so intent on the battle of wits, he'd lost sight of the girl with the crush. *Not good, Dane.*

"Come on. Let's get you back home."

She sauntered clear up to him and touched his chest. She walked her fingers up the buttons on his shirt until she reached the knot in his tie. "This is a very sexy tie."

He realized she'd taken off her glasses at some point and batted doe eyes at him. He wrapped his hand around hers and drew it away from him.

She pouted. "Did you know I've been fascinated with you for years? I wonder what it might be like to kiss you."

He ran his eyes along her lips, trying to push that image out of his mind.

"Would you get into my car, please?" He opened the door for her, but she leaned against it, pulling the elastic out of her hair and shaking it in a way that might have left him desiring her. But he hadn't forgotten that she worked under him. This could get him in more trouble even than the stunt he'd pulled with that sys admin, Connor. Maybe.

He thought he could sober her up with a cold reminder. "Your dad would not be very happy about this."

"Screw him. He told me I can't work with you anymore."

"Oh, so he found out." He knew that. He remembered Noelle's email. He'd wondered how long it would take for him to berate his daughter. Poor thing. He was almost tempted to carry her into his house just to help her get even. Geraldo deserved it. But he'd grown to like Selena, and the last thing he wanted to do was have Geraldo on his mind if he took her in his bed. He knew how that went.

"He did." She clenched her fist and punched nothing in particular. "He said I have to go back to New York, but I told him I wouldn't. This is a prestigious internship program. And I'd never get into another at this late date. He has to let me stay."

"Did he agree?"

"Yes, but." She lifted her eyes up to his. "But he told me he wants me to work under a different mentor. I couldn't get him to hear reason. He's got the wrong idea about you."

Dane chuckled. "Maybe not."

Her eyes narrowed. "Oh, like he's one to talk." She shook her head. "He's the worst, most controlling, selfish—" Her voice dropped. "It's my life. He can't treat me like one of his employees."

Dane wanted to press her to go on, but she swayed a little. She needed someone to protect her. There were predators about. He dipped his head to look into her eyes, voice lowered. "Is that why you came here tonight?"

"I thought. I just thought."

"I might mentor you on the sly maybe? Teach you about securities at eleven p.m. on a Tuesday in my kitchen?"

She stepped away from the car and laid her hand on his cheek. "I just thought you might have other things to teach me."

He hoped she couldn't see his eyes roll in the darkness. This was the weakest come-on he'd ever witnessed. "Look, Selena. You're a beautiful girl. But I'm your supervisor. And that means you're off limits."

"Not anymore. Not if I work with another mentor." The girl was learning to work the loopholes. Her hand slid down until her palm skimmed his neck inside his shirt collar, and he shivered. "And I've thought about this for such a long time."

She was cute as hell. But she was an intern, he reminded himself. The worst cliché. Taking advantage of her would be so easy, it would be criminal. Possibly literally.

"No, still."

"Nobody would have to know."

He considered it for a half a second. Nobody *would* have to know. And the risk was tempting. If he wasn't absolutely sure he was being followed, he might have taken her up on it. He had half a mind to anyway. But he wasn't nearly drunk enough, so he pointed to his car. "Get in. I'm taking you home."

He dropped her off and ended up walking her to her door with her holding onto his arm. This would be exactly the kind of scene he didn't need anyone documenting, but he couldn't drop her at the curb. His car stood out in any case. He waited while she pulled out her key. Her dark hair fell over her shoulder, and he resisted the urge to push it back. But she lurched and giggled, reminding him that she still hadn't sobered up.

She held up her key triumphantly, then squinted one eye at the keyhole. Once the door opened, she turned back, stood on her toes, and planted a quick kiss on his cheek. "Goodnight, sexy."

He laughed as he walked back to the car. Normally, he recoiled when the interns professed their adoration, but she'd somehow charmed him with her wide open devotion. Maybe because he really liked her.

It gave him an idea.

Wednesday

O ne exception to Dane's habit of standing at meetings extended to developer scrums since he needed his laptop open while the technical lead, Steve Dworkis, projected his desktop on a large screen at one end of the table.

Steve manned the mouse, and the cursor bounced across a Visio diagram. "And as you can see, the original design just isn't scalable. It's cheaper and meets our immediate needs, but we'll end up revising this in a couple of years if too many clients adopt it. Also, I should point out that the maintenance costs will be greater in the long run."

Dane nodded. "So what would you propose instead?"

"We've been discussing shifting the paradigm."

"Speak English, man."

This guy was a competent developer, but he was bucking for a promotion to a management position, and he'd started talking like he thought he'd be moving up the corporate ladder any day.

Steve spoke to the rest of the group. "If we're willing to refactor and retrofit older code, we could—"

Dane shook his head. "No. We're not going to rewrite the whole system for this project."

"But hear me out. It would set us up for a whole new set of functionality."

"And who's going to pay for this? We have one client asking for it. If we tell them it's a million-dollar redesign, they'll go somewhere else. Are we going to eat those costs? Are you going to pay for it, Steve?"

Steve straightened his tie. "It's good long-term business sense, Dane. You should know that."

"Why exactly? You think any of us will be doing business like this in ten years? You know we'll have to redesign the system soon enough anyway. Why do it under the umbrella of a hidden piece of functionality?" Dane actually agreed with Steve, but he'd been around longer, too. "Look, Steve. You win the logical argument, but you're not going to win this battle. Stick around, and when the pressure comes down to overhaul the whole system, I'll personally recommend you to manage the project. It will be high profile, and you'll get all the kudos. You do it now, through the back door, and you'll sleep well at night knowing you do good work, but if anything goes wrong, you'll be the scapegoat. You do realize that, right?"

The fight went out of Steve. "Okay, Dane. We can do it as proposed."

"Great. Then can you get the estimates to me by later today?"

"Sure thing."

Dane scanned the rest of the developers. "Anything else on the agenda?" Silence.

He shut his laptop, feeling the mild content of having actually done something productive. He should go to more meetings, he decided. Maybe instead of leaving this company, he'd take it over. He could pull a Geraldo. Just buy up all the stock on the sly and push out the actual owners. They never set foot in this region of the country anyway. They might not even realize they'd lost an asset.

Deep in thought, he walked out of the conference room and ran into Noelle who looked immaculate as always. He could smell whatever mix of coconut, ginger, citrus concoction she'd lathered up with that morning, and he pictured her naked under a stream of water. "Good morning, Noelle."

He tried to walk past her, but she laid a hand on his elbow. "Dane. I was actually looking for you."

Steve glanced at them as he went past. Dane took a noticeable step back from Noelle for show. "Yes?"

"Can we talk for a minute?" She nodded toward the now empty room.

He held the door and watched her as she entered. She'd always been a beautiful woman. He couldn't understand how she was still single. She wasn't a player, but maybe she was working too many hours to commit to someone who wanted a woman at his beck and call. She was the kind of woman Dane would have loved to land—smart, self-possessed, driven. He wouldn't have minded if their lives had moved around each other like a double helix. As long as their naked bodies could have connected once in a while, he wouldn't have expected her to wash his underwear.

But she hadn't wanted that with him.

As Noelle settled into the seat Dane had recently occupied, he slid his hand into his pocket and flipped his phone so he could glance at the screen. A few taps, and the device became a recorder. He cringed a little, but he could delete it if it made him come across too sinister.

Dane considered taking the chair on the opposite side of the table, but instead went for Steve's former seat at the head of the table and just around the corner. "What's up?"

"Listen. First of all, I wanted to apologize for last Friday night. I felt awful for giving you the impression I considered it a date, and then I must have made you feel embarrassed when I said what I did."

Dane had been frustrated but not embarrassed. If he'd been embarrassed, this conversation would not be doing much to change that fact. "It's not a problem, Noelle. We had a nice dinner. That's all. You were right. We work together, so we should just keep things professional."

She ran her finger across her hair. Her hair was perfect, but she always tidied invisible loose strands when she was nervous. It was an endearing habit that had always captivated him.

"I'm glad you understand. It's been so long since—" Her nose wrinkled. She couldn't even bring herself to say it out loud.

Since she would have anything to do with Dane. Since she'd almost said yes.

"Noelle, why did you come to work here of all places?"

"Why wouldn't I? It was a good offer, and I needed the job."

"You had a job." He studied her for any signs she might balk if he pushed, but she straightened her posture. "Would you at least tell me why you left R&M in the first place?"

She inhaled sharp as if he'd asked her why she'd scorned *him*, a question he hadn't ruled out. She let her hands settle on the table between them. "I was no longer happy there."

"What did Geraldo do?" The idea of Geraldo pushing himself onto her against her will made his adrenaline course through his veins. He didn't miss the irony in his reaction.

She laughed. "I told you already it was what he didn't do."

Could she have been after Geraldo? Dane's fists clenched. The thought of Geraldo besting him twice made him ill.

"Did he spurn you or something?"

"Oh, God, no. It's just that he's been promising me a promotion for years, but he never delivered. That plus I haven't gotten more than the standard cost of living raise in all that time. I finally decided I needed to go."

That was it? Or was she hiding something else? "So now you're here."

"Now we are here."

He sighed. "Noelle, what do you expect from me?"

She stared at her hands, picking absently at her thumbnail. "You know I never intended to hurt you before, and I don't mean to now."

Dane had a million thoughts racing through his head, but he kept his face even. Fuck it. This might be his only chance to get an answer. "Why did you kick me to the curb? What did I do? I spent weeks trying to understand, but you wouldn't give me any explanations."

That red spot appeared on her cheek. What did it mean? Was he making her uncomfortable? Was she ashamed? Was she preparing to lie?

"I want to apologize for how I handled things before. But Dane, people talk. And your reputation—"

His *reputation*? Did she think he was juggling other women? He wanted to protest, but it wouldn't matter. She had formed an image of him, and that's what he had to work with. He sat back and crossed one foot over his knee, the picture of nonchalance.

"I don't know what to tell you. I could say that everything anyone's ever said about me was untrue, but it's probably not. Maybe it's exaggerated. Who knows? I stopped reading my own press when I left R&M because I didn't recognize myself in any of it." That sounded pretty good, he thought. Humble, with a hint of self-awareness. Noelle leaned in. Maybe she was buying it. He raised one eyebrow. "But I'm not a saint."

Her eyes tinged with fear or excitement, and she reached her hand out to his. "I know you're not. I haven't met a saint yet. But I don't believe you're as ruthless as Geraldo painted you. I have to tell you I've spoken to some of the people who remember what happened. To a one, they feel you were treated unfairly. Why hasn't the press picked up on that?"

Dane shrugged. "That's all old news. The only times I end up featured in an article now are when they compile lists."

"Ah, yes. Forbes ten most eligible financial leaders. Are you eligible Dane?"

Was she flirting, now? He smiled. "Do you want me to be?"

She tightened her grip on his hand. "For now, can we be friends?"

He drew his hand back and assessed her body language. He recognized the longing in her eyes, the flush painting her cheeks, and he knew that her refusal was equal parts self-denial and fear of the unknown. She wanted him, but she hadn't yet given herself permission to act on that.

He thought about how Selena's profession the night before had affected him, how even now, it made him more intrigued with the young girl.

On gut instinct, he decided to make a bold move across the board into her territory. "I don't want to be friends, Noelle." He hoped he'd read her right, or this might cost him the game. "We tried this before, and I was miserable. It's too difficult to be around you without wanting more." He closed his eyes and inhaled to emphasize his exposed vulnerability. Would she laugh in his face, or would she take pity on his apparent weakness?

He opened his eyes to gauge her reaction. Three blotches marred her neck and cheek. He licked his lips. "When you came here, all my old feelings reignited. I can no longer pretend I don't want more from you than friendship." He paused and gave her a deep penetrating eye fuck as he said, "I've always been in love with you."

"Dane."

He stood. "I can work with you. I've been doing it since you came here. But friendship is asking too much." He buttoned his suit coat as he stood and took a step toward the door. "If you change your mind about our relationship, you know where to find me."

He walked out into the hall, holding his breath so he wouldn't laugh. He'd either just screwed the pooch or set into motion the rest of his summer.

Sophie,

My head is killing me. Nothing as bad as the time you had acute sinusitis, and I realize this was my own fault and not caused by a bacterial infection like yours. Nonetheless, I'm very sensitive to light and sound. I'd love to stay in bed all day, but I start working with Val today.

I'm sure you'll be happy to know my dad has demanded I work with anyone other than Dane. You weren't the one who told him I'd gotten that internship I hope. No, of course you wouldn't do that. I might decide to change rooms in the fall if that were the case.

What's worse, my dad's now apparently going to call me every day to ask me everything that goes on here.

Anyway, I have other reasons to want to avoid Dane. I may have come on to him last night, and I'm mortified. It's kind of a blur.

Selena

Dane exited the stairwell on the fourth floor. He entered the breakroom and grabbed a packet of coffee without looking. After his Styrofoam cup filled, he walked slowly out, focused on his stir stick.

He rarely came up to this floor, and everything looked foreign. He scanned the people with their cheery plants and festive lights draping cube walls, like they were at home instead of the office. He sensed Rosamund's influence in the relaxed atmosphere. His eyes skated along the cubes until he located her, squinting at her monitor. He considered stopping over to chat, but that wasn't his primary mission. He could make a social call another time. Rosamund began to cough heavily, making up his mind. He didn't need to be picking up any kind of summer illness.

Nobody else seemed particularly interested in his presence. He blew on the hot liquid and proceeded toward his ultimate destination.

Morty sat in a large corner cube. It was open to the whole floor, so Dane had no intention of talking frankly to him here. He sauntered over and put his elbow up on the low cube wall. "Hi, Morty."

Morty's arms jerked. If he'd been holding his own cup of coffee, it would have ended up in his lap. "D-Dane. Hello. You don't usually grace us. What can I do for you?"

Dane glanced around his desk. A tower of Styrofoam cups leaned against the far wall. Various stacks of paper merged into one another. Brown rings covered any visible counter space. How had this slovenly man ended up in this position? He had a suspicion competence played a very small role in his hiring. He could smell Val's influence in this. "I just stopped by to ask you if you'd ever been to Miller's bar on Sixth."

"No. I can't say that I ever have." Morty attempted a smile, but it looked more like a cringe. He only managed to show his stained teeth.

"Well, that's a pity. I plan to go there tonight after work. I hear they have a great happy hour special. Well, I guess I'll see you around."

Dane put his hand in his pocket, and a twenty dislodged itself and dropped to the floor. Dane pretended not to have seen it and turned to walk away.

"Just a minute." Morty's head peered around the cube wall. Dane closed his eyes, hoping this imbecile wouldn't say anything stupid. Morty scratched his head and white flakes floated to the floor. "Do you want to meet me for drinks?"

"Well, Morty. Now that you mention it. We should do that. I'll be there around five-thirty."

Morty wrinkled his nose. "You know I'm married, right?"

Seriously? Dane bit back his honest reaction. "Of course. Just a couple of guys getting a beer after work. Sound good?"

Morty's yellow teeth made another appearance. "Yeah." He smiled a little wider. "Yeah. Why not? I'll see you there."

Dane held his composure until he'd entered the stairwell and then heaved in a huge breath and started laughing.

When he got back to his desk, he found a yellow sticky stuck to his laptop. It read: *Coffee* in perfect penmanship. He closed his door behind him as he headed back out. *Good thing nobody expects me to work.*

Val's coffee had grown cold, and she was about to abandon her post at the back of the café. She decided to check her phone one more time to read through any emails or messages that might have come during the last thirty seconds. Since she received roughly one thousand emails a day, she wasn't surprised to discover three more. But they were all the sort of crap she usually filtered out. She'd need to create more rules to get rid of the new influx of emails congratulating Alanna on her five years of service. That chain could go on all day. But she created a reminder to add her own saccharine response to the rest of the voices.

The chair across from her moved against her foot, and she glanced up to see Dane pulling it out to sit. "You might as well meet in the lobby as here. I thought we agreed to stop coming here." He scooted toward the table with a glance around at the other patrons.

"I couldn't think of any other place that we could get to quickly. I didn't expect you to take so long. Where were you, anyway?"

"Working?"

Val snorted. "Oh, right."

"You know, sometimes I do."

"Oh, okay."

"Did you invite me over here to insult me? I could go read the last letter my dad wrote me if I wanted to be abused."

Val rolled her eyes. "Are we doing this again?" Given her childhood, she found it difficult to muster up any sympathy. Dane's father had once told him he was "disappointed" with him and then left him six million dollars. Val's dad had repeatedly told her he wished she'd never been born. The only thing he left her were scars.

Dane's expression hardened. "Right. So I was just leaving."

She reached out and grabbed his wrist. "Wait. I needed to tell you something."

He stayed, but his body remained turned in his chair like he might leave at any second. "Go on."

"Selena has asked me to find her another mentor."

His face didn't register anything but boredom. "You could have emailed me that information."

"No, but I wanted to talk about why." She bit her lip, gleefully anticipating his reaction to the turn of events.

"I'd expect it's because Geraldo knows she's here." He had the audacity to look smug.

Val held her breath for a count to modulate her tone. "How'd you know that?"

He touched his forehead. "Psychic."

"Fine. Don't tell me." She sat back and crossed her arms. He couldn't be begged, so she waited.

A charmer's smile crept across his face. He knew she'd wanted to tell him. "Selena told me about her dad. She came to my house last night."

Val's spine went rigid. "She did what? Why?"

"Maybe to get back at her dad. Maybe because she has a ridiculous crush on me. It doesn't matter. I straightened her out and drove her home."

Possibilities were piling up in Val's mind. She leaned forward and talked low. "Do you think you could take her out on a date?"

He ran his tongue along his upper teeth, and it protruded under his cheek. "That would be incredibly risky. You know that."

Val did know. A day before, she would have found it the worst news. But now, at least on paper, she couldn't deny what a brilliant move it would be. Geraldo's most valuable piece lay exposed before Val's most ruthless player. "But she obviously worships you. She's the one coming onto you after all. Surely you could use that to your advantage. You wouldn't have to sleep with the girl. Just take some selfies out clubbing or whatever you do. It would drive Geraldo insane."

Dane pushed the chair back, but he didn't stand. "Look. You wanted to send her away from here with her ethics corrupted, and believe me, she's well on her way. On Monday, she was calling me out on legally gray trades, but it took very little encouragement to get her looking for ways to skirt the letter of the law. She even suggested she's got some dirt on her dad."

Val nodded. "Yes. I got that impression myself."

"She thinks it's a game. Wouldn't you rather work your magic on her? Besides isn't questionable trading your territory? I think it would be good for her to learn from the master."

"Oh, please." She didn't let him see that he'd flattered her. Maybe it would be good for Selena to fall into her hands. "Yes. Okay. With you, there will always be a whiff of corruption anyway." She wrapped her hands around her now cold coffee mug ignoring Dane's displeasure at that jab. "But it couldn't hurt for you to whisper sweet nothings in her ear and take her somewhere romantic."

"That's a dangerous game, Val."

She smiled. "I know." She noticed he hadn't said no, and her goading was making him angry. She loved when she got under his skin. It made him easier to knock off balance, but it also made him sexier than usual. "Don't think you can handle it?"

He leaned back and pierced her with his blue eyes. "You'd have me do everything for you."

She'd always found his arrogance ridiculously attractive. She hoped to draw him in with one more juicy bit of speculation. "Aren't you wondering how Geraldo found out Selena's even here?"

He cocked his head, with a bored expression, like he was ready to listen to her suppositions, but refusing to show any curiosity.

Val didn't wait for him to ask. "I'm convinced it's Noelle. Remember the list of contacts from last week? They must be colluding."

"Colluding? Noelle? I doubt that."

"Okay, but it's possible she accidentally told him, don't you think?"

"She is certainly talking to him, but I have something for you." He reached into his coat pocket and produced his phone. "One sec."

He fumbled in the other pocket for a set of ear buds and attached them. She put one end in her ear and waited for him to find a recording and forward to a specific point in time.

He hit play, and Noelle's voice began speaking. "*I told you already it was what he didn't do.*"

Val looked up. "When was this?"

Dane held a finger up to his lips. "Listen."

She missed something Dane said, then heard Noelle again. "*Oh, God, no. It just that he's been promising me a promotion for years, but he never delivered. That plus I haven't gotten more than the standard cost of living raise in all that time. I finally decided I needed to go.*"

When her eyes widened, Dane went to stop the recording, but Val grabbed his hand. She wanted to listen to the end. He didn't protest and leaned back all casual as though he didn't have a care in the world. Val had taught him that posture. Still, he looked delicious when he was being devilish, and everything he said to Noelle made her grin wider.

Until.

"You told her you loved her?"

He grabbed his phone back and dropped in his pocket. "Did it not sound sincere?"

It had. Too sincere.

She was beginning to regret hiring her.

If Noelle had nothing more than thwarted ambitions to lay at Geraldo's feet, she was no use, and Val could dispose of her. She needed to change the trajectory of this game immediately. She needed to get Dane to change his play. "What do you propose?"

She bit her upper lip, considering. "Get her to say something to you that could constitute an act of sexual harassment."

Dane scoffed. "Oh, is that all?"

"You've already laid some groundwork. You could use that as evidence you'd had a pretext to document her interactions with you. Push her."

"She's hesitant as hell, Val. If I push her any more, she's going to bolt."

"Fine. If you don't care, I'll get to the bottom of this."

Dane sighed. "She's not going to come out and threaten to fire me if I don't sleep with her. You expect too much. She's never going to be that reckless. Noelle's as straight-laced as they come."

"Her intentions don't matter, Dane. What people are willing to believe is the only thing that matters. Just finish what you started, and maybe—" she traced a finger along his wrist, tickling the skin below his cuff "—we can have that night together soon."

"You know if you keep moving the goalposts on our wager, I'm going to start to doubt your sincerity."

"It's quite simple, Dane. If you want to prove to me you don't care about her, sacrifice her."

He yawned. "I need to head back. My emails won't delete themselves."

Val stood. "Seeing as how I waited here for you for half an hour, I'm leaving first." She walked out of the coffee shop, directly into a torrential downpour.

Dane watched the lines of water sluice across the window for a minute before running a Google search on his own name and looking for any news articles he hadn't read yet. Right when he'd clicked on a link to Forbes, Anthony poked his head into Dane's office, a behavior that ranked among Dane's top pet peeves.

"Can I help you?"

Now that Anthony had walked into the office, he appeared shy and uncomfortable. He rubbed the back of his neck and shuffled his shoes.

"What do you need, Anthony? I don't bite unless asked to."

That brought a smile, and the boy relaxed a little. "I'm so sorry to trouble you. It's just that. Well. Rumor has it that you no longer have a mentee and—"

Dane looked longingly at the article he'd been about to read and said a silent farewell to his free time. "And you'd like to know if you could replace her?"

Anthony nodded and lurched further into the office. "I'm every bit as eager as Selena. I learn quickly. It would be an honor to learn from you. And I'm planning to win the intern contest. I'll work harder than anyone else."

"What about the others? Is there nobody else who might object?"

"But I got here first." Anthony's tone reminded Dane of a teenager. He hadn't heard a whine that petulant since he'd started shaving.

"That might work in musical chairs, but we should probably make sure nobody will file a complaint of favoritism."

Anthony smiled at the word as though he had been named a favorite. "Of course. But then if nobody minds, you'll teach me?"

Dane sighed. "Yes." It would be all vanilla mortgages and by-the-numbers securities, but he'd teach the kid the trade. Anthony felt like the kind of intern who would come back again in a year. It wouldn't hurt to have another ally on the trading floor. That was how he'd started paying Leonard to do be his eyes an ears.

He assumed that was the end of the conversation, but Anthony continued to stand, examining his hands until Dane asked, "Is that all?"

Anthony took another halting step forward and then seemed to make up his mind all at once, hurrying over to the chair facing Dane's desk. "I was hoping you might be able to give me some advice."

"If you end up interning with me, I'll give you plenty of advice."

"About girls."

Dane regretfully closed his laptop completely and gave Anthony his full attention. "What do you want to know?"

Anthony swallowed. "It's just that you're obviously very, uh—" He shifted a little. "I completely missed an opportunity to take a girl out—er, I mean, a woman. She asked me to go out with her, to talk about finances outside of work. I didn't realize until much later that she meant it as something more than that. But now I don't know if I've totally blown it. She hasn't paid me any attention all day."

"All day? Does she work here?" Then he remembered. "Is it Selena?"

Anthony looked stunned, but then his eyes cleared, and he said, "Right. Selena."

Dane would have thought the kid would remember having confided in him about the girl just a week before. His hero worship of Dane must have blotted out the details. "It's no big deal. Ask her to do something casual with you, like coffee. If she says no, it won't be too awkward."

"You think she'll say no?" Anthony's freak out had killed Dane's mood.

He was on the verge of telling Anthony he no longer stood a chance since Selena's gaze had shifted to an older, more experienced man. But he decided to take pity. As long as Dane wasn't encouraging Selena, Anthony might stand a chance. It almost made him want to get involved with her just to prove to himself he could still beat out a young guy. Maybe Val was right, and he was just out to prove he was still vital.

He proposed a different obstacle. "She might be reluctant to date her direct competition."

Anthony's forehead creased. "I honestly don't think that will be a problem, but how can I convince her?"

He leaned in. "What you're going to do is find her right now, wherever she is. Tell her she's been on your mind all day. Tell her you regretted the missed opportunity to take her out. Ask her if she'd let you take her to dinner. And if—when—she says yes, you better find a decent restaurant to take her to. No road signs on the walls."

Anthony almost looked convinced. "But what about the casual date? The coffee?"

"Look. You could do that to test the waters, but she'll know that's what you're doing, and she'll doubt your intentions. Go for broke, man. If she likes you at all, you can win her over with a big gesture."

"I'm going to do it." He jumped up. "Thanks. You're awesome."

Finally, Anthony left Dane alone with his thoughts. There were days Dane wanted to quit this pointless job. His bi-weekly paycheck went straight to his accountant who used it to pay the taxes he owed on his massive fortune. If there was anything left from that, Dane considered it spending cash. He could make do without the job. But on days like this, he remembered what made it fun. Alone in his house surrounded by money, he'd never have anyone to play with.

My dearest Geraldo,

How are you enjoying the summer in Germany?

Honestly, I don't care, but one needs to begin with pleasantries. I know you find it as dull as I do, so I'll cut to the pertinent. Your daughter has been to see me, and the poor dear is rather distraught over your refusal to allow her to maximize her training here with us. A child like that might have words to say about her overbearing father, wouldn't you think?

I assure you that she will no longer be mentored directly under anyone other than myself. I trust that will satisfy you? If you have an issue with this arrangement, I suggest you come and fetch her yourself. She seems rather eager to learn everything I have to teach her. I'm eager to hear everything she has to tell me.

Val

The bar had no atmosphere, but it had plenty of cheap liquor which made it a top destination for the down and out. As such, none of his co-workers frequented this seedy hole in the wall. Dane ordered a glass of scotch and then wiped the rim with a napkin. He didn't trust the napkin either but figured the booze would kill the rest of the germs.

Morty came in, sodden and disheveled. He wound his way back to Dane's booth and took a seat.

"What's your poison, Morty? Would you like a beer?"

Morty shook the water droplets from his limp hair. "You're buying, right?"

"That was the deal."

"In that case, I'll have a Michelob."

"Sure thing." Dane got up and asked the bartender for the beer. He brought it back and set it in front of Morty.

Morty took a long sip and let out a satisfied sigh. "My wife only lets me drink light beer. This was real nice of you, Mr. Russ."

"It's Dane." Why did people think they needed to kowtow to him like servants all the time? "So Morty, the reason I asked you here was quite simple."

"Oh, there's more?"

Did the guy really think this was a social outing? "I'm aware that you're being paid to follow me." He wasn't completely sure, but Noelle had indicated she'd planned to use the auditor. And the auditor was Morty. It stood to reason.

Morty tried his best to feign ignorance, but his eyes shifted around when he said, "I don't know what you're talking about."

"Look, Morty. I know. I can go and let it be known you were caught."

He sat up straighter. "No. You can't tell them. They'd stop paying me."

"Them?" That took Dane by surprise. "You were hired by Noelle Constance, right?"

"Y-yeah. Right. Just Miss Constance."

Dane rubbed his chin. Who else would have hired him? And why? "So if I go tell Val Montgomery you were found out, she would—"

Morty's eyes went wide. "No, please. Don't. I'll stop following you. I promise."

"I don't want you to stop following me, Morty. In fact, I'm going to help you out. How much are you making every time you tail me?"

"Now, I'm making one-fifty. Miss Constance would only pay me half of what Miss Montgomery offered." He frowned, nursing an ill-founded grudge.

"For the job you were already doing?"

"Yeah. But she doesn't know it."

"I'm going to pay you two hundred."

"You're going to pay me to follow you, too? Forgive me, but why?"

"Morty, you're going to report back some amazingly glowing things about me. Would you like to start tonight? I have an hour free, and I thought I might visit an old folks' home or maybe an animal shelter."

"Clever, sir. But can it wait? My wife is waiting for me at home, and I have to clear it with her before I stay out past seven."

Dane bit back a smile. His spy wasn't allowed out at night? He wished he'd known that earlier in the week. "She wouldn't clear it for you to earn five hundred dollars in an evening?"

"When you put it that way . . . I'll give her a call."

MARY ANN MARLOWE

Val opened the door to a soaking wet Dane. She kept discovering new favorite versions of him. She let him in and led him back to the drawing room. She hadn't seen him looking so relaxed in ages.

He slipped out of his suit coat and sat in a chair, laughing. "I had to come over and tell you about my crazy night."

"Okay. Would you like a drink? Or a blanket?"

He looked down at his wet clothes. "I could probably use a towel."

She could see his nipples clear through the white shirt. She forced herself to walk down the hall to the guest bedroom and find him a towel. When she came back, he'd already fixed himself a drink and sat with his ankle crossed over his knee and a wry smile on his face.

She sat down across from him. "So you had a crazy night?"

He rubbed his hair with the towel and then dried his face. As he started to blot his shirt, he said, "Why on earth did you hire Morty Becker to follow me?"

She might have protested the truth of that accusation, but he was laughing. "I wouldn't have expected you to find that so funny."

"Oh, I didn't at first. But after the night I've had, it's hysterical." His laughter did seem almost manic, and he leaned forward with his elbows on his knees. "So tell me why?"

She tilted her head. "All right. It was just a whim. The night we met at the nail salon, it occurred to me that you were so paranoid I should hire someone to give you cause. When you thought Morty had followed you to the gym, I hired him to fuck with you. I didn't ask him to gather any information on you, though."

At first, she did ask Morty to report back on Dane's activities. He was already gathering the information. Why not get what she was paying for? But the possibility of learning about how many women Dane took home only made her jittery. The whole purpose of Morty shadowing Dane was to keep him on his toes. Not for his sake. She wasn't worried he'd do anything to get into trouble. But she liked that he only felt he could trust her. It kept him coming to her to confide and scheme. Nobody else understood him like she did.

And it's why he'd never leave this company without her.

"And when I was pretending to quit smoking? When he followed me around the office?"

She frowned. "What about it?"

"You had him follow me then, right? It might have been Noelle, but—"

"It wasn't me."

Dane's eyes narrowed, but he let it go. "I found out Noelle also hired Morty to follow me."

"How?" Intrigued, she covered her mouth with her fist.

He grinned. "I have my ways. And also Morty's a terrible spy. I just had to ask him, and he outed the both of you."

She wasn't pleased. "I guess his gravy train has come to an end."

Dane's hands flew up. "No. You have to keep paying him. I promised I wouldn't tell you."

"Then why did you?"

"As if I couldn't tell you this." He looked radiantly happy, so she relaxed and enjoyed this side of him. It was a rare opportunity to see his gorgeous smile. Usually these days, it was tinged with a cynicism she recognized all too well in herself.

"So tell me."

He got up and walked over to where she was sitting. "I'm gonna come over here and borrow your warmth if you don't mind." His wet shirt sleeve touched her bare arm, and she shivered.

"Maybe you should remove that?"

Instead, he wrapped the towel around her shoulder and scooted closer. He looked into her eyes as he began to talk. "I met Morty at the bar on Sixth. Once I got him to admit to his activities, I offered him even more money to follow me and document my many exploits. He agreed, the shady bastard."

Val laughed at Dane's ironic humor. "Yeah, what a creep."

"Morty Becker it would seem is only loyal to the highest bidder."

That was good to know. Perhaps it was time to get Morty fired. Or give him a raise. "And he followed you back to your place to prove how dull you've become?"

"You know me better than that. I went on an adventure."

"Oh, no."

"First, I went through a drive-thru window and paid the cashier for the car behind me. Of course, that car was Morty's and he recorded the cashier gushing about my generosity as my car pulled away into the night."

"Then what?"

"I phoned ahead to a nearby hospital and got in touch with one of their directors. I let her know I wanted to make a sizable donation, anonymously, and wondered if she would agree to meet me in the lobby. This made for a nice photo op for Morty." Dane's lips pursed in smug arrogance, and she nearly leaned forward to kiss them.

"So what happened?"

"Well, then the director told me she wanted me to see the facilities I'd be helping with my donation." He sighed. "She took me through the children's ward and introduced me to some of the kids who were sick. I ended up sitting in the corner, reading to them for about an hour. It was actually quite moving." His smile dropped, and he sucked on his lower lip, eyes far away.

"I hope Morty got it all on video."

"Oh, of course." The wicked smile came back, and his eyes focused back on hers. He hovered, inches from her, and he was no longer laughing. He laid a hand across her cheek. "God, you're so beautiful."

His lips brushed hers, and she let him draw her to him. She felt herself letting go and reached deep inside to find the power to resist him. His mouth had moved down to her neck, and his hands were working the top button of her shirt. "Dane." Her voice sounded like sand paper, raw from desire. "No, Dane. Not now."

He grabbed her shoulders. "Are you seriously going to make me finish some stupid wager before you'll have me? I'm right here, right now, Val. Why do you keep pushing me away?"

She half considered taking a chance on Dane's continued attempts to bed her. She wanted to believe that all it would take to put a stake through this Noelle debacle would be to give in to Dane's charms and spend a strings-free night in his bed. If only she trusted him.

If sex could fix her current situation, she would have slept with Dane already.

No, she didn't want to be the one he spent his pent-up lust on until he'd finished his game. She was no side quest.

Besides . . .

"Dane. I'm not alone."

His eyes opened wide. "Oh." He stood and grabbed his suit coat. "Of course. I should have asked before I came over." He walked around as if he were looking for something lost. "I guess I'll be going."

"Dane." Val wanted him to stay, but it was made awkward by the naked man in her bed upstairs. She could send him away, sure, but it would only lead to inconveniences. "Tomorrow?"

He leveled her with a gaze and let his eyes drop down the length of her body. "Tempting. You're the most desirable woman I've ever seen. But you always light the fuse and leave me frustrated. As much as I'd love to wait a full twenty-four hours to dip my wick, I think I may have other plans then." He didn't wait for her to lead him out, and by the time she'd reached the foot of the stairs, he'd already closed the front door behind him.

She swallowed down her disappointment and took the stairs slowly, wiping the wetness from her cheeks. But it was fortunate she had a reason to turn him away. If she had given in, he'd have taken her on the floor of her drawing room, and that would be that. She wanted their night together to mean more.

When she opened the bedroom door, Anthony sat up, silk sheets draped over his legs. "Miss Montgomery."

She unbuttoned her shirt and let it fall to the ground. Anthony had been so skittish when she first came on to him. She wasn't sure what had gotten into him today, but if she had sent him away, she was sure he'd never have come back again. And she so wanted someone young and beautiful and inexperienced as a summer toy.

She sat on the edge of the bed and ran her hand down Anthony's chest. He didn't have the build of Dane, but he responded eagerly to her touch, and that pleased her. She teased his cock, knowing full well he wouldn't know how to return the gesture. Yet. She unzipped her skirt, picked his hand up, and laid it on her bare abdomen. He took the hint and slid the rest of her clothes off. Then she showed him what else to do.

"I told you to call me Val."

Thursday

Dane found the group of interns huddling together near their cubes, gossiping about whatever they thought they knew. Anthony wore the smile of an investment banker's son who'd never had a real struggle his whole life. It was distinctly different from the obsequious expression from just a week before. From just yesterday come to think of it. Maybe Dane had lost Selena's obvious infatuation to a kid after all. But surely he could coax her back with a bit of flirting. If he wanted to. Piece of cake.

"Anthony. Can I talk to you?"

Anthony looked up, and his cocky smile grew even more arrogant if possible. He clapped one of the guys on the back and exchanged a Douche Lord handshake with another. "See you guys later."

Dane hated that he'd come to tell Anthony he'd decided to mentor him since nobody else was fighting him for it. He hoped the kid wasn't bragging about banging Selena. He didn't care what he did on his own time, but he respected people who let their reputations be built for them. Bragging was crass.

Anthony's self-congratulatory post-coital victory lap only increased his motivation to win Selena away from him. Assuming it hadn't been a one-night stand. No, Anthony had asked about dating Selena, not getting her to sleep with him. She must have been more willing than he'd expected. It didn't surprise Dane after she'd come on to him the other night.

They approached the office, and Dane hung back to let Anthony go on in. As he closed the door, he refrained from gossip and focused on the business at hand. "So if you still want me to mentor you, you're in. I seem to have grown unpopular."

Anthony frown-smiled with smug knowledge. "Actually, I pulled a few strings."

Dane raised his eyebrow. He couldn't take much more of this. "With the interns?"

"Well, yeah." He finally had the grace to appear somewhat humbled. "I promised to show them how to code mods for *Minecraft*."

"You program?"

"No. I just write mods."

Dane let it go. "So are we good? You'll be ready to start this afternoon?"

"Yeah. Thanks." At least he'd dropped his bullshit privileged rich kid act for the time being. "And that was good advice yesterday."

"Oh, yeah? Things worked out?"

"Totally." Anthony pressed his lips together, and the smugness resurfaced. Dane got the feeling Anthony thought he'd gotten one over on him. Did Selena tell him she'd tried and failed to attract him? That made no sense at all.

Dane gave him what he thought was a fatherly look of concern. "And you're not going to let it affect your work here, right? Or let it become office gossip?"

Anthony blanched. "No, no. Of course. She doesn't even want anyone to know about it."

"Okay. You should respect that." Maybe he'd misjudged the kid.

"I will. I'm just glad she's interested in me. *Me*."

Dane didn't bother to clue Anthony into the fact that he was obviously better looking than any of the other interns, even if he wasn't the sharpest. Of course Selena would go for him. He was surprised Val hadn't fished him out for herself. Then again, she still might. He nodded to Anthony. "Well, I'll see you here later then?"

Anthony left, and Dane went back to check if any of the meetings of the day might interest him. The answer as always was no, except for possibly one with the developers. He liked sitting in on high-level design. He'd let the teams work out the implementation, and he always eyed their patches because he missed coding so much. He'd have to look into this *Minecraft* and see if it might be something he could do in his spare time. Maybe he'd make his second fortune as a *Minecraft* coder.

A movement out his window caught his eye, and he just had a moment to realize it was Noelle before he instinctively dropped onto the floor and hid behind his desk. He heard a tap as the door cracked open. *Why do people always just walk into my office?* He waited, hoping she wouldn't come in. How would he explain why he was sitting on the floor like it was storytime?

He wasn't at all prepared to have the next conversation with her. For one thing, his phone with its voice recorder was in his jacket out of reach.

"Excuse me?" Noelle's voice wasn't loud enough to be directed at him, and he heard someone outside the office answer, "Yes?" She continued, "Do you have any idea where Dane went? I was hoping to catch him in his office."

"Nope, I didn't see him leave." It sounded like Subhra

Bishnu who sat in the cube nearest his office. He usually had on his headphones and worked face down, tapping out code or banging out functional design documents or writing furious emails to everyone about build deadlines. At some point someone had given him a red stapler, and he kept it prominently displayed with no apparent idea that it was meant as a joke.

Noelle closed the door. Dane waited a good minute before sitting back in his chair. When an idea struck, he jumped up, grabbed his jacket, and opened the door to his office, making sure Subhra saw him coming out.

A light summery scent lingered in the air that Dane couldn't precisely define except that it belonged to Noelle. It played with his memory, but not some long ago nostalgia from New York. This smell took him back to the previous Friday night, driving with Noelle in his passenger seat. It made him recall her legs as she climbed in. It made him remember the feel of her lips when she began to bend to him.

He squeezed his fists. He wanted Noelle's resistance to thaw, but he didn't want to expose himself to those feelings that had left him vulnerable and raw when she'd hurt him before. He wasn't about to open himself up to that.

Subhra looked up at him and then back at his laptop. A beat later, his head jerked up. "Hey. Were you in there the whole time?"

Dane raised a finger to his lips. "Shhh. I was hiding."

Subhra crossed his eyebrows. "Why?"

"Long story."

Subhra narrowed his eyes, obviously curious, but not enough to ask any more questions. "Okay." And he went back to looking back and forth between his three huge monitors covered in Putty terminals, remote desktop connections, browsers opened onto the app, and his programming interface. It looked like insanity, and Dane felt a stab of envy that he'd been removed from the controls. When he finally left here for good, he might just immerse himself in *Minecraft* coding. He needed to first find out what in the hell *Minecraft* was.

Dane ducked into the stairwell, listening for any sounds and finding it empty. He took the steps two at a time and exited on the third floor. He looked both ways, as though he were crossing a busy street. When he saw Noelle swing out of the elevator bank and catch his eye, he nodded and strolled casually to the breakroom.

He leaned against the counter and waited. Within moments, Noelle appeared in the doorway with a haunted look in her eyes. She stopped and raked her eyes down him. He held his breath.

Dane was blocking the coffee maker, but he didn't move, waiting to see how she'd respond. She quickly made up her mind and walked straight over to where he stood, placing her mug in the machine behind him, forcing him to slide to his right. The shift placed him directly in front of the assorted coffees. Noelle lifted her eyes and looked directly into his.

Her chest rose and fell heavily as she wound an arm around him, grazing his shoulder and retrieving a packet of Columbian coffee. She stood so close, he could smell her hair, run his eyes down her neck, and peek at her cleavage. He could have snaked an arm around her waist and pulled her to him. And he believed she might let him.

He blew gently against her skin, encouraged to discover that marble could shiver. Her mouth fell open, then closed, and he would have bet money she was thinking about kissing him.

This was what he wanted from her—unlocked desire for him.

He pictured lifting her onto the counter, standing between her legs, his lips on her neck, listening to her moan as he rocked into her.

Noelle stepped away to drop the coffee into the machine. The tent in his pants left no doubt where he stood, but he didn't bother to camouflage it.

As the liquid sputtered, she finally spoke. "I may have been wrong about you, Dane."

He held his breath. Was this it? Had he won?

He was on the brink of asking her out, but she ran a hand over her hair, taking control of her expression. The genie pulled itself back into the bottle before he'd made a wish.

She shot a glance at him. "But I think you may have been wrong about me, too."

He watched her perfectly shaped fingers open a packet of sugar, admiring her neatly polished nails. Her hands trembled, but she managed not to spill a grain.

"You want too much too soon." She sighed.

Highlights glimmered in her hair, picking up light and making him picture decorative tinsel. He'd never noticed that her blond was so different from Val's, so full of brightness and life. Her skin too. Soft and unlined beyond the light creases under her eyes. And she must have been an inch taller because Dane would only need to tilt his head forward and his mouth would be on hers.

"It's not that I want to say no to you." She stirred her drink, then turned to face him again, red blotches marring her cheeks.

He let his eyes fall on her lips, and she exhaled one shaky breath.

"But you're playing with fire," she whispered. "Stop. Please."

She picked up the mug and carried it from the break-room. Dane stood stock still until his impure fantasies would allow him to walk comfortably. He hadn't said one word.

Nefarious

My beautiful Val,

Why must you always be so sharp with your tongue. You wound me deeply. To answer your first question, Germany is lovely. Thank you for asking.

As to your second question: Am I satisfied? That's an odd question coming from you. Am I satisfied that my daughter has been rescued from a lecherous dilettante? No, not really. Am I satisfied she will be protected from him in your care? Probably not. But as I cannot come there and physically drag away an adult against her will, I'm left with the slightly less odious choice of having her remain under your tutelage. At least with you, she won't be exposed to such open disregard for decency. It might be a deception, but you're good at pretending, aren't you? I don't have any secrets I worry she might spill. Do you?

But am I satisfied?

You never asked me that question before your betrayal. Does Dane even know the depths of your treachery to him? I've often wondered at that. Why would you turn your back on him only to follow him into exile? Oh, you won't call it that anymore, I'm sure. I don't suppose the enigmatic Val will ever let me in on her motives.

So let me answer the question since you left.

Yes, I'm satisfied. I've worked you from my system and more importantly I've torn your spider fingers out of the woodwork at this company. You built a strong company, Val. And still, it nearly collapsed when you left without warning. But it's stronger now than ever. All this without you.

Yes. I am quite satisfied.

Geraldo

Val,

Thank you for last night. I hope we can do that again. It was . . . enlightening.

Anthony

Val considered calling Anthony down to chastise him for the stupidity of his email. But after she read it a second time, she decided it didn't really say anything in and of itself. If he wasn't talking, anyone might read it and think she'd taught him something. It was her job after all.

And she knew he wouldn't talk. She'd managed to find an intern to play with almost every summer. First, she made sure they were placed under another mentor, so the immediate problem of her supervisory position would be mitigated. The threat was never entirely removed, but she had other pressure points to lean on to keep them from talking. For one thing,

Anthony hoped to work here next year. It was in his best interest to keep this affair quiet, even if it didn't work out so well for him.

But it behooved him to make sure it worked out well for her. And he seemed so inclined.

She considered Geraldo's email. Was she satisfied? Would she ever be satisfied?

The last time she'd felt momentarily content had been in that transcendent night when her loneliness had abated if only for a few hours.

In her youth, she'd kept most people her age at arm's length, only assessing what they could do for her. And then she'd met Dane, and although he'd started out a pitiful thing, he offered her understanding and eventually friendship. She'd missed that limited window between when he'd morphed into the dazzling creature and when he realized he no longer needed her.

Things might have been different if she'd recognized his potential sooner. She'd come so close.

What if he'd waited for her one more night that first New Year's? What if she'd stayed with him and let Geraldo twist in the wind?

Would they have dated, fallen in love, married, and had a normal life?

She couldn't envision the alternate reality to what they had, but she deeply craved it.

Dane was the only man who knew her. As much as she was willing to be known anyway. Dane was the only man who had loved her in spite of, maybe even because of, who she was.

She dreamed of telling him everything, sincerely confessing her vulnerability. But once she did that, he'd hold all the power. What would he do with it?

Was she satisfied? A long way from it.

How had things gotten so fucked up?

It was Dane's fault. Why'd he have to go and get so desirable?

Fuck it. She wiped her eyes. She had work to do. She gathered up her laptop and headed down to the conference center to set up for her morning presentation.

To all staff, employees, and interns:

REMINDER. Tomorrow will be our annual company trust-building outing. Bring a change of clothes as it will be hot tomorrow. There will be carpools leaving here at noon. You are free to drive yourself. A map has been attached.

See you there!
Leanne Weber

Selena arrived promptly at one to begin their session. She'd reverted back to the conservative wardrobe of the week before. Val preferred the more modest dress but wondered what had stopped the girl's descent into male fantasy attire and whether it coincided with her change of mentor.

The other two interns came in five minutes later and had to play catch up. Val usually ended up with whichever interns hadn't picked someone else or who weren't mutually picked by another mentor. She didn't offer to mentor normally, but she enjoyed teaching. Usually.

In this case, she'd been left with two less than brilliant interns who couldn't tell a discount from a haircut. She'd given them extra work to do at home. Selena hadn't needed to do it, but she spent the evening preparing for today. Val liked that about her. She was young and eager. It was a shame they'd have to lose her next year. It was a shame they'd have to ruin her before she even left.

With all her ducks, she walked down to the training room so she could set the two slower students on an exercise that would at least help them understand basics that they'd failed to master already. This always happened whenever she agreed to take somebody's nephew or daughter into the program. Those were two spots a talented future trader could have filled.

Selena started to take a seat at a terminal, but Val touched her arm. "Come with me. Martin Chiu told me he's going to short sell some stock."

Selena blanched. "On the trading floor?"

"Where else? Come on. This will be fun."

Val glanced at her remedial students to make sure they were set and led Selena back down to the second floor and down the long hall that opened onto the cacophonous live trading floor. Most of these kids would drool to get a chance to answer these phones and plug in the actual trades.

Martin had his desk phone handset cradled between his shoulder and his chin. He was talking a mile a minute, and when he saw Val, he tapped the back of his arm, right where his watch might have been if he were wearing one. Val ignored his silent scolding and pulled over a chair. She talked low to Selena, "Sit. Learn."

Phones buzzed all over the floor, voices carried from dozens of other desks. The far wall was lined with clocks showing every time zone with a city listed above each. New York. London. Frankfurt. Tokyo. Sidney. Above these, TV monitors displayed all the news networks. Except the one that showed

Wimbledon. Val wondered how many people in this room had side bets on the match.

Martin put his hand over the microphone and said, "Sale's made already. Where have you been?"

Val sighed. "I had to square away my other interns. Have you closed the short?"

"No. Of course not." He looked at Val like she'd grown an extra head.

"Just checking, Martin." She indicated Selena. "This is Selena Valencia. I thought she might like to see you in action. Any chance you'll close today?"

He shrugged. "If I could predict the market, I wouldn't be here anymore, would I?'

"Well, someone thinks it's going to tank soon, or you could have waited five minutes to negotiate the deal."

"Don't get your tits up, Val. The price is already starting to drop. I didn't want to lose a hundred grand for an object lesson. Let her practice shorting in the training room if it's so important."

"Ah, Martin, my tits have nothing to do with it."

Martin laughed. "Look, I'll call you if anything changes. It might not be until tomorrow though, if at all. We're watching a possible takeover, hoping it falls through and the stock tumbles. It's a nail biter this one."

Selena spoke up. "What happens if the takeover goes through?"

"It's hard to say." Martin glanced up at his Bloomberg terminal that looked like an air traffic control system crossed with hospital vital statistics. Graphs in purple and navy showed a trajectory. "Most likely, the stock will stabilize and we'll be lucky to break even. We'll try to buy it all back before it can rise."

Val touched Selena's shoulder. "Come on. I promise I'll let you know if anything happens. Let's go back to my office."

"What about the other interns?"

"Surfing the net the second we left the training room. I'd love to have some one-on-one time."

Selena beamed. "Lead the way."

If Selena were anything like Val, just breathing in the air of the trading floor made her want to fan herself. It made her need a cigarette. It made her want to go to bed with even the most unattractive trader.

As they entered the room, Val casually asked, "Well?"

"Thank you for thinking of me. Even without getting to watch Martin in action, I learned a lot. Is it always so stressful?"

"Stressful, yes. And exciting."

"It seems like it would be so easy to make the slightest mistake. There's so much to lose."

"And so much to gain."

"True."

"Would you like a chance to work on the floor before you leave here?"

Selena gushed. "Oh, God yes."

"Good. Then consider it done." Val sat in her chair and slowly turned it toward the window. "How is everything else going today?"

"I really enjoyed practicing on the Bloomberg terminals this morning. That was timely."

Val needed to turn this conversation, or Selena would talk shop the whole time. Val used to be exactly the same way once. "Are you making any friends here?"

Selena frowned. "Not really."

"No? I guess it can be hard when you're obviously one of the top interns. I was a lot like you. I'd get so caught up in succeeding, I'd forget to put myself out there. I lost out on a lot of opportunities to socialize."

"I did put myself out there, actually. I got shot down pretty hard."

Val schooled her face so as not to show her glee. Finally, she'd brought up Dane.

"Friendships take time to develop."

"I thought things were developing, but I guess I read the signs wrong."

"Wait. Are you talking about a friend or . . . something more?"

Selena took off her glasses and touched the edge of her sleeve to her eye. "It's stupid. I guess I have a little crush. It's no big deal. He's not interested." She shrugged in contrast to the look of hurt on her face.

Val started off with the party line. "Well, you know it can be difficult to carry on an office romance."

"I know. And that was my stance at first, but I didn't expect to feel an attraction to anyone here." She laughed through an almost sob. "It gets complicated so fast."

Now Val put on her human face, her understanding aunt face. "Oh, honey. We've all been there. It can be hard to follow the rules when you want what you want."

"But they are the rules. I should just get over this. Summer will end soon enough anyway, right?"

"Hold on, now. It may be a gray area, but unless we're talking about a direct supervisor, there's no reason you can't date a co-worker."

She looked relieved, but then she slumped. "It doesn't matter. He's made it obvious he's no longer interested. If he ever was."

Val tapped her fingers. "There's always something you can do. You are a woman after all. You hold the keys. What you choose to do depends, though, on what you hope to achieve."

"What do you mean?"

"Are you looking for a boyfriend? A long-term romantic commitment that could lead somewhere after the internship ends? Or do you just want a summer fling?"

"I hadn't thought it through. I don't know. I mean, I guess I wanted a fling that could lead somewhere?"

Val shook her head. "It doesn't work that way. You have to make a decision. Your actions will depend on which way you want to go. Whatever you're doing now will net neither result though."

"So if I wanted a boyfriend?"

Val hoped she could convince the girl against this. Dane didn't have girlfriends. He might keep her all summer, but with Noelle on the table, the most Selena might get would be the space between projects. And once he finished with Noelle, Dane became Val's. Preferably, he'd give up and come crawling back to Val to re-negotiate terms. Maybe she could get him to go in for simple revenge.

"That's going to be the difficult sell because you've already scared him by alerting him to your interest. So you are going to have to back way off and make him think you aren't interested. You'll have to make him think he wants something he can't have."

"But that could take all summer."

"Women have to wait around far too long for men to pursue us. But we always have the trump card, and we can always short cut the game, if all we want is a moment in time. It's when you want to possess them that you get yourself in trouble. You end up giving yourself away in the process."

"So what if I just want a fling?

"Much easier. And actually, the fact you put yourself out there works in your favor. Despite what I just said, now that he knows you want him, whenever he sees you, he's going to think about sex. So you're already a step ahead. Crook your finger and he'll come running."

"But he's already shot me down."

Val couldn't help smile her mischievous grin. "I find men always need a reason to say no to sex. They rarely need a reason to say yes."

"So I just flaunt it?"

"Pretty much. You're beautiful and smart. He'd be a fool to turn you down. But bear in mind, if you choose that route, you're almost guaranteed to walk away from any chance at romance. It could still happen, but in my experience, men are dogs. You might win their hearts, but they're born ready to hand over their dicks. Take whatever and whoever you want, Selena, and you could still have a very fun summer."

Val always marveled at the influence she could wield over men with nothing more than the simplicity of her own body. She didn't fool herself into believing there was anything special in the act. From a young age, she'd never hesitated to use her sex to obtain whatever she needed. Her high school counselors, church leaders, friends' dads, and neighbors' husbands would provide food, shelter, and sometimes money in exchange for what she was willing to do to them. Some, like her uncle, had tried to take it from her—but never for long.

Selena laughed. "You're just so much cooler than I expected." Her shoulders relaxed, and she said, "Thank you for listening to my personal dilemmas. It's nice to have someone I can trust to come to for advice."

"I'm sure your father wouldn't care for me telling you all this."

"My father doesn't need to know everything I do. Besides, it's not like he pretends to be such a saint." She blushed. "Oh, sorry. I mean, I know you—"

"No need to apologize. You're absolutely right about him. He holds himself to a different standard." She patted Selena's knee. "Like all men."

"It makes me so mad that he gets away with treating me like a child. He treats the women he dates like they're possessions. And the women who work for him—"

Val leaned in. "Yes?"

"Well, you ought to know."

"I never worked for Geraldo. He worked for me."

Selena pushed her glasses up. "I hadn't thought of that. I only started paying attention to his"—her eyes flew to Val's—"your company since I started school."

"It's not my company, and whatever Geraldo's doing with it has nothing to do with me. What have you observed?" Why hadn't she thought to record this conversation?

"He's so disrespectful. Do you know that since you left the company, no women have been promoted to any of the top management positions? Not a single one."

Perhaps this really was why Noelle had left. "You're right. That is reprehensible."

"Part of me wants to go to work for him to change the culture. Part of me wants to work elsewhere."

"You could report him."

Selena's eyes widened. "I couldn't. I mean, I'm in no position to."

True. But Noelle could.

Val patted Selena's knee. "Let's get to work. I think you'd maybe like to leave a little early today, no?"

Selena nearly bounced in her chair, and Val wondered if she should give Dane a heads-up or just let him enjoy the sudden bird that was about to fly to him. He might think himself too ethical to take advantage of her, but Val knew Dane. He'd have fantasized about doing Selena over his desk at least forty-eight times since she'd offered herself up. If she delivered herself to him, he'd be hard-pressed to turn her down a second time.

And Val would collect the evidence.

Dane had spent a couple of hours with Anthony, but when it became apparent Anthony's mind was occupied, he told the kid to go work in the training room and come back after he'd either had a cold shower or spent whatever pent up energy was keeping him preoccupied.

Anthony apologized with a boys-will-be-boys grin Dane hated.

Once Anthony had gone, Dane poured himself a shot of bourbon and kicked back, but he also felt cooped up and decided to go for a walk around the facilities. Unlike Val, he enjoyed getting out and talking to the other employees from time to time. And now that Noelle knew how he supposedly felt, it would be good to confront her with himself and make her consciously decide for or against him at every step.

Not to mention, he wanted to see her, catch her smell, watch her skin redden, sense her pulse racing. Her resistance was an aphrodisiac, especially since it was wavering.

As he exited his office, he ran straight into Selena, coming from the direction of Val's office. She smiled at him in a friendly way. He immediately thought about taking off her glasses and pulling that elastic out of her hair, but he shook it off.

"I'm going to get a coffee in the breakroom. Care to join me?" He was relieved she didn't seem at all awkward about the other night. He'd been avoiding her in case she started crying or accused him of leading her on. Or worse, if she'd come offering herself again. He felt himself stir and fought back images of unbuttoning her blouse. He wished she'd never come onto him in the first place. Not that he hadn't already imagined half these things, but they were fiction before. Now his fantasies had one foot in possibility.

"Sure. I was in the mood for some as well."

Subhra and Steve were in the breakroom already, so Selena and Dane waited quietly.

Steve said to all of them, "I just got an email reminder that we're having a day of trust, Friday."

Subhra groaned. These were typical nerds. He used to be just like them, and he remembered dreading any kind of outdoor activity. The sun, the heat, the physical exertion. All of these things were antithetical to a life of sitting in a dark room engaged in social interaction at the end of a blinking cursor. It would do these guys some good to get some exercise. Not that he had any interest in participating in a team-building event.

"I'll see you all out there. Maybe we'll be on the same team?" Dane tried to smile like he'd actually welcome that, but the other guys' smiles looked as fake as his probably was. They all respected each other, but none of them really liked Dane. He'd switched teams at some point, and they saw him as a developer in name only. But he had the final say, and they resented that.

At last, the two developers left. Selena popped an envelope into the coffee maker with her mug below and then turned to face him. "Listen. About the other night. I wanted to apologize. I was upset with my father, and I don't know what came over me."

"It's okay, Selena. It made for an interesting turn of events. But it's nothing to worry about." He gave her a smile meant to be endearing. "An old guy like me can't really complain about attentions from a beautiful younger girl, right?"

She blushed. "You're not old. And for the record, you're definitely hot."

He knew that, but he still loved the flattery. "How are you settling in with Val?"

"She's great. I probably should have tried to work with her originally." Her eyes went wide. "I mean, I learned so much from you so quickly, and I'm glad I got a chance to work with you and get to know you. You have no idea how honored I am to have had that privilege. But I don't know. Val has been so helpful and friendly. I feel like I've got a trusted mentor and friend in the same package. I'm just sorry to have left you in the lurch." She looked down at her coffee. "I understand you're mentoring Anthony now?"

How adorable. She couldn't look him in the eyes when asking about her new lover. "I am. And I understand he's shown some interest in you."

She looked up quick. "Did he say that?"

Crap. He forgot Anthony had told him she wanted to keep it quiet. "I probably shouldn't step into this."

Her eyes narrowed, but she let it drop. "So maybe sometime we could go get a real coffee. Or a drink?"

Did she know she was sending mixed signals? "Selena."

"I know. My father would freak out. Well, he can tell me I can't work with you, but he can't keep me from talking to you, can he? I wasn't finished learning about securities. But I know you're busy, so it's okay. I'll just make sure to find classes in the topic at school next year."

Dane knew he should steer clear of Selena now that she was in Val's custody, but his vanity sought validation that he could seduce her yet. Maybe Val was right, and he could pursue her now. A little. He couldn't stop the corner of his mouth from rising. He'd come to like Selena. She was beautiful and smart, and now that she wasn't starry eyed with hero worship for him, she'd relaxed and talked to him like a friend. "Maybe we could talk outside of work. About securities, of course."

Her smile lit up her eyes. "That would be so cool."

He laughed. "Or maybe you could teach me about this *Minecraft* thing."

"It's a deal."

Dane looked at his watch. "You better hurry along and get back to work. We can talk later."

She bit her lower lip and batted her eyelashes before abandoning him in the breakroom.

Anthony,

Would you like to go out with me tonight on a quasi-date date? It doesn't have to be anything—it can be whatever you want it to be. I just thought it might be fun to hang out and see what comes of it.

I was considering going to see a movie, but if you wanted, you could come over to my place, and we could watch something here.

Selena

Friday

S*elena,*

I had fun last night. I hope we can hang out again.
Are you free tonight?

Anthony

Dane had tried to get out of these corporate trust-building events for the past three years to no avail. The traders weren't required to attend because the markets were open. Dane argued someone needed to be around in case there was a production issue. The response had always been, "*Bring a phone and your laptop. You can work remote if you need to.*"

So he stood around in the mid-June noonday sun with sweat running down his cheek, trying to figure out how not to get grouped with anyone who hated him. There wasn't much point in picking people out to pair up with because more often than not, the directors would make a point of placing people with whoever they wanted with no regard to preference.

Still, he looked around and found Noelle walking between groups and socializing. Val stood toward the back, smoking one last cigarette. There was a nervous but festive feel to the air. Everyone was glad to be away from the office, but nobody liked doing these exercises with people they rarely spoke to about things that didn't revolve around work.

Noelle worked her way over to him, and as casually as if they were barely acquainted, she greeted him. "Good afternoon, Dane. Are you ready for this?"

He indicated his T-shirt, running shorts, and lightweight hiking shoes. "Not in the least."

"I might have overdone it myself." She wore a perfectly white tank top, a pair of khaki cargo shorts, and brand-new purple hiking sandals. He wanted to see her get dirty in all that.

"You look beautiful. As always." He pretended to be flustered and looked away. In reality, he was already itching, and he could feel a river down his spine. More than anything else, he wanted to be standing under his shower in his air-conditioned bathroom. *With her* preferably, but at the moment, he was too uncomfortable to care either way.

Noelle twisted her mouth in school-marmish disapproval. "Dane."

"I'm not trying to make you feel awkward. Just stating a fact."

She touched his forearm. "We'll talk again soon."

"Tonight maybe?"

She hesitated. It was only for a micro-second, but he saw her consider the question. It was as quickly discarded. "That wouldn't be the best idea."

"Well, maybe I'll get lucky, and you'll land on my team." He had a particular smile he'd developed, not accidentally. He'd practiced it in the mirror, and then he'd practiced it on girls. He'd honed it into a lethal weapon. It was wicked, but at the same time, it was charming, inviting. He leveled it at Noelle, and watched her pupils dilate and her breathing hitch.

"That would be—" She swallowed. "I need to move on. Thank you." She took a step away and looked back with an awkward laugh. "I mean, goodbye. Have fun today."

As she left for the next group of co-workers, Dane looked at his watch and counted the minutes until he could go home.

Val sidled up next to him, eyes following Noelle's trajectory. "You two are so cute. Maybe you'll be holding hands by Christmas."

Leanne clapped to get everyone's attention. "Rosamund couldn't make it today, and unfortunately she had our group assignments. We're going to improvise."

Dane's brow creased. "Huh. Wonder what's wrong with Rosamund."

Val shrugged. "She's old. Old people get ill."

"Right." Dane worried his lower lip with his teeth. "Still."

He recalled seeing Rosamund coughing the day before, but he pushed it from his mind. Nothing he could do.

Leanne called out, "Anyone who's an Aries, form a group over here."

Dane's heart sank at the realization the groups would be based on astrological signs. He wouldn't be partnered with either Val or Noelle since their birthdays were months away from his. But when they called the Scorpios together and he saw Selena step into the group, he smiled. One friendly, familiar face always made these things less of a chore.

A bearded twenty-year-old wearing a visor and a whistle approached Dane's group. "Good morning. My name is Kevin, and I'll be leading you through some exercises today. Please stay close to me at all times and listen to the instructions I give you. I don't just talk because I like the sound of my voice. There will be times when my instructions hold keys to how to solve the exercises. So pay attention." He scanned all the faces. "Who can tell me my name?"

Patricia, the nearly retired sales representative, spoke out first. "Kevin!"

Dane rolled his eyes. He'd never understood the urge to be the teacher's pet. He knew the answer, but why set high expectations from the beginning? It was easier to impress when you came in from behind.

Selena caught his attention and made a grimace of solidarity. Dane shook his head in like-minded disgust of the whole situation.

Kevin took them about a hundred yards into the forest and stopped. The first exercise was to toss a ball around, introduce themselves, then lob it at the next victim. This exercise was further complicated by having to name something they liked. "I'm Dane. I like bourbon," did not go over well. But Selena laughed.

The next series of activities involved figuring out how to move the whole group along a narrow log, around a stationary object without falling off. At first, the group couldn't speak, but they could communicate through gestures. After failing long enough, the guide told them they could speak, but they had to come up with a universal decision before they made any moves. Dane had no intention of taking the lead on this until he became so frustrated with the disorganization that he started barking out orders.

The leader gathered them together to ask what they'd learned from the activity, and they all said some variation of, "Don't cross Dane in games of organized team cooperation."

If it meant they finished all this an hour earlier than everyone else, he didn't care.

But then the next event was more hands on, literally, as they helped each other up and over a wall. Everyone had to get over somehow. He ended up in the position of lifting the smaller team members which became a weird sanctioned gropefest. He hoisted Selena by the upper thigh and placed one hand on her butt to push her to the top of the wall. He barely resisted throwing in an added squeeze. He wasn't sure she'd respond well to it. Then when it came time for the group on the far side to help pull him up and over, he made it halfway over and was about to jump to the ground when he felt a hand sliding up his inner thigh. When he landed, Selena shot him a saucy wink.

Throughout the rest of the activities, Dane and Selena made a game of trying to find ways to inadvertently touch each other in places that would be off limits in the office. He had no idea how many people were aware of their misconduct, but he figured it went over their heads. Everyone was pinching each other by the time they got to the last obstacle.

The final task wasn't as intensive as the rest and seemed simple enough. They were only required to lower a hula hoop from waist height by supporting it on one finger per team member. It was a good final exercise because everyone kept laughing at how impossible it seemed to keep the hula hoop from rising up higher and higher until it floated above their heads.

Finally, Kevin brought them all in together and praised them for working hard. He went over a few of the things they'd learned together and then told them that they'd finished a little early, but they were also farther into the woods than all the other groups and needed to head back.

As the rest of the group moved away, laughing and rehashing some of the funny moments, Selena grabbed Dane's hand. He held still and watched the others disappear around a bend in the trail, then turned toward her.

Her lip caught between her teeth, as though deciding on her next action. Without warning, she reeled him closer and slid her hand under the hem of his shirt, tracing the skin along his back.

He sought her eyes for any sign of hesitation. Finding none, he leaned forward and pressed his lips against hers. He broke the kiss and said, "I'm sorry, but I couldn't help it. I've been wanting to do that all day."

"I thought you were afraid it would be inappropriate?"

"I thought I taught you about loopholes?"

She glanced behind her at the empty path, at the isolation of the forest. She hooked her index finger around his and led him deeper into the woods, behind a wide tree and drew him closer. She pressed herself hard against him, and he shivered. He pushed her back against the tree and kissed her deep. She responded with a soft moan. It was the more exciting because he hadn't even imagined this possibility out here.

Encouraged by her reactions, he touched the edge of her T-shirt and pulled it up, exposing the pink lace of her bra. With a snap, he popped the front clasp and ran his thumb across her nipple. The sounds she made in response had him completely erect, and he bent his head to suck on her tits. He couldn't believe she was letting him. This wasn't the shy girl he'd met a week ago.

Her hand dug into his hair then began reeling his shirt up his back, and he straightened up so she could pull it over his head. She touched his chest. "God, you are even more beautiful than I imagined."

Any thoughts he had of stopping this before it went any further were completely upended by her admiration of his body. He gave her a questioning look and touched the button on her shorts.

She said, "Yes," and he unbuttoned and unzipped, dragged shorts and panties down. She had on goddamn sexy underwear. "Were you planning this?" he asked.

"How could I have? I didn't know you'd be in my group."

"But you hoped."

"I've been hoping for a solid week, Dane."

He grazed her body with his hands. She stood against the tree, naked from her waist down. He kissed her again, nudging her legs apart. When he ran his finger against her, she groaned. She was soaking wet and ready. She dragged her nails down his chest to the waist band of his running shorts. Her hands plunged under the fabric and found him. Her thumb felt damn good stroking him, and he reached to his back pocket before he remembered he didn't have one.

"Fuck."

"What's wrong?"

"My wallet's in my car."

She laughed. "I'm not charging anything."

"No wallet. No condom." He pressed against her, wanting so bad to throw caution to the wind and fuck her hard against this tree. "Shit." He couldn't let the entire opportunity go to waste though. He kissed her hard against the neck, with his hands on her hips. Then he walked his kisses down and dropped to his knees. "Fuck," he said again when his knees hit sticks and dirt. He reached over for his shirt and spread it out. Selena, bless her, hadn't moved an inch.

He laid a hand on her thigh and his mouth on her closely groomed pussy. A little too late, he wondered if she might be a screamer.

She moaned. "Oh" and "ah" and "Oh God, Dane" and then she panted. When she started giving him directions, he nearly came in his pants. "Harder . . . Right there." He drove his fingers up inside her, and that's when she started to really groan. The sound was too much, and he stroked himself while he worked her. He shot out into the dirt, on her feet, onto his T-shirt. He didn't give a fuck. He watched her face as she went over the edge, and her entire body bucked.

She opened her eyes and looked around. "Oh, shit. Was I loud?"

He smiled and stood up. "No louder than one of those howler monkeys."

"I can't believe we just did that." Then she looked down at his pants. "Are you? Should I? Do you need?"

"I'm good. But my shirt's a disgusting mess."

She shook out her clothes and put them back on. Once she'd straightened her shirt out, she asked, "What now? Do we go back separately? Will everyone notice we're gone?"

Dane rubbed his shirt in the dirt, figuring he could blame it on the day's activities. They started back up the path, walking a foot apart. Dane touched her shoulder. "Could I convince you to go the long way back to the parking lot and spend the rest of the day at my house? I'd love to do that again, properly. If you're into it."

She veered over so her hand brushed against his as they walked. "Um. I would love to, but—"

"You have a date with Anthony?"

Her eyes widened. "How did you know?"

"I didn't. But I figured it out. He said he was going to ask you out."

"What? When?"

"A few days ago. Maybe Tuesday."

"Well, he certainly does take his time. I ended up asking him out last night."

Dane's forehead wrinkled as he tried to piece together the scraps of his memories. He was sure Anthony had scored with Selena at least two nights ago. "You didn't go out with him before that?"

"Nope. I mean, I asked him once before, but he'd already decided to go out with a group. That's the night you came out with us. You know. That night."

"So you went out last night then?"

She gave him a cockeyed smile. "You jealous? We just went to the movies."

He shook his head. "Just trying to square the details. I like to know things."

"I'm not sure if he likes me or not." She looked at him. "Should I be talking about this with you? I mean, we just . . ."

"Believe it or not, I make an excellent girlfriend." He laughed. "You can confide in me. Or fuck me. Just don't fuck me over."

She took his hand. "You're nothing like what I expected. I really like you."

Dane smiled. "I really like me, too."

She punched him softly. "So raincheck?"

He pulled her wrist up to his lips. "How would you like to go out on the best date of your life? Say the word, and I'll blow your mind."

She bit her lip. "Not tonight."

"Tomorrow. I'll pick you up at seven? Say yes?"

He loved the look of utter glee that crossed her face. He loved the prospect of wooing her away from Anthony.

"What should I wear?"

"What size do you wear?"

"Six."

He stood back and took in her height. "I'll have something sent to you. Can someone accept a package tomorrow afternoon?" He'd just have them deliver several sizes. She'd never be able to date another man again. He smiled, surprised that he found a thrill in the knowledge that he'd make her feel so happy. And he wished he could be there to see her reaction.

"I can be there."

The edge of the trail came into view. Before they exited the forest, he pulled her off the path and gave her one last kiss. "I'll see you at seven."

He walked out of the woods and merged into the groups of people until he could get back to his car.

Val watched Dane wend through the crowd and go straight to his car. Typical. He was more sociable than her in so many ways, but he sucked at showing it. She, on the other hand, worked a party like nobody else, even though she didn't enjoy it. She always found it odd that they both behaved exactly counter to their own true natures and wondered what drove them to do so. It was like they were always in costume.

She'd spent her afternoon letting others cooperate with the decision-making and pretending to have learned something new from the activities even though she'd done these so many times now, she knew everything they wanted the team members to take away from the exercises. She hated the heat and the sweat and the strange hands touching her without her consent. She hated the stupid jokes that people made every single year. She hated the waste of a productive afternoon.

She walked through the crowd until she located Anthony. She'd been looking to take him aside since they arrived, but until now, the groups had all been too focused. In the disorganization of the returning teams, she hoped to have a quick word without anyone noticing. She touched his elbow and led him further from the edge of people. She whispered in his ear, "Where were you last night?"

He looked surprised. "Last night?"

"Yes. We had plans. I don't like being made to wait. Next time, call if you can't make it. It's simple courtesy."

He scratched the back of his head. "I'm sorry, Val. I must have misunderstood."

She pursed her lips. "Very well, then. Should I expect you tonight?"

He didn't look her in the eyes. "Not tonight. But maybe—"

"What plans could you possibly have made tonight?"

Right then, Selena broke free of a group and called over. "Anthony?"

Val took in Anthony's guilty expression and Selena's suspicious curiosity. She took a step away. "I'll talk to you on Monday, Anthony. Have a nice evening." She spun around and walked away, trying to figure out which of the million signs she must have missed. Had she completely misunderstood that much?

But as she reached her car, another piece clicked into place. If Selena was chasing Anthony, then she'd mistaken her interest in Dane. And that meant Dane had probably just spent a very frustrating afternoon in her company. She was tempted to drive over to his place and pick up the pieces.

"Val? You look lost."

Val turned to find Noelle approaching. "I was just trying to remember if there was anything left at the office I needed to attend to. Where are you headed?"

"Home."

Noelle managed to look pretty despite the loose hair and smudges of dirt on her cheek. Val appraised her, imagining how Dane must see her, what he must like about her, what he'd want to do with her. And she suddenly understood why he'd need to possess her. Not only did she refuse him once, she was the sort of woman who refused most men. And she'd fight against him every step of the way. She was a prize he had to have. And Val didn't stand a real chance as long as Noelle was still in play. "Would you like to go grab a drink?"

"I'm a mess. I should really go home and shower."

"You look fine. Really. And look at me. But if you like, I could meet you a little later? I have no plans."

"Sure. When and where?"

They made the arrangement, and as Val drove home, she weighed the available options. Noelle was a rook, and she could be moved to the side, out of Dane's reach. Without the temptation, he might move on to Selena. Selena might be all eyes for Anthony now, but she'd shown her hand. Dane would know that. And if Dane took Selena, Val could reclaim Anthony. Her pride demanded it. But it was short-sighted.

For what she really wanted, she needed to find a way to move Noelle straight forward, right at Dane. And that would bring Dane back to her. It would be so much easier if she could murder, abduct, or fire Noelle. Or simply wipe her off the board.

The shower was every bit as heavenly as Dane had imagined. He stood under the water, enjoying the memory of what was and the image of what might have been if he'd had any clue that he'd find himself half naked in the woods. It would have been sweeter still if he'd convinced her to ditch the schoolboy to come home with the experienced man, but tomorrow would be entertaining. He was already making plans in his head. He was already picturing the look of delight on Selena's face when the new dresses arrived. He could at least make her happy while he was ruining her for all other men.

Dane loved women. He loved everything about them.

He turned off the shower and dialed the number of his friend Margaret, a buyer for Armani in New York. She answered on the second ring. "Dane. Please tell me you're in town."

"If I were, you'd already be under me."

She laughed. "God, I miss you. It's so boring here. Couldn't you fly out for the weekend?" She lowered her voice. "I have a new line of lingerie you could test out."

Yes, he loved women. "I'm going to have to reconsider my weekend plans." He sighed. "But I was hoping you might help me with that."

"You've got a young one?"

"Early twenties. No wardrobe at all." He fumbled his way one-handed into a pair of boxer briefs.

"Where are you taking her?"

"You wouldn't know it. It's as upscale as you get in the Midwest."

He put the phone on speaker as he pulled a T-shirt over his head.

"You'll be wearing a tux?"

"I don't think so. Something elegant though."

"What size is she?"

"Six."

"Busty?"

He felt through his drawer for a presentable pair of cargo shorts and hopped on one foot as he put his leg through.

"Of course."

She laughed. "All right. I might be able to help you out. I'll contact some people in the morning. Can you email me her address?"

"Sure thing, Margaret. I owe you."

He slipped his feet into a pair of European leather sandals and made his way downstairs.

"After you pay me for everything, then we can arrange how you want to square the favor. I have some ideas."

"Keep talking."

He grabbed his keys off the side table, walked outside to his car, and settled into the driver's seat ready to listen to Margaret's filthy imagination.

Val held the scotch in both hands, watching the ice clink from side to side as she sloshed it about. "And how is it you're not seeing anyone?"

"I have tried." Noelle blew a raspberry. "This industry doesn't make it easy on a girl."

"Tell me about it." Val took another swallow, savoring the smoky backbone. "This is good scotch."

"Yeah. Would you believe my father started me on the stuff? Now I only keep the best on hand. Would you like another?"

They sat in Noelle's kitchen, having decided it wasn't worth going through the motions of getting ready to go back out again. Noelle's place wasn't far from Val's, so they ended up at her house. Noelle stood and brought the full bottle over. "Now it's a party." She held up her glass, and they clinked.

Val kicked off her heels and settled into her chair. "I can't believe you and I weren't better friends at R&M."

"I didn't recall that you had many friends. Except Dane, of course. And Geraldo."

That was all Val needed to steer this ship the way she wanted. "Ugh. Geraldo. I don't know how I didn't see him for what he was sooner."

Noelle looked into her glass and narrowed one eye. "Can I ask you something? You won't laugh?"

"Yes. And no. I won't laugh."

Noelle shook her head, and her hair tumbled around her face. She'd taken it out of the tight twist an hour before. "No, I can't. It would be a breach of confidence."

Val pushed Noelle's scotch glass toward her and said with a German accent. "Ve haf vays of making you talk."

For Noelle's great stock of scotch, she didn't seem to have a habit of drinking it. And it was beginning to show.

Noelle wrinkled her nose and grimaced and bit her lip all at once, shame-faced, mustering the courage to do something she knew she shouldn't, but that she really wanted to do anyway. "Okay. So Dane told me he's in love with me. That's ridiculous, isn't it? Has he ever said anything like that to you?"

"Dane said that? That's interesting. I've really only heard him profess his love for one other woman."

"Not you, then?"

Val snorted rather than lie.

Noelle nearly whispered. "Was he really in love?"

"Oh, quite." She gave Noelle what she thought was a gentle smile. "But the girl didn't know what she had until too late."

"Or maybe she did." Noelle snickered.

Val didn't laugh. "No, I think that girl came to regret her choices."

"Do you think he got over her?"

"Possibly." Val leaned in, confidentially. "But I think he'll always harbor some feelings for her. I think he has a romantic notion that there can be a happily ever after."

Noelle ran a finger around the rim of her glass. "Dane's a romantic?"

"Hopeless."

Noelle stared down at the table. "He's just lying, right?" She lifted her eyes. "What if it's some kind of emotional manipulation to get something from me. But why would he go to the trouble? Is it just because he likes a challenge?"

"Dane? Like a challenge?" Val laughed like it was a ridiculous idea. In fact, Dane loved a challenge. If Val had slept with Dane the first time he'd come onto her, their relationship would have been altogether different. "He might still carry a torch. But if you don't respond to him, he'll stop pestering soon enough. He won't wait around forever. He has some sense of self preservation." God, Noelle should see through this bullshit considering how long he'd pursued her in New York.

"So you think he means it?" Her eyes goggled. "I don't really know what to think of him. I'd come to work here convinced I'd need to steer clear of him. And within the first month, he conned me into going on a date with him." She smiled a wide, tipsy smile. "It was a great date. He knows how to impress a girl." Now she frowned. "But I can't tell if all that is him posturing, on his best behavior." She swallowed the rest of her scotch. "Do you think I should give him a chance?"

Val's eyebrow began to rise like the helium hula hoop at the trust exercise, and she stopped herself from giving everything away in one look. "Oh, I don't know. What could it hurt?"

Noelle chortled. "Seriously? You warned me too well what it could hurt. He could make a fool of me. He could have a change of heart and leave me broken hearted. He could probably give me chlamydia." She smiled. "Allegedly."

"You want me to encourage you to walk away? Or are you asking for permission to say yes?"

"Maybe. I'd hoped we might start out as friends first before rushing into anything."

"Have you seen his car?"

Val expected to earn another laugh, but a tear rolled down Noelle's cheek. The scotch had caught up with her. She let out a sigh. "I do love that car."

"And Dane?"

Noelle focused on her glass, lifting her eyes as though they were fighting gravity. "Perhaps."

Val grabbed the strap of her purse hanging from the chair, slung it over her shoulder, and stood. "Then it's easy.

March up to him first thing Monday and tell him in no uncertain terms you want him."

"Yeah, that would look great to the board of directors." She started to stand but wobbled. "I should go over there, tonight."

Val hesitated. Dane would love that, but it would be better if this played out with some witnesses. "Not tonight. Dane's probably out on a date by now."

Noelle's gasped. "You think?"

"I told you he won't wait around forever." The knife slid in. A little twist to drive it home. "But if he *is* out, he's probably just trying to take his mind off you."

Noelle slumped. "What if it's too late?"

Val didn't believe in God, but she prayed Dane would record every word Noelle would say to him Monday morning.

"I'm gonna head home, but take the weekend to think it through. I'm pretty sure you know what you want. Why deny yourself?" She leaned in to give Noelle a hug. "We women have to work too hard as it is."

Noelle's hand flopped up in a drunken wave. She didn't get up or escort Val to the door. When Val turned back, she was staring into her glass like it held the answers. Val hoped she'd remember their conversation tomorrow.

He was being followed. The car had tailed him off the interstate and through several turns. Dane pulled over to the side of the road and let the car pass, laughing as the brake lights flashed. Poor Morty wouldn't know if he should keep driving or stop and wait. They were the only two cars on this side street. Dane could turn around and make Morty change course. Instead, he got out and climbed on the hood of his car, waiting.

Morty parked down the lane, far enough for plausible deniability maybe. Dane checked his watch. It was dinnertime, and Morty wouldn't want to be out in the suburbs trailing Dane around. He could probably lose the guy, but he wanted to be sure. When he heard the car door slam, he jumped down and started walking.

"Morty? What are you doing?"

"Where are we?" Morty was heading his way. At least he wasn't going to play a game, but he hadn't answered.

"Who sent you out tonight?"

"Beg pardon?"

"Was it Val or Noelle?"

"You did, sir. You asked—"

Dane closed his eyes. Right. "I think you misunderstood me. I'm not playing tonight."

"Well, since I'm here . . ."

Dane slid his hand into his pocket and produced a wallet. He slipped a one-hundred-dollar bill out and held it up. "For your troubles."

Morty took the cash. "A hundred? Thank you, sir."

Dane slipped out a second bill. "And you won't report my whereabouts tonight?"

"Couldn't if I wanted to. I'm not sure where you're headed."

"Good. Now scram."

Morty took a few steps backward, then turned and climbed back into his car. Dane waited until his headlights disappeared down the lane and around the corner before making his way back to his own car. Then he made a U-turn and followed another nondescript lane, deeper into the country than Dane usually ventured. It amazed him how quickly the city fell away, leaving nothing but fields.

He pulled in the drive and skipped up the front steps, double checking that nobody waited in the evening shadows to take his picture. This wasn't something he wanted passed around for speculation.

He rang the bell, trying to overlook the peeling paint and the spiderweb cracks in the panes of glass. The door creaked open, and Rosamund's eyes opened wide before she doubled over and began to cough heavily. She recovered enough to say, "Dane, what are you doing here?"

"I heard you're not feeling well. Everything okay?"

"Just the crud. Nothing to worry about."

"I thought you might like something warm and a little company?" He held up the bag he'd carried out of the Chinese restaurant. "It's not chicken soup, but close enough. Wantons in broth?"

"You've always been too good to me." She opened the door and let him in. "Come in."

He stepped into the foyer, nodding in approval at the improvements he could discern from that vantage point. "How's the water, Rose?"

"I haven't had any problems since you had the well pump replaced. Thank you, again." She headed down the hall to the kitchen where she pulled out a couple of mugs from a hutch. "Tea?"

He sat at the table and produced a deck of cards. "Fancy a game?"

She smiled and slid open a drawer. She dropped a pad of paper covered with penciled tabulations in front of him. "We never finished the last game. I was winning."

Dane glanced at the date scrawled at the top, wincing with guilt at how long it had been since he'd last paid a visit. "What were we playing for? Your hand in marriage, was it?"

Rosamund ladled the soup into a bowl and carried it to the table. She pulled her bathrobe tight as she dropped into a chair. "Now, you know I'd lose on purpose if that were on the table."

"Yes, well. That would indeed be your loss."

She leaned in. "Don't let them tell you who you are."

Dane chuckled. "Who's *them*?"

"Everyone. The press. The gossips." She dipped her spoon into the greasy liquid and blew to cool it before slurping it up. "Mmm. That's good."

"I know who I am, Rose. At least I think I do. The press gets it right even when they get it wrong."

"I know you, Dane. You've got a heart of gold."

Dane shook his head. His heart was black as tar. "You only think that because you're the great love of my life, sweetheart."

She snorted, then reached over and laid a twisted hand on his. "Whoever ends up with your affections will be one lucky lady."

"Whoever ends up with my affections is likely to burn them to the ground. That's why you're the girl for me."

Rosamund's eyes narrowed. "Now you listen to me, boy. You need to stop playing around and decide what you want. Your problem is you take nothing seriously."

Dane didn't dispute her. How could she understand that the things he wanted were mutually exclusive. She was right though. He'd need to make a decision. If he didn't, Val would make it for him.

He shuffled the cards and began to deal. "I think we were playing for a new front door?"

Saturday

D ane straightened his tie and knocked. He was enjoying the anticipation of finding out exactly what magic Margaret had pulled off. Selena opened the door with a radiant smile.

"Look!" She spun around and showed off a navy knee-length gown with a neckline that left little to the imagination. Margaret had dressed her up to show her off. "They came by earlier with a couple of choices. OH! And look at the shoes!" She stepped back so he could take in her full length. High heels matched the dress perfectly and brought out the muscles in Selena's calves. She had gorgeous legs, and he thought of a half a dozen things he wanted to do to her right there in the doorway.

"You look beautiful. I knew a cocktail dress would look stunning on you."

She curtsied and then reached up to tug at his tie. "And you, sir, look devilishly handsome."

He caught her hand in his. "Are you ready to go? We have reservations."

Before she closed the door, she yelled into the apartment, "I'm heading out! Don't wait up!"

"Roommate?"

"Yeah. One of the interns. Susan?"

"I take it she knows what you're doing tonight?"

She stopped short and waved a hand over her dress. "Kind of hard to hide it. But if you're worried, I didn't tell her who with. She didn't seem to care anyway."

They approached his car, and he opened the door for her, but instead of climbing in, she turned to face him. "I never thanked you for doing all this. I feel like *Pretty Woman*."

He laughed. "Thought you weren't charging anything?"

"It's true. You get the pleasure of my company for free."

"Not quite." He held his hand toward the passenger seat. "But no worries, your company entertains me. It's an even trade."

After they'd both climbed in, and he got the car on the road, she said, "The other night when you drove me home, I never told you how sexy this car is."

"The car?"

She shifted toward him. "And the driver." She laid a hand on his thigh.

He gripped the steering wheel and set his teeth. "Selena, please don't take this the wrong way, but I really don't want to wreck this car."

She took the hint and drew her hand back. "So where are we going?"

He gave her a side-eyed smile and didn't answer. When he parked, she said, "I've never been downtown here. Don't you miss Manhattan?"

"Sometimes."

He led her to the elevator and up to the restaurant overlooking the city. The maître d' led them to his usual table, and

Dane watched Selena as she took in the view. "Such a tiny city, isn't it?"

Dane realized he wasn't dealing with an inexperienced twenty-something. He was dealing with a New Yorker and the daughter of a wealthy man. He'd need to step up his game if he wanted to impress her.

The waiter brought the wine list with an expectant eyebrow raised. Dane asked Selena, "Do you drink wine?"

"Sometimes."

Dane shook his head subtly to the waiter and said, "We'll have a bottle of your finest red." He scanned the menu and settled on a mid-list wine that she'd probably like. He saw no reason to waste a one-thousand-dollar bottle on someone who wouldn't know any better.

Once the waiter had decanted the bottle and poured the glasses, Dane felt Selena's toe on his ankle, moving under the hem of his trousers. He was beginning to feel like a cat toy. Not that he minded, but he still had memories of his date with Noelle and her cutting verbal sparring. But he had a bird in the hand.

"What would you like, little bird? The steak?"

They talked easily through dinner. Dane let Selena take his hand and even rubbed her thumb back. When that brought a satisfied grin from her, he squeezed her fingers and then brought them to his lips. The whole time they made casual conversation, she batted her eyes and smiled in a way he assumed was meant to be seductive. He came to the realization that she wasn't inexperienced with the world, but she was completely inexperienced with men. And he found it more endearing than off-putting. But it had the unwanted side effect of making him feel protective of her.

And so when the meal came to a close and they climbed in the car, he took the exit back toward Selena's. She noticed right away. "Are you taking me home?"

"Did you have a nice time tonight?"

She turned completely sideways in her seat. "You didn't?"

He reached over and took her hand. "I did. You've been wonderful company."

"You know I can't ask you in. I have a roommate."

"Yes."

"So—" Her face fell. "Is it me? I thought we'd go back to your place. I thought we were going to—"

He pulled in to a parking space in front of her door. "Look, Selena. Yesterday was great. Completely impetuous and unexpected." He shot her a smile. "And delicious."

"So what? You only do things when they aren't premeditated? That seems fruitless."

"And yesterday, I didn't realize you were interested in Anthony. But now I do. And I don't want to complicate that."

"Anthony? Nothing is happening with him. We hung out and talked. Yeah, I like him, but if that's why you drove me home, you should know I'd rather be with you."

He took her chin in his hand and looked back and forth between her eyes. "You have to understand that I don't share my toys." Not true, normally. But this was about competing with a younger man.

Her lip curled slightly. He thought she was going to tell him to go fuck himself. It's what she should have done. It's what Val would have done. Noelle would have slapped him. Selena leaned her head forward and took his thumb in her mouth.

"And, Selena, you can't tell anyone about this. Not even your closest friend. Do you understand?"

She climbed across the median console, sat in his lap, and began unfastening his tie while her lips trailed kisses down his neck.

Dane threw the car in reverse. As he slowly drove out of the parking lot, he slid his hand up Selena's dress and pulled her underwear to the side. He swerved onto the main road, one hand on the steering wheel, one hand between Selena's thighs as she ground herself into his groin.

His phone buzzed as he pulled into the driveway. When Selena walked through his front door, he opened the email and glanced once at the picture Morty had sent. It was a great shot of Selena with her foot halfway up his pants leg and his lips on her hand. He might have to give Morty a raise. Val would be very pleased.

He lifted his eyes to find Selena unzipping her dress in the middle of his living room. He tossed the phone onto the floor, along with his tie and his already unbuttoned shirt. He crossed the floor in two strides and pulled the dress down over her shoulders, running his hands along every inch of her exposed skin. She arched her back, and he caught her in his arms and carried her upstairs where he intended to spend the rest of the night making her show him exactly how she liked it.

Week 3

Monday

Val swiped to the left and brought up the next picture on her phone. Dane got a haircut Saturday morning. Swipe. Dane went back to the children's hospital and read to the children's ward. Swipe. Dane went for a jog. Swipe. Dane left his house in a suit. Swipe. Dane sat at his favorite table at his favorite restaurant with Val's favorite intern.

She hovered over the screen, studying Dane's expression. She was pleased he'd sent her the photo but wasn't sure if his intentions were altogether altruistic. He could have held onto this little bomb for some future payout, but he knew she'd want it in her on-going war on Geraldo. It would make a wonderful addition to the list of ways Geraldo's daughter would soon disappoint him.

Still, Dane wouldn't send it out of the generosity of his heart. There was a reason Val asked Morty to hold back the pictures he took. Dane probably thought he could make her jealous in order to melt her stubborn resistance and get her to cave to his seduction on his timeline.

But there was still Noelle to deal with.

No, she'd play the game to the end. She wouldn't crawl to him.

Val knew the risks she was taking. She was beginning to worry Noelle meant more to Dane than he even realized. What if she had as far back as New York? What had Val unleashed?

If she could get him to destroy Noelle, then she'd know he was completely hers. But if she gave in before forcing him to prove Noelle meant nothing to him, she could lose everything.

She swiped to the next picture and chortled at an image of Dane apparently coming out of mass on Sunday morning along with a whole crowd. The next picture showing Selena waiting patiently in his car undermined his carefully planned illusion. It also hit Val in the gut harder than she'd expected. Selena had spent the entire weekend with Dane. She couldn't think of the last girl he'd actually spent time with.

Val moved through the rest of the pictures, all taken for Noelle's benefit. She laid her phone down and stood to stare out the window. What would she do about Selena now? The damage had all been done. Would she let Dane keep her?

A flash of light caught her eye, and she watched as Dane's garish car swung into the parking lot. Why he didn't keep a more practical car for everyday use made no sense to her. But she did love seeing him climb out of the driver's seat. Especially since he was alone.

External Security Camera #1 Footage

9:12: *Dane Russ's car pulls into a parking space at the northwest corner of the parking lot.*

9:13: As he is getting out, Noelle Constance crosses into view, walking directly toward Mr. Russ.

Ms. Constance appears to speak, but Mr. Russ begins to walk toward the building, and she follows.

9:14: Ms Constance touches Mr. Russ on the arm. Mr. Russ stops and points toward the southeast corner of the parking lot.

External Security Camera #2 Footage

9:14: Mr. Russ walks to a picnic table. Ms. Constance sits first. Mr. Russ sits facing her.

9:15: Ms. Constance appears to speak. Mr. Russ shakes his head, then appears to speak.

9:16: Ms. Constance reaches across the table and lays a hand on Mr. Russ's. Mr. Russ withdraws his hand. They appear to converse more. Mr. Russ raises a hand in the air.

9:17: Ms. Constance appears to speak. She stands and moves around the picnic table directly next to Mr. Russ. Ms. Constance bends and appears to kiss Mr. Russ. Mr. Russ jerks his head back and appears to speak. He looks up toward the building, then stands. Ms. Constance appears to speak. Mr. Russ walks away.

*9:18: Ms. Constance leans against the picnic table
and covers her face with her hands.*

Dane drove to work alone, although he'd only just
dropped Selena home so she could change for work. She teased
him that she planned to spend the entire morning hiding under
his desk, licking him until he brought the entire office running
to find out why he was screaming.

He reminded her that she was strictly prohibited to train
under him. So she suggested he climb under the desk and lick
her. If he'd known she would be such a hell cat, he might not
have bothered with Noelle.

But while he loved sex, Selena was just a distraction from
his larger goal. A very fun distraction.

He hoped Val had found his weekend enterprise both
amusing and frustrating.

He parked at the far end of the lot to keep his car away
from the main thoroughfare of crazy drivers. He grabbed his
jacket and straightened his tie, thinking back to the morning when that tie was the only item of clothing Selena wore.
Damn. He was going to be at half-mast all day at this rate.

Halfway across the parking lot, he heard heels clicking
fast, coming toward him. "Dane?"

He turned to find Noelle, blinking in the morning sun,
moving toward him like a homing missile. "Good morning,
Noelle. You look particularly radiant today."

She produced the warmest, most penetrating smile he'd
ever seen on her before. "I was hoping to catch you today."

He began moving away from her toward the building.
"Can we walk and talk? I'm a little late." He didn't wait for
her answer.

"I've been thinking . . ." she said from behind his left shoulder as her heels click-clacked. She grabbed his elbow. "Dane, honestly. I won't let anyone fire you for being late."

He stopped and raised an eyebrow. "You'll wield your influence just for me?"

"I'd like to talk to you without running out of breath."

Dane glanced over at a picnic table. "You want to sit over here?" He led her to a seat visible from every window in the front of the building. If he looked up now, he might find Val watching them. Or any number of gossips. Dane made sure to keep his distance. He sat down across the table from Noelle, hands rested just out of reach.

"I think maybe we got off on the wrong foot together. That was my fault."

He shook his head. "No, I'm aware that my reputation precedes me." He scratched his chin. "What are you saying? Have you changed your mind about me?"

She hesitated. "Yes. I think so."

"Noelle, yes or no? You're killing me."

"I'm sorry." She reached across and took his hand. "I don't think you understand how scary this is for me. I—"

Dane pulled his hand away. "Scary? I'm scary now?"

"No, I mean—"

"You think I'm some monster who's going to gobble you up? If you look at our history, I'm the one who's put himself out there again and again. I'm the one who's been rejected over and over. And yet, you're scared?"

"Yes, but you—"

He held up a hand, and she snapped her mouth shut. "Do you even like me?"

"I do like you, Dane."

"But are you attracted to me?

"Isn't it obvious?" Her voice came out a rasp.

"Not really. You touch me like I'm toxic. The last time I tried to kiss you, you seemed horrified."

"You need proof?" She stood up and walked around the table, leaned forward, and pressed her lips to his.

Dane was so shocked, he jerked his head back. "See? I don't bite."

"Maybe I want you to."

Dane's jaw dropped. What had gotten into her? "All you have to do is ask."

"I'm asking."

"For what exactly?"

"I've thought it over and decided maybe I'll give you a chance. I'll let you take me on a date if that's what you still want."

"You'll *let* me take you out?" He started to stand. "Excuse me if I say that's not exactly the level of enthusiasm guys are hoping to hear."

"What do you want me to say? That I promise to love you and cherish you from this day forward 'til death do us part?" Noelle's voice dripped sarcasm. "Seriously, Dane. I thought it would be nice to get a chance to know you better. I'm open to another date."

Dane was so tempted to say yes. All he'd hoped for when he'd started this whole charade was a reversal of rejection. And here he had her wanting to date him for real. If he thought it could be that easy, he might have let go of everything else and accepted. But it would still be on her terms, and he wanted to break down her walls. He wanted her begging. "No. I don't think so."

"I don't understand. You've done nothing but stalk me since I came here. You tricked me into going out with you." Tears welled in her eyes, and Dane swallowed a feeling he didn't usually entertain, one that felt like remorse. "I should be taking out a restraining order, but I thought there was more to you than your awkward attempts to ask me out. And now I'm saying yes. Why are you turning me down?"

"Look, Noelle. A part of me wants to take you up on your—whatever you call this. I want to take you out, get to know you better, wine you and dine you, and damn, I want to kiss you." He wasn't even lying. But he wanted to play to end game. He wanted her resistance to more than slip; he needed it to shatter.

Noelle sputtered out, "But—"

"You have no idea how hard this is, but I'm done chasing after you. I'm not a charity case. If the best you can do is capitulate to my desires, I'm afraid this relationship would have a very poor prognosis."

"You're being unreasonable. If you don't think we need to get re-acquainted before jumping into something, then forget it."

"Noelle, you don't need to know me better to decide what you want. You already know me. And you know where to find me if you decide you're interested in giving it an actual go." He made a show of scanning the windows. Val would love to hear this conversation.

As he left, Noelle sat back against the table, unaware that she'd put one foot into a tangled web, and the spider surely watched from her window above.

From behind him, he thought he heard laughter. Or sobbing. He nearly turned around to find out, to drop to his knees, to tell her yes, whatever she wanted, but he was in the middle of a game with three potential outcomes, and he had no choice but to play.

Outcome one: Blitzkrieg.

He was confident he could seduce Noelle and have a delightfully torrid one-night affair and then end things. It was all he'd set out to do. The prize, besides the sex, would be the sweet taste of revenge, but he'd lose any chance of anything more with Noelle, the elusive outcome number two.

Outcome two: Sustained Occupation.

If there were any chance he could build a legitimate relationship with Noelle, he might set aside the long game he'd been playing with Val. But even if he did exactly what Noelle was asking, took his time, drew her out, gained her trust, he knew she'd eventually see through his deceptions, know him as the black-hearted villain he was. He'd just end up losing her the old-fashioned way. And he wasn't about to give her a second opportunity to destroy his soul. Not when he had his eyes on another prize.

Outcome three: Scorched Earth

His sights had always been set on Val, and in order to gain her trust, he'd have to forget about any possibility with Noelle either in his bed or his life. He needed to drive Noelle so crazy that she'd say or do something foolish enough to put herself in jeopardy so Dane could deliver her on a platter. It was the only way to hook Val on the line—if Val actually honored the wager.

He hoped this would work or he'd be risking everything for nothing.

He ran his hands through his hair.

God, how he wished he could come up with a fourth scenario where he could win Val's trust and keep Noelle. He was practical, however. Val would never consent to being the other woman. To take a shot at Val, his aim had to be true.

Sophie,

I'm sorry I haven't been writing. Everything is fine. I just got busy with the internship and started to have a social life.

About that. I know I said I wasn't going to get involved with anyone—and I really haven't!—but I have been having fun. Two of the hottest guys in the office are both competing for my attention. I'd love to tell you more than that, but then I'd have to kill you ha ha.

*I'm exaggerating a bit. That one guy, Anthony, took me to a movie on Thursday, and then on Friday, we hung out talking. He's so much nicer than I expected. He wanted to go out again on Saturday, but I'd already made plans to go out. And I really wish I could tell you about that, but it's confidential. You might guess it though. *cheeky grin**

And I know you're going to chastise me for playing when it was so hard to get into this program, but if you were here, you wouldn't blame me. I'm at the top of my group. I'm the only one who has mentored under both Val AND Dane. Val even took me on the live trading floor before anyone else. They seem to have a lot of confidence in me. If Dad wouldn't disinherit me for it, I'd probably apply to work here next year. I'm a shoo-in for the guaranteed job they offer. But I may have convinced Anthony to apply at R&M next year.

How odd that I'd be working for my dad at Val's and Dane's old company. It almost feels like a betrayal. Maybe I'll use my new credentials to go work somewhere altogether different. Maybe Solly?

Also, for your information, when I asked Val about dating Anthony, she encouraged me to pursue whoever I wanted to. Isn't she the coolest?

Suffice it to say, I'm enjoying my internship.

And it does make me feel a little guilty, knowing you're there buried under summer school home-work. You should have those headaches checked out. You could be overworking.

I promise I'll check in regularly.

Ta,
Selena

Val paced behind her three interns. Matt yawned and dropped his chin onto his hand, propped up on his elbow. Blake slumped in his chair and sighed. Selena crossed her legs, staring intently at the monitor as she clicked through screens answering all the questions and moving on. It was obvious when she finished the test because she made a gesture like an atomic bomb had detonated on her keyboard. The girl had become arrogant in such a short time. Val could use that.

"Let's take a ten-minute recess." She needed a break, too. She'd spent the morning filing paperwork and overseeing a particularly brutal staff meeting. She'd come to realize that she was going to have to find someone else to run the intern-ship program because every year, her regular underlings began to mutiny in her extended absence. She'd dealt with the slight insurrection, but now her mind was split between the intern-ship and the fires that might start burning out of control.

And they were only in the third week.

Matt and Blake bolted from the room and headed down to the smoking area. Val considered following suit, but she was sick of those two. What she wanted was a stiff drink. Maybe she'd pay a visit to Dane. She moved toward the door, but Selena stopped her.

"Val, I wanted to thank you for your advice last week."

"Oh?" She paused and then decided to come take a seat next to the girl. "So did you end up having a fun weekend with Anthony?"

Selena blushed. "No, actually. We just hung out."

Stupid boy. Val was glad to hear it but wondered why Anthony would choose to hang out with Selena rather than come home with her. She realized she was tapping her finger and stopped. "So he wants to move slowly, is that it? You're dating?"

"I don't know what he wants. I enjoyed spending time with him, and he asked me out again for Saturday, but I turned him down. I'm trying to figure out how best to let him down without hurting his feelings."

"Wait. You managed to hook him, but you've lost interest?"

"I don't know. I'm still interested in him, but I met someone else and—"

Val tilted her head as if this were news to her. "That was sudden."

Selena's smile was bursting off her face in the way of someone hiding the best secret. "Not really. I met him earlier. I never thought he'd be interested in me. But he was."

"Someone in the program?"

Selena shook her head. "He doesn't work with me."

Val snorted without meaning to. The girl was learning to lie and not badly. "So what's he like? Cute?"

"Beyond cute. He's sexy."

This had surpassed Val's tolerance for suffering. "Well, I'm glad things worked out. But how did my advice help you?"

"I got the attention of two different guys I like because I let them know how I felt. I wouldn't have had the courage to be so obvious without your words of wisdom. And now I have to figure out which one I prefer."

Val bit her tongue. Selena seemed to think she was shopping for non-perishables. She couldn't know that when she turned Anthony's invitation down on Saturday, she set a ticking time bomb on that potential relationship. "Well, good luck deciding. Is there any reason you can't just see them both?"

"D—" She shut hurt mouth and restarted. "I don't think either of them would like that."

"Possibly. But what they don't know won't hurt them."

Selena adjusted her glasses. "I don't know how to juggle. To be perfectly honest, this is all totally new to me. I mean, I've dated back at school, but I usually scare boys away."

"You're too smart for a lot of men, Selena. Have you spent much time around truly smart men? Men who are secure enough in their own intelligence to respect yours instead of fearing it?"

"I thought I had. Although my father set me up on so many dates with sons of his friends that ended up badly."

"And let me guess, they condescended to you but still expected you to put out by the end of the night." Selena's face grew red, and Val pressed on. "Or you talked too much, and they felt intimidated by your wit and dropped you off politely without much more than a chaste kiss goodnight?"

"Is it so common?"

"For women like us? It can be very hard to navigate a sea of worthless idiots and come up with a man who can match us intellectually. And physically." Val pointed toward Selena's neck. "Don't tell me you burned yourself with the curling iron."

Selena's hand clapped over the hickey. "I'm so embarrassed."

"Don't be. You shouldn't feel compelled to put out for the cretins who expect it as payment for an evening spent in their odious company. Never sleep with a man who can't keep up with your mind. But neither should you refuse yourself the pleasure of an enlightened man." She waited until Selena looked her in the eyes before she said, "Especially someone with the experience to teach you what you otherwise might take years to learn."

Selena's eyes popped open. "How did you guess?"

"Oh, please. You'd be crazy not to. But remember our conversation last week. Dane's a lot of things, but a boyfriend is not one of them. Enjoy him while you can." She stood to go. "And, Selena, don't throw away your budding romance with Anthony, if that's what's going on. He'll never be able to compete with Dane in nearly any way. You know that already. But he might be able to fill in the gaps."

She left the training room, pondering the many recent developments. She hated when people did things she couldn't anticipate and forced her to reconsider her entire strategy.

Perhaps playtime with Anthony had come to an end.

Val could sit back and enjoy the dog fight that would result when Selena got caught between the two men. After all, Selena had served her purpose. She deserved a moment's reward.

On the other hand, Val wasn't quite ready to give Anthony up. She'd miss the young man's eagerness when he was in the throes of hero worship. Surely she could find a replacement quickly enough.

Decisions, decisions.

Val headed for the stairwell. Maybe she needed that cigarette after all.

Anthony sagged in the seat. Dane had created a fairly simple test for him, but he dragged the mouse around with lethargy, sighing heavily between each exercise. Dane wasn't sure he was even bothering to read the questions.

"Is gravity affecting you more than everyone else today, Anthony?" Dane pinched the bridge of his nose, barely tolerating this display of gloom. "Would you rather go home?"

Anthony shoved an empty chair away from Dane's desk, and it rolled until it hit the wall, though it had slowed in momentum considerably so that the resulting collision was anticlimactic. "Can I talk to you about something personal?"

Dane closed his eyes to hide their intense rolling. "Can you finish this test first? Don't you want to move on to the trading floor?"

"What's the point?" Anthony's face was buried in his palms, and Dane wanted to grab him by his shirt collar and shake him.

"Stand up."

Anthony lifted his head out of his hands. "What?"

"I said stand up. We're going out."

"What about the test?"

"The test is bullshit. We're going to go get a drink. I'm tired of watching you sit around here moaning." He grabbed his suit jacket off the back of his chair and started toward the door. When Anthony remained seated, he turned back. "You coming? Or would you rather calculate net rate?"

Anthony's eyebrows furrowed, and he glanced from the computer back to Dane. "But—"

"It's my test, and I'll say you passed it. Normally, you would have. I made it ridiculously easy. So come on."

Dane drove to the restaurant where he'd come out the night Selena invited him to hang with the interns, set them up in a booth, and ordered a couple of beers, figuring Anthony probably hadn't cultivated a hard alcohol problem. Yet.

"So you want to tell me what the dying patient routine is about? Did you get some bad news?"

"I'm in love." Anthony groaned.

"That is bad news." Dane smiled at his own joke, but when Anthony's frown deepened and he looked like he might start to cry, he walked it back. "I'm kidding. Are we talking about Selena?"

"We went out together twice. I thought I showed her a nice time. I went out of my way to let her see that I respect her. I mean, I love talking with her and want to get to know her better. Obviously, I'm attracted to her, but we've only been out twice, so I wanted to let her see that I'm not all about the sex. I thought I was doing everything right."

"But I take it your feelings aren't reciprocated."

"Worse. I think there's someone else."

"What makes you think that?"

Anthony squeezed his fist tight on the table next to his glass. "I asked her to go out with me on Saturday night, and she turned me down because she already had plans."

"That doesn't mean anything."

"So I went over to her apartment on Sunday to see if she'd like to go for a walk, but she wasn't home. Her roommate said she hadn't been home all night. She'd gone on a date the night before." His voice cracked. "And she didn't come home."

Dane listened to Anthony with apparent interest, unsure exactly what advice he ought to give. He could defend Selena's honor and fill Anthony with hope that he'd misunderstood everything. He could come right out and tell Anthony that he was the other man. Neither option much appealed to him for various reasons, not the least of which was the prospect of being stabbed in the heart with a steak knife. He went for the third option.

"You should have slept with her."

Anthony looked like he'd been slapped. "What?"

"The evidence you've presented tells me you've been friend zoned. And someone else picked up on Selena's interest, and she ran with the one who could give her what she wants now. Today." He shook his head, laughing. "You might have over-planned your game, Anthony."

Anthony's eyes were dark and angry. "I was respecting her."

Dane snorted. "No. You were respecting yourself. Did she ask for you to respect her to the point of neglect?"

The curl on Anthony's lip warned Dane that he needed to tone it down quick. But anger was better than whining. "Do you play chess, Anthony?"

He narrowed his eyes. "I have. Why?"

"When you play chess, there are times to be defensive and times to be offensive. You can't think of end game before you've made your first move. And you can't make your second move without watching your opponent and seeing what they do. You have to adjust according to how they play the game."

"You think I failed to read Selena?"

"I think you came to the table with a preconceived notion of your imaginary opponent. And you acted accordingly. And Selena may have decided to go find a table with a better player."

"What should I do now?"

"You could take up checkers."

"Enough with the analogies. You nearly lost me with the chess game. I just want to know what I can do to win her back."

Dane crossed his arms and leaned back. Was he really about to give himself competition? He thought about it. He'd enjoyed the hell out of Selena over the weekend. She was like candy—sweet, delicious, fun. And she was smart enough to keep him entertained, but she lacked the backbone and wit of someone like Val. Or Noelle. And he was growing bored with Selena.

Why not let Anthony have another shot?

"What you want to do is get her alone today. Ask her to come talk to you in the training room. And when you get her alone, take her by the hand and kiss her. Really kiss her."

"At work?"

"Absolutely. The more forbidden, the better."

"But what if we get caught?"

"That's what will make it exciting. Press her against a wall, run your fingers through her hair, get physical." Dane was starting to regret his decision. Selena would be eager to let Dane take her over one of the tables in the training room. That would be worth tempting fate over.

"I can't believe you're advising me to be so . . ." He covered his mouth. "Wouldn't that be sexual harassment?"

Dane burst out laughing, unintentionally. "Oh, Anthony. You're going to make a very nice friend for Selena."

Anthony swallowed. "But you really think it might work?"

"If she likes you at all, she'll be all over that. But you have to read her responses. If she resists, stop immediately. She'll let you know." He paused, worried about Anthony's reluctance to properly seduce the girl. "You *have* been with a woman, right?"

"Of course." Anthony's face relaxed into a stupid grin. "Recently, in fact." His expression tightened back into the soulful scowl of the brokenhearted. "But that was different. And I'm going to put an end to it."

Dane appraised Anthony. "You're involved with another woman, right now?"

"It's kind of complicated." His eyes darted away from Dane and caught on some object in the distance. "But I can't talk about it."

"You sure? I'm a good listener." And damn curious now.

"Maybe some other time." He blew out through his lips. "But I don't know how she's going to take it when I tell her. She was already jealous when I stood her up last week."

The wheels were turning. "You had a date with her last week?"

The cocky grin Dane had seen Anthony sporting last week returned with a vengeance. "It wasn't a date. She told me it meant nothing. She actually called it a 'dalliance.' Who says that?"

Val said that. Dane tapped his finger on the table. How could he exploit this information? "You know what? I think you should give her one more night of fun before you end it. Let her have tonight."

"But you said to go get Selena right away."

"I did, didn't I?" He nodded, thinking. "Well, the thing is, if you respect Selena the way you say you do, you should put an end to the other relationship first. Right?"

Anthony sipped his beer, not committing to an answer either way. He waited for Dane to get to the point. But Dane didn't have a point yet. He was still trying to figure out how he could get Anthony to do something so obviously wrong.

"Last week, I recall you asked me about a woman you were interested in. That wasn't Selena, was it?" He hoped the kid would be honest about this at least.

"No." He licked his lips. "But I'm not fickle. I liked Selena before. It was just that I admire the other woman so much. And she showed some interest in me. I couldn't resist."

"It's okay, Anthony." That was the angle he needed. "If you admired her so much then, I'm assuming you still hold her in some esteem?"

"Oh, yes. Very much. She's incredible."

"And she'll be disappointed when you break it off?"

"I suppose so."

"There you go then. You'll give her another night with you, enjoy it for what it is, and then in the morning, let her know you've decided to let her go." Dane threw a twenty onto the table. "You ready to head back now?"

Dane added Selena to his To-Do list. He'd need to get her out of the way to keep Anthony from becoming distracted from Val. Plus he now had a stop to make to Morty's floor. This had been a very eventful day and it wasn't even two o'clock.

Dane,

I came down to your office, but you weren't there. Could you come see me? Or call me tonight?

Noelle Constance | CEO Fleetwood Capital LLC

I can't stop thinking about you.

Noelle Constance | CEO Fleetwood Capital LLC

Dane,

We're all on the trading floor. You should come down here so I have something interesting to look at.

Selena

Dane got back to his office to find a backlog of emails. He paused on Noelle's and Selena's. It had been a pretty good couple of weeks. Where to go, where to go?

He considered the layout of his board. He was easily circling in on check. Could he make it check mate?

It was nearly three o'clock. The interns would be on the trading floor for another hour at least. Dane left his office and took the stairs to the third floor. He passed the now empty training room and knocked on Noelle's office door.

She opened the door and stepped back to let him in. Her finger went straight to her mouth where she started to worry her ring fingernail with her teeth. She'd chewed it to the quick. "Thank you for coming up. I needed to see you."

She turned away to walk back to her desk. Dane closed the door and came up inches behind her, a breath away from her neck. He refrained from touching her, but she had to feel his presence. She stopped, and her shoulders rose and fell.

He laid a hand on her waist and slowly slid it around the front of her, drawing her into him. She leaned her back against his chest, and he breathed in her hair, her fear, her awakening desire. Before she could gather her resistance, he stepped around her so he faced the door—and more importantly the small window embedded in the door—so he could be sure nobody witnessed him wrapping his arms around Noelle. When she didn't resist, he kissed her with the confidence he hadn't shown on that first date.

She didn't pull away this time, but he stepped back. "Noelle, is this what you want?"

She nodded, but her face registered surprise and uncertainty. He pulled her to him, kissing her, pressing his body hard against hers so she'd be in no doubt of his physical desire. He didn't have to pretend he wanted her. She'd denied him for too long, and now she was on the verge of giving herself to him. He nearly lost himself in the intoxication of her kiss.

His sole intent had been to break through the rest of her barriers and make her confront her desires, make her get a taste of him, make her want him, and make her know she wanted him. When he walked out of here, he wanted her unsatisfied, hungry, desperate. From this moment on, she could try, but she wouldn't be able to stop herself from ruining herself for him.

But he couldn't get enough of her. He ran a hand up her thigh, along the hem of her dress, up to the edge of her underwear. She gasped, and he relented, but he didn't retract his hand altogether. He clamped tight onto the back of her thigh and ground himself into her. When she moaned, he heard himself echo her.

A small voice he didn't recognize urged him to step away from her and give her a chance to survive him. He nearly heeded it, but the protest came too late; he'd already committed himself to this course of action. He needed her.

He unfastened his belt. When he unzipped his pants, she finally came to her senses. "Dane. Stop."

He dropped his hands and stood back, studying her confusion with an interest that was no longer merely calculated. He licked his lips and watched her eyes. She was fighting against a primal desire to fuck him in her office and a need to remain above such base desires. Part of him wanted her to give in right now. He wanted her more than ever.

But his wager with Val required more than a shag in Noelle's office. An inter-office romance was a gray area ethically, but it would be flimsy proof of harassment. If he was going to satisfy Val by compromising Noelle, he needed Noelle to pursue him. He'd never conquer Val until she believed she'd beaten him at his own game. Until he'd definitively sacrificed Noelle.

He'd known it from the start, but standing on the precipice, he found himself unable to do what was necessary. His mind and body warred for control.

This was the price of getting to Val.

It was almost a relief when Noelle shook her head and said, "I've made a mistake. I'd like you to leave."

Almost. His willpower faltered, and he stepped closer again, inches from her face and sensed the goosebumps prickling her skin, the shuddering of her breath, the heavy beating of her heart. "Noelle," he whispered. "You know you want this."

She backed up. "I told you I wanted to take things slow." With a trembling finger, she pointed toward the door. "Please leave. Now."

"This isn't a game." He almost wished he'd been recording this conversation for that line alone. Val would be amused.

He considered kissing her, making her change her mind, but he didn't want to take her against her will. He wanted her to crumble and give herself completely. Taking a step away, he said, "When you've decided to commit one way or another, I'll be waiting."

He left her office wondering if he'd crossed a line. What if she never wanted to see him again? He swallowed down regrets. He'd known going in he'd never beat Val without losing almost everything else.

Before he'd hit the stairwell, his confidence returned.

Of course she'd want him still. He'd felt her body melting into his. He'd felt her resistance breaking. *Patience*. She'd be running to him before the end of the week.

With renewed confidence, he sauntered to the trading room, still buzzing with energy when he crossed the threshold. He scanned the room, locating the various interns watching the action. Most of them appeared dazed by the reality of trading. For the past two weeks, they'd gotten a crash course in the tools, and many of them took their lessons with a bored nonchalance, like they'd been studying a textbook. Now the cold possibility of losing someone else's money froze them in place. They watched and learned, but many of these kids would go back home and change majors. Understanding the markets and developing a stomach for the never-ending stress of predicting and second-guessing were two different things.

Selena sat in the middle of the room, arguing with one of the traders named Alan. She pointed at the Bloomberg monitor and then put her finger back in Alan's face. After a minute, Alan shrugged and backed down. He held the phone headset out to Selena, and her face fell. She reverently took the headset and put it on. Then she started talking fast. Dane leaned against a wall and enjoyed the show. After a few minutes, she looked over and saw him, and her face lit up. She stood the entire time she negotiated with the broker on the other end of the phone, typed in some numbers, then victoriously punched the enter key. She took off the headset and dropped it to the table. Alan clapped her back, looking as proud of her as Dane felt. And he had no idea what she'd even done.

He crossed the room. "How's it going?"

Alan shook his head. "She's got the knack. I wanted to go conservatively in on this security, but she saw a possibility to add a little risk for a sweet gain. I didn't think she understood the ramifications of the trade, but after she laid it out, I knew she was right. You trained her well. I just hope the risk pans out."

"Can you release her back into the wild?"

Alan laughed. "Yeah. She did good for a first timer. I hope you don't plan to hire her next year. I'll be out of a job." He winked.

Alan had nothing to worry about. Val had no intention of letting Selena work here next year. All her efforts would be in vain if she didn't return to R&M to work for her father. Dane would miss the little spitfire.

Selena grabbed her things and thanked Alan. As she left the trading floor with Dane, she said, "You're taking me away from my duties."

"I wanted to see you in my office." He led the way down the hall and opened the door. As soon as she entered, he closed the door behind him and locked it. He pulled her into the corner and kissed her.

"Mr. Russ. I'm not supposed to be in here."

"Did you know that nobody can see into this corner of my office through the window?" He unbuttoned the top of her shirt and ran a finger across her neck.

"So we're invisible?" She reached for his belt, unfastening it like a pro. She'd lost all her shyness with him around three o'clock Sunday morning, after she'd told him she liked his dick in her the best when she was on top. She unbuttoned and unzipped his pants and reached in to find him ready for anything. She slid down his waistband and dropped to her knees.

Dane groaned as she worked her mouth around him, running one hand up the base and the other across his balls, exactly like he'd shown her. Her lips circled around the head, her tongue firm, up and down the soft sensitive flesh below. She'd gotten good at that in record time. His knees barely held him, as the pleasure intensified. "I'm going to—" She pumped him faster, harder. "Selena, I'm about to . . . oh fuck." He couldn't hold it, and she sucked him off until he could only drop to the floor in exhaustion.

He pulled her over into his lap. "Whatever you want, you shall have."

"Dinner?"

He laughed. "I was planning on that anyway. Where do you want to go?"

"Your place." She was insatiable.

"Your wish is my command." He wiggled back into his pants. "But can we head out now? I'm suddenly starving."

Tuesday

Val,

I thought you might like to know that the project is coming in a bit ahead of schedule. You should definitely prepare for a live demo as early as Friday. I trust you'll still want to be a part of the integration testing.

Dane

Dane had emailed Val sometime during the night, obviously cocky, probably drunk. She wondered why. He'd always avoided communication as transparent as corporate email. His message was coded in work jargon, but any fool could decipher it. It made her nervous, and she wasn't sure why. She looked out the window at Dane's empty parking space. He was usually so cautious. Was he planning on quitting? Was that why he'd thrown caution to the wind?

Bombs away.

She didn't like it, but surely she was just paranoid. Where would he go?

She sat down and fought through her initial reaction. Maybe he was just as anxious as she was to reunite. The two of them were meant for each other.

Friday. She'd have him by the end of the week. Her biggest concern should be whether she could turn that one night into a future. It had been a long time coming.

But Noelle had to be out of the picture first, and Dane had to be the one to swing the blade. Would he? Oh, he preened as if he was just as ruthless as Val, but he'd never had the fortitude of someone forged in fire, like herself. He fed off ego-stroking like a drug addict, and in his victory over Noelle, he might mistake that intoxication for love. Worse, he wouldn't be mistaken.

Surely, he could manage this one thing. He might need a push in the right direction.

She sat at the computer and hit reply on his email.

Don't forget this project requires documentation. The demo cannot proceed until you've squared away any remaining legalities.

She hesitated before sending. Dane might want to leave a trail, but she planned to be working here the following Monday. Chances were slim that anyone would find anything incriminating in what she'd written, but why take the chance? It would wait. She'd have to trust Dane knew the rules of engagement. She'd have to trust him to want to return to her victorious, if for no other reason than his pride.

Her attention turned back to her plans for Geraldo. Geraldo, who had put her in this predicament in the first place. Granted, the decision had been hers, but how was she supposed to know everything would fall apart? She still blamed him.

As soon as she'd gotten his calling card, she'd gone to him right away and appealed to his pragmatism. He'd never loved her. He'd juggled multiple women even while she'd let him cage her. She'd expected him to be angry and jealous, but he'd been more reasonable than she might have feared. Cold, even. Still, he gave her an ultimatum: She could leave the company immediately, or Dane had to go.

Who could blame her for trying to get out with everything intact—her money, her power, her pride?

Dane.

Dane had never thanked her for helping him leave without incident; he never would forgive her if he knew how she'd managed that.

Four more days, and this tiresome chapter of her life would be over. After all this time, she'd make damn sure Dane came to her with no attachments. Starting next week, they could be the featured couple on financial magazines.

And then maybe they'd start their takeover of Fleetwood Capital while watching R&M collapse from within. With Noelle removed from play, Val would have to focus the next six weeks on building the Trojan horse that was Selena.

A movement out the window caught her eye, and she watched Dane park and walk across the lot, quickly but not hurrying. He walked like a man who owned the world.

Like every man did.

Selena,

Can you meet me in the training room after work?

Anthony

Dane,

There's a conference in New York City this week. I was invited to attend, but the board has very strongly urged me to stay here until I've settled in. I'd like for you to go in my place. You've missed the first two days, but there's a flight out this afternoon, and you'll be able to catch the last most important panels.

You can, of course, expense the trip.

Noelle Constance | CEO Fleetwood Capital LLC

Dane took the stairs two at a time and opened Noelle's door without knocking. Rosamund Shirley sat across from Noelle, hands on her knees, with her head now turned to face Dane as he intruded.

He ignored Rosamund and rushed straight up to Noelle's desk, finger raised. "What the fuck are you thinking?"

"Excuse us, Rosamund." Noelle stood, smoothed her skirt, and waited until Rosamund had left the office. "Good morning, Dane. I trust you've read my email."

"A conference? Are you banishing me as punishment?"

She swallowed. "It's not punishment, Dane. I just thought it would be good, for *both* of us, if you took some time away."

He stepped around her desk and closed the distance between them. "Good for both of us? I think what you mean is that you want me away from here. All you have to do is tell me you don't want me, and I'll leave you alone. You don't have to send me away."

She sat erect, carefully composed, but her hands shook in her lap. "Dane. I need time to sort out my feelings, to gain control of myself. You—" She shook her head, jaw working silently. Then she muttered, "I can't even think when you're around."

He thought he'd wanted to see her broken, but something inside him yielded. A wave of fear he might have blown it staggered him, and he dropped to his knees, grasping her fingers. "Please. Please. If I mean anything to you, just keep me here. We can start over. I'll take you to the movies. Or we could just go get a coffee. Anything. Noelle, please."

She closed her eyes and a tear rolled down her cheek. "Dane, please. Just go."

God, it was just like the last time. He let go of her before he humiliated himself a second time. Letting her push him away without a fight. Again. "Okay. I'll go."

As he left her office, an unfamiliar pain twisted his gut.

Margaret,

Guess who's coming to town? I believe I owe you for that favor. I'll be staying at the Marriott at Times Square tonight. I should be arriving around 6.

Dane

Val's door opened, and Noelle practically poured into the office. Val quickly opened the voice recorder app on her laptop and hit the big blue circle before she stood and helped Noelle to a chair.

Noelle shook her head. "What have I done?"

"You're going to have to bring me up to speed, Noelle."

"I chased him away." Her bloodshot eyes rose, pleading. "I had to, right?" She twisted her hands, and Val noticed her fingernails, once manicured perfection, had been chewed to stubs.

"We're talking about Dane? Did something happen?"

"Everything happened. I told him I wanted more. And I do. But I'm so terrified." She closed her eyes, but tears continued to roll down her cheek. "I've fought and fought, but it doesn't matter, does it?"

Val remained silent, stunned by this outpouring of grief over a simple seduction. She'd begun to fear Dane's feelings for Noelle were more than the result of his deflated ego. She never would have guessed Noelle's feelings were reciprocal. Not to such an extent. He'd inadvertently tapped a powder keg.

Maybe he *would* wrap this up by Friday. Val reached into her top drawer and unwrapped the brand-new box of Kleenex. "Here. Tell me all about it."

"Thank you." Noelle plucked out a tissue and blew her nose. Then she began to worry the paper in her hand, wadding it, kneading it, shredding it. "I can't tell you how grateful I am that you're here. Did you ever go through anything like this?"

"With Dane?" Val smiled. What if she told Noelle exactly what she'd been through with Dane?

"Oh, of course not. But surely you've had your heart broken."

Rather than answer that, Val brought the conversation back to the topic of interest. "Is your heart broken?"

"Well, he's gone."

"What do you mean?" An acidic taste filled her mouth. "Where has he gone?"

"New York City." Noelle's face was ugly from crying. "I sent him to the STA conference in my place."

The conference would run through the weekend. A muscle in Val's cheek twitched. "Why would you do that?"

Noelle's head jerked up, but at least she stopped crying. "I told you. I can't fight him here. I had to get some distance."

Val's eyes closed with the realization that Noelle might have found the trump card Dane hadn't expected her to play. Who would have anticipated she'd pack him off to get him out of the picture? It might not matter in the end. Val recognized Noelle's false bravado as a coward's defense.

Noelle sniffed, but she'd calmed down considerably. "You have no idea how tempted I was to tell him to stay. Or to get on the next plane to follow him to the conference." She laughed, hollow. "I know I can't do that. Can you imagine what that would look like? The board would eat me alive."

Val didn't bother to point out that it already looked bad that she'd used her influence to resolve a personal issue with Dane by making him attend a conference in her stead. "Well, he won't be gone forever."

Noelle nodded. "Right." But she didn't look convinced. "I've only bought myself a few days' respite."

Val would have loved to encourage her to fly to NYC on the next flight, but she didn't want to get her hands too dirty. Noelle would find herself unable to resist the lure of temptation. She'd give Noelle a day to pine, and then point her in the right direction.

Dane was a lucky bastard. His banishment might end up working out even more in his favor. No matter what, Val felt confident that she'd have Dane back very soon. If she had to wait another few days, she could be patient. Sooner or later, Noelle was going to chase after Dane and pour out her heart. He'd capture his queen.

And then Val would sweep the board.

Since Noelle had more or less pulled her emotions together, she thanked Val and left. But not five minutes later, Anthony entered. *I should put a take-a-number machine outside.*

"What can I do for you, Anthony?" She'd gotten little sleep the night before, thanks to him. She didn't want to have to hold his hand through any relationship angst in the daytime.

He sat down and examined his hands. "I don't know how best to say this, so let me just come out with it."

She took in a breath and let it out impatiently. "Can this wait until after work? If it's about how you don't like to be so secretive, fine. We can even go out and get a drink together. But I'm actually trying to do work."

His frown brought out her own. "It's not that. I wanted to tell you it's been nice."

She raised an eyebrow at him. Did he think he was ending this? "Nice?"

He cleared his throat. "Nice. Uh . . . great. I mean, I've had a really lovely time with you. I have so much admiration for you."

"Anthony, please cut to the chase. I don't have time for middle school speeches."

"There's someone else." His eyebrows drew together. "I'd really like to remain friends with you, but—"

Val's eyes rolled to the ceiling, and she licked her teeth. "I don't see what that has to do with us."

He swallowed. "I thought you should know. I won't be able to see you anymore."

"And you decided this since this morning when you were happily lying in my bed?" She unbuttoned the top of her blouse far enough to reveal the lace of her bra.

"No. I decided it before, but I thought it would be better to let you have one more night?"

"You thought I'd rather be fucked by someone who was thinking of dumping me?"

"Val—"

She raised a hand. "Anthony, you can pursue someone else, but I picked you out of all the possible people I could have spent the summer with. I expect you to follow through. Nobody else needs to know. As you know, I prefer it that way. Unlike some people, I really don't care what you do when you're not with me."

His eyes widened. "You can't force me to keep sleeping with you. You realize that would be harassment, right?"

Val stood and walked around her desk. She pulled a chair close and laid one hand on his crotch. He already sported a tight bulge. He turned his head and squirmed but didn't stand and leave. She popped the button, then found the tab of his zipper and slowly lowered it. "Is this harassment, Anthony?" She opened his fly all the way and ran her fingers through the opening in his slacks, through the opening in his boxers and gripped his hardening erection. She helped adjust him so she could stroke him. He closed his eyes, breath quickening. She kept one eye on the rectangular window to her office. "Would you like to come over tonight, Anthony?"

"Yes. God, just don't stop."

She pulled her hand back. "I'll see you tonight."

Selena,

Something came up and I need to leave earlier than I expected. I'll talk to you tomorrow.

Anthony

Normally, traveling to New York was quick and painless for Dane. But this felt like exile. Long and torturous. As soon as his anger abated, his frustration welled up, and he clenched his fists, wishing he could take all this pent-up fury on one of the innocent bags in the luggage carousel.

He kept an apartment on the Upper East Side, so he normally wouldn't even need to pack for a quick trip to the city. But Noelle had booked him a room at the same hotel where the conference was being held, and he wanted to keep up appearances. So before boarding the plane, he'd gone back home and packed a bag.

He hated staying in hotels, but as soon as he walked into the lobby, he felt a pair of arms around his waist and turned to find Margaret, dressed in a short plaid skirt with knee high socks and penny loafers.

"Well, hello, sexy schoolgirl."

"Hello, Professor Russ. Could I see you after class?"

Dane checked in and whisked Margaret up to his room and promptly forgot why he hated hotels.

Noelle,

Thank you for setting me up in the executive suite. It's not quite home, but I've been welcomed with open arms from the second I arrived. I'm currently sitting on my bed, enjoying a gorgeous view, remembering kisses so recently exchanged. It's probably best that you aren't here to see me in my naked vulnerability. I'm physically and mentally exhausted from hours of torment, my flesh marked by flagellation.

However, since I came, I've experienced a blessed sense of peace. If only I could have given you such a powerful release. Even so, whenever I close my eyes, I can almost taste your lips on mine, and I'm left wanting more. I don't mean to burden you with my frustration. It's a temporary weakness, I assure you. As I sit here, writing this, I am literally touched by the promise I might purge myself of any residual desire as soon as I recover my strength.

Please excuse me for exposing myself so freely.

—D

Wednesday

N oelle burst into Val's office, looking uncharacteristically disheveled. Had she slept at all?

"Val, have you seen the pictures Dane is sending from the conference?"

Val rubbed her eyes with her palms. "Good morning, Noelle. Where is he posting them?"

"He's emailing them to the company's list." She paced back and forth, chewing her thumbnail, while Val brought up her Outlook.

Val scrolled through her unopened emails aware that Noelle kept throwing her furtive glances. When Val found a handful from Dane, she said, "Ah." He'd gotten up early to schmooze, and every picture he sent showed him with an arm around a different pretty young woman. He was so obvious, Val nearly rolled her eyes, but Noelle's haunted expression gave Val every reason to admit that Dane's ham-fisted efforts weren't going to waste. "So he's enjoying the conference, I see."

Noelle rushed around the desk and gawked over Val's shoulder. "Do you know who that is?" She pointed at one of the girls in the photos. "I don't recognize her."

"No, I don't know. Let me see if I can zoom in on her name tag." She blew up the picture and with the enlarged name tag, the girl's cleavage became nearly lifelike. "Does it say Karen?"

Noelle resumed her pacing, her hand destroying whatever remained of a once orderly hairdo. "This is crazy. I'm driving myself crazy."

"Calm down, Noelle."

"I should want him to find another woman. I should be glad that he wants to forget about me and move on. Why am I letting my imagination go?"

"Sit down, Noelle. Surely, you're just overreacting." She frowned. "Although Dane does have a number of acquaintances in the city."

Noelle dropped into a chair, but her hands continued to fidget. "I deserve this. I sent him to the conference to get him away, to get him out of my sight. I drove him to seek solace with some other woman." She stared at the floor, eyes vacant. "What am I going to do? I can't get him out of my system." She balled her hand into a fist and pressed it against her forehead. "I can't be in love with Dane Russ. I can't be obsessed with a guy who has 'acquaintances in the city.' What am I going to do?"

Val came around her desk and stood behind Noelle, rubbing her shoulders. "You can't get him out of your system by sending him away, Noelle. You're going to have to confront your feelings. And him."

"Should I make him come back?"

Val considered the optics. If Noelle made him come back, it might appear like she was abusing her power, but that could be explained away. No, Noelle needed to chase Dane to New

York. She'd look desperate. The board wouldn't put up with even the hint of scandal. "What if you went to him?"

"The board said I'm not supposed to go to the conference. I would have gone myself if they hadn't forbade me to."

Even better. "You're the CEO, Noelle. You can do whatever you want. And it's only a couple of days."

Noelle's breathing slowed as she relaxed and gave into the urges she'd clearly been resisting for hours or even days. "Yes. If I go see him in New York, we can talk things out."

"I'm sure Dane would like that. I've never seen him quite so agitated."

Noelle twisted around and faced Val. "Do you think he's sincere? I mean, his reputation—"

"His reputation was built on a lonely man's futile search for the right woman." Val hoped this was true. She hoped when he came back to her, she'd have him body and soul. And so she gilded the lily. "Noelle, I think that woman is you."

The twinkle returned to Noelle's eyes, but it only highlighted the turmoil going on there. "I can't thank you enough, Val. I'm going to check flights right now."

Val thought for a second. Could she get Noelle to leave a smoking gun on top of everything else? She rubbed Noelle's arm. "But do make sure to send him an email if you decide to go. He should be aware of your intentions. It's only fair."

Noelle nodded. "Oh, right. Of course." She stood, clearly eager to act on her decision.

Val caught her by the elbow. "And Noelle, it might not be the worst thing to let things take their course."

Dane,

*I'm catching the next flight to New York. I know
I said I wanted some distance to sort out my feelings, but since you've left, I can't think at all. I'm
in misery. I may get in trouble with the board for
leaving right now, but I can't work, I can't sleep, I
can't breathe. I need to see you and settle this. I'm
coming straight to your room when I arrive. I hope
you'll meet me there.*

Noelle

The knock on the door was so light, Dane almost didn't
hear it.

"Thanks for your company, Margaret." He gave her one
last kiss before showing her out. "I promise I'll contact you
next time I'm in town."

Margaret laughed. "Next time, let's do more than talk."

Dane opened the door for Noelle, who looked like she'd
drunk four pots of coffee and snorted a line of cocaine. Her
normally neat hair had been twisted and pulled until the fas-
teners no longer functioned as anything but moral support.

Her eyes flitted from Dane to Margaret. "Who's that?"

The pained expression that pinched her features gave
Dane a small sense of satisfaction. He was mortified that he'd
spent the entire night pouring out his frustrations to Margaret
when she'd been more than willing to help end them. He'd let
her get some sleep while he took a stroll down to fetch breakfast and made an appearance at the conference. Considering
Noelle's appearance, his selfie bait had worked.

"Noelle, this is my friend Margaret. She works in the fashion industry. I was consulting with her. Margaret, this is Noelle."

Margaret giggled. "Nice to meet you." She slipped out the door. "See you around, Dane."

Noelle hesitantly walked into the hotel room, looking around and taking it all in—the half-drunk glasses of champagne, the food on a pair of plates in the living room, the unmade bed. "Who was she?"

"A friend. I told you that."

She spun around. "What was she doing here?"

"Relax, Noelle. I ran into her in the lobby. I hadn't seen her in a long time and wanted to catch up." He inched closer to the skittish woman. "Noelle, don't jump to conclusions. I knew you were coming here."

He'd wanted her to jump to conclusions. If she wanted to wield his reputation against him, let it ricochet back on her. He hoped her devastation would match his. He expected her to walk right back out the door.

Instead, she stayed and surprised him when she said, "It doesn't matter. I don't even care if you slept with her. I don't care who you've been with before if you'll be with me now."

Her shirt had come untucked, and her skirt had wrinkles that made Dane wonder if she'd slept in the clothes she had on. She wasn't wearing any makeup. Her nose was raw, and her cheeks tear stained.

He'd never wanted her more.

"Tell me why you're here." He took a few more steps toward her. When she didn't back away, he crossed to her and took her hand.

"I've quit fighting." Her eyes lifted, red from tears, dark circles from exhaustion. "I couldn't stay away. I can't stop thinking about you." She let out a soft sob. "I could lose my job, and I don't even care. I had to be with you."

He took her hand. "Why?"

"Isn't it obvious? I'm in love with you."

It was what he'd wanted from her when he'd started this game. This was the moment to break her heart and walk away without telling her why. He'd never envisioned a more perfectly orchestrated opportunity.

But seeing her desperation, hearing the words he'd never expected her to say, slaked his thirst for vengeance. He couldn't send her away now when she was giving herself to him. All his careful calculations couldn't have prepared him for his absolute need to give himself in return.

He reeled her in and kissed her, not gently. He sucked on her lower lip and pushed his tongue into her mouth, wanting to consume her.

He couldn't resist the disaster of her.

Her knees buckled, and he caught her up and carried her to the bed, sweeping the sheets and blankets completely off onto the floor. He unbuttoned her shirt as she breathed desperately in and out. Her skin felt like velvet as he skimmed up her stomach. He paused for a moment before unsnapping the front catch on her bra.

She sighed. "Yes. Dane. Yes."

He leaned down and licked her nipple, and her groan brought him to total arousal.

Goosebumps appeared on her flesh wherever his fingers landed as he undressed her. She shivered. He was mesmerized by her every reaction. And she responded with needy kisses and frustrated attempts to work the last buttons on his shirt. He laughed and helped her out with the shirt but let her open his belt and unzip his pants. He slipped out of them and lay beside her, running his hand along her body. "I've wanted you for so long."

"I can't resist you. I've tried. But I can't stop wanting you."

The words unfurled something inside him. He hadn't known how long he'd needed to hear her say them.

She worked her fingers into his hair and pulled him closer. Their lips met briefly, but he wanted to watch her as he ran a hand up her thigh and slid a finger into her. He stroked her with her own wetness, turned on by the arch of her back and the shallowness of her breath. He kicked her knee over with his and settled between her legs so he could circle her clit with his tongue, loving how she wriggled and moaned. She rocked her hips, pressing against his mouth searching for release. He buried his finger deep inside her, in and out, and increased the pressure and the rhythm with his tongue, with his lips, with his thumb until she bucked and curled away from him.

He wiped his face on the fitted sheet and crawled back up beside her, kissing her forehead. She moved languid, sensual, his. He wrapped an arm around her and lay beside her, just holding her. She must have been more exhausted than he'd known because she drifted off on him. Sighing, he got up and dragged the sheet and blanket back over her. Then he rummaged around in his suitcase for his pack of condoms and threw them into the drawer next to the bed. He called room service and requested dinner and more champagne, then jumped in the shower. After he dried off, he threw on a bathrobe, then settled on the edge of the bed to watch Noelle sleep. She'd never looked as beautiful as she had when she'd surrendered to him. Tonight, at last, she would give herself to him completely.

Sophie,

So much has happened in a week. Remember when I thought two guys were fighting for me? Well, one of them has left town. Then the other one asked me to meet him after work. The first time he asked, yesterday, he bailed on me at the last minute, which ticked me off. But maybe he'd lost his courage. He asked again, today, and when I met him, he kissed me! And he told me he really likes me and hopes we can be more than just friends.

I don't care what you think about it. Anthony is a great guy, and I think this will turn into something that lasts more than just the summer. He told me he had been trying to take things slow because he likes me so much and didn't want to scare me away. As if. He's so adorable.

This internship has been the best decision of my life. And we're just getting started! We still have a little over five more weeks. I'm going to have some things to teach you!

Selena

Geraldo,

Are you attending the STA conference this week? As much as I would have liked to go, Noelle decided to send Dane. It would have been lovely to catch up with you. Maybe next time.

Val

The food arrived, and Dane let the waiter set it up on the table. He slipped the boy a twenty and sat down, contemplating whether or not to wake Noelle, sleeping in the adjacent bed. He wanted her alert and present when he finally took her. He needed her to want it even when she was no longer desperate and hurting. He wanted her whole.

He uncovered the dishes, and the smell of the food permeated the room. Noelle stirred and sat up. Dane watched her stretch and come back to the world slowly.

He stood and brought her the other bathrobe. "Did you sleep well?"

"I can't believe I conked out on you. Sorry." She looked past him. "Did you order food?"

He ran a hand across her cheek, gently pushing a strand of hair behind her ear. "Are you hungry?"

She smiled. "Are we talking in innuendo again?"

"Do you want to?"

She reached up and took his hand, twining her fingers with his. "I want you." She lifted his hand and kissed his wrist. "You always smell so good. What is that?"

"Right now? Just me. I took a shower."

"Without me?"

He laughed. "I thought the water might wake you." He stood. "Come on. Let's eat."

She followed him to the table, but even before they sat, she laid her fingers on his neck and chest. She reached into his bathrobe and touched his abdomen. "You're hard as a rock."

"Yes. I am." He smiled at her, and she laughed. He poured her champagne and lifted the glass to her. "We once drank to tonight. What shall we toast now?"

"To now."

"To now."

She took a sip of the champagne and then picked up a strawberry. "I didn't even know I was so hungry. This is perfect." Dane lifted the strawberry from her and pressed it to her mouth. She took a bite, and her eyes transformed from clear and alert to sultry and desirous.

She got up and walked to where Dane sat, lifted one leg across his lap, and straddled him. She reached back for a strawberry and offered it to him. "You have the most gorgeous lips. I don't know how I resisted them for so long. I've always wanted to kiss you."

"Have you? It took me long enough to convince you."

"I tried to get over my attraction. I'm glad I finally get to allow myself the pleasure of you." She kissed him and brought her pelvis closer, so his cock pressed against her through the terry cloth. He grew hard immediately and ground himself into her. She rocked her hips and sucked on his lips. He reached into her robe to touch her gently. She pulled it off and threw his open, so she could rub her wetness against his bare skin. It was regrettable that his condoms were across the room, out of reach.

He could wait for this. For her.

"Noelle, did you mean what you said?"

"That I love you?"

"That you don't care about my reputation."

She dropped a kiss on his temple. "Should I?"

"No. Did you think I was sleeping around before? Is that why you cut me off?" He had to know.

She tilted her head back to better look in his eyes. "If I'd only thought you were womanizing, I might have confronted you. It was the way Val made it sound like you were laughing at me while you were sleeping with all those other women."

"Val said that?"

He clenched his fists. Val had been there to pick up the pieces after he'd shattered. If she'd orchestrated his destruction, he'd—

Noelle lifted her hips, and he would have slid right into her, but she held back, teasing. She looked so delicious, and his anger evaporated, leaving behind a single thought: He no longer owed Val anything but revenge. His years of loyalty had been in service to a lie.

He took Noelle's hand. "Come with me."

He brought her back to the bed, praying she wouldn't have a sudden change of heart. He sat down and slid the condom out of the package. She took it from him and wrapped her hand around his erection, stroking him slowly before rolling the condom onto him. He moaned her name.

She repositioned herself across his lap and kissed him while she worked him deep inside her. She rose and fell, dragging pure pleasure across the length of him. He couldn't take it anymore. He picked her up and laid her onto the bed so he could drive into her. She wrapped her legs around his back and gripped him to her. The sounds she made nearly caused him to come before he was ready, but he gained mastery of himself and then took control of her. He kept up a steady rhythm until she jerked and then held stiff as a board for a half a second before her muscles relaxed.

He flipped her over onto her hands and knees and grabbed her hips, fucking her hard until the orgasm came swift and powerful.

He fell beside her on the bed and wrapped an arm around her, snuggling her into his chest. "Are you done with me now that you've had your way?"

She laid a hand on his abdomen. "I was wondering the same thing."

He wanted to explore this, take his time, experience this new feeling away from Val's machinations, at least for this stolen island of time. "Can you stay with me? You don't have to go back, do you? I want you to stay."

"I want to stay. I don't need to go back until Sunday. We can go back together."

"Good." Maybe he wouldn't go back at all. Maybe he was done with Val. Free. He relaxed and ran a hand down Noelle's soft skin. "I could get used to this."

"And what then, Dane?"

What if they didn't go back?

Thursday

Dane woke up to a delicious sensation and came to consciousness as he realized Noelle had his dick in her hand. "Good morning."

"What time is it?"

She shrugged. "Three, I think." She moved down between his legs and ran her tongue up his shaft.

"Oh, God." He looked down just as she put her lips around him and took him in her mouth. The sight of her looking up at him while she sucked him off turned him on even more. "I'm so in love with you."

She lifted her head. "You're gonna love this." She produced a readied condom and slid it onto his now fully erect cock and then climbed on top of him. She reached back to fondle his balls as she rode him. It was so erotic and exciting he came within minutes.

"Fuck. I'm sorry, but you can't be that sexy and expect it to last."

She dropped beside him. "That was exactly what I wanted. I wanted to watch you when you came. I didn't get to see it last night."

"You're full of surprises."

"You know what else I want?"

"No, what?"

She looked across the room. "See that table?" When he nodded, she went on. "You don't know how many times I've fantasized about you coming into my office and bending me over my desk to take what you want."

"I'd need you to get dressed for that."

"Why?"

"Because in my fantasies, when I bend you over your desk, I slide your underwear down from under your skirt before I take you."

She shuddered. "Can we do that later?"

He laughed. "I had no idea you were so naughty."

"I'm not. But for some reason, my imagination is vast when it comes to things I want you to do to me."

"What else?"

"Did you bring any ties?"

He raised an eyebrow and went to his closet, producing a purple silk tie, one of his most expensive. Her wicked smile made him instantly hard again. He really could fall in love with this girl.

Room service woke them late in the morning. They'd slept, some. Mostly, they'd explored every inch of each other and whispered their secret fantasies, but when they were spent and lying beside each other, they'd confessed their hearts' desires. Dane tipped the bellhop, then set a plate before Noelle. She tucked in like she hadn't eaten in weeks.

Dane smiled, watching her. "We should stay here."

Noelle wiped the corner of her mouth. "You don't want to go to the conference?"

"Oh, that. No, I don't want to share you with any of those bastards downstairs. But that's not what I meant."

"Oh?"

"I mean, we shouldn't go back to Fleetwood. We should just stay here."

"Run away, Dane? If you want to make this thing work, you can't just keep me in a tower, hidden. And you can't go and create a brand-new life."

"But we don't need Fleetwood." For the first time in years, Dane finally didn't care what happened between him and Val. He could let go of his anger. He could forget his obligations. He wanted to take this girl and run. "Wouldn't you like to create a brand-new life? We could go anywhere."

"Where would we go, Dane? We have a life. We have jobs."

Dane shook his head. "Noelle, I don't have a job. I have a distraction." He forked a sausage and waggled it in the air, giggling at the image. "Do you want my sausage?"

"Seriously, Dane. We should probably go mingle, get some fresh air, feel like civilized people for a few hours."

"Or we could pack our bags and be in Key West by tonight."

"Key West? What would we do there?"

"At first, we'd relax, enjoy the weather, each other." He laid down his fork so he could reach over and stroke her fingers, show her he was being serious. "But I know you want to do more than that with your brains. So we'd start a company together."

"A company? Wall Street of Florida?"

"No finance. I'm done with finance." Before he'd met Val, he'd never had any interest in finance. "I'm thinking we could get into gaming. You know, I used to be heavily into all that, a long time ago."

"I remember. You used to wear T-shirts with *World of Warcraft* stuff on them."

Dane raised an eyebrow, impressed. "You remember that?"

"Of course. I used to game until I had to buckle down and get real."

"See? It's meant to be. Maybe we'll hire that kid Anthony. He's got promise."

"And so you've planned out our entire lives? You're not impetuous, are you?"

"It's not impetuous. I've been dreaming of moving there for years. I've never had sufficient motivation to leave everything behind. But if you came with me, it could be paradise."

She narrowed an eye. "That sounds wonderful, Dane. You'll forgive me if I want to give this day-old relationship some time before I throw away a career I've spent my life building."

"So you're not saying no? Just not right now?"

She squeezed his hand. "We'll see what the future holds, okay? I would love for us to spend the rest of our lives growing old in Key West, running a gaming company together. But you know you're a complete rake, Dane. You have a terrible reputation."

He ran a hand through his hair. "I do. I'm a scoundrel, Noelle."

"It would be pretty stupid of me to fall for someone like you. I should probably just go join a convent or maybe try Internet dating."

"You would die in a convent. And imagine the creeps you'd meet on the Internet."

"I seem to gravitate towards sexists and womanizers." She sighed.

"But none of them will understand you like a certain disreputable cretin you already know."

"Let's take it one day at a time, okay?"

He grinned. "You go ahead and do that. I'll just be waiting for you to come to your senses. You know I've been in love with you since the first day I saw you."

"You are so full of shit, Dane. But I've waited three years for that shy bad boy to commit to me."

He chuckled and kissed the back of her hand. "You've turned out to be a dangerous vixen."

She snorted. "Get dressed. We're going downstairs. I'm feeling naughty, and I want to show you exactly how dangerous I can be."

Her eyes met his, and he swallowed hard. For the first time, he realized, he was in major trouble.

Friday

*V*al,

I wasn't planning on attending the conference, but then I remembered I hadn't been in a couple of years. I thought it would be nice to run into acquaintances and network. It's always good to keep up with other traders and learn about new legislation from experts. I was roaming around and happened to see Dane, but he was quite occupied and didn't look open to conversation.

Speaking of which, you didn't tell me that Dane and Noelle were an item. I took some pictures of them together. Don't they look lovely? I thought you might like to see what a team they make.

I'll be in touch,
Geraldo

Val scrolled through the pictures. Dane and Noelle weren't even trying to be secretive. He had his arm draped over her shoulder, casually. She leaned into him, secure and content. She practically glowed. And Dane's face had lost its edge. Her hair looked like she'd just rolled out of bed. His tie looked like she'd used it as boat rigging. They both mooned like they were fucking in love. That wouldn't do.

That was supposed to be Val on Dane's arm. Val would burn it all down before she let Noelle take her place.

She tugged at a lock of hair, twisting it in her fingers, thinking. She got up and paced to the window, tapping her nail against the glass. The absence of Dane's car in the parking lot pained her. She could always count on him to be around to keep her entertained. Boredom left her irritable.

It was time to fetch the interns off the trading floor anyway, so she left her office and took a left down the hall. Her eyes landed immediately on Selena and Anthony, locked in each other's gaze as they smiled and laughed about God knew what.

Her irritation flared. She walked through the desks with her hand raised to get the interns' attention and bring them upstairs to the training room. They'd all resist. Now that they'd gotten the adrenaline rush of the floor, most of them couldn't tolerate being relegated to the bullshit exercises. She didn't blame them. And her heart wasn't in taking them through another round of debriefing about their experiences on the floor.

As soon as they were off the floor, she announced, "Why don't we call it a day. Good work, everyone."

Their eyes lit up, and they all looked at one another as if to make sure they hadn't misheard her. But without waiting for her to change her mind, they filed off past her. When Anthony walked by, she said, "Anthony, a moment?"

He touched Selena's elbow. "Go on. I'll catch up in a minute." He pursed his lips. "Val?"

"Would you come with me?"

She led him back to her office, but he stayed several feet away. She'd coaxed him into another night, but his enthusiasm lasted as long as his orgasm. And then he'd gone home. He wasn't going to give her another chance to seduce him which was fine. She didn't need him anymore, provided she could exert her influence on Dane, but she wouldn't let anyone treat her with disrespect.

She pulled the door closed and walked to her laptop.

"Has Selena told you she was seeing someone else until recently?"

He inhaled. "Yes. But it's over now. She's chosen me, just as I've chosen her. Please understand."

Val sneered. "Oh, get over yourself. I thought you might like to know who your rival was." She spun the laptop around to face him, revealing the photo of Selena playing footsie with Dane at the posh restaurant.

Val's shoulders relaxed as she watched the blood drain from his face. She took satisfaction in his distress. She'd love to see him try to maintain a serious relationship with Selena knowing all the while Dane had been the one fucking her. She nearly smiled at the delicious melodrama. Anthony raked a hand through his hair. "I don't understand. Dane? But then why did he encourage me to go after her?"

Val's stomach lurched. "He did what?"

"I told him how I felt about her, and he said I should let her know." His eyebrows drew together. "He told me to give you another night, first."

"Oh, God." Val dropped into a chair. "Of course he knew you were seeing me."

"I didn't tell him anything."

She bit her lip. "Okay. Okay. Fine." It wasn't fine. Information in Dane's hand was a ticking time bomb. She'd have to find a way to detonate it first. What had he already started?

She remembered Anthony stood across from her. "You can go."

His expression of shock mirrored hers, but he staggered back out of the office.

Val turned to her laptop and opened her email program. She hit Reply.

Geraldo,

So good to hear from you again. I enjoyed your descriptions of the conference. You can't imagine my surprise to see those pictures of Dane with Noelle. Dane's been very busy. A friend of mine took the attached photos while he was dining recently. I'm sure you'll find these every bit as tantalizing as the ones you sent me. Selena is a lovely girl. Congratulations.

Take care,
Val

Saturday

ane woke with the sun. The light entered through the
hotel windows and brightened the whole room. He
turned over on his pillow to find Noelle propped on her
elbow, watching him. She smiled. "Did you know you laugh
in your sleep?"

"Do I?" He punched and fluffed the pillow behind his
back and leaned against it. "Did you know your eyelashes flut-
ter when *you* sleep?"

He'd never spent so much time watching the same woman. She revealed so many different facets the longer he spent
in her company. She kept up with him verbally. Since the first
night, she hadn't treated him with quite so much reverence, and
he loved her willingness to call him out on his bullshit without
making the bullshit an obstacle to showering him with her kisses. She kept up with him physically. They'd spent themselves in
every way they could imagine, and then they imagined more.

Between sating their lust, they dressed up to go down
to the conference but spent more time at the bar, teasing each

other until they couldn't wait to return upstairs. Sometimes their clothes came off. Often they didn't. They worked around it. They drew the line just shy of fucking in public. Whether anyone knew what they were doing in private didn't matter to them, but Noelle didn't want to completely ruin her career with a scandal. Dane no longer gave a fuck.

Dane kissed the crook of Noelle's elbow, watching her eyes close with the pleasure of his touch. He loved that he could bring that look to her face so easily. "How have we spent this many years apart? Think of all that time."

She stretched and threw an arm over his exposed chest. "We have right now. Let's not regret the past. Let's plan for the future."

"Whatever you plan, just make sure I'm there."

She slid the sheet down the rest of him and smiled at the morning wood. "You're there."

He flipped her onto her back and pressed his body against her. "Are you there?"

"I'm there."

He slid in, the motion familiar now. He loved how her head fell away from him at the moment he entered. He loved how she cooed when he laid gentle kisses on her neck. He loved how she groaned when he sucked on her skin. She rocked her hips in time with his, and they found a rhythm that caused their hearts to beat quicker, their breaths to increase. He wanted the moment to last longer, but then he couldn't help chase after the bliss of a second even though he knew it would come to a crashing end. As long as he could keep her when it was over, everything would be fine.

They looked into each other's eyes as they reached for climax. He hugged her to him and said, "I've never been happier than I am in this moment."

He phoned for breakfast service, and they showered together, dressed, and then ate. Dane casually lobbied Noelle to drop everything and run away with him. "We have nothing waiting for us." Nothing and no one but Noelle could drag him back to the drudgery of his former existence. He'd kissed the sun. He had no desire to fall back to earth.

Noelle took a more pragmatic approach. She'd laid out a timeline that involved the two of them working at Fleetwood, moving in together, sharing the routine of their former lives. And he'd agreed because at the end of her plan, they left together. He couldn't persuade her to leave immediately. He was just happy to know she wanted him in her world. Val wouldn't like it one bit, but she'd already exhausted her ammunition on him. There wasn't anything she could do about it.

She laid his suit on the bed. "Come on. Let's head back down to see if there's anyone worth rubbing elbows with or any speakers who might enlighten us."

He actually wanted to get out of the room. "Sure. I'm getting cabin fever anyway."

After wandering through the conference, Noelle yawned and excused herself to get an hour or two of needed sleep. "Will you come join me before lunch?"

Dane wrapped his hands around her and sent her off with a pat to her ass that made her jump and giggle. Then he settled in at the bar over a glass of scotch. It was only ten o'clock in the morning, but he was at a conference that felt like a vacation. And why not celebrate the unexpected turn of events?

A body slid onto the stool next to him. He turned and came face to face with Geraldo. "Geraldo. I'm surprised to see you here. Did someone put chum in the water?"

"As a matter of fact, they did." His accent was so subtle, but when it came out, it always gave Dane the impression he was talking with a Telenovela villain. Selena had no accent at all. Her father hadn't raised her bilingual in the hopes of acclimating her to this country where, as he'd often complained,

English as a second language somehow marked him as less formidable. Dane knew better than to underestimate Geraldo.

"And who do I have to thank for your odious company?"

Geraldo waved a finger to the bartender and indicated he'd have the same as Dane. "I understand you took my daughter out for dinner, recently?"

"Ah, Val." It was only a matter of time before she used those pictures to get under Geraldo's skin. If she'd played them now, then Geraldo was a missile she'd armed and sent directly at him.

Geraldo showed no reaction. "How do you think your new girlfriend would feel about that?"

"What, are you going to blackmail me? You don't think my reputation precedes me?"

Noelle might get upset over seeing him with Selena, but he wasn't worried enough to fall under anyone's coercion.

"I think you overestimate your charm, Dane." He took a sip of the scotch that had arrived. "Do you wonder why Val tipped me off?"

"Val has her reasons. They usually aren't what you might expect." Dane had known her a sight longer than Geraldo. "She may be hoping you'll tell Noelle so she'll leave here in a shameful public display. Maybe she just wants me to come back to her." Dane shrugged. Val's motives were never obvious.

Geraldo's smile barely touched his lips. "I'm not so sure. After all, Val has betrayed you on more than one occasion."

"Are you referring to her choice to return to you—what was that? Three years ago?" Dane sucked on his teeth. "I've forgiven that. She thought she was protecting me after all." He told himself to shut up, but Geraldo's smug confidence made him want to punch him. He hated that Geraldo still thought he'd won this many years later.

Geraldo sniffed in disdain. "Protecting you from what? If Val wanted to protect you from heartache, then why did she leave you? And if she wanted to protect you from me, then why did she ask the board to vote you out?" He tilted his head, watching Dane.

Dane tightened his fist and let it go. "You're lying. She tried to bring them around after *you* instigated a jealous witch hunt. When she couldn't win sympathy for me, she advised me not to fight against it."

"Don't you ever wonder why? Why not fight against it? You could have swayed the board to take your side. You were always well liked." He laid a hand on Dane's knee and squeezed. "Think about it, Dane. Why would Val want you to leave your company quietly? Was she protecting you? Or did she sacrifice you to suit her own needs?" He released his grip and pulled out a cigar from his suit pocket. "Do you mind?" He lit up the cigar without waiting for an answer.

Dane barely registered the question. "You aren't making any sense. It's me you came after. You were punishing me for taking Val from you for that one night. You've always resented me for taking her away for good. You resent me now because she followed me. Look at you, even now, trying to manipulate me toward whatever end. What are you up to?"

Geraldo shook his head. "I've never held a grudge against you. You're right about me wanting revenge. But not against you. Although I confess, I never cared whether you suffered collateral damage. I don't like you, and I don't want my daughter near you. I think you are every bit as devious as Val is, but you were always her pawn, same as me. I realized what she is a little too late. Maybe the gentlemanly thing to do would have been to warn you sooner. But would you ever believe me? Would you have even cared?"

"I have no need of warning. I know what Val's capable of." He gritted his teeth. "But you've forgotten history. Val quit the company, too. If she was trying to protect her position there, she had a hell of a way of showing it."

"Actually, I gave her a choice. I wouldn't have tolerated her to remain on the board if she'd stayed with you. She could have left, and you might still be on the board." He chewed on the end of the cigar. "You know, it was her idea to vote you out—to prove to me that she didn't care about you, that that night had meant nothing—to save herself." He barked a laugh. "I almost believed she cared about me. Then she walked away right after you left. Turns out, she was just rearranging the pieces on her chessboard."

This all sounded way too familiar. "But why? She could have just asked me to leave with her."

"And take the chance you'd choose the company over her? Oh, Dane. She wanted to make sure that her constant companion remained by her side. So congratulations, she did choose you over me. You win."

"Then why hasn't she ever given me another chance?"

"She plays a long game, Dane. And she won't trust you until she's won." He puffed on his cigar once more and stubbed it out. "She doesn't think you have it in you to beat her, you know. She's had you on a string long enough."

"But it's you she's always competing against. She's never let go of her resentment against you—over losing our company."

"Not at all. She resents losing control of *you*. I'm just an excuse—a convenient straw man."

Dane felt nauseous. "Why are you telling me all this?"

"Because she pointed me here to cause you trouble, and I don't like being her monkey. I should tell you that I came to find you yesterday, but you were occupied with other affairs. I sent some photos off to Val. I'm sure she'll be interested to see you're making the most of your time here."

What would Val do if she knew Dane had already conquered Noelle and hadn't returned immediately?

The pictures of Selena might not devastate Noelle, but Val could reveal every detail of his plan to compromise her, and that would be the end.

Worse. She could ruin Noelle's career with an email to the board. But only if she got there first.

"I have to go." He threw a twenty onto the bar.

Geraldo laid a finger on his sleeve. "Don't play her game, Dane. She'll win at any cost."

"Not if she thinks she's already won."

He took the elevator up to the suite, flipping on the voice recorder as he opened the door. He stood in the threshold for a moment, already regretting the loss of paradise. It had been a nice dream.

As he entered the hotel room, he strangely wondered if this was how Val had felt that New Year's Day.

Val's morning had been punctuated with boredom. She'd waited for some kind of reaction from Geraldo, but he'd disappointed her entirely. He might have at least written Selena to make her come home.

The weekend ahead would be dreary with nobody to play with. If Geraldo hadn't taken her bait, Dane wouldn't be home until tomorrow. She hated not knowing. Had her email caught in Geraldo's spam filter?

Dane's public displays of affection could jeopardize everything, and time was running out.

She paced the floor, contemplating what moves she had left to make.

She could have emailed the photo of Dane with Selena directly to Noelle herself, but while that would have likely driven Noelle to leave Dane, Dane's ego would demand he waste precious time fighting to win her back. After the way things ended before, Dane wouldn't stand to be rejected a second time. He'd return unmanned and humiliated, even more hell-bent on vengeance, and this game would never end.

True, Geraldo might have gone straight to the hotel and shown that picture to Noelle to destroy Dane's budding romance. But she didn't think Geraldo would waste ammunition. That wasn't his style. He might be angry at Dane for touching his daughter, but he would still calculate his best move.

She was counting on Geraldo to see the photo as leverage. Surely he would prefer to threaten to expose Dane to Noelle if he wouldn't stay away from Selena. There was no benefit to Geraldo wrecking Dane's relationship with Noelle. He *would* be motivated to scare Dane away from his daughter.

Geraldo would never expect Dane to take a bullet rather than give him the pleasure of blackmailing him. A threatened Dane was an angry Dane. And an angry Dane made mistakes. Dane's knee-jerk reaction would be to neutralize Geraldo's threat at any cost. To do that, Dane would see no choice but to confess his tryst with Selena to Noelle himself, and that would bring his affair to a dramatic and messy conclusion.

And then his only remaining move would be to snatch victory from the ashes and return to Val, claiming to have chosen the moves she'd forced, claiming to have won the wager.

If Geraldo did as she intended . . .

She tapped her fingernails on her desk, imagining a perfect scenario.

She needed Dane to make his final play and lay an accusation of harassment at Noelle's feet, ruining any hope he might have of winning her back once the dust settled. Hopefully, he'd done as she'd asked and recorded some incriminating statement. The evidence they'd collected would support the initial claim. Eyewitnesses would corroborate her odd behavior. And the spectacle of Noelle chasing Dane to New York after the board had expressly forbidden it would seal the deal. As soon as Dane set the wheels in motion, Noelle would be forced to resign.

The company wouldn't put up with CEO misconduct. Not after Ted Rasmussen. Noelle would be gone by Monday.

She shivered at the image of Dane's triumphant return. She could almost taste his lips.

What in the hell was going on in New York?

Around three, just as she was beginning to lose hope, she heard the banging on her front door.

When she opened the door and Dane walked in, she relaxed into a smug smile.

"Dane."

He kicked the door closed. "It's done." He grasped her wrist. "I've come for my reward."

Val yanked her hand free. "Reward for what?"

"Noelle came to me in New York. It's over now." He reached up and unfastened the top button on her shirt. "And you owe me. Shall we do this right here, or should we go upstairs?" He reached the second button before she drew back.

"You know that wasn't the deal."

Dane pulled out his phone and waved it at her. "I've got what you want."

"Are you prepared to follow through? Do you have enough to take it to the board?"

He stepped close again and dug his fingers into her hair. "I do."

"Show me."

"Read this." He scrolled until he found what he wanted.

He held out the device and she read the email Noelle had sent him before chasing him to New York. It was perfect. "Oh my. She's practically begging to be fired. What else do you have?"

"One second." He messed with the phone and then hit play.

Noelle's voice filled the room. "*I could lose my job, and I don't even care. I had to be with you.*"

He held up a finger. "And—"

He loaded the second recording. "This is from this morning."

Noelle said, "*Is it lunchtime?*"

Dane hit Pause. "I'd come back to the room and started packing."

He hit play, and Noelle's voice sounded concerned. "*What's going on? Is everything all right?*"

"*I'm going back home. Stay here. We have the room until tomorrow.*"

"*You're making me worry. What happened?*"

"*I'm leaving.*"

The recording ended. Dane loaded up another. "I had to call the front desk to arrange a cab to the airport. Here's the rest."

Noelle's voice pitched higher. "*Will you wait five minutes for me to pack?*"

"*You can keep the room.*"

"*Please, Dane. Give me a minute.*"

"*I don't think you understand. I'm not even going back to work. I'm bored, and I'm leaving.*"

"*If you walk away, you'll lose your job. You'll never work in this industry again.*" It sounded like a threat. Val could definitely use this. She'd want to cut all this drama out.

She smiled as Dane added the emphasis. "*You think that threat will induce me to change my mind? I'm not some low-level employee. I'm leaving it all.*"

"*What about us? Don't you want me?*"

"*Goodbye, Noelle.*"

A door clicked shut.

Val grinned. "Write the letter. Then I'm yours." Her voice gave out, and her breathing increased. She was so close to winning everything.

Dane pulled his laptop from the bag and carried it to her sitting room. He sat on her sofa and typed as Val dictated the words of the email to the board.

"Write this exactly: 'I'd like to file a formal complaint of sexual harassment against my boss, Noelle Constance. I have evidence in the form of audio recordings and written documents to prove that she's used her position of authority to demand sexual favors of me.'"

Val paced the floor as she spoke. She'd written and rewritten those words in her head for days. It was a pleasure to finally light the fuse. She asked to read the email before he sent it. She dropped into a chair, sighing. "Include the attachments. All the evidence."

He nodded and unlocked his phone. "Give me a second to upload the files to my drive so I can zip them."

"And edit out the part before she threatened you."

He nodded. She waited for him to put all the pieces together into a single attachment.

Finally, he said, "Just adding the email addresses now."

"Be sure to CC me." Val stretched languidly. She felt like the cat who'd caught the mouse. The past three weeks—no, the past three years—had been leading to this moment.

"And sent."

She clapped her hands and reached for her phone. She opened the email and read eagerly. "Oh, delicious. But you forgot to copy Noelle." She hit the forward link and scrolled to find Noelle's email address in her contacts.

Dane bounded toward her, snatching at the phone. "What are you doing?"

Val spun away before he could thwart her, disappointed that he'd failed that little test. She held the phone out where he could see it and hit send.

He yelled, "Do you know what you've done?"

Val chuckled. "Yes, I do." She dropped her phone onto the sofa, like a mic. "I just shot an arrow. Unless I've misjudged, and I rarely do, I made a direct hit to the heart."

Dane raked his hands through his hair, eyes wild, like a trapped animal. His display of weakness disgusted her.

"Do you think Noelle wasn't going to find out when the board brought the charges against her? Were you thinking you could send that email and then fix everything before she found out?"

"Of course not." He squeezed his fists, then slowly pulled himself back together, apparently as insouciant as ever. "I'm here, aren't I? You can stop aiming your weapons at Noelle."

There was the Dane she knew and loved. But it was a lie.

"You foolish boy." She smiled. She loved knocking him off balance. "I wasn't aiming at her." She had to laugh at his confusion. "I was aiming at *you*."

He narrowed one eye, and she knew she'd hit her target.

"You are so stupid. You always want what you can't have. God, you're pathetic. You managed to coax Noelle into your arms, and you've pissed it away to win a wager? You think you can beat me while you keep Noelle ignorant of your betrayal?"

She ran a finger down Dane's cheek. "The sad thing is that even now, you don't know what you've lost. What I've cost you. You loved that woman. You've loved her since the first time you lost her." Dane's mask cracked enough for her to see beyond his anger, beyond his need for revenge. She watched as the last of his hope crumbled. "Oh my, God. You really didn't know, did you? You realize that once she reads that email, she'll never want to speak to you again."

All at once, his demeanor shifted, as if he'd made a decision. He stood straight, eyes now hard and focused. He stepped into her, grabbing her by the shirt collar. "May I remind you: You *did* lose the wager. I've come to collect."

There he was. "Yes. That was the point of all this. I wondered if you were really so vain you'd rather sacrifice Noelle than lose face with me."

Dane took a step, forcing Val to stumble back.

"Oh, Dane. You are so adorable. Did you really think you could win?"

His eyes dilated black. "What are you talking about? I have."

"And what? You're going to take me like the spoils of war?

"You promised. I won. Now you're mine. Tonight. You don't have a say."

Dane held her shoulders and pressed his mouth against hers. Despite his brutality, she nearly collapsed with the pleasure of his long-dreamed-of lips. His anger fueled her desire. She wanted him to force her down, to take her. His teeth raked her neck, fingers unfastened her shirt.

Her hands reached for him, but she regained control, grasped his palm, and twisted hard, breaking his hold on her. He was such a mess, she wanted to let him have his way, but not like this.

"Regardless of the situation, it's still against the law to take a woman against her will."

He froze in place, but he only seemed to be recalculating.

She chuckled, goading him. "I know what you're planning. You think you're going to take your revenge on me for what happened years ago."

He leered, his whole face a mask of hate. "Years ago? Try minutes."

"Oh, truly unfortunate." She jerked her arm free and walked toward the front door. "Perhaps it would be best if you come back a little later when you've calmed down." This had to end with her on top, or not at all. "I'll have you again, but not until you're in control of yourself."

He closed in, encircling her wrist, calmer than before. "It's now or never, Val."

But she was stronger. She flung the door open. "Well, then. Never."

She returned to her sitting room and poured herself a drink. When she heard the door slam shut, she collapsed onto the sofa, hurled the tumbler at the wall, and screamed.

Dane drove recklessly through the subdivision, slowing only for the speed bumps. A slight rain had left the roads slick, and he skidded to a stop in front of Noelle's house. One tire bounced over the curb. He left the car running as he sprinted to her front door. He rang the bell, then began knocking. When she didn't answer, he called her name. He ran to the back door and tried peering through windows. She hadn't come home yet.

Or she'd left.

He pulled out his phone and sat down on the front stoop to start typing a text message, but the rain made the screen unresponsive to his touch. He got up and sat in his car. Water flooded down the windshield turning the world outside into a smudge.

Please call.

He laid his head on the steering wheel, waiting and hoping. Had she already seen the text? He just needed to find her to explain. He looked at his black phone and accepted that she wasn't responding. Her phone could be off. Maybe she went to the movies. A laugh erupted from his throat, and it hurt his chest. He sounded like a lunatic even to himself.

He drove quickly to his own townhouse on the wild hope she might be there. A car sat out front, but it wasn't Noelle's. As Dane slowed down, Anthony stepped out. Dane parked in his driveway and got out of his car, watching the younger man cut across the grass to face him.

"Anthony?"

Anthony kept walking until he was a foot away, then drew his arm back. A split second before the fist landed in his face, Dane dodged and came up behind Anthony. He caught his arms up under Anthony's elbows from behind.

"Whoa, there. What's this all about?"

"You were the man Selena was seeing." Anthony cried out through tears, "You lied to me. I trusted you."

Dane looked up to the heavens for patience. "You're not actually going to fight me, are you?"

"Val showed me pictures. You were with Selena the whole time you knew I wanted to be with her." He slumped and began to sob.

Dane sighed and pulled out his phone, scrolling. "And who were you with when you knew you wanted to be with Selena?" He held up the screen to show Anthony the pictures he'd had Morty take earlier in the week. Anthony and Val walked hand in hand from her car into her house.

"You had me followed?"

"I had Val followed."

"But why?"

"I know you don't want to believe it, but Selena came to me. I didn't seduce her against her will. Can you say the same about Val with you?" Anthony shook his head. "And do you know who pushed Selena into my path?"

Anthony's eyes jerked up. "Why would she do that?"

"Because she's not who you think she is." Dane pushed the phone into Anthony's hand. "Here, take my phone. There are pictures and emails and recordings on here you can use. And I recorded my last conversations with Val today. There's enough here to get an investigation started."

"How?"

"Get it to Rosamund. She can take it from there." Anything that implicated Val would take him down, too. But she'd never expect him to self-detonate. "Look in my sent emails. The last one I wrote might interest you."

The evidence on his phone would finish the job of destroying him in Noelle's eyes, but there was no other option open to him. Noelle was always going to the cost of his last move. If he wanted to best the queen, he had to make his one shot count. He'd sacrifice every piece on the board—himself included. Hell, he was prepared to die to take Val out once and for all. At least death would mean freedom.

And even so, this might not even work.

Anthony stared blank at the phone. "What are you planning to do?" The color had drained from his face. He looked up, eyebrows furrowed. "Dane?"

Dane patted Anthony's shoulder, said, "Good luck, kid," and turned toward his front door. When he got the key in the lock, Anthony called after him. Dane closed the door, locked it, and poured himself a glass of bourbon.

The cold irony was that he could never be worthy of someone like Noelle until he exposed all the truths that would make her despise him. Val was right: She'd never want to speak to him again once his treachery was laid plain.

He'd swallowed half the glass when Anthony began knocking on his door. "Dane?" *Knock knock!* "Are you okay? Dane?"

The knocking faded as he closed the door to the master bedroom. He swallowed another finger of bourbon and further insulated himself in his bathroom. He stared into the medicine cabinet mirror and didn't like what he saw.

Noelle,

I've received an email from Dane Russ that we need to discuss. I've been unable to contact him. Would you please give me a call at your earliest convenience?

Maxwell Baker

Week 4

Monday

Val dressed for work like she always did. She peeled the dry-cleaning plastic from one of her many crisp dress shirts, zipped up her skirt, and ran her hands down the fabric to straighten it. She wore no pantyhose but slipped on a pair of business-appropriate heels. She'd already fixed her makeup and hair. She checked her lipstick one last time and stood back from the mirror pleased with her appearance.

On her way out the front door, she slipped her phone into her purse. She'd given up on hearing from Dane anytime soon. He'd gone into hiding. In time, he'd have to come back around. She'd screwed him over before, and he'd stuck around. Angry, but there.

As long as he never found out exactly how little control she'd actually given him, he'd continue to think they were equals. He'd return to the game board.

But today was her victory. She'd beaten every other woman. Today she'd savor the downfall of a rival. On a whim, she drove over to the donut shop and bought two dozen assorted pastries and a box of coffee.

She carried the food into the meeting room and laid them on the sidebar, smiling at the others sitting around the long table. She didn't have to fake her ebullience. Her smile was met with sour expressions, even hostility. Typical Monday morning.

The board had set up the meeting at the last minute, and Val suspected they'd have something more important than usual to discuss. The chairs around the table were mostly all taken, but the head was vacant. Noelle's absence from the office only furthered her certainty that today, they'd announce the CEO's forced resignation. She only regretted Noelle wouldn't be present to bear the humiliation publicly. No matter, with Noelle out of the way, Val would once again become invaluable to Dane. *Why hadn't he come in yet?*

Val sat down in Noelle's place. She considered for a minute whether she'd accept the offer to finally take up the executive mantel. She'd always turned it down, but why not? It might be a fun change to run a company again.

The tech support guy, Chris something or other, got the screen projector working with the cameras, but without Noelle, there was no slide show to display. All they saw were their own faces looking back at them, and the list of attendees' names.

Val unlocked her phone to find Dane's email, but he'd zipped the file with the incriminating evidence. She wanted to download the audio of Noelle to play back in case anyone in the room hadn't yet heard it. While Chris finished up, she reached into her bag to drag out her laptop and powered it up.

Maxwell Baker spoke up first. "I don't know if all of you are aware, but Noelle Constance has taken a leave of absence."

Val smiled triumphantly, but nobody in the room reacted with the level of shock she desired. She spoke up. "Maxwell, can you please expand on this?"

The laptop came to life. She opened Outlook and found the email. She right-clicked and downloaded the zip file.

"Actually, yes Val. She let us know that she was severely disillusioned with certain activities and is no longer sure she wants to maintain her position. She wanted to resign, but we urged her to reconsider. She's taking time to recuperate in New York."

This wasn't at all what Val wanted to hear. "What are you talking about? What about the sexual harassment suit?"

Amy Waterson broke in. "I'm glad you brought that up, Val. We weren't sure if you were aware of the charges."

Val scoffed. "I'm aware of the email Dane sent."

"Dane? We did receive an email from him on Saturday." Amy's face on the screen appeared shrouded in darkness, but Val could make out her confused expression. "Have you spoken to him?"

"Not since Saturday." She checked her expression. She didn't need them to know she'd been with Dane when he'd started the unfolding drama.

Amy frowned. "Val, you do know it's a fire-able offense to use corporate power to compel an employee for sexual favors. Possibly criminal as well."

"Of course." Were they really going to make her spell it out? She unzipped the downloaded file and opened it. "I assume you've reviewed the documents Dane provided?"

She went to click on the audio file, but there was only a single Word document in the zip. How could that be? He'd said he'd uploaded the audio and email records. She'd heard the audio. Where were the emails?

On screen, the board members shuffled, and then Maxwell spoke up. "Val, the only thing Dane sent Saturday was his resignation letter. We haven't been able to contact him since."

She double-clicked the Word document. It began:

Dearest Val,

Had you bothered to double check the email addresses—

She looked at the list of email recipients, really looked, and saw the names of all the board members. Except. *No.* He'd misspelled each so slightly she would have had to be expecting it. The email never made it to anyone. He'd tricked her?

She scanned further down the file.

See I know you care more about appearances than substance, which is why you may never read this file I'm actually planning to attach. Did you think I was going to hand you—

Maxwell said, "We did receive some documents from Rosamund Shirley and—" he looked down, presumably at his laptop monitor "—Anthony Knight?

Her eyes jumped down the page.

After we send this email, you'll think you've won. And it's true, you might win the battle. I know you're capable of ruining me. Meanwhile, you took your eye off your rear flank where I've amassed my own forces. It may cost me everything, but I will win this war.

Checkmate, Val.

Cold water ran down her spine. *Why?* The faces in the room all turned toward her, curious, leering, secretly laughing.

Maxwell was still talking. "Val, did you coerce Mr. Knight to spend the night with you last Tuesday evening?"

"No. I've never had to coerce anyone?"

"He says differently. We do have photographic evidence showing the two of you entering your house. Do you deny you had sexual relations with an intern?"

She stood. "I don't know what you're talking about." They had no proof. She wouldn't supply it. "I never laid a finger on him."

Amy Waterson asked, "I'm troubled by the audio we've obtained. What do you have to say about this?"

Val's voice filled the room. "*Get her to say something to you that could constitute an act of sexual harassment.*"

Val stood. Dane had *taped* her? "That son of a bitch." She'd find him and murder him.

Amy continued, "Were you conspiring to sexually harass Noelle Constance in order to frame her?"

Val scanned the room. Everyone was against her. "I'm calling this meeting to an end."

"Val, please sit down."

She held a finger up and pointed it at every face. "I will sue all of you if you make any further accusations against me. They're all lies. I will get a lawyer." She turned to walk out of the room, but one heel on her shoes gave way, causing her to stumble. She caught herself, held her head up, and walked from the room.

She staggered up the stairwell to the second floor, gripping the handrail the whole way up. She had recordings, too. She'd turn this around and destroy Dane. As she approached her office, she became aware that the interns were standing and watching her. Anthony leaned against his cube wall, glowering.

Val picked up her pace, deciding between fight or flight. Her office door was a foot away, and she longed to hide away, nurse her wounds, and come back stronger than ever. But she looked once more over her shoulder to find Anthony, smug, victorious. And she lunged for him.

She seized his suit coat and hissed in his face. "You liar. You wanted *everything* I gave you. Nobody will believe differently. I'll make sure you never work here or anywhere else I have any influence." She heard snickering coming from all around. She stopped and looked at the interns who had all worshiped her from the first day. Selena held her phone up, recording her meltdown. It would be all over the Internet in minutes. She fled into her office where she leaned against the wall and slid to the floor, hyperventilating.

She had time to send one text message before security arrived.

Wherever you are, I'll find you. You won't get away with this so easily. You will always be mine.

Two large men accompanied Rosamund Shirley and Morty Becker into her office. Rosamund stripped her of her company phone and laptop before the burly men took her by either arm to escort her from the building.

She shook them off. "Don't touch me. I'll go without protest."

They never left her side down the elevator and into the parking lot. As they helped her into her car, she glanced up at the windows, wondering how many people looked down at her.

Tuesday

Front page *Financial Times:*

Val Montgomery Faces Multiple Accusations of Sexual Misconduct

Eight new accusations of unwanted sexual advances follow on earlier revelations that Val Montgomery pressured a yet unnamed intern into a sexual relationship. The new allegations come from former interns and employees of the Fleetwood Capital and R&M, the company founded by Ms. Montgomery along with Dane Russ.

Noelle Constance released a statement reporting that Fleetwood Capital has immediately terminated Ms. Montgomery's employment, adding, "We are deeply saddened by yet another scandal of this nature."

Financial Times *spoke with Geraldo Valencia, current* CEO *of* R&M, *who said, "I am shocked. If these allegations are true, and I have every belief that those making the accusations are truthful, Val should be shunned by all polite society."*

Dane Russ could not be reached for comment.

Dane wiped the grit out of the corners of his eyes. The buzzing sound he'd been dreaming continued as he adjusted to his surroundings. Where was he? He lifted his head off the carpet. Home. On the floor. Hallway. Had he passed out?

The buzzing continued, and he realized it was the front door. Had Anthony ever left? He vaguely recalled that he'd woken up another time, eaten some food, and then continued drinking. His mouth wouldn't open.

"Dane!" A woman's voice.

Val's come to kill me.

He crawled to the top of the stairs and lifted his shoulders. He managed to sit up, but his head fell against the wall. He wished he could die. For the hundredth time in the past however many days. How many days? He looked across the hall and saw the empty bourbon bottle. Was that the same bottle he'd started with, or had he broken into his reserves? Did he have anything left in the house?

Knocking replaced the buzzing. "Let me in, Dane! I know you're in there!" *Knock knock knock.* "If you don't open up, I'm calling the police."

Who cares?

The door handle rattled, and the whole door began to shake. "DANE!"

"Coming," he croaked. He coughed and pulled his head back up. Lights floated in his eyesight, and he dropped his forehead into his hands. "I'm coming!" he yelled at the continued attempts to break in. "You're going to break the door." As if it mattered.

He grabbed the rail and heaved himself up. Halfway down the stairs, his knees gave out, and he nearly fell down the remaining flight. Finally, he stood at the front door. He ran his hands through his hair and looked down at himself. He'd thrown up at some point apparently. His mouth tasted like a morgue. He opened the door.

Rosamund's eyes grew wide. "Dane! What's happened to you?"

He stepped back and let her come in. "I happened. To the world." He leaned against the wall and slid back down. "Just let me die."

"When nobody could contact you, we feared the worst."

He jerked his head up. "We?"

"The board . . ."

They weren't his concern. "Noelle?"

Rosamund patted his hand in lieu of an answer.

"Come on, young man. Get up." She pulled weakly, and he helped her by standing and following her into the living room. He fell onto a sofa. She went into the kitchen and came back with a glass of water and a couple of pills. "Take this. Have you eaten?"

He swallowed down the pills and lay back again. This was the strangest dream. "Rose, this is a strange dream."

Rosamund sat beside him and took his hand. "Lord, son. You reek."

"Do you want me to change? I can shower."

"I'll live." She narrowed her eyes. "But tell me, what were you thinking? Did you set out to ruin your life?"

"Just Val's." He coughed, and his head exploded in sharp needles of pain. He sat up and rubbed his temple. "I fucked up. I fucked everything up."

She laughed. "Yeah, well. A little."

"God, I'll never see her again." He pressed his face into his palms. "Was it worth it? I shouldn't have taken Val's bait. But she would never have let me be. I thought if I—"

"It's over now."

Dane slumped. He'd known he would lose her if he lit that fuse. "This was never supposed to go beyond Val and me. I never meant to hurt so many people."

"You were a victim, too, Dane."

He snorted. "You have no idea, Rose. I'm every bit as bad as Val. Maybe worse."

Rosamund laid a hand on his. "Did you know that anything communicated on corporate resources belongs to the company? Do you know who has access to monitor all exchanges of information?"

He waited for her to say what he already knew.

"Human Resources."

"And?"

"I've personally gone through thousands of system emails. We've confiscated Val's phone and laptop. Did you know she made recordings, too?"

He wasn't surprised. "Great. I already resigned, so they can't fire me. Should I expect a lawsuit anytime soon?"

She chuckled. "Oh, you were always so dramatic. But no. Nobody else has reviewed all the documents, and I made sure to share only what was relevant and necessary to the investigation into the accusations against Val." She arched an eyebrow. "But I reviewed everything."

"So what did you learn?"

"I learned that you did us all a great favor by exposing her. And I learned that you need to get as far away from her as you can."

"Before she kills me?"

"Before she gets her hooks in you again."

Dane laughed, but it hurt and turned into a cough. "Way ahead of you there."

"Where will you go?"

"I'm going to look for someone I liked years ago."

"Noelle?"

He frowned. "Myself."

Rosamund squeezed his hand, then stood. "You have a good heart, Dane." She ruffled his hair. "But you've made some terrible decisions. When you get yourself together and have a less cryptic address, please send me a postcard."

Once she'd let herself out, Dane showered, shaved, and dressed in a pair of cargo shorts and a worn T-shirt with a graphic of a joystick on the front. Then he booked a one-way ticket to Key West and packed two suitcases. He'd let a service haul away everything he left behind.

He'd head south and detox from a decade of poison. Alone.

Partial dump of emails recovered from the corporate hard drive.

Dane,

The board informed me that you resigned, or retired, however you want to name it. I am honestly contemplating the same. After reading the attach-

ment included in the email Val forwarded to me, I understood what you were trying to do. But I'm shocked and disillusioned by the layers of deceit and rot woven into this company.

I don't know if anything you said to me last week was true or if I was just a joke to you, but could we at least talk?

Noelle

Rosamund,

Could you look in on Dane? I'm still in New York, and I can't reach him. I'm worried he might hurt himself.

Noelle

Miss Constance,

Dane is fine. He just needs some time to focus on himself.

Thank you for your concern,

Rosamund

Rosamund,

That's exactly why I want to talk to him. My last email to him bounced. Could you let me know how I might reach him?

Noelle

Rosamund,

Did you get my last email?

Noelle

Rosamund?

Weeks Later

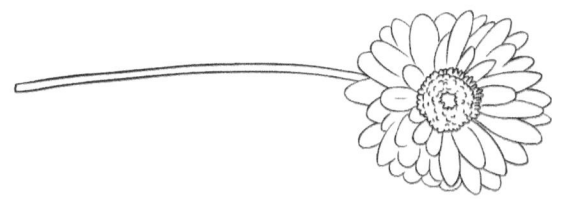

Someday

D) ane reached around the pile of game theory books, searching for his phone, although he knew the chime would be nothing but spam.

I ought to permanently set it to Do Not Disturb.

He'd only created the Gmail account to register for various gaming communities. Over the past few weeks, he'd installed *Minecraft*, *Roblox*, and *Undertale* and bought every console on the market, along with the most popular titles. It had started out as simple research, and for a few days, he was able to convince himself that spending twenty hours a day in a video game could be construed as productive. But now, with his hair out of control and nothing in his cabinets but pretzels and beer, he'd finally begun to admit he might be self-medicating with virtual reality.

He'd honestly intended to face real reality and do some soul searching. And he *had*. Some. He'd met a man of the cloth and a woman wearing crystals, but exploring every aspect of Hyrule was a lot less painful. And more fun. Not to mention, his island in *Animal Crossing* wouldn't maintain itself.

He unlocked the phone to discover an email from the guy at the surf shop in town.

Hey Dan!

Got something here for you. I can swing it over sometime this week. If you want it today, you'll need to stop in!

Bruce

In town, he was known as Dan Ruse. It wasn't much of a disguise but easier than going into the witness protection agency. Only his legal documents were in his real name. Not that he expected anyone to recognize him outside the financial community. But he didn't want the *Financial Times* to trace him and hound him either. He wanted quiet. He wanted restoration. He wanted absolution, but he didn't expect that. He'd settle for peace.

He scrounged up his sunglasses and put on a proper shirt and sandals before heading out his front door. His house was a modest two-bedroom on Admirals Lane he'd picked up for a mere two million. It had a private backyard, a small pool, and a yard crowded with palm trees. A short jog would bring him to a walkway overlooking the Gulf of Mexico. He loved the wraparound porch and the quaint picket fence that gave the place curb appeal. He scanned the paint for signs of wear, ready to play the role of handyman at the first chip. He'd never owned a house before, and he'd fallen in love with his peaceful yellow bungalow.

He'd materialized the dream he'd cultivated for so long. If only it hadn't cost him everything but money.

The Florida heat surprised him every time he stepped outside. He'd known it would be sweltering, but he hadn't been prepared for the reality of living inches from the sun. He wouldn't trade it for northern winters or the frigidity of a life he'd assumed was his own. How had he fed a soul-sucking vampire for all those years? Half his life in service to what? What had he ever done that was useful or good?

Had he always been a shallow wreck of a human?

Thoughts like these had kept him mired in video games for the past several weeks. He needed to face them, maybe find a therapist. He had a lot to decouple from years living alongside Val. Val, who was in jail awaiting arraignment. Did he deserve a different fate? Had he been any better than her? Was he a free man only by virtue of being a man? Or had he been lucky enough to tiptoe to the line of criminality without going over?

With a stream of sweat already working its way down his neck, Dane headed down Admirals Lane to Front Street and turned right. To the west, down the side lanes, he'd soon be able to make out the cruise ships docked near Mallory Square. To the east, inland, up Eaton Street, sat the church he'd wandered into when he'd first arrived, searching for penance and finding none. How could a man's soul be saved when he no longer had one?

Like some kind of cliched new-age spiritual, he found what he was looking for to the south in a yoga studio run by an older woman who didn't tell him what he wanted to hear but tolerated his harmless flirting and accepted him into her fold. It wasn't the yoga that had brought him closer to what he was seeking, though the stillness of the focused exercises purged the noise of the games and forced him to pick apart every bad decision he'd ever made, every wrong he'd ever committed. What he found there were regulars who welcomed him into their community. They didn't know they harbored a fugitive, but he came to realize he wasn't the only one there running from demons. There was a certain relief that came from communing with the damned. Recovering alcoholics, sex addicts, gamblers, and cheaters. He could see it in their eyes. They could probably see it in his as well. But he hadn't come here to hide from who he was. Just to find a way to pay for it.

At last, Mallory Square came into view. This was a major tourist destination, but that was what he loved about it. Every time he walked over here, it reminded him he was on vacation from his life. He might one day have to face a real punishment—prison or hell—but this was his purgatory. A chance to turn it around and be a better man.

He waved to Pete, the guy who'd taken him out on a snorkeling expedition the first week he'd arrived in town. A few shops down, he ran into LaToya, a local artist who had a side hustle pushing henna tattoos on the tourists. He stopped for a minute to ask, "Have you considered my idea?"

LaToya gave him a slow side-eye. "I didn't think you were serious."

"Why not?"

"Because it sounds like a waste of money."

"Let me worry about that. Can you do it?"

"Yeah, I can do it." She brushed back a long tangle of thin dreads. "You're seriously gonna pay me to draw cartoon characters?"

"They're not cartoons. They're avatars."

"Whatever."

"I gave you my card, right?"

She tapped her nonexistent pocket. "Daniel Ruse. Yup."

"Call me. We'll talk."

He reached Bruce's shop and knocked on the counter to draw someone out. Bruce poked his head up from behind a surfboard. "Hey, Dan dude!"

"You have something?"

"One sec." Bruce went behind the counter and squatted, then came up with a single letter. "Aw, they spelled your name wrong, but I figure this is for you."

The envelope said *Dane Russ* and had no return address. He smiled. "Close enough."

He left the shop, tearing the envelope open. He probably could have just given Rosamund his real address, but paranoid worries didn't die so fast. He trusted Rosamund with his life, but people could intercept her mail. It was taking enough of a risk to let her know he was here.

He stood still in the middle of the pedestrian traffic to read what she had to share.

Dane,

Your accountant came out to the house last week. You know you really didn't need to leave me such a sizable sum of money. But since you did, I was thinking . . . It's about time I retired, and there's nothing for me here. What's it like in Key West? I understand they like the olds in Florida. Maybe you could direct me to a decent rental. I think with the money you've passed to me, I'll probably die before I can spend it. And I don't have any family here. The closest thing I've ever had to a son recently moved away. And I miss him.

I get an occasional email from someone else who's looking for you. Your privacy is safe with me, but she seems eager to talk. Let me know.

I'm considering your last marriage proposal very seriously. I'm holding out for a destination wedding.

Love you,
Rosamund

He laughed. Of course he wanted Rosamund to move to Key West. He stopped at a tourist boutique to buy a postcard and then settled in at a café to respond. It was such a lovely day, he ordered an iced chai latte and grabbed a table outside to jot down a message. While he was mulling his choice of words, he thought he heard his name.

He glanced up, but it had to have been his imagination. He tried to shake off the fear he'd been discovered. He didn't want to hide in his house forever.

"Dane?"

That time it was unmistakable. He turned and saw a ghost. He nearly scrambled out of his seat from the shock.

"Noelle? What are you doing here?"

"I can't believe I finally found you." She came around the table and dragged out a chair.

His heart hammered like he'd fallen from a vast height. He'd never expected to see her again, and yet there she was, looking like she'd merely been out for an afternoon stroll.

On the surface, she looked as relaxed as any vacationer, hair down, a slight tan on her skin, casual shorts and a T-shirt. He flashed back briefly to the corporate trust-building day and wished he could reverse time. If he could, he might have fallen at her feet and begged her to run away with him. He might have warned her to get as far from him as she could. He might have fled straight to Key West without corrupting her along with everything else he touched.

She'd been right about him then. He'd only won her back through cruel manipulation.

"How did you know where I am?" If Rosamund hadn't talked, was someone tailing him again?

"Oh, please." She rolled her eyes "You *told* me you'd be here. You weren't very subtle about your plans. I've actually been here for a week asking around. Nobody's heard of Dane

Russ, but someone pointed you out, thinking I had your name wrong."

"Well, here, I'm Dan."

She snorted. "It's not that different."

"It's enough."

"So?" She gave him a once-over, probably taking in his disheveled appearance and judging. "You look well. Is Key West everything you'd hoped it would be?"

"It's quiet. But I forgot that old saying: *Everywhere you go, there you are.* Being alone with myself is its own kind of hell."

"Are you okay?" Her brows drew together. "I've been worried sick. You literally dropped off the grid. I figured if you weren't here, you were dead. I was determined you'd be here."

"I've been here. Trying to figure out how to undo myself." He narrowed his eyes, searching for a better way to explain it. "I haven't been a good person. I don't know if that's permanent or malleable. I keep looking for ways to just buy salvation."

She sat back and studied him as though she could be the one to decide the fate of his afterlife. "Why didn't you even say goodbye? You could have at least sent word where you'd gone. Were you planning to make me spend my life without some kind of explanation?"

"I was doing you a mercy, Noelle. I worried you'd follow me."

Her mouth twisted into a frown, and he noticed how tired she looked, the sallow under her eyes, the overall disappointment he'd spinelessly tried to avoid facing.

She heaved out a ragged sigh. "I'm sorry. I know you probably don't want to see me, but I wanted to talk to you. At least once more. I couldn't just let you disappear from my life without another word."

"I needed to disappear, to take a break from everything. I came here hoping to find myself."

"You didn't need to do that alone."

"I'm not alone."

"Oh." She blinked like understanding suddenly dawned. "Of course. I should have thought . . ." She started to stand, to leave, hands shaking as she reached for the strap of her purse.

Belatedly, he heard how she'd misconstrued his words. He could say nothing, and she'd go. That would be the best thing for her. She'd move on and never look back at the good-for-nothing who'd wrecked her life. But if by his omission, she believed he'd taken solace in the arms of any other woman, he'd end up hurting her in a new and different way.

"Wait!" He threw his arm out. "I just meant I'd made friends here. I've never had friends before. It's nice."

She sat back down, but her tanned skin had drained of all color but the splotch of red near her jaw. Her chest rose and fell like she'd had the fright of her life, and he hated himself for how he continued to lure her into his woe-begotten life. His heart clenched for reanimating an emotion he should have left well enough alone.

"I'm sorry for reeling you back in, Noelle." Her mouth curled down, lips trembling, and he squeezed his fists to resist the urge to reach across and take her hands. "You were safely free of me, but I couldn't stand to be rebuffed, so I made it my mission to seduce you."

"Was that all it was to you? Did you lie to me?"

Ah. Dagger straight to the heart. Maybe he'd get to do penance one victim at a time.

He could lie to her now, but he'd made himself a promise to leave the machinations to his former life. It would be a slippery slope to his old self if he started playing deceitful games in some vain ploy to gain Noelle's forgiveness.

He laid his hands on the table and leaned forward to gaze in her pretty eyes as he confessed. "I lied to a great many people."

She scowled. "Did you lie to *me* specifically when you told me you loved me?"

Perhaps some truths were too toxic to be spoken aloud. "Does it matter? Why would you want that from someone like me?"

"It matters. You matter."

However she'd come up with that false notion, he needed to disabuse her of it before she convinced herself he was worth saving.

He looked out at the endless sky as if the words he sought dwelled in the clouds. There was a sense of boundless freedom in the knowledge that this sky stretched out over infinite ocean. He could board a ship and lose himself to adventure like the pirates of old. But he'd lived a kind of pirate life already. What he wanted was to set down roots, become part of a community, add value. He was tired of sucking the life out of everything and everyone around him.

"Noelle, thanks for coming here, but I'm the anti-hero in your story. What you saw in me was a mirage."

"Do I look like a saint to you?"

"Yes."

She laughed quietly, then tilted her head with a little shake. "You do think highly of yourself, don't you?"

"Not really."

"You're not just flawed like the rest of us, you're an arch-villain. You're not just searching for answers, you're lost, damned, irredeemable."

"Are you here to bring me religion, Noelle? Absolve me of my sins?"

"I'm here to tell you that the fact you know you have flaws is in itself evidence you're not as contemptible as some.

You're not nearly as corrupt as you think you are. Do you think Val will accept any blame in this?"

That was a laugh. "No. She'll go down swinging."

"She did. Or so I heard. She's trying to bring a counter-suit against the company, against me."

Dane hadn't followed the news. He'd buried himself in innocuous games and willed himself to stay alive another day. That was the best he could manage. "So you're saying there's relative evil?"

"You're not evil, Dane. You're a bit of a scoundrel, but I know you. I've seen your true nature, and you're not a total miscreant. Without a corrupting influence, you even focus your talents on good works."

"You can't place my decisions on Val. We're two separate people. We each carry our own blame."

"And unlike her, you're kind. You help people."

"For every act of kindness you could uncover, I've done something worse. And you should know I faked all that charity Morty Becker documented for you."

"I'm not talking about that. You forget I worked next to you at R&M. You had so much passion for developing new technologies, and not for your own gain. It was one of the things that I loved about you even then—all that dorky enthusiasm. You were so enamored with simplifying trading so average people could understand it. You had all the wonder of a child discovering the world. I'm going to guess since you've been here, you haven't spent your days lying on the beach. Tell me what you're working on?"

He smiled. She'd made him sound like a half-decent man. He brushed his eyelid with the back of his hand. He'd never seen himself the way she'd just described him. Had *she*?

So he laid out the idea that had him excited for the first time in years. "It's kind of a role-playing adventure, but simple. I've noticed some of the most popular games are almost retro in their feel. I'd want it to be open-sourced so anybody could contribute and change it. I've been lining up local artists and coders to start work on a prototype."

"You've only been here a few weeks. You're already giving work to the locals?"

"I mean, yeah?" He scratched the back of his neck, feeling an odd sense of pride and humility all at once. "I've mostly been buried in game theory. It's likely I'll burn all my time and money on a total flop, but I have a lot of both. At least I'm spreading it around."

"And that makes you feel good? Giving other people honest work? Helping the economy?"

"It's the least I can do, Noelle. But it doesn't erase years of leeching off people like an emotional vampire."

"Before I came looking for you, do you know what I did?"

"Had your memory wiped?"

"Funny, but quite the contrary. After I got that bizarre email from you that Saturday, when I couldn't reach you, I wandered around, lost, trying to understand what had happened. I ended up at Kitty Monroe's, and we talked about you. You know, before—when you were pretending you wanted to date me—I'd reached out to some of the board at R&M to ask them to send me dirt about you. It was Geraldo's idea."

Dane's blood went cold at the memory of her emails. "Noelle—"

"I know. I shouldn't have snooped, but see? We've all got dirt on our hands."

He could have laughed at her trying to come down to his level, as if to prove that every sin could be overlooked if everyone was a little bad. "Noelle, I already know about all that. I fucking read your emails."

She froze and blinked. "Oh, right. The guy in IT mentioned that. Anyway . . ." Her hand swanned as if waving away a pillar of smoke, like she could dismiss an ethical breach with a flourish. "When I went to see her, the way she spoke of you was nothing like the things she'd written."

"Of course not. I'd coerced Kitty and every single one of those people to put in a good word for me, Noelle. It was all lies."

"Really?" She didn't look scandalized. In fact her grimace made her look underwhelmed. "It's funny. When Kitty first wrote me, I didn't question her account because it rang so true. It fit the image *you* cultivated. The bad boy with the heart of gold. Sound right?"

"Half right."

"Well, Kitty did have some grievances to air she'd apparently been holding onto."

Dane gritted his teeth, wondering when this slow death by Festivus would end.

"She said you always thought you were smarter than everybody in the room and more than likely had broken multiple laws before draining the company of capital on a severance package you shouldn't have taken."

"Wow. And this is how you planned to convince me I'm just a saint in wolf's clothing?" All this reminiscing over Dane's treachery was beginning to tire him out. He'd been flagellating himself just fine on his own. He started to stand. "I think I've heard enough."

"No. You haven't quite." Her smile melted. "I asked her if there was anything truly good she could recall, and she told me about the things you did for people that nobody ever talked about. Is it true you paid off the loan on some food truck outside R&M headquarters?"

Had he? "I don't remember that."

"Kitty said the guys who owned it swore it was true. They said, you'd struck up a conversation with them every time you'd stopped for their chicken shawarma."

"Oh, the chicken shawarma. My guilty pleasure. Seven bucks for street meat heaven." Maybe he could pay for those guys to move to Key West.

"Well, one day they apparently told you they were closing up because they'd missed a few payments on their truck. When they got home that night, the bank told them the loan had been paid in full."

"So how do they figure it was me?"

"The bank told them."

"Oh." He'd probably had his accountant do it. "I have no recollection of this."

"Because you're naturally charitable, Dane."

He snorted. "Hardly. If I paid off that truck, it was pure selfishness. If I don't remember it, it's because money isn't charity to me. That would have been a financial investment into my own happiness. I wasn't buying that truck for them; I was buying it for me."

"Okay. Then tell me about Rosamund?"

"What?"

"If money's so easy, why did you personally take the time to keep her company? Bring her food? Check up on her and make sure she was secure?"

Dane swallowed. "I don't know what you're talking about."

"Morty Becker isn't as terrible an investigator as you thought he was. You do realize he worked for me, not you."

"Leave Rose out of this." He snatched the letter he'd been writing and stood. "It's been fun catching up. Maybe I'll run into you again sometime. Where are you staying?"

She pushed her chair back. "I thought I might stay with you."

Vertigo caused the ground to tilt, and he grasped the table for support. "You can't, Noelle."

She came around the table and laid a hand on his shoulder, steadying him. "Why not? I'm here."

"You shouldn't be."

"Because you don't want me?" She asked it like she knew the answer already, but he wouldn't make it that easy for her.

"I'm not fit for anyone. I need time."

"You've had time. Tell me you don't want me, Dane. Tell me the truth."

The truth. Why had he made that vow? He evaded with a different truth. "I'm a broken man, Noelle. I'm not the man you thought I was."

"I know who you are, Dane. Tell me you don't want me, say you never loved me, and I'll leave here."

He could do it. With his eyes closed, he could tell her it was all a game, a joke at her expense. He could break her heart with finality and keep her out of his dangerous clutches.

"Look at me, Dane."

He lifted his eyes. Hers were blue pools of disaster for him. He couldn't look away. Those were the eyes he'd seen in a New York City hotel room he'd named Paradise. But once you leave Shangri-La, you don't get to go back. Once you break a woman's heart, it will never be whole.

His breath rose and fell like the moon pulling the tide, and he couldn't form the lie that would save her from him. "I can't."

Noelle laid a hand on his cheek. "Don't you know that I love you, too?"

He waited a beat for her to qualify it. "*I love you, but . . .*" *But* he needed to atone for his sins. *But* they were never meant to be.

It never came.

"Noelle, what we had was . . ." God, what word could encapsulate the everything of those few days when he'd had her body, mind, and soul. When she'd looked at him like he was the person he'd pretended to be. "It was serendipitous."

She laughed. "Hardly."

"It wasn't for you?"

"Serendipity is an accident of circumstances, Dane. Do you really want to tell me you've ever just fallen into anything that remarkable by happenstance?"

"What would you call it, then?"

"Preordained."

"Doomed."

"Blessed."

How could she keep seeing him that way after everything else. He shuttered his eyes and sought a way to escape her relentless pursuit of his beleaguered soul. Before he found the strength to bolt, she pulled him into a hug that felt like true acceptance, and he wanted what she was offering, desperately needed it like rope to a drowning man.

But he pushed her back. "You don't get it, Noelle. I cheated. I lied. I hurt people." His voice rasped liked sandpaper. "I'm the bad guy in this story. I don't *get* a happy ever after."

She sniffed as though offended. "Well, *now* you're being a little bit selfish."

"What?"

"Are you going to send me away? Break my heart? Make your sacrifice mine as well?"

His fingers raked through his hair. "You deserve better. You'll find someone who'll earn your love."

"Excuse me? I'm not a cookie or a gold star someone wins for checking off a series of good deeds. If you're working to earn anybody's love, it should be your own. I don't need you to self-immolate for me."

He pinched the bridge of his nose. "It might take me my entire life to rediscover the person I once was."

"Dane, hear me when I tell you that I'll gladly help you do that work, but for *you*. I love you the way you are."

He swallowed back the painful tightening in his throat. Nobody had ever said that to him. Nobody but Rosamund. He whispered his last plea. "You're making a mistake. You should go home."

"Unless you can tell me you don't want me here, *this* is my home."

The last bit of glass sheltering his heart cracked, and he clutched his chest as though he could actually die from happiness. "Will you promise to leave me when I don't measure up?"

"No, Dane. I'm not going to abandon you whenever you show yourself to be human. I might call you on your bullshit, but I promise to stick by you until you find a way to believe you already do measure up."

His knees buckled from the relief of this woman strong enough to hold him up while his fight gave out.

He grabbed her wrist and pulled her toward him. "Yes, I want you. I've never stopped wanting you. Damn you. You shouldn't want this."

She wrenched her arm free and lifted a finger to his temple, tracing a line into his hair. "There has never been a man on this earth I've wanted more."

The dam on his resistance broke, and he wrapped a hand behind her head so he could reel her in and kiss her, kiss her like she deserved, with reverence. Noelle's entire body softened as he drew her closer, lined their bodies as one.

The catcalls of passersby broke the spell, and he pulled back, wiping tears from his cheeks with the back of his hand. He breathed out, "I love you so much." With the awareness that they had an audience, he admitted defeat. "I do believe we should continue this at my bungalow."

He couldn't believe he'd be able to share his new paradise with the woman he loved.

"You know, we might want to make a detour to this shop I discovered over that way." She waggled her eyebrows, and Dane suspected he knew the store she meant.

"That's in the wrong direction."

She grinned like a saucy waif. "Worth it."

"Why? What did you have in mind?"

"You'll see." She folded her lips into her mouth, like she was holding back a state secret.

"Kinky?"

She nodded, and he remember the paradoxical freedom in having his hands cuffed behind his back by one of his own ties. Could she force him to his knees, make him repent of his sins? He shuddered.

"Not illegal?"

Serious headshake.

"But sexy?"

She kissed him full on the mouth. "And is your kitchen stocked up? I don't plan to leave your house for at least a day."

She held her hand out for his, ready to lead him toward some fantasy sex shop she'd encountered while searching for him.

Who was this woman?

And he saw it all clear as day, because she was the woman he'd courted under cloudy New York City skies, years ago, before the floor had dropped out and he'd become consumed with vengeance. She was the woman who'd made him believe he was capable of an emotion as precarious as love.

He hated himself a little for deciding to take it, to take the bite from the apple of temptation and allow himself the happiness he'd never once deserved.

But when she looked back at him with that wanton desire, with that guileless adoration, he almost saw himself in her eyes. He could picture himself as the man he once thought he could be.

And he raced after her with reckless abandon, risking everything for the magic of possibility.

What if paradise could be regained?

What if love could be real?

Was there anything more dangerous?

Acknowledgments

Long ago, in what feels like a parallel life, I went to see a movie that changed the course of my academic career. Sitting in that theater, I was so stunned by the brilliance of *Dangerous Liaisons* that I decided on the spot to specialize in 18th century literature in the graduate program in French literature I'd just started at the University of Florida. I loved the book so much, I read it every year, and by the time I was working on my doctoral dissertation at the University of Virginia years later, I focused one chapter on the strategic masterpiece. My first thanks belongs to Choderlos de Laclos, a French general who's been dead almost since the French Revolution. This homage to his work is nothing more than a dim shadow compared to what he accomplished. To this day, I'm still in awe.

I always knew this book wouldn't be for everyone. I figured it might only be for me, and it's honestly been a struggle to get past obstacles, both internal and external, that have kept this project buried in a drawer for so many years. My deepest gratitude to my circle of writing friends, without whom, I would not have continued to dust it off and keep revising. If not for Jennifer Hawkins, first and foremost, who propped up my faith when I had all but given up on this project, I would have quit years ago. Thanks especially to Elly Blake, Kelli Newby, Kelly Siskind, Kristin Wright, Summer Spence, and Ron Walters who are like a set of bellows constantly blowing renewed confidence my way. Thank you all for always reading, always advising. To Maureen Marshall, and my Team Twue Wuv buds, Amy Jones, Gwynne Jackson, and Michael Asbrock, thank you all for jumping in for the final push to get this ready for the world.

To my readers, I know this isn't what you're used to from me, but thanks for taking a chance on a weird little foray into the dark. There will be more straight-up contemp romance to come.

If you enjoyed this book, please consider leaving feedback on Goodreads or on whichever ebook retailer you buy books from. Reviews help authors reach readers.

Keep up with me for news, freebies, and bonus materials.

https://www.maryannmarlowe.com/newsletter-sign-up/

And check out my other books:

I Want You To Want Me

I Want To Rock With You

I Want To Know What Love Is

I Don't Want To Miss a Thing

Want To Be Starting Something (prequel novella)

Nefarious

Falling in Luck

Holding Out For a Gyro

Crushing it (as Lorelei Parker)

Find out more at maryannmarlowe.com

Love rock stars?

I WANT YOU TO WANT ME
by Mary Ann Marlowe

My best friend recognized the international rock god before I did, but by then it was too late. I'd already slept with him.

In my defense, I'd gone out to the club to support my brother's music career, and Adam stopped by the merch table shrouded in a hoodie, sporting grungy jeans and a threadbare T-shirt from a long-forgotten AC/DC concert. How was I supposed to recognize him?

God, it gets worse.

When he asked me what I do, I half lied, "My company's developing a perfume." I couldn't tell him I research boner pills on laboratory mice. Besides, it was true that a coworker had tossed me a vial of some experimental fragrance as I left work. It smelled nice so I tried it on.

Adam leaned in. "What's it like?"

I scooted over. "I'm wearing it."

Gaze locked on mine, he lifted my wrist and brushed his sensuous lips across my skin, breathing in whatever chemical I'd loosed on him. Just like that, an electric charge sparked up my arm. I sucked in a sharp breath, and his eyes dilated black, like this intense desire had surged back toward him.

"Mmm," he said. "You smell intoxicating."

I must have, because he flirted with me, bought me beers... invited me back to his place. I knew I shouldn't go home with him. We were perfect strangers. But God, I wanted to. I wanted more. I wanted *him*. I thought he wanted me, too.

So when my best friend ran an image search the next day, proving the guy I'd hooked up with was THE Adam Copeland, I had to ask: How had I, a biochemist from suburban New Jersey, attracted that sexy out-of-reach rocker?

And what the hell was in that perfume?

Read on for a preview...

chapter one

Eden

My pen tapped out the drumbeat to the earworm playing through my laptop speakers. Glancing around to make sure I was alone, I grabbed an Erlenmeyer flask and belted out the chorus into my makeshift microphone.

"*I'm beeeegging you…*"

With the countertop centrifuge spinning out white noise, I could imagine a stadium crowd cheering. My eyes closed, and the blinding lab fell away. I stood onstage in the spotlight.

"Eden?" came a voice.

I swiveled my stool toward the door, bowing to Stacy and Kelly as they entered. "Thank you. Thank you very much."

Stacy shrugged out of her jacket and hung it on a wooden peg, unimpressed by my performance. "You're early. How long have you been here?"

"Since seven." The centrifuge slowed, and I pulled out tubes filled with rodent sperm. "I'm gonna leave a bit early to head into the city and catch Micah's show."

"At that filthy club?" Kelly curled her lip. "There are never even any guys there. It's always just a bunch of moms."

I gritted my teeth. "Micah's fans are not all moms." When Micah made it big, I was going to enjoy refusing her backstage passes to his eventual sold-out shows. I had faith in him.

I'd never admit that she was right about the crowd that came out to hear my brother perform. But unlike Kelly, I wasn't there to pick up random guys. I spun a test tube. "Whatever. Sometimes Micah lets me sing."

Kelly's voice turned singsong. "Ooh, I think Eden's got the hots for her brother."

"Don't be ridiculous, Kelly." Stacy rolled her eyes and gave me her best *don't listen to her* look.

The clock on the wall reminded me I had seven hours of prison left. I hated the feeling that I was wishing my life away one workday at a time.

Thanh peeked his head around the door and saved me. "Eden, I need you to come monitor one of the test subjects."

I followed Thanh down the hall to the exam room. Behind a window, a cute blond dude sat with a wire snaking out of his charcoal-gray Dockers. Thanh instructed him to watch a screen flashing more or less pornographic images while I kept one eye on his vital signs.

I bit my pen and put the test subject through my usual Terminator-robot full-body analysis to gauge his romantic eligibility. I wagered he held a desk job in programming, accounting, or maybe architecture. His fading tan, manicured nails, and fit build lent the impression he had enough money and time to vacation, pamper himself, and work out. No ring on his finger. On paper, he seemed to fit my basic mental checklist to a *T*.

Even if he was strapped up to his balls in wires.

Hmm. Scratch that. If he was financially secure, why was he participating in a clinical trial for boner research? And if it wasn't for the compensation, I didn't want to know. *Never mind*.

Thanh sat next to me, punching buttons on the complex machine monitoring the erectile event in the other room.

I stifled a yawn and stretched my arms. "Don't get me wrong. This is all very exciting, but could you please slip some arsenic in my coffee?"

He side-eyed me. "Why are you still working here, Eden? Weren't you supposed to start grad school this year?"

"I was." I sketched a small circle in the margin of the paper on the table. I'd already had this conversation with my parents.

"If you want to do much more than what you're doing now, you need to get your PhD."

I sighed and turned in my chair to face him. "Thanh, you've got your PhD, and you're doing the same thing as me."

When he smiled, the corners of his eyes crinkled. "Yes, but it has always been my lifelong dream to help men maintain a medically induced long-lasting erection."

I cracked a smile, but his joke barely took the edge off my mood. "I'm not sure this is what I want to do with my life. I've lost that loving feeling."

"Well, then, you're in the right place."

I snickered at the erectile dysfunction humor. The guy in the testing room shifted, and I thought for the first time to ask. "What are you even testing, today?"

He reached into a drawer and brought out a vial containing a pale yellow liquid. When he removed the stopper, a sweet aroma filled the room, like jasmine.

"What's that?"

He handed it to me. "Put some on, right here." He touched my arm.

I tipped it onto my finger and dabbed both wrists. "What's it supposed to do?"

He raised an eyebrow. "Do you feel any different?"

I ran an internal assessment. "Uh, nope. Should I?"

"Do me a favor. Walk into that room."

"With the test subject?" It was bad enough that poor guy's schwanz was hooked up to monitors, but he didn't need to know exactly who was observing changes in his penile turgidity. Thanh shooed me on through the door, so I went in.

The guy's eyes were now on me. As the machine behind me buzzed, I thought, *Is that a sensor monitoring you, or are you just happy to see me?*

"Uh, hi." I glanced back at the one-way mirror, as if I could telepathically understand Thanh's instructions.

The guy sat patiently, like he expected me to do something. I adjusted one of the wires, and he went back to watching the screen, as if I were just another technician. Nobody interesting.

I backed out of the room. As soon as the door clicked shut, I asked Thanh, "What the hell was that?"

He frowned. "I don't know. I expected something more. Some kind of reaction." He started to place the vial back in the drawer. Then he had a second thought. "Do you like how this smells?"

I nodded. "Yeah, it's nice."

"Take it." He slid it over. "Let me know if anyone comments on it."

I shrugged and pocketed it, curious why Thanh was wasting his time testing aphrodisiacs.

When four o'clock finally rolled around, I swung into the ladies' room and changed into a pair of comfortable jeans and a T-shirt. I'd taken the perfume from my lab coat, and before dropping it in my bag, I dabbed a little on my neck, breathing it in. I went nose blind searching for the undertones.

As I passed through the lab on my way out, Kelly gave me a once-over. "I have a low-cut shirt in my car if you want something more attractive."

"I'm fine, thanks," I said, trying to sound appreciative of her uncharacteristic generosity, but our styles were wildly at odds.

When she added, "At least let me fix your makeup. Are you even wearing any?" I heard the insult hiding in her offer.

I pretended she wasn't bothering me. "No time. I have a train to catch."

She sniffed. "Well, you smell nice anyway. New perfume?"

"Uh, yeah. It was a gift." I zipped my computer bag and said, "Gotta go. See ya tomorrow, Stacy."

Stacy waved without turning her head away from whatever gossip site she'd logged on to, and I slipped out the door.

As I stood on the train platform waiting for the 5:35 Northeast Corridor train to Penn Station, my mom called. "Oh, there you are, Eden. I'm making corned beef and gravy tonight. Why don't you come by before you go out?"

I didn't know how to cook, so my mom's invitation was meant as charity. But since her own ineptness in the kitchen was the reason for mine, her promise of shit on a shingle couldn't lure me from my original plans.

"No, thanks, Mom. I'm on my way into the city to hear Micah play tonight."

"Oh. Well, we'll see you Sunday I hope. Would you come to church with us? We have a wonderful new minister and—"

"No, Mom. But I'll come by the house later."

"All right. Oh, don't forget you've got a date with Dr. Whedon tomorrow night."

I groaned. She was relentless. "Is it too late to cancel?"

"What's the problem now?"

She wouldn't understand why he gave me the ick, so instead, I presented an iron-clad excuse. "Mom, if we got married, I'd be Eden Whedon."

Her sigh came across loud and clear. "Don't be so unreasonable."

"I keep telling you you're wasting your time."

"And you're letting it slip by, waiting on a nonexistent man. You're going to be thirty soon."

The train approached the station, so I put my finger in my ear and yelled into the phone, "Next year."

"What was wrong with Jack Talbot?"

I thought for a second and then placed the last guy she'd tried to set me up with. "He had a porn mustache and a *Don't tread on me* tattoo. Also, he lives with his parents."

"That's only temporary," she snapped.

"The mustache or the tattoo?" I thought back to the guy from the lab. "And you never know. Maybe I'll meet Mr. Perfect soon."

"Well, if you do, bring him over on Sunday."

I chortled. The idea of taking a guy over to their ridiculous house before I'd secured a ring on my finger was ludicrous. "Sure, Mom. I'll see you Sunday."

"Tell Micah to come, too?"

My turn to sigh. Their pride in him was unflappable, and yet, I'd been the one to do everything they'd ever encouraged me to do, while he'd run off to pursue a pipe dream in music. So maybe they hadn't encouraged me to work in the sex-drug industry, but at least I had a college degree and a stable income.

"Okay, Mom. I'll mention it. The train's here. I have to go."

I climbed aboard and relaxed, so tired of everyone harassing me. At least I could count on Micah not to meddle in my love life.

chapter two

Adam

I stumbled off the bus, sick to death of testosterone and noise.

"Give me a hand with these?" Shane called over, grabbing a drum case from the trailer.

"Leave it for the crew," I called back. After all, there were some perks to our success.

"I *would*," he said, leaning hard on the sarcasm, "but I don't want to stand out here all day waiting for them to show. Someone might try to steal our gear."

I sighed, remembering the guitars and amps we'd had stolen over the years. And that was when our instruments weren't worth a hell of a lot. A couple of years ago, we'd driven a broken down van across the country, eking out a living in smoky bars and the occasional run-down theater.

Now, with the name of the band covering every single conveyance, it would be hard to hide. It was always hard to hide now.

Syd stepped off the bus and ambled over to the trailer. "Okay, let's get this over with."

Noah joined us, blond hair a wreck from another month on the road. Somehow he made that look work, earning him the role of the pretty one of the band in the media write-ups. On the bus, he was known as the surly asshole, yet he worked through women like he was sampling chocolates. I couldn't relate. Women on tour were like carbonation, sparkly and tempting, but by morning, there'd be nothing left. I had no interest in flash. I had even less interest in anyone who only wanted me for the pop fizz of a night with a rock star.

"I'm going to sleep for a month," Noah groused. "Maybe a shower first."

"Definitely a shower," Shane jabbed. "You smell like wet p—"

"Guys," I interrupted, before they started bickering again. I was so tired of the constant bickering. "Get some rest tonight. Tomorrow's gonna be hectic."

"Yes, Dad," Noah said, blowing me a kiss.

Shane's eyes widened. "Madison Square Garden."

"I know." I blew out a breath. That was a big get for us, and I'd worried we wouldn't sell enough tickets to fill the venue. I was convinced every day this dream we'd worked so long for would come to a sudden end, and I wouldn't have banked enough money to keep making music even as a hobby, let alone a career. I didn't want to be a flash-in-the-pan in my career any more than I wanted to be someone's one-night stand.

But this was our home turf, and New York had always welcomed us. Still, I'd held my breath until Jane, our booking agent, texted, *Sold out show! Congrats!*

Success came with its own very well-advertised burdens, and I hadn't come up for air in months. Right now, I needed to take life one step at a time, and my next step was to follow up on the leads our manager, Hervé, had sent for Syd's replacement while his wife gave birth to their first child. Great for him, but bad timing for us. We were set to go to Europe in a couple of weeks.

Syd grabbed his guitar case, shaking his head. "Man, I'm glad I won't have to miss out on playing the Garden."

"Yeah. Same," I said, patting his shoulder. But as soon as he disappeared into the old garage we'd converted into a rehearsal studio, I turned back to Noah and Shane. "Do either of you want to come out with me tonight to Tribeca? I want to check out another guitarist."

Noah grimaced, reached for a large drum case, then headed toward the studio, ignoring my question. Shane made an apologetic face. "I'm gonna pass. Just"—he shot a glance at Noah's backside—"make sure whoever we pick isn't grouchy all the time?"

I didn't like to gossip behind each other's backs, but Shane and Noah had been best friends since high school, and if Shane was annoyed with Noah, then it wasn't just me picking up on the bad vibes. "He's been worse than usual," I admitted.

"We played D.C. again," Shane offered with a shrug. "Makes him cranky when we pass so close to home. So close to—"

"Lucy, right?"

He nodded. "I think something happened between them. He's more unbearable than usual."

No lie detected. "Okay, so prioritize attitude over talent. Got it." We didn't have a ton of leads to replace Syd on such short notice, but I'd be glad to find someone who wouldn't drag down the mood on the bus.

Shane ran a hand through his cinnamon hair. "And would it hurt to find someone ugly for once?"

I laughed. Shane wasn't ugly in the least, but he hid behind the drums, so writers focused on his actual musical skills—if they mentioned him at all. And the girls flocked to Noah. Or me. I wouldn't mind having another pretty boy on tour to attract all those adoring girls looking for someone who didn't exist.

This last leg, it had been worse than ever before, now that we had a certified number one hit, a gold record, and a Grammy for our last album. The venues were bigger. The crowds were louder. The fans were scarier. And the groupies... Well, they were like proverbial fish in a barrel. And none of it felt real. Shane watched Noah with envy, as he bounced from one shallow hookup to another. But I wondered if I'd created a prison for myself. I envied Syd a little bit. He'd met his wife while we were still poor and unknown, and he had his priorities straight, willing to risk his spot in a band he'd invested so much in.

Maybe if I'd been in a steady relationship before all this had happened, I'd trust someone might want me for me. But now? There was no way to tell, and the last thing I wanted was to take advantage of one more girl with stars in her eyes, when all she could see was Adam Copeland, front man to the band The Most Wanted, and not me. Would anyone ever see *me* again?

By the time we finished unloading the trailer, I barely had time to drop my suitcase off at home before turning around and heading into the city. I pulled my hood up and donned a pair of sunglasses, hunching down to avoid wandering eyes. It wasn't that I hated the fame. It was all still so new to me, and I hadn't quite wrapped my head around the fact so many people connected with my music. Whenever anyone recognized me now, it reminded me how far we'd come, how all our hard work had paid off. But I was exhausted and not in the mood to deal with strangers.

The club looked vaguely familiar, though they'd started to blend together after a while. Nobody prevented me from walking through the front doors and into the darkness within, so I headed straight back, past the unmanned hostess station, past a merch table, where a girl with dark hair unloaded T-shirts for tonight's main act, past the empty stage, until I found the tiny green room near the back door.

"Micah?" I asked, and the blond lying on the ratty sofa with his forearm over his eyes sat halfway up, a grin breaking free as he came all the way to standing, hand outstretched and shaking mine before I'd stepped all the way in.

"Oh, my God. Adam Copeland." He pumped my arm. "I wasn't sure you'd make it."

"Hey," I wrested my hand free, and gave him a once over. Shane was going to hate that Micah was blond. And maybe as pretty as Noah, though more rugged, more boyish. He looked older than Noah and Shane by a few years. Closer to my age, maybe. I hadn't had time to research his entire bio, but I didn't need to know his astrological sign to know he could play guitar. And so far, he seemed at least a fair site cheerier than Noah. Not that it was a high bar to reach. "It's great to finally meet you."

Micah retreated into the room a little farther, allowing me to enter. "I haven't even mentioned this to anyone, not even my family. I didn't want to jinx it or disappoint them if this doesn't pan out, but man, I'm excited about the possibility. I fucking love your music."

"Yeah?" People always said that to me, to my face anyway. The reviewers and even the fans had more critical words in writing, but I'd take the compliment. And returned it. "We were blown away by the videos we've seen. You're very versatile." That was an understatement. Tonight, Micah was playing a solo acoustic gig, but he'd performed in various rock bands, as a stand-in or studio musician, and the dude could handle his own. He should've been fronting his own band, but if he were, I wouldn't be here.

"Ever since you contacted me, I've been studying your set lists and learning as many songs as I can. Syd's amazing, by the way. I assume he'll be coming back?"

I shrugged. "Yeah. We're only looking to replace him for the European circuit for now. We'll see how it goes."

"I'm happy doing whatever. It would be a total trip to play with you guys."

There was more to hammer out, but that would come later, once we'd narrowed down our choices. "So do you mind if I hang around tonight and watch your set?"

His smile turned megawatt, and I could see him one day on the cover of a magazine. Shane would not be happy at all. "I would love that. Just so you know, this is going to be pretty low key, but I *can* write rock songs, too, not that you need any help there."

He was starting to gush, and it was actually endearing. I couldn't help but like the guy, and I wondered if we might be friends even if we went with a different guitarist. I needed to make the smart choice and find someone competent who could weather night after night, playing our music skillfully, but emotionally, I was already hoping that guy would end up being Micah.

I edged into the hallway, back to the still empty club. The girl at the merch table now leaned on her elbows, waiting for the doors to open, bored and idle. She eyed me as I approached, wary, like I had no right to be there. Her blue-black hair framed light skin, which gave her the look of some fairy creature. She was pretty, but not conventionally so. There was something interesting, even captivating in her look.

Maybe it was the way she glowered at me, like I might rob her blind, that caught my curiosity. For the past month, I'd only seen dollar signs, adoration, or lust in anyone's eyes. Something about this girl's blank disdain unlocked a little piece of the real me, the one I tucked away to keep safe from the unreality of my public life. I wanted to win her over, turn her scorn into approval, but I wanted to do it as me, not with my name or my fame. I pulled my hood tighter and walked straight over to the counter.

As soon as she realized who I was, this cool, disinterested dryad might flit back to another realm, to be replaced with a fawning admirer, chasing after someone and something I only pretended to be. But as I neared the counter, her eyebrow arched with suspicion, not recognition, and my need to charm her without the obvious weapons at my disposal, grew stronger, almost like a compulsion. I let her see my face, risking myself for a hit of pure connection.

In a former life, Mary Ann Marlowe was a PhD student in French literature. She wrote her dissertation on *Dangerous Liaisons,* and the fascination never wore off. She changed careers in the aughts to become a computer programmer and wrote mortgage-trading software on Wall Street for five years. She spent ten years as a university-level French professor, and her resume includes stints as an au pair in Calais, a hotel intern in Paris, a German tutor, a college radio disc jockey, and a webmaster for several online musician fandoms. She grew up mostly in the midwest, but she's lived in twelve states and three countries and loves to travel. She currently lives and works in central Virginia with her family and one surly cat.